# Wealth
# Health
# &
# Peace
# on
# Earth

**The Life You Were Meant To Have...**

How To

# Make Everyone Wealthy, Heathy & Safe on Earth *Including the Poor!*

Mark Hamilton

NEOTHINK® BOOKS

Published by The Neothink® Society
In the United States of America



LIBRARY OF CONGRESS
CATALOGUE-IN-PUBLICATION DATA
Hamilton, Mark
Wealth Health & Peace on Earth
ISBN 0-911752-91-9

Printed in the United States of America

December 2016 [WHPE] [15,000]

# Table of Contents

# Introduction

Imagine everyone is wealthy, healthy and safe, including today's poor. Imagine our standards of living beyond anything ever seen before. But how?

Consider a single law, a Prime Law, that removes initiatory force (opposite of self-defense force) from society and government. If we take away initiatory force, then we no longer have government as we have always known it. By definition, we have a business. Indeed, revenue collection can no longer function through implied force; instead, the people have to voluntarily pay for the value. Therefore, we have a business. The value must be so good that we want to pay for it. The value, of course, is national protection and economic prosperity.

Just imagine our government as a competent business run by competent businessmen who protect our country and stimulate our economy. With such competent national security and unleashed freedom (via removing strangling regulations under the Prime Law), standards of living will soar as demonstrated on the pages to follow. Read further to discover this super-competent businesslike protection and freedom and resulting universal wealth. What follows is the greatest path ever conceived to universal wealth, health and peace.

# Introductory Idea

## A Better Life: The Life You Were Meant To Have

For years I studied many of the most successful people today and throughout history. Over and over again, I observed the extraordinary drive of extraordinary people. I concluded that extraordinarily driven people rise to greatness. And I believed *few* people had that extraordinary drive to rise above others.

Over time, however, I realized that actually *many* people have that extraordinary drive, yet only a handful ever rise to greatness. Whether in business or the arts, millions of people possess the drive and the dream.

Moreover, over time I have come to see how *chance* plays a huge role in business and the arts. And if given the chance — the opportunity — *many* people have what it takes; they will rise with a superhuman drive...rise to greatness. More often than not, it takes that *opportunity*, that lucky break. Given the opportunity, *many* people can become that Steve Jobs, that Katy Perry.

And therein lies the real problem — the culprit — as to why we don't live the spectacular lives we were meant to live: in this country the *opportunity* is not here for us!

We long for "something more" out of life because *something more is within our reach*; we can have it *if we had the opportunity*. But the opportunity never comes. Indeed, do you ever feel that there has got to be something more to life? You sense there is something more because *there is* a better life you are meant to live but unknowingly are blocked from.

In a bountiful, free country like America, the people should enjoy well-paying jobs at the very least. In fact, I will go so far as to say that in America, people should be well-off, even today's poor.

But today in America, something is stopping that from happening. Something is wrong from top to bottom, from left to right. And that something wrong is stopping our rightful prosperity.

The American system just no longer works. The people running the system do not really matter in the long run; they simply fill a bad system. They vary quite a bit, from liberal left to conservative right, but they just fill a bad system that blocks the life you were meant to have.

What makes the American system bad? It is a system built upon rule by force. The whole system is built on a destructive premise that allows rule-by-force, which increasingly enables the destructive rule of man and steady demise of the masses. A privileged ruling class of men and women — politicians and bureaucrats — forcing others to live by their rules backed by force, whether liberal or conservative, leads to the long and steady demise of the non-privileged, non-ruling working class.

Natural laws of protection are necessary for those in society to peacefully coexist. All other man-made laws beyond the natural laws of protection are erroneously built on a system of rule by force, building a privileged ruling class whether liberal left or conservative right. The people running the system will come and go, cycle left and right, but the system itself is bad.

America put the most and best obstacles in place to resist the rule of man and block its destruction of the working class and our opportunities. But over two centuries those obstacles are no longer able to hold back the rising rule of man. The fall of the working class is now upon us. Our opportunities are gone.

The problem goes on and on because the masses focus only on the political candidates and their political parties. But that is the sleight-of-hand of the ruling class. We look closely at the candidates put up for election without seeing the real deceit — the bad system built upon force, steadily growing a privileged ruling class (with its destructive rule of man), steadily draining the non-privileged, non-ruling working class. Opportunity becomes a remnant of the past.

## New Wealth: The Wealth You Were Meant To Have

The Obamas, Bushes, Clintons of our time function in a bad system. Conservatives fighting liberals, liberals fighting conservatives...by being caught up in that passionate fight, we all miss the real enemy — the bad system built on force. Liberals and conservatives just fill that bad system built on force. The bad system itself is taking us down.

The answer is elegantly simple once we see beyond the battles inside the system, beyond the battles between conservatives and liberals. Once we see that the entire system built on force is bad regardless of who fills the system, then we can change civilization dramatically for the better. We need to step outside of the existing system into something new, as provided in the information that follows.

The bulk of this book was written from the perspective of saving our country and its citizens from the inside out by providing a new system that will make all people wealthy, including the poor. One change, an amendment to our U.S. Constitution, would send the prosperity and peace of civilization beyond anything ever seen before on Earth.

To make that change (that would make everyone wealthy) easier to grasp, let's imagine a new country...a new paradigm that shows just how prosperous a country free of the rule of man can be. Let it serve as a model for our country — any country — with the Prime Law (i.e., a law that ends the bad system built on force and ends its rule of man) as its constitution or supreme law. And realize to get this prosperous new system in our own country is exactly one constitutional amendment (the Prime Law Amendment) away. Indeed, as a constitutional amendment, the Prime Law would end the bad system built on force and its rising rule of man in America.

## A New Paradigm

Imagine a new country with the Prime Law of Protection (as seen on the next page) as its supreme law, a protection-only government run as a competent business, with no force...indeed, with revenues voluntarily paid. That idea initially seems incredulous. But on closer look, one realizes that in such a civilization with record-breaking prosperity and peace, the people will want to pay for the conditions that make their standards of living higher than any civilization throughout history. This would become the first and only civilization in which the prosperous citizens would *voluntarily*, without coercion and force, pay their government.

Instead a voluntary tithe would bring in the revenues. People immigrating to the new country would first sign a covenant stating that in order to move there and live there as residents and citizens, they will tithe ten percent of their income to the

*The Neothink® Movement*

## Introductory Idea

# A New Country

## Based On

## The Prime Law

**(The Fundamental Law of Protection)**

**Preamble**

*The *purpose* of human life is to prosper and live happily.

*The function of government is to **provide the conditions** that let individuals fulfill that *purpose*.

*The Prime Law **guarantees those conditions** by forbidding the use of initiatory force, fraud, or coercion by any person or group against any individual, property, or contract.

**Article 1**

No person, group of persons, or government shall initiate force, threat of force, or fraud against any individual's self, property, or contract.

**Article 2**

Force is morally-and-legally justified only for protection from those who violate Article 1.

**Article 3**

No exceptions shall exist for Articles 1 and 2.

country's protection services. The tithe will be a contractual agreement for all immigrants: To live and benefit in this purely free civilization in which protection is provided, immigrants must contractually agree to tithe ten percent of income to the country's protection services. That tithe is the communal commitment, the societal agreement to live and benefit in the beautiful society.

A resident or citizen may freely choose where to spend his or her ten percent. A management company will form known as "government" that will hire private protection services to bring safety and peace to the citizens and residents. A citizen or resident may place his or her ten percent with that management company known as "government". Or he/she may spend his or her tithe with a rising competitor to the "government" management company. The "government", a protection-only management company, allocates its revenues to private protection services...from Prime-Law-based military, police, courts, prisons, legal professionals/scholars...to disaster preparation and relief. In all circumstances, "dollars" (i.e., the country's currency) do the voting as opposed to political elections.

A Democracy = citizens vote
(Elect Politicians)

- versus -

A Prime-Law Society = "dollars" vote
(Hire Protection Services)

Protection services are the only purpose of the protection-only prime-law government. Citizens and residents vote for their protection services with their "dollars". The division of labor would naturally bring out a competent, expert management company called "government" to collect and allocate protection funds to the best protection services. The military would consist of different protection companies. A similar competitive situation would apply to police protection and for professionals and scholars who develop the laws and provide the justices who most accurately serve the Prime Law. ANY failure to uphold the Prime Law — the supreme law of the land — would result in severe loss of trust, and "dollars" would flow to competitors who accurately uphold the Prime Law.[1]

Those expert professionals/scholars/businesses studying/providing/protecting laws that purely uphold the Prime Law are, of course, subject to the Prime Law.

Competing protection services will keep competence and value front and center...no more bumbling bureaucracies as we see in democracies. Instead super-competitive, super-competent businesses protect us. Those multiple, competing businesses are natural watchdogs on each other. This is a new concept of civilization and government. This concept should have evolved into existence between two to three thousand years ago, but the few wanting to lead the masses through the use of force has prevented this concept of civilization from ever rising until now. This is a purely free civilization where leaders have no use of initiatory force, no power to subjugate others. Leaders exist only as long as people are willing to pay for their services...pay for their *values*.

With "dollars" voting for protection services (as opposed to elections voting for politicians), the *very best results* prevail. "Dollars" voting means the protection services are constantly making necessary improvements, a rapid evolution to the best values...a rapid evolution that benefits mankind. Our future requires this rapid positive evolution of protection to outrace the rapid destructive evolution of state-sponsored terrorism and potential nuclear proliferation among rogue nations.

People voting within a democracy, say, every two or four years, can be largely deceived and controlled by illusions. And consider that voting happens only every four years for, say, the U.S. President, in contrast to constant pressures on results and

---

[1] If the richest 10 Americans sold their entire lifetimes of worth, everything, and combined all their money, it would amount to less than 10% of just one *annual* budget of America. At a national level, the rich could not overwhelm the government against what is best for everyone when "dollars" do the voting. "Dollars" voting is a sound, valid approach. And the rich will never do something to hurt the system that allowed their success. The rich, just as everyone (all the people will be rich) must, of course, adhere to the Prime Law.

values when "dollars" do the voting every day! Dollars flow to the best services. A presidential election and re-election get us into nearly a decade of an administration instituting destructive policies and ideologies that are essentially irreversible. And the example and influence of a president's destructive ideology for eight years upon young children plants harmful mental views in their young minds.

Voting with "dollars" brings civilization the greatest values quickly. This is a completely different, brand-new concept of civilization and government based on no initiatory force within government, eliminating all subjugation while creating a businesslike, values-first, protection-only government.

Multiple protection services would rise and evolve for our benefit. We will gladly financially support those services that guarantee our peace and prosperity. You must read the pages that follow to understand how we will be the wealthiest civilization that ever existed and how we will gladly support that which guarantees our prosperity: our protection services. The new-concept Prime-Law Society that hires its government surpasses the age-old democracies that elect their governments.

The new country would make The Prime-Law its Constitution: pure freedom, pure protection with no initiatory force permitted, not even in government. The Prime-Law Society is a new dimension of civilization, for EVERY civilization throughout history allowed initiatory force within its government. With the Prime-Law Constitution, NO OTHER PURPOSE of government exists beyond protection. And if we were to start a new Prime-Law country, the government would rise as a service we voluntarily pay for. Competing services will have the freedom to rise too. In essence, we HIRE our government. We hire AND fire our government! Doesn't that feel right to you?

In such a society, there is no administration backing an ideology through force — through laws and regulations that the citizens must obey or suffer civil and criminal consequences. Such initiatory force no longer exists, only self-defense force exists. And children no longer live under destructive ideologies as their example. Instead they observe the drive to create values that people love so much they voluntarily pay for. What a beautiful observation for children to make and to strive for: a value-creation-driven life!

Self-defense protection involves a system of justice, including criminal laws and courts that deal with crime and uphold the Prime Law, civil laws and courts that deal with money, property, injury and uphold the Prime Law. Self-defense protection involves a system of prime-law-enforcement that includes jails and prisons, local, state and federal police. All these services will be hired and fired with our "dollars" doing the voting.

The use of initiatory force as found throughout ALL OTHER governments — all ruling classes — throughout history...will be banished through the Prime Law. This entirely new dimension of civilization, the first and only civilization with initiatory force banished from its government, ends subjugation and for the first time opens the pure prosperity-path mapped out on the pages to follow. The prosperity-filled Prime-Law civilization with a protection-only government is laid out like a safety net, here ready to catch America when her great fall occurs.

Initiatory force and subjugation would forever be banished by a Prime-Law Constitution (and by a Prime-Law Amendment to the U.S. Constitution). By removing initiatory force from civilization including from the government, the pure value-creation nature of society emerges; the pure value-building nature of immigrants flocking to the new country emerges. Pure and beautiful value-creating businesses fueled by pure and beautiful value-building citizens and immigrants would power the rise of this new world.

A major military defense would not be needed for some time. Protection would initially come in the form of police and a prime-law-based justice system. An infrastructure would need to be built first...an opportunity for utility, transportation, and communication companies interested in getting in early for excellent market shares.

The new country would strive for *recognized* sovereignty in order for its people to gain *recognized* citizenship and renounce their home country's citizenship and escape from their home country's taxes, regulations, sinking standards of living, and to instead enjoy the soaring standards of living in the new country. The inevitable soaring standards of living are described in Volume

Two, *Split-Run*. In there I hypothetically describe splitting America into two — one half with America's existing political policies and the other half with the Prime Law as an amendment to the U.S. Constitution. In *Split-Run*, you will see exactly how a civilization under the Prime Law will make everyone wealthy, including the poor.

In such a wonderful place of prosperity and peace, where the standards of living surpass any civilization in the history of the world, the citizens and residents would know that the Prime-Law civilization with a *protection-only* government is the reason for their soaring standards of living. So, only in such a nation would they gladly *voluntarily* pay for their Prime-Law, Protection-Only government. In America, internal revenue collection must be backed by force in order to continue receiving taxes from citizens. But in Prime-Law-America, internal revenue is sent in voluntarily by citizens and residents[1] who gladly protect their precious gift: their wealthy and peace-filled lives.

Immigrants coming to the new country would sign a covenant in order to come live in the beautiful society. The immigrants flocking to the new country must contractually agree to tithe ten percent of their income to live there. If they do not agree, then they should not come to the beautiful society. Deadbeats will be ostracized[2] by society. Second and third generation citizens must tithe ten percent of their income or face ostracization. If unhappy with "government", citizens and residents may put their ten percent tithe elsewhere to accredited protection services (accredited by private, reputable services). Private tracking services will be sure citizens and residents are paying their ten percent to protection services. The payment is a voluntary tithe, and anyone may withdraw their tithe from "government" and not be a criminal. But to enjoy society and not face ostracization, one must put ten percent of income toward protection services. Private tracking companies will make any deadbeats known to

[1]Residents in the new country would in most cases be a short, quick step away from becoming citizens leading value-creation lives.

[2]Ostracization is a very powerful technique that can exist without the use of initiatory force. If private businesses of all sorts refuse services and products to a deadbeat, it will become virtually impossible for that deadbeat to live in that society.

society.

Revenues happen through this voluntary tithe. That money provides the internal revenue for a protection-only government, as described over the pages to follow. This protection-only institution named "government" would essentially act as a management company hiring and firing the appropriate businesses and professionals to provide the greatest protection of its citizens (including protection-only laws, courts, jails, prisons, police, military). Therefore, ongoing competition would exist among protection businesses and professionals. And that competition will also work *within*, internally among the "government" management company itself, as in any business. *Performance* not elections, *results* not rhetoric, keep the "government" a value-creation institution.

Bottom-line is: income-earning citizens and residents would tithe ten percent of their income to their country for protection only. For the first time in history, they will want to pay this, for in the new initiatory-force-free dimension, everyone will be rich as described on the pages to follow, including today's poor.

Again any resident or citizen may allocate his or her ten percent tithe directly to accredited protection businesses if he or she prefers as opposed to the management company called "government". Private tracking services will be sure ten percent per income-generating resident and citizen is provided to protection services. Most people will find it most efficient to put their ten percent in "government".

But no one is a criminal if delinquent or even if he or she withdraws, for private tracking companies would expose deadbeats, and they would be ostracized, not turned into criminals as in America...but ostracized.

However, in the new freedom paradigm of no initiatory force, deadbeats will only exist in theory, for everyone will be rich as shown on the pages to follow, and everyone will pay to keep it that way.

What follows is the map into the Prime–Law civilization within America...as distinguished from starting a new Prime-Law country. I spent several years developing this dimension of civilization never before experienced on Earth. This prosperity-dimension delivers the life you were meant to live. Now, you will see our existing world as hopelessly stuck in the only dimension ever known — the dimension of initiatory force and subjugation. The new world eliminates initiatory force, and as you will see, without initiatory force in government, all people will be prosperous, even wealthy; businesses will be beautiful value creators; citizens and immigrants alike will be precious value builders. Wealthy citizens and residents, beautiful value-creating businesses, government hired and fired, our "dollars" doing the voting...it's a new dimension of civilization that you will now discover. It's our answer.

For the love of our children, take a close look at the following information that offers a good system, ending the rising rule of man and its privileged ruling class. The following information opens the door to the better life you were meant to have but were always blocked from.

Make Contact

If the Prime-Law Amendment impassions you, then join with others. Meet quality people to pursue this goal. You need to get organized. Make contact at: MarkHamilton@Neothink.com

Volume One

For the Love of Our Children

# New Start

## Providing the New

*Era of New Thinking,*

*A New Dimension*

*Universal Wealth, Health, Peace*

# Era of New Thinking (Neothink®)

After a schoolyard fight, the boys get sent to the principal's office. The first question the principal almost always asks is: Who started it? *"Who threw the first punch?"*

Why?

We inherently know natural law. It is okay to defend ourselves with force, but *not* okay to initiate force, hence the age-old instinctive first question: "Who started it?" The only moral use of force is self-defense force to protect oneself from initiatory force.

Government regulations forced on us are more complex and confusing than a schoolyard fight, but the fundamental principle still remains: IT IS *NOT* OKAY TO INITIATE FORCE. Regulations forced on business, for instance, if not a form of self-defense force, are immoral and wrong *initiatory force*.

Natural law applies across all time, all cultures, all lands. For example, across all countries, throughout all generations, the first question a school principal instinctively asks boys fresh from a schoolyard fight is: "Who started it?" or "Who threw the first punch?"

The new Twelve Visions Party is based on a supreme law: The Prime Law, which is based on the supreme natural law: no initiatory force.

All governments including the American government immorally violate the Prime Law, the supreme natural law. Some examples in America are the increasing, subversive regulations across many industries. Indeed, those subversive regulations are examples of initiatory force.

The simplest way to understand initiatory force is to understand that the only moral use of force (i.e., forcing actions through regulations, laws, litigation) is self-defense force for the physical protection of the people and their property. By recognizing that self-defense force is the only moral use of force, one can immediately identify the regulations backed by force crippling the energy industry, for example, as *immoral initiatory force*.

The new Twelve Visions Party with its Prime Law has one objective: End Initiatory Force. The Prime Law is the tool to do this. If the Prime Law were embraced by the American people and then grew in popularity to become an amendment to the U.S. Constitution, the freedom and prosperity of every American citizen would soar beyond all previously known experiences as shown over the following pages. And that is precisely why I wrote *The Twelve Visions* (300 pages, nf), *Superpuzzle* (1200 pages, f), and this Platform (318 pages): to show the American people and the world the heights of freedom and prosperity each and every citizen would enjoy and pass on to their children and grandchildren. And that is why I formed the new Twelve Visions Party: to spread these ideas to the American people and to the world and to hopefully someday shift our government-by-force to something much different via the elegantly simple Prime Law Amendment. That change will make everyone wealthy, including the poor. Discover over the pages to follow the wealthy life you were meant to have (and can still have).

*Universal Wealth, Health, Peace*

## A New Dimension of Civilization

Babies are born into a world ruled by illusions. We go from cradle to grave taken in by and giving power to those illusions. Consider the illusion of money: currency not backed by tangible value such as silver and gold by definition means its value is an illusion. Yet, we go from cradle to grave taken in by and giving power — buying power — to that illusion. The problem with illusions is: reality eventually asserts itself. As demonstrated throughout history, the longer the people support illusions, the more devastating the correction when reality sets in. Throughout history, when reality eventually asserts itself, unbacked currency collapses.

Consider the illusion that government (beyond protection of its citizens) provides value. People go from cradle to grave taken in by and giving power — ruling power — to that illusion. Throughout history, when reality eventually asserts itself, big government (government beyond protection of its citizens) collapses civilizations.

Beyond its one valid purpose of protecting its citizens, government by definition does not create or produce values. But people are taken in by and give power to its well-orchestrated illusions. Indeed, politicians provide well-orchestrated illusions of bringing values to society, but the one and only real value government brings to society is *protection*, as demonstrated inside this book. Any so-called "values" beyond protection are illusions that will eventually collapse and bring civilization down.

The reason people follow and give power to illusions such as our unbacked currency and such as our growing ruling class is explained in my Neothink® literature. In short, the reason we follow our leaders and their illusions reaches back to our primitive minds and thousands of years living in a following mode, following the imagined gods, god-kings, oracles, pharaohs — following leaders — as opposed to the modern mind's capacity to integrate reality and lead itself.

My breakthrough Neothink® Discovery and my Neothink® Manuscripts teach you how to become the powerful, illusion-free Self-Leader. The Self-Leader easily integrates reality and sees through illusions and charts his or her own course to a monetarily and emotionally rich life.

Until you become the Self-Leader, you will follow and give power to illusions all your life. Unbacked currency has buying power; the politicization of society has ruling power. All that power and so-called "value" sit upon illusions, and the general populace lives from cradle to grave supporting those illusions.

In the end, following illusions as opposed to integrating reality will lead to disaster – from currency devaluation to hyper-inflation to the economic meltdown of our country...from shrinking freedom to growing rule of man, socialism, tyranny.

Unfortunately, we see those consequences already starting to happen. We know we are in the early, intro-catastrophic era.

Can we stop the looming catastrophic era? Yes, and the process sits inside this book. Will we stop it? No...our hard-wired primitive mentality follows leaders and their illusions and will not stop until the illusions collapse as reality sets in. When those illusions collapse, we will then see the world as it is. And it will be too late.

If you want to stop following illusions, read this book. Check out the Neothink® Society and my Neothink® Manuscripts. My Neothink® Manuscripts shift our minds into the modern Neothink® mentality that integrates reality as opposed to following illusions...that charts its own course to financial and emotional wealth as opposed to following and serving leaders. In short, you become the Self-Leader and live a financially and emotionally rich life.

I started the Neothink® political movement (described on the following pages) to fundamentally change our government of illusions that the people fatally follow...to a government of values that brings the people the world's greatest protection service under the Prime Law, as you will see inside.

I founded the Twelve Visions Party to catch our fall when reality sets in and the illusions come crashing down, making this new political party relevant to every American *right now, today.* Moreover, the new Twelve Visions Party can turn everything around *right now* if enough people read this book. After you read it, do not let this life-saving information stop with you. Pass this book on to someone else to read, and insist they do the same. That single action of *passing it on* can start a peaceful revolution to save our future.

With increasing failure of America's currency, government and economy, the people will begin to, one by one, break from the illusions and, for the first time, discover the Twelve Visions Party, *America's safety net.*

The Twelve Visions Party takes us into a new dimension never experienced on Earth: the dimension in which *initiatory force* is prohibited in the ruling body, banished by the Prime Law. Therefore, for the first time, the destructive rule of man cannot exist. Indeed, the rule of man requires initiatory force to exist, and politicians and regulatory bureaucrats must weave well-orchestrated illusions to downplay and disguise their growing rule-by-force. Without initiatory force, with the Prime Law that banishes initiatory force in our government, we will for the first time live in pure freedom without politicians' and bureaucrats' rule by force and without their illusions. We will enjoy a prosperity never known before, as demonstrated within this book.

To enter that never-before-known dimension requires never-before-seen fundamental building blocks — the fundamental documents and prime literature upon which the new dimension is built. Those building blocks to a never-before-known world of pure freedom and extraordinary prosperity and peace, those documents that will end initiatory force and its illusions, will not look like anything seen before in this world. The Prime Law, the TVP Platform, the TVP Bylaws, the Neothink® Prime Literature — the building blocks from which rises the new world free from the insidious rule of man and his illusions — will look very different than other laws, platforms, bylaws, and literature.

Ending the destructive rule of man — the disease of civilization — ends our leaders' control, power, and wealth at our expense. Man's inherent dark desires and egos no longer have power in the new TVP Government, lifting us to a prosperous new world.

The Twelve Visions Party with its Prime Law is a worldwide movement to bring civilizations around the world into the new dimension free of initiatory force and its virulent rule of man.

Internally throughout the TVP, perspectives on national boundaries, national affiliations, even national jealousies and prejudices, unhealthy envy and egos must step aside among the visionaries bringing the new world to civilizations everywhere. The sole focus of visionaries everywhere must be on one thing only: on effectively eradicating initiatory force and its insidious rule of man, as presented within this book. This political movement is for all peoples of all countries. The Twelve Visions Party will end the ruling class and unite the non-ruling-class everywhere.

The Twelve Visions Party rises from over thirty years of developing the Neothink® Literature. This small book was written and distilled over several years. It is **the** fundamental document for taking civilization out of its only dimension ever known on Earth and bringing civilization into a new dimension never known on Earth: That new dimension is a world free of initiatory force, free from the virulent rule of man. This book is the fundamental document to disarm leaders of their age-old weapon against the people, *initiatory force*, and to end their ruling classes *everywhere*. The result will be universal wealth, health and peace on Earth.

The TVP transcends borders, races, religions and natural resources. Its mission is: a world free of initiatory force and its rule of man. The job of this worldwide movement is to cure civilization, each and every civilization, of its disease — the rule of man. That is the single, collective goal of the universal TVP Movement.

# The Greatest Kept Secret of All Time For Universal Wealth, Health, Peace *Hidden for 3000 Years*

Your leaders have prevented you, your parents, your children from living an amazing, wealthy life. For 3000 years leaders of all civilizations have shared this secret. They have even waged wars and starved their own people to guard this secret. By leaking this secret inside these pages to enough people, you and your loved ones will eventually live like millionaires.

Universal wealth comes to America with *one simple change*. The simple change will eradicate poverty and multiply the people's wealth. It will make all people wealthy, including the poor! And your leaders do NOT want you to know this simple change — their most highly-guarded secret! For, this simple change that delivers universal wealth will end their control over the people.

The change is elegantly simple — so simple that it just might catch on with the people and sweep across the nation. If it does get swept into action, then the people's buying power and standard of living will multiply as dramatically as we observed in the computer industry during the personal computer revolution. Poverty will perish. Everyone will become wealthy. And our leaders will lose their privileged positions of power and wealth.

What could possibly be such a simple change that would 1) cause a spectacular boost to our wealth and 2) eradicate poverty?

By forbidding just ONE thing among our leaders, EVERYTHING changes dramatically for the better. That one thing is *initiatory force*.

By forbidding initiatory force among our leaders, the political machine can no longer impede progress and burden everything good. A Great Technological Revolution would drive down costs and drive up our buying power as rapidly as we witnessed in the unimpeded computer revolution, but across the entire economic landscape. As with the computers, your buying power over *everything* would multiply many times over. You would become wealthy; *everyone* would become wealthy including the poor.

To understand the rightness of this prosperity-explosion requires a deeper philosophical understanding of human life, which I thoroughly expose throughout my thirty-plus years of writings in my Neothink® Manuscripts. To simplify that philosophical understanding for those who have not read my literature, let me ask one simple yet profound question: **Why should one adult control another?**

Only one type of force is necessary among humankind and that is: *self-defense force*. Although *initiatory force* has ALWAYS existed in *every* ruling body including the American political system, it is unnecessary and actually very damaging to humankind. But people believe it is necessary, and they **do not know it is extremely damaging to their prosperity** because initiatory force has always existed within all political systems. It is the leaders' greatest kept secret! People have never seen the other political paradigm of *no initiatory force* to compare to.

There is one very simple law — the Prime Law — that would successfully remove initiatory force from our political system via making the Prime Law an amendment to the U. S. Constitution. (The tenets of the Prime Law were blocked by every government since leaders first enjoyed their power thousands of years ago):

## The Prime Law

(The Fundamental Law of Protection)

### Preamble

• The *purpose* of human life is to prosper and live happily.

• The function of government is to **provide the conditions** that let individuals fulfill that *purpose*.

• The Prime Law **guarantees those conditions** by forbidding the use of initiatory force, fraud, or coercion by any person or group against any individual, property, or contract.

### Article One

No person, group of persons, or government shall initiate force, threat of force, or fraud against any individual's self, property, or contract.

### Article Two

Force is morally-and-legally justified only for protection from those who violate Article 1.

### Article Three

No exceptions shall exist for Articles 1 and 2.

*Universal Wealth, Health, Peace*

This simple yet profound law would eradicate poverty across America and multiply prosperity for every American as explained throughout this book. This simple yet profound law would also remove the leaders' power and control over the people, which is why they have fought to keep this specific knowledge from leaking for thousands of years. The resulting economic freedom would send buying-power soaring. The unregulated computer revolution was a small forerunner to the Great Technological Revolution that will send buying-power soaring a hundredfold, even a thousandfold, making everyone rich. This entirely new approach, for the first time based purely upon self-defense force or protection only, will make everyone wealthy, including the poor.

The new protection-only political system rises from the entirely new idea that no initiatory force exists in our government. At first, the idea seems ridiculous, for no political system has ever existed without the power of initiatory force. And that is because the leaders would not allow it. But when reading this book, the resulting wealth, health, and peace becomes evident and overwhelming. This is the people's greatest gift; the leaders' worst nightmare.

A new political system ushered in by a new political party can take us into the new dimension of *protection-only politics*. The name of that political party is the Twelve Visions Party, named after Twelve Neothink® Visions of our wealthy and peaceful world after the Prime Law Amendment to the U. S. Constitution, as you will see inside.

A fundamental change to a protection-only government effects everyone in America spectacularly for the better. Today America and tomorrow the world discovers the new political system that brings us the wealthy, healthy, and peaceful Twelve Visions World...a world in which *everyone* is wealthy, including today's poor! When enough people read this book, the change will come. Pass this book to a loved one or friend after you finish reading it.

*Making Every American Wealthy*

There is a way to end poverty, hunger, disease. There is a

way to make *everyone* wealthy. Ending poverty and making *everyone* wealthy requires an entirely new dimension of governing. The Twelve Visions Party with its Prime Law takes civilization into that new dimension never entered before on Earth. In that new dimension, all people will experience a wealthy lifestyle, even today's poor. In turn, our leaders lose their improper power and prestige.

Until now all forms of governing: tyrannies, dictatorships, fascism, communism, socialism, democracies, republics, even so-called capitalism in our world all fall under the one and only dimension of governing experienced on Earth. That one and only dimension allows varying degrees of initiatory force in the governing body. Never before has initiatory force been explicitly banished from the governing body.

Now with the Prime Law, for the first time government, law, and the people's prosperity can go into a new dimension. That new dimension is a civilization free of initiatory force, which means free of the rule of man. There has *never* been a civilization free of the rule of man. Our leaders would have *never* allowed it. The results will be soaring new technologies that drive down costs as explained throughout this book. Your buying power in this next dimension will soar as never seen before. That soaring buying power will pull the poor out of poverty and push everyone into the wealthy elite class. The Twelve Visions Party with its Prime Law takes us into the new dimension of no rule of man. Poverty and hunger will vanish. Diseases will be eradicated. Everyone will be rich.

The pages to follow explain all this, but here is a summary:

Rule of man destroyed all civilizations throughout history. The greater the move away from rule of man, the greater the prosperity. America is the shining example. But without the Prime Law, over time rule of man adapts, evolves and takes over and takes down civilization. It is happening now to our America, to the greatest country that ever existed on Earth.

America was founded on the most rule-of-man-resistant governing body ever conceived. But without the Prime Law, America was still stuck in the only dimension ever known on Earth — the same dimension in which initiatory force exists in the governing body. Therefore, the rule of man eventually took over. And the rule of man is now taking America down.

The Twelve Visions Party with its Prime Law takes us into another dimension never known on Earth in which initiatory force does not exist in the governing body. This new dimension will end poverty, hunger, even disease, and will make you rich. It will also end the leaders' power, end rule of man, which is why they have never allowed this idea to leak.

The Twelve Visions Party with its Prime Law is *the* answer to all our problems. The dangerous debt goes away with the Prime-Law-based, Protection-Only Budget. Poverty goes away with the unburdened, rapidly advancing new technologies driving down costs. Diseases go away with unburdened, rapidly advancing new medical technologies and life-saving drugs. We enter a new dimension never known before, the dimension of no ruling class, the dimension of pure freedom. Without a ruling class, civilization will advance at never-before-known speeds. All the arguments against this new dimension will quickly subside in light of the results that eradicate poverty, hunger and disease — that raise *everyone's* standard of living to that of a millionaire or more.

But to go into the next dimension is not easy since it has never been so much as envisioned before, and that is why I founded the Twelve Visions Party with its Prime Law. The TVP is bringing to civilization a new dimension that eradicates the rule of man, ending the ruling class. Make no mistake, not even our beautiful America experienced this other dimension, which is why we are going down today. The Twelve Visions Party is a precious but fragile gift being offered to mankind. Accept this gift.

*The Seven Immediate Effects of the Twelve Visions Party With Its Prime Law*

**First and foremost, the immediate effect of the Twelve Visions Party will be the end of poverty.** Rule of man is inextricably linked to poverty. The Twelve Visions Party with its Prime Law is the party to end rule of man and poverty.

Only the TVP can take us into a new dimension where rule of man does not exist...where poverty does not exist. Why? The

Prime Law. The Prime Law eradicates initiatory force. Without initiatory force there can be no rule of man. Of course, your leaders do not want you to know this.

So the first, foremost and immediate effect of the Twelve Visions Party will be the end of poverty.

**The second stunning effect of the Twelve Visions Party will be the rapid eradication of many diseases.**

The rule of man's regulatory bureaucracies politicize the medical industry and destroy it. When we end the rule of man, and their regulatory bureaucracies can no longer politicize the medical industry, then research-and-development money will dramatically pour into the medical industry. The results will be rapid and uninhibited medical progress in an environment of no debilitating web of political regulations retarding progress.

The Twelve Visions Party with its Prime Law and Protection-Only Budget will depoliticize the medical industry. The war against disease will then move very fast with nothing political holding the geniuses back, supercharged by record amounts of research-and-development money pouring in. Cancer, heart disease, and possibly the ultimate disease — aging itself — will be cured within a decade in the Twelve Visions World.

**The third welcomed effect of the Twelve Visions Party will be the eradication of terrorism and crime.**

The entire might and focus of government will be protection. There will be no competing funds.

Today for example, entitlement money competes with national defense and national security. Because politicians (i.e., man) run the country, their vote-collecting entitlement money ultimately "wins", which jeopardizes national security.

Why does entitlement money eventually "win" the battle of the budget over protection money? Well, entitlement money buys votes. Rule of man — man running our country with selfish re-election fever — pushes for vote-buying entitlement money, which jeopardizes national security.

When we remove the rule of man, when the Prime Law is an amendment to the U. S. Constitution, at that time our civilization moves into another dimension...into pure freedom in which government's sole purpose is to protect its people. All money, all focus goes toward protection, which would minimize terrorism and crime unlike we have ever seen before. Moreover, people may lose their modest entitlement money, but they will quickly live like millionaires as explained in the pages to follow. (Also, social security will be paid back with interest as seen on the pages to follow.)

**The fourth needed effect of the Twelve Visions Party is minimizing unemployment.**

To best understand this, let me go into something I write about in the pages to follow in which I talk about a *split-run*, a term used in the direct-mail industry. I use the scenario: *let's split-run America.* In other words, let us say half of America continues on her current path, the other half splits off into Prime-Law America (i.e., an America with the Prime Law). In Prime-Law America there would be no taxes. Now, no taxes seems to just about everybody as something undoable, but the reason it seems undoable is because our minds are stuck in the only political dimension known on earth.

You see, taxes (i.e., forced taxes) are intrinsically part of the only political dimension we have ever known...rule of man with initiatory force as our governing body, our ruling class. So we are not able to look at the possibility of no taxes with any sense of credibility. Without forced taxes, today's political dimension would disintegrate, making the idea of no taxes impossible. However, in the new dimension of no initiatory force and no rule of man and no ruling class, in my scenario of Prime-Law America, I ask: what would happen in such a country where there's no taxes?

Well, first of all, businesses would move to Prime-Law America. Suddenly that becomes the place where the jobs are, and hard-working people would follow for work in Prime-Law America where the jobs are available, where there are no taxes. Prime-Law America would boom. There would be a demand for real estate, for buildings, factories. Homes would be built and bought. We would see a rapidly booming economy with essentially no unemployment in an environment of pure freedom. We would experience the prosperity explosion I have written about for the past 30 years. Everyone would live a wealthy lifestyle as the cost of living is driven down to fractions of what we currently experience through a Great Technological

Revolution. And people would gladly pay for a government that provides the conditions for this millionaire-like universal prosperity and peace.

People *will pay* for prosperity and peace. Yes, people will voluntarily pay for a government that provides the conditions for them to live like wealthy millionaires in a world of safety and peace. We just do not know this because we have never entered this new dimension of no initiatory force. Ultimately the government would run as a protection service, as a business structure as I describe in Volume Four.

So to recap the fourth needed effect of the Twelve Visions Party: it would eliminate unemployment as the country booms in this other dimension.

**The fifth effect of the Twelve Visions Party would be greatly improved quality of life.** Standards of living would soar. Our buying power would soar. Our wealth would be something we never experienced before.

We would enjoy our lives. We would live the lives we were meant to live. In this new dimension, unburdened new technologies and unburdened geniuses of society would lift our buying power and quality of life to unimaginable new heights.

We have seen one microcosm of this recently, and that was the computer revolution. Imagine that computer paradigm that was very lightly regulated, during which computer buying power multiplied thousands of times...imagine that same freedom-paradigm spreading across all industries. That image, that same phenomenon is what we would experience in Prime-Law America, otherwise known as the Twelve Visions World.

**The sixth effect of the Twelve Visions Party would be the superior quality of education in a Twelve Visions World.**

Today we have to ask *why*, in the greatest country on our planet, *why* do we see so many children graduating high school illiterate and incompetent? The answer to that question baffles just about everyone.

But the answer to that question is: we have such a high illiteracy rate and incompetency rate of graduating high school students because the rule of man politicizes our school systems. That is *the* answer.

Therefore, the Twelve Visions Party that eradicates the rule of man would eradicate illiteracy and inferior education. Again, there is no explanation for illiteracy and inadequate education in this prosperous country other than: the rule of man politicizes education. The Twelve Visions Party removes the rule of man. Education becomes what it should be. Children will graduate as integrated thinkers, as self-leaders, as value creators as explained in Volumes Two and Three.

**The seventh effect of the Twelve Visions Party: it will quickly stop America's fall into insolvent bankruptcy.**

The Protection-Only Budget, the budget that adheres to the Prime Law, would almost immediately cut our budget in half. As I write about in the pages to follow, there would be a huge event I refer to as the Great Displacement Program, which would be the selling off to the private sector every aspect of government that has nothing to do with protection. And we would use that huge sale in the trillions of dollars, including selling government land, to pay off Social Security.

So the seventh effect of the Twelve Visions Party is: it would quickly get a handle on our runaway deficits and debt. It would stop America's irreversible fall into bankruptcy. Subsequently, as the Twelve Visions Party spreads around the world, it would stop the world's fall into insolvent bankruptcy and remove the debt from our children's and grandchildren's futures.

### *The Prosperity Option*

The Twelve Visions Party with its Prime Law will take the world into a new dimension never known before. For three millennia the prosperity option has been held secret. The three-thousand-year-old secret is the Prime Law, **the prosperity option**.

There are two dimensions of civilization, but only one to date has been known on our planet. In that *traditional poverty dimension* we have the history of the world. Initiatory force is allowed in the governing body. The rule of man steadily rises, and the ruling class gradually takes over. Agenda-laws, regulations, litigation hold everything back. The non-ruling class gets pushed down into an underclass. Over time, poverty grows; freedom shrinks. Mankind fails his potential; ultimately tyranny and poverty prevail.

Now there is another option. It is the prosperity option, which has been held secret for 3000 years. In the *new prosperity dimension*, we have the Twelve Visions World. Initiatory force is not allowed in the governing body. The Prime Law permanently banishes initiatory force. Rule of man is eradicated. The non-ruling class is truly free. There are no agenda-laws, regulations, litigation to hold back civilization. The non-ruling class rises into a wealthy elite class as prosperity spreads throughout society; pure freedom reigns. The leaders lose their ruling-class power. Mankind soars to fulfill its potential; peace and prosperity prevail.

This sheds light on the importance and value this new non-political party called the Twelve Visions Party is bringing to civilization. The Twelve Visions Party will make this a better world for us, our children and their children.

### *3000-Year-Old Secret*

I am going to sharply define the highly-guarded 3000-year-old secret that would send any nation and all its people to the richest levels the world has ever known. For millennia, the political leaders of the world have waged wars and even starved their own people to death in order to guard this secret. Once it is out, America and all her people will become wealthy, and I am going to further reveal the secret in this section.

In order to open our flight to riches, I must first close our fall into poverty. In all civilizations throughout history, the more powerful and imposing the *rule of man*, the more tyrannical and poor the society. America's prosperity will end, and her fall into poverty will continue under steadily growing rule of man. If we do not eradicate the fundamental ingredient that nourishes the rule of man, we will steadily sink into poverty and eventually into tyranny.

That fundamental ingredient is *initiatory force*. For man to rule over others — over large populations — requires the ability to *force* those populations to obey their political leaders. Yet, how can government lead a nation without that power of force?

Let us look more closely at the concepts of "lead" and "force": let us take into account *parameters*. The government should *lead,* with use of *force* if necessary, when it comes to *protecting us* FROM FORCE or THREAT of FORCE. Protecting the people was the original intent of our government. And as you will see in the pages that follow, protecting the people is the *one and only* valid purpose of government. In other words, *self-defense force* against those *initiating force* is the proper role of government. Government *should lead* when it comes to *protecting us*...lead with the use of *self-defense force* if necessary, which includes the military, police protection, courts, justice, prisons. With those parameters around the government's role "to lead" and "to use force", the government plays a vitally important role toward our prosperity and well-being.

Should government go beyond protecting us to impose its left-wing or right-wing political agendas upon us? Should politicians and bureaucrats impose those agendas upon us through their laws and regulations that are backed by force? If those laws and agendas go beyond the parameters of *self-defense force* necessary to protect citizens and their property...then those laws and regulations enter the parameters of *initiatory force*. Within the parameters of initiatory force comes the rule of man: men and women forcing their political agendas — left-wing or right-wing — upon the populace. If we disagree with those agendas, what then? We are forced by man-made agenda-law to obey. With those expanded parameters around the government's role "to lead" and "to use force", the government plays a deadly role against our prosperity and well being.

With initiatory force, government power goes beyond its one valid purpose of protection. Government transforms from a valuable *protection service* into a destructive *ruling class* that steadily replaces economic freedom with political power, which inevitably pulls a nation down into poverty (and eventually tyranny) as is happening now in America.

All laws and regulations within the parameters of self-defense force are good and necessary. All laws and regulations that go beyond those parameters of protection...laws and regulations that push political agendas — liberal or conservative — enter the parameters of *initiatory force* and must be eliminated in order to end rule of man and, consequently, end poverty and eventual tyranny.

But how can we, the people, get control of our government, embrace laws and regulations based on protection and *self-defense force* and eradicate laws and regulations based on political agendas and *initiatory force*? **How do we begin to stop rule of man, poverty, and eventual tyranny?**

I have the answer. It is called the Prime Law. The Prime Law was developed as *the* tool to embrace good laws and regulations for our protection and to eliminate bad laws and regulations for our politicians' and bureaucrats' agendas. The Prime Law can cap and clean the massive spill of bad political laws and bureaucratic regulations and get back America's clean sea of economic freedom.

In 1787, this looming leak of bad political laws and bureaucratic regulations was not yet seen by our founding fathers. Today the out-of-control, rule-of-man leak pollutes our economic freedom nearly to the point of no return. We have one last chance with the Prime Law. Its separation of bad political laws and regulations from good protection-only laws and regulations can save America. This clean separation was missed by our founding fathers and is the missing ingredient to a perfect constitution that clears out and keeps out the insidious rule of man and forever eliminates poverty and tyranny.

The Prime Law as an amendment to the U.S. Constitution would purify America's freedom and lift all of us to a prosperity no civilizations of the world have ever seen before.

So, let us ask one last time: beyond the function of protection, should politicians and bureaucrats be leading our lives? Should we allow the rule of man? I say NO. I have developed an entirely new political system — or better described as a nonpolitical system — to lead the country, limiting government and its leadership to protection only while eliminating the rule of man.

We must first remove the ruling-class political weapon of *initiatory force*, leaving our government with only one form of force — nonpolitical self-defense force against those violating us by using or threatening initiatory force against us. The Prime Law is our tool to accomplish that otherwise impossible feat.

*A New Dimension*

The Prime Law changes everything, for with it we enter an entirely new dimension of law, government, and civilization. This new dimension is a brand-new paradigm never seen on Earth. All law and politics and civilizations throughout history and currently, including America, are in the same dimension defined by the presence of initiatory force in the governing body.

Historically, the more checks and balances of power and divisions of power such as in America, especially early America, the better civilization does within that only dimension known to man in which the governing body is permitted the use of initiatory force. In other words, the more obstacles put in place to limit government's use of power — limit initiatory force — the more civilization thrives.

However, as we are witnessing in America, no matter how many obstacles are put in place, still, civilization stuck in that dimension that permits initiatory force in its governing body will ultimately be pulled down by rule of man, by the ruling class that has ever-increasing access to initiatory force — its ruling power.

Never has there been a civilization on our planet in which initiatory force was NOT permitted in its governing body. Such a civilization would enter a new dimension never known on Earth. The Prime Law brings civilization into that utterly new dimension.

The most prosperous civilizations throughout history only moved towards that new dimension. America came closest, but still remained in the only dimension known to man — the dimension in which initiatory force is inherently in our governing body, which eventually strengthens into a ruling body backed by force.

Despite all the checks and balances and obstacles put in place, man creating, interpreting, and executing law backed by initiatory force axiomatically leads to the destructive rule of man — imperfect man influenced by ego, power, prestige, ignorance, selfish agendas, and inspired by control over others. Man creating, interpreting, and executing law backed by and bound by the Prime Law, on the other hand, leads to pure freedom and unprecedented prosperity.

Explicitly removing initiatory force from civilization including and especially from the governing body brings civilization into a never-before-known dimension — a paradigm of prosperity never known in our world.

I am sometimes asked if the Twelve Visions Party is about going back to our founding fathers' original concept. The answer is NO; we are about making civilization leap forward into an entirely new dimension never known before: the entirely new dimension of NO initiatory force.

We are not setting up checks and balances and divisions of power to *restrict* government's use of initiatory force as did our forefathers. No, we are taking civilization into an entirely new dimension by *banishing* initiatory force within our government.

Only the Prime Law can take us into that entirely new dimension. When people try to compare us to other political movements such as the Constitution Party or the Libertarian Party, the comparisons do not hold. Those political movements are stuck in the traditional dimension. They may move in our direction, but they could never take civilization into our entirely new dimension void of initiatory force...not without the Prime Law. The Prime Law makes us unique, for it causes law and governance to leap to a new dimension never entered before...a dimension where rule of man becomes impossible.

Without rule of man, civilization will flourish. Initiatory force in the hands of government is unnatural (violating natural law) but has existed as our ONLY option for so long that it seems normal. Civilization would flourish with definitive removal of initiatory force and, consequently, removal of rule of man. This is a new concept. Imagine a civilization, a country with no initiatory force, no force-backed political agendas, only protection. Early America came closest, but was missing the Prime Law. It is hard to imagine a government without initiatory force, but that image has been simplified for you on the pages to follow. This is a breakout concept that will change America and then the world. The Prime Law is the 3000-year-old secret on how to become and remain the richest nation on Earth. Now, let us open our flight to riches...

*Universal Wealth, Health, Peace*

## How To Become and Remain The Richest Nation on Earth

All the people can live like millionaires, including the poor. Let me explain...

During the computer revolution of the late 20th Century, computer buying power multiplied so dramatically that ordinary families could buy computers that a few years earlier only millionaires could buy. The computer revolution's paradigm was elegantly simple, as follows: **the ruling class had little control over the computer industry**.

The TVP takes that same paradigm and applies it to ALL AMERICAN INDUSTRIES. Buying power can multiply a thousand times, not just for buying computers...but for buying EVERYTHING. When the Prime Law nullifies ruling-class control over all industries, the resulting TVP-induced, unhindered Great Technological Revolution will spread that same "get-millionaire-rich" paradigm beyond the computer world across all industries. With the new end-rule-of-man thus eliminate-the-ruling-class political system, with the Prime-Law Amendment to the U.S. Constitution, you will be able to buy what a few years before only millionaires could buy!

The new political party, the Twelve Visions Party (TVP), embodies that new political system. The TVP ignites the most real and ambitious get-rich program for the people in the history of mankind. The TVP Platform is named: *Make All The People Wealthy, Including the Poor!* That title is literal, not figurative. The Twelve Visions Party *literally* delivers the largest, most ambitious get-rich program since the beginning of civilization. The entire non-ruling class, essentially *all people* will be the beneficiaries! They will live like millionaires without lifting a finger! People will become a thousand times richer!

If buying power multiplies a thousand times, then *you* become rich. Consider this late-20th-century quote from Bill Gates: *"Another sign of a healthy, competitive industry is lower prices. The statistics show that the cost of computing has decreased ten million fold since 1971. That's the equivalent of getting a Boeing 747 for the price of a pizza."* Through the TVP, that get-rich phenomenon applies universally. That get-rich phenomenon happens through computer-industry-like economic freedom under a protection-only government purified by the Prime-Law Amendment and Protection-Only Budget (or Prime-Law Budget). *All people* will get rich, including the poor! And although the Twelve Visions Party has a comprehensive list of protection-only planks in its National Platform, the bottom-line results will be rapid and universal wealth (and health) for all citizens, including the poor. It is the largest, most realistic and most comprehensive get-rich program ever conceived.

Consider the Twelve Visions Party *a legitimate get-rich plan for the people...the biggest get-rich opportunity of all time.* The plan is quite simple: the rule-of-man ruling class on top of our society pushes us all down into a suppressed class — all of us. If not for those political and regulatory leaders pushing every industry down, then *you* would be rich; the ENTIRE suppressed class from all racial and social backgrounds would rise up into a wealthy elite class! Universal wealth, health, and peace is a beautiful thing and, for the first time, is possible through the Twelve Visions Party. Simply remove the rule-of-man ruling class through the Prime Law. We will be a thousand times richer just as the mostly unregulated, free computer industry of the late 20th and early 21st century during which buying power multiplied a thousand times in a few short years! The TVP is *the calling* for the entire non-ruling class, the suppressed class...the underclass.

If we remove the rule of man through the Prime Law (i.e., the Prime-Law Amendment), then the costs of living will fall and the people will rise up at all levels — the poor, the middle class, the successful, the self-made millionaires — the entire non-ruling class will rise up very rapidly into a **wealthy elite class**. As the costs of living dramatically decrease, EVERYONE will become rich, including the poor! The Twelve Visions Party provides a practical plan for removing the ruling class. Therefore, the Twelve Visions Party provides the people with the greatest get-rich opportunity in the history of the world.

The computer revolution was a forerunner to the coming all-encompassing, TVP-induced **Great Technological Revolution**. If someone tells you the computers' exponential multiplication of buying power was an anomaly due to the invention of the silicon chip, then pages 147-159 of this book give another indisputable example of this get-rich phenomenon 100 years ago before high-technology altogether. The computer revolution was an anomaly *due to the absence of the rule of man!* The TVP is here to eradicate the rule of man, the ruling class, and, consequently, liberate the suppressed class and send the entire suppressed class soaring up to the wealthy elite class. Universal wealth is absolutely possible; it just has never been seen before.

### *Defining the Suppressed Class*

I ask both the poor and the middle class: how would you like to see your little bit of spending money buy ten times, a hundred times, a thousand times more goods?

I ask both the struggling and successful self-made business owners: how would you like to keep all of what you make without paying nearly half your money to the government? How would you like to have no more state and federal regulations burdening your business and cutting back your profits?

The poor, the middle class, the struggling business owners, the rich business owners are in the same family, although they are played against each other by the ruling class. But they are in the same family of the *non-ruling class*...or the *suppressed class*.

When the suppressed class is free from the ruling class, then the self-made business owners soar ahead and compete for our business; they drive down our prices, which in turn drives up our buying power making the poor and middle class more prosperous. Remember the computers.

### *Society's Two Families*

Society consists of two families of people: *the ruling class* and *the non-ruling class* or *the suppressed class*...that is, *the ruling family* and *the suppressed family*.

Because of decades of media abuse, most people today do not understand their family relationship. For example, clever people in *the ruling family* influence people in *the suppressed family* to dislike each other. We are led to believe we dislike, even hate those in our own family...those geniuses of society who are actually our greatest benefactors.

We don't realize that those geniuses of society whom we are led to hate are actually part of our own suppressed family, part of the non-ruling class or the suppressed class. They are the successful parents who want to make their children successful too. Those geniuses of society, if left alone by the ruling class, if not targeted, maligned, regulated, attacked and pushed down by the ruling class...those geniuses of society would raise the standard of living for all of us so fast and so dramatically that the less fortunate would quickly live prosperous and fulfilling lives. In fact, even the poor would soon live like millionaires.

The computer revolution gave us our most recent example during which computer buying power multiplied a thousand times in a few short years. The invention of the assembly line starting with Henry Ford's automobile was another example...when people could suddenly buy cars and other mass-produced goods that only millionaires could previously afford. There have been other examples, too, including an eye-opening example in this book involving the railroad industry. There are examples throughout history involving the airline industry, the food industry, the publishing industry, the housing industry, the appliance industry, the medical industry and more. All such examples have a common thread: the ruling class was not yet hovering over those industries at the time of their prosperity-explosions for the people. They all have yet another common thread: their prosperity-explosions for the people were all stopped by the ruling class as you will see when you read the heartbreaking story of James J. Hill later in this book.

The geniuses of society are like our successful parents who want to raise us to be successful and happy too (although we have been led to dislike or even hate our "successful parents"). Henry Ford was so generous he was taken to court and thought to be going crazy for dramatically overpaying his employees and undercharging for his cars! Of course, his genius worked, and he raised the standard of living of the entire country. If the geniuses of society were left alone by the ruling class, and if the people were not fooled by the ruling class, then the geniuses would raise our standard of living and win our love just as the employees and customers loved Henry Ford. But by maligning and suppressing our greatest benefactors under relentless bad press, suffocating regulations and abusive litigation, their ability to send our standard of living soaring to new heights is destroyed. Through clever use of lies and propaganda, the ruling class leads us to dislike the geniuses of society as we remain suppressed in financially and emotionally inferior lives.

I have spent over thirty years researching and uncovering this well-hidden secret of the ruling class. Political leaders have suppressed the tenets of the Prime Law for 3000 years. I have written thousands of pages of evidence exposing this 3000-year-old secret-suppression by the ruling class. I have also prepared in the TVP Movement the rapid solutions to liberate us from our Great Suppression. As you will see, my rapid solutions will bring us stunning explosions in our standards of living. With my solutions, all the people will live like millionaires in the Twelve Visions World. We saw it happen to the computer industry; now it can happen across all industries. The Twelve Visions Party along with its Prime Law are here to make that happen.

*Points to Remember:*

The ruling class causes us to dislike or even hate the geniuses of society, the very people who will actually make us rich, *including the poorest among us.* Indeed, even today's poor *will be rich* in the new TVP political system. The unhindered geniuses of society will make all of us rich by dramatically lowering costs of living and innovating cost-free technologies just as they did in the computer industry. The Twelve Visions Party provides the practical protection-only political system.

The ruling class convinces us to admire or even love our charismatic political leaders, the very people who will eventually make us all poor...including the middle class, even the rich eventually. Our political leaders are members of the manipulative ruling class who were never around the computer industry during its prosperity-explosion for the people. They suppress us and suppress the geniuses of society who could MAKE US ALL

RICH. The Twelve Visions Party opens our flight to economic freedom and personal riches.

The most ambitious get-rich plan since the beginning of time is upon us. It is up to you now to recognize this rare opportunity. YOU and your loved ones are the direct beneficiaries. This new direction has NEVER BEEN DONE before and NEVER CONCEIVED at this scale. Bringing down the ruling class sends the huge suppressed class at all its levels soaring up to the wealthy elite class. Including you!

How exactly will this happen?

The rise of the Twelve Visions Party with its Prime-Law Amendment and Protection-Only Budget (i.e., a Prime-Law Budget) will eradicate the rule of man to free all industries — *pure* freedom. The unimpeded geniuses will drive down costs and drive up buying power until we all live like millionaires without us having to lift a finger. America or any country that adopts the Twelve Visions Party with its Prime Law will become and remain the richest nation on Earth.

*Universal Wealth, Health, Peace*

# The Beautiful Society

The actions of animals, man included, are guided and shaped by survival. In today's society that allows initiatory force, irrationality thrives, and actions of politicians and bureaucrats actually require more and more irrationality just to survive. Indeed, imagine the political arena now in America; irrational and dishonest behavior is actually part of the composite for political survival. A completely rational and honest person would not survive in today's political arena!

When I explain the beautiful society to people, they often have a hard time because they have never seen and therefore cannot conceive a society truly free of irrationality. I am often peppered with questions such as: "What would happen if a very powerful business (you fill in the blank with something sinister)?" Or, "What if society and its businesses started hurting the environment?" Or, "What would happen if those with money and influence started to control our products and therefore influence who we become?" And so on and so on.

Whereas I can thoroughly answer each and every one of the endless such questions and demonstrate how a Prime-Law society would always remain the beautiful society with no corruption or depreciation of freedom and prosperity, instead something deeper can wash through one's conscience like a cool ocean wave that puts all the doubters at ease. You see, mankind shapes its actions based on survival. In this other dimension of no initiatory force, survival pressures will guide man to rational actions and will drive out irrational actions. By contrast, in today's society steeped in initiatory force from our government, the opposite is true as survival pressures guide man to irrational actions. But when initiatory force is eradicated and a Great Technological Revolution drives down costs of living so low that we all become wealthy...well, irrational actions no longer make any sense and actually hurt one's survival. Lies, deceit, fraud, illusions that give politicians and political businessmen advantages today will reverse in tomorrow's no-force dimension and will hurt politicians and businessmen. Irrational actions for the first time will work against any and all advantages. Imagine a person in that other no-force dimension wanting to rob a store. Whereas in today's opportunity-stricken dimension such an irrational and immoral action happens rather frequently, why would anyone in the other prosperity dimension ever desire or need to take that irrational action? Everyone will be well off to begin with, and the irrational action would risk all that prosperity for nothing — for less prosperity and severe consequences. There simply will be no more demand for irrational actions in the other dimension of no initiatory force. In fact, all survival pressures in that other dimension will push people into rational actions only. Irrationality disappears along with deceit, fraud, coercion and initiatory force. The Prime-Law society becomes and permanently remains the beautiful society in which everyone prospers, even today's poor. There will be NO irrationality; survival will guide mankind into pure rationality. That beautiful society gives us the life we were meant to have!

By understanding that irrational actions vanish forever, those endless "what if" and "what would" questions (all based on irrational actions) can go away in one swoop. The Prime-Law society is the beautiful society in which *all* the people are rational, wealthy and healthy with eternal peace and prosperity. Keep this in mind while reading this book: in the new dimension of no initiatory force, survival pressures push everyone into purely rational good-for-society actions and drive out irrational bad-for-society actions. You just have never seen anything like it before.

## Evidence

The evidence of the poverty path versus the prosperity path is obvious and overwhelming. To easily see proof of poverty as a result of initiatory force within the ruling class versus prosperity as a result of restricting initiatory force within the ruling class, just look across the political-economic landscape of countries today and throughout history. Consider the poverty in the Middle East and throughout Africa — countries loaded with ruling-class initiatory force. By contrast consider the prosperity in America in which the U.S. Constitution resists initiatory force within the ruling class. Unfortunately, the U.S. Constitution has battled against the disease of mankind — initiatory force and its rising rule of man — for over two centuries and is battle worn and weary. It needs reinforcement. It needs new and absolute strength to stop the rule of man (initiatory force). It needs the Prime Law Amendment.

Volume Two

Make All the People Wealthy

# SPLIT-RUN

## AMERICA (SPLIT-A)

## VERSUS

## PRIME-LAW AMERICA (SPLIT-B)

*SETTING FREE THE GENIUSES OF SOCIETY:*

*ERA OF RAPID ADVANCEMENT*

*AND*

*FLOURISHING PROSPERITY*

## What is a Split-Run?

The large marketing industry — direct-mail — sends advertisements to you through the mail. The reason direct mail dwarfs other forms of advertising such as television, radio, newspapers and magazines is because of its effectiveness. And the reason direct mail is so effective is because of something called **the split-run**.

Here is how it works: in an advertisement-mailing (called "a run"), every two names get "split" — the first name and address (split-A) gets mailed the established advertisement ("the control"); the second name and address (split-B) gets mailed the test advertisement ("the challenger"). That is known as an a,b *split-run*. The response (i.e., the orders) quickly and undeniably tells us which approach is more effective. There is no guesswork: the numbers tell us what works and what does not work. We need no "brilliant" professors or "expert" analysts telling us what we should do. The numbers tell us everything we need to know.

Veterans in the direct-mail industry shake their heads when they hear some marketing "expert" saying "*I think* this..." or "*I think* that..." For, living by the unlying and unthinking numbers, direct mailers *know* their answers are correct.

During the fourth-quarter 2008 worldwide financial implosion, I heard over and over economic "experts" on television and on the radio saying, "I think..." "I think..." "I think..." I noticed that they were wrong as much as they were right. In other words, their many opinions meant nothing above the odds.

One day, when I had heard one-too-many "I think..." I blurted, "God, I just want to split-run this country!"

*Bingo*. The light turned on in my head. Over the next few weeks, I wrote *Split-Run*. As you will see, one split takes us down the sad road to poverty while the other split opens our flight into prosperity.

## Imagine...No Taxes!

In *Split-Run*, we hypothetically a,b split America. Split-A is the control — the half of the country with the same political and economic policies that exist now backed by initiatory force and rule of man. Split-B is the test — the half of the country with different political and economic policies void of initiatory force and rule of man...starting with *no taxes*. Remember, income tax in America is backed by force — initiatory force. (I will explain later how the government will generate its money without coercion, but one step at a time.)

No taxes. What happens? Well, I know I personally move to Split-B, *Prime-Law America*. In fact, with no taxes, most people owning a business move to Split-B — move to Prime-Law America. Of course, businesses are where the jobs are — so more and more people who are badly wounded by the suppressed job market in Split-A — in America — move to Prime-Law America to find good jobs.

Prime-Law America booms. Factories and office buildings fill up and more get built to accommodate the new businesses rushing in. Homes get bought and more get built to house the job-searching people rushing in.

In short, the smartest job creators, both burgeoning entrepreneurs and established business owners, and the hardest-working people ambitious for work flock to Prime-Law America. The economy and standards of living soar in Prime-Law America. Meanwhile, the lazy moochers stay home, in America. The economy and standards of living sink in America.

Moreover, with no taxes, the smartest job creators and hardest working people rush into Prime-Law America not only from America, but from around the world. They leave behind their sinking economies and tax-crazed countries. Indeed, the smartest creators and hardest working people *in the whole wide world* end up in Prime-Law America! Prime-Law America becomes the booming melting pot America once was. Prime-Law America is the beneficiary of a worldwide brain-drain!

Schools, infrastructure, construction, real estate, publishing, clothing, farming, energy...all industries produce and boom. Very quickly, Prime-Law America becomes the envy of the world. Prime-Law America experiences unprecedented prosperity as America experiences unprecedented poverty. Sister America sadly suffers another Great Depression.

## Immigration — Let the Creators Come!

Prime-Law America not only has no taxes; it also has no welfare, no handouts. So, as in the early days of America, only the best of the foreigners – the smartest job creators and hardest workers — come to Prime-Law America. We get the best in the world — the best value creators, best job creators, and the hardest working people from around the world. The lazy moochers never come, for there is no welfare for them. They have to work for their existence in Prime-Law America, so the inherently lazy foreigners stay in their existing countries and continue receiving from the large "social good" programs.

Early America was known as the land of opportunity. People from all around the world came to America to build or contribute. None of those early immigrants came here with the idea of taking from our government. They came here with a dream and a passion to fulfill that dream.

Those early immigrants contributed enormously to America's rising prosperity. Some of those immigrants built the original industrial empires in America. Prime-Law America is the revival of that time of passion and production.

Meanwhile, America continues her stiff resistance to simple, hardworking immigrants. At the same time, America grows her welfare programs that ultimately motivate immigrants toward entitlements and laziness. America gets pulled under the weight of her growing welfare state as she begins to drown in debt.

## Small Government / Rich Main Street

Prime-Law America booms...growing, building, producing as the smartest creators and hardest workers rush here from America and from around the world. In this booming economy, standards of living keep rising.

Why? It all started with *no taxes*. Now, the smartest creators come to Prime-Law America to build their businesses here. The hardest workers follow to work for those businesses.

Well, *no taxes* and *booming economy* give us the data — the unlying numbers — we need to determine the role of government in Prime-Law America. Essentially in Prime-Law America, the government will *get out of the way*. That was the case in early America when our country was the envy of the world. Now, American industry is mired in regulations, legislation, taxes. America, Split-A, is stuck and sinking in ineffectiveness. America is falling.

Prime-Law America, on the other hand, is free of government drag. The role of government returns to *protection only*, which includes national defense, justice, courts, police, prisons.

In 1787, the U.S. Constitution supplanted suppressive rule of man with nearly flawless rule of law. A single, missing integration allowed power-seeking man to steadily "misinterpret" the Constitution and gradually weaken its power to limit government. Like a resurging disease thought to have been eradicated, the rule of man has adapted and gained strength against rule of law, against the U.S. Constitution. The missing integration that would have permanently protected the U.S. Constitution from the resurgence of rule of man is the *Prime Law*. In Prime-Law America, the ratification of the Prime Law as an amendment to the nearly flawless original U.S. Constitution makes the difference between America's less and less effective Constitution and Prime-Law America's incorruptible Constitution. The Prime Law, as defined later, guarantees a get-out-of-the-way government. The Prime Law is the difference between sinking into poverty (split-A America) versus soaring onto prosperity (split-B Prime-Law America).

## Universal Wealth
## The Great Technological Revolution

The huge bonanza that Prime-Law America enjoys that early America did *not* enjoy is high-technology. Unregulated, rapidly advancing high-technology drives costs to fractions and multiplies buying power, making consumers wealthier and wealthier.

Let us look at one industry that rose so quickly that the government did not know how to entangle it in regulations and legislation: the personal computer industry of the late twentieth century and early twenty-first century.

Specifically, within that industry, consumers' buying power

multiplied a thousandfold. In other words, computer consumers became computer rich. Indeed, computer consumers could purchase computer power that only multi-millionaires could buy just a few years earlier.

Now, in this modern era of high-technology, imagine that wealth-phenomenon spreading throughout all industries...a natural "millionaire phenomenon" today once government *gets out of the way*.

America's mainstream media, however, continues to play the blame-game and promote the out-of-context lie that lack of government regulation caused the 2008 financial collapse. Prime-Law America, on the other hand, just winks and smiles as the brightest creators and most ambitious workers emigrate from America to Prime-Law America. As the wealth in America evaporates, the wealth in Prime-Law America explodes. *All* the people become rich in the ensuing Great Technological Revolution that drives prices down to fractions as seen in the computer revolution, the forerunner. The people's buying power quickly multiplies a hundredfold or more.

## Universal Health
## The Great Technological Revolution

The health care in America continues to deteriorate. Making the problem worse, bureaucratic regulations have caused more and more doctors to slave longer and longer hours for less and less money.

The good doctors shake their heads, pack their bags, and leave for Prime-Law America.

The medical industry in America, perhaps more than any other industry, is submerged in bureaucratic regulation. Therefore, the medical and health-care industries, deprived of freedom (the oxygen to creative progress), have been severely *retarded* by big government.

Prime-Law America frees the medical and health-care industries. Doctors, surgeons, research doctors, scientists can make good money again. They can create values without being punished. Insurance premiums collapse as frivolous lawsuits cannot stand up to the Prime Law (revealed soon). Government gets out of the way in Prime-Law America. Medical research investments soar as cost-prohibitive FDA-like regulations vanish. The most competent doctors, surgeons, research doctors, scientists and pharmaceutical companies flee America for Prime-Law America just as fast as they can!

Furthermore, without the regulatory web catching and eating alive all aggressive research and progress, Prime-Law America becomes the health beacon of the world.

Free as the computer industry, the Great Technological Revolution moves into the health and medical industries. Prices begin dropping. Health care costs plunge. Like the computers, health care, cures, and medicine become cheaper and cheaper yet better and better. Very quickly, the most affordable and best health-care in the world welcomes all those coming to Prime-Law America.

As America calls for more and more FDA regulations to control the pharmaceutical companies, regulate medical research, and approve medicines in order "to protect the people", Prime-Law America just sighs. Indeed, there is no longer a need to point out and argue the many faults of a ruling class, for people can just get up and leave now — leave for Prime-Law America.

Prime-Law America not only becomes the fastest growing and most prosperous nation in history, it also becomes the most healthy! Prime-Law America enjoys the brightest research doctors and scientists in the world backed by the largest pools of investment-money for costly research projects finally free of cost-prohibitive self-serving political regulations. With the most brilliant doctors and scientists backed by unprecedented research funds, Prime-Law America routinely produces medical breakthrough after breakthrough; and with a get-out-of-the-way government, the investment companies can bring those lifesaving medical breakthroughs to the people at increasingly affordable prices. ...In sister America, just the most simple insurance policy becomes unaffordable.

## Remarkable Safety & Peace

Never in the history of the world has a government existed with *strictly* one purpose: **protection**. Early America came close, which is why early America's get-out-of-the-way, protection-only government created the conditions for her rapid rise to the envy of the world.

Without the Prime Law in place, however, the U. S. Constitution was vulnerable to the resurgence of the rule of man. Government steadily grew beyond its one proper purpose of protection. Instead of a protection service, government eventually became a ruling class. It has become so bad that today the President of the United States is expected to "fix" the economy. The President should focus on his proper role of Commander-in-Chief of the military and homeland security.

In Prime-Law America, the government is a protection service only, not a ruling class. It focuses on protection only and everything that protection involves such as justice, courts, police, prisons, national defense. With every dollar and every action going toward protection, the effectiveness of that protection surpasses the protection of all other governments, which are focused far beyond their one valid purpose of *protection only*.

Crime prevention becomes unsurpassable in Prime-Law America. Moreover, the creative and hardworking people who emigrate to welfare-free Prime-Law America could never possess the lazy criminal-mind. Furthermore, society is so prosperous with a get-out-of-the-way government, crime largely loses its appeal. Indeed, with prices falling to fractions (as seen in the computer industry) causing buying power to soar, essentially making all citizens rich, the motivation for monetary-based crime vanishes.

In Prime-Law America, crime vanishes. In America, wealth vanishes and crime rises...and rises. **...So far, the test Split-B Prime-Law America delivers a far better response than the control Split-A America, especially involving the three most important conditions of civilization: wealth, health, and peace.**

## Voluntary Pay

Prime-Law America is the only place on Earth that is booming with an abundance of jobs, peace, falling prices...a place where people are wealthier and healthier than they have ever been...while America and the rest of the world sink into job losses, home losses, fear, panic, collapsing standards of living.

Prime-Law America is also nearly free of crime and is the safest place on Earth. For, here government's sole function, its every thought and action is *protection*. Moreover, the people coming to Prime-Law America are the smartest value-and-job creators and most ambitious workers in the world. With no welfare, no government handouts, the lazy moochers and criminal minds do not bother to come to Prime-Law America. They stay home where their socialistic governments hand out elaborate entitlements. The criminals also stay home because crime *does not pay* in a country with a protection-only government.

As America and the rest of the world sink, the people in Prime-Law America enjoy wealth, soaring health, peace, happiness, and love. The juxtaposition of America and Prime-Law America shines a bright light on misery versus luxury, poverty versus prosperity. The contrast is stark. Political rhetoric and demagoguery no longer tell the out-of-context story. Instead, the split-run and the unlying numbers tell the whole story.

America and the whole world succumb to depression. The citizens of Prime-Law America feel how precious their **conditions** really are. And they *want to pay* for the protection service — the government — that guarantees their **conditions**. This new government idea that *gets out of the way* adopts the original U.S. Constitution with the following addition — the most basic Prime Law of Protection the founding fathers of America missed:

## The Prime Law

(The Fundamental Law of Protection)

### Preamble

*The *purpose* of human life is to prosper and live happily.

*The function of government is to provide the conditions that let individuals fulfill that *purpose*.

*The Prime Law guarantees those conditions by forbidding the use of initiatory force, fraud, or coercion by any person or group against any individual, property, or contract.

### Article 1

No person, group of persons, or government shall initiate force, threat of force, or fraud against any individual's self, property, or contract.

### Article 2

Force is morally-and-legally justified only for protection from those who violate Article 1.

### Article 3

No exceptions shall exist for Articles 1 and 2.

Living in the only prospering country in the world, a country setting new records for standards of living and safety while the rest of the world collapses into a catastrophic era of poverty and terror, citizens of Prime-Law America gladly, patriotically pay for their Protection-Only Government. That Protection-Only Government backed by the Prime Law guarantees the conditions for Prime-Law America to become the wealthiest, healthiest, and safest country in the history of the world. Beyond that, Prime-Law American government *gets out of the way!*

The question of: "Will people pay for their government if they don't have to?" is answered as follows: In Prime-Law America — YES. In America — NO. That is why America has resorted to a force-backed IRS. By the way, the Prime Law would never allow a force-backed IRS and would have prevented the resurgence of the rule of man and his insidious force-backed ruling class in America.

## The Government Trap

In the incredibly complex and confusing world today, what do we do? Imagine a person in America loses his job and, in the shrinking job market, he cannot get another job. He then loses his home. He has a family, wife and children to shelter and feed. Well, he is in the government trap. He needs government assistance to survive. He needs food stamps to feed his precious family. He looks to the government, for what else can he do? Where else can he turn?

However, with the arrival of Prime-Law America, he does not turn to food stamps. He immediately moves his family to Prime-Law America and gets a great job! This is just common sense.

In Prime-Law America, freedom begets the Great Technological Revolution, which begets falling prices and rising buying power just as we saw in the mostly unregulated computer revolution, the forerunner. Therefore, as citizens grow wealthy in Prime-Law America, the government trap never happens here.

In America, as more and more desperate business executives and desperate citizens fall into the government trap and turn to government for "rescue money," Prime-Law America just sighs and shakes his head at sister America. While they put out their hands, the truly creative business executives and hardworking citizens leave America for Prime-Law America and drive the economy in Split-B to unprecedented heights.

## *Common Sense* and *Split-Run*

In 1775, America's problems were complicated and confusing. Most Americans did *not* want to go to war with England. The situation was too complex for Americans to get clear answers and conviction.

As a response to the King's abuse of power, Thomas Paine published *Common Sense*. His pamphlet begins metaphorically in a simple place with a handful of persons. Then a few more persons arrive, and civilization begins. Seeing civilization in its most simple state, at its origin, cuts through the complexities...and common sense shines through! That little pamphlet brought America together to stand united against the King of England.

Similarly today, America's problems are complicated and confusing. The financial collapse starting in 2008 has Americans scared and confused. The situation is too complex for Americans to get clear answers to the problems including their feelings on socialistic government intervention.

As a response to the complex financial crisis and the government's confusing abuse of power, I completed *Split-Run*. My pamphlet begins with the hypothetical split-run, the a,b split between the existing control, Split-A America, versus the test, Split-B Prime-Law America. Prime-Law America starts fresh and free of the political entanglements of America. Seeing Prime-Law America in its most simple state, at its origin, cuts through the complexities...and common sense shines through! This little pamphlet can bring society together to stand united against *bogus* government and virulent rule of man. (Remember *proper* government is protection only, backed by rule of flawless law — the Prime Law.)

## Investments

Companies, jobs, construction, housing boom in tax-free Prime-Law America. So stocks and real-estate values go up. Moreover, capital gains taxes do not exist in Prime-Law America, so investors from around the world invest in Prime-Law America. In fact, Prime-Law America becomes the investment capital of the world.

Furthermore, with a relatively low-cost, voluntary-pay, get-out-of-the-way protection-only government, Prime-Law American industries do not get politicized and shackled with regulations as in America and around the rest of the world. Cost-prohibitive bureaucratic regulations do not exist in Prime-Law America, which dramatically lowers the costs of research and the risks of failure. Businesses and investors, therefore, pour money as never seen before into research and development. Those investments in research and development bring Prime-Law Americans rapidly advancing new technologies. Greater and greater life-enhancing products rise throughout all industries, from the health industry to the transportation industry, for lower and lower prices. Those rapidly evolving new technologies and products drive up standards of living and drive down costs of living.

Those investments in research and development are the best investments that do not create a bubble. Those investments in Prime-Law American industries stimulate the Great Technological Revolution unlike anything seen before. Those investments dramatically increase manufacturing and create more and more jobs. Business booms; investors invest; prices fall; prosperity soars.

Back in America, industries fall apart and collapse. Money evaporates; jobs vanish. Businesses go bankrupt. People go jobless and homeless. Government goes on the offense. With much media-driven fanfare, the president's top priority is "to fix the economy." Prime-Law America does not argue the point. Prime-Law America just raises his eyebrows as sister America's best benefactors emigrate to Split-B and make Prime-Law America stronger.

## Manufacturing

Prime-Law America becomes the best place in the world to house manufacturing companies and manufacturing jobs for several reasons: First, *no taxes*. Second, *no cost-prohibitive regulations*. Third, *no government-enforced unions*.

Those are three immediate, standout reasons that manufacturing companies and their jobs flee to Prime-Law America.

Another reason quickly arises: the truly free Prime-Law America experiences the Great Technological Revolution. No other country does; even American industries are too politicized to enter into the remarkable Great Technological Revolution. Indeed, only truly free, nonpoliticized industries can enter into the Great Technological Revolution.

The Great Technological Revolution becomes perhaps the greatest benefit of all to manufacturing companies. The steady cost-saving and production-improving technological breakthroughs are a boon for both profits and production.

America's manufacturing businesses, on the other hand,

continue dying. Manufacturing jobs go overseas for cheaper labor and less-regulatory conditions. And now, with the creation of Prime-Law America, whatever manufacturing is left in America makes a quick exit for Prime-Law America. America becomes less and less competitive, overrun with regulations, unions, taxes, lawsuits, unfriendly media and class-envy. Prime-Law America stands back and nostalgically watches the fall of the once-great nation.

America sinks into catastrophic conditions as politicians, bureaucrats, and mainstream media continue to cry out for "social justice" and more regulatory controls on business. Prime-Law America just sighs as the job creators and hard workers pack their suitcases and head for the land of the free.

## Estate Planning

Prime-Law America has no estate tax. Prime-Law America has no need for an estate tax, for there is no big and growing bureaucracy to pay for as in America. Therefore, with no estate tax, wealthy dynasties in America and around the world emigrate to Prime-Law America. In fact, the majority of business owners and investors emigrate to Prime-Law America, for human nature does not agree with turning over half of one's property to strangers for redistribution — half of what took one's entire life to build for one's children...just to owe half of its appraised value to a socialistic government that will spread one's wealth around!

In many if not most cases, the deceased parents' business must be sold so the children can pay the estate tax. Now, as clear as it is to see how wrong that socialistic force-backed government policy is, and how that was NEVER intended in the original U.S. Constitution...rule-of-man politicians and their media cheerleaders justify the family-business-destroying estate tax. And because over half of Americans depend on entitlements, that take-from-those-who-earn-and-give-it-to-strangers-who-do-not-earn mentality flourishes in America.

In fact, the irrationality grows increasingly grotesque to the point that the greatest contributors to society — the job creators and wealth creators — are somehow perceived as the villains of society. Moreover, their profit — their private property — is expected to be taken by government and redistributed to strangers — by and large to those lazy moochers on entitlements. And finally, at the end of those admirable job-and-wealth creators' lives, after they spent their entire lives creating jobs and benefiting society and earning and building their reward, their private property — their businesses or their investments — the government claims half of the appraised value for redistribution. The children have to sell the business to pay for that redistribution of wealth.

As obviously wrong as American government and its growing ruling class has become, as blatant as the violation is to the U.S. Constitution, the socialistic politicians, bureaucrats, judges, and media justify their wrongful acts. And the majority of Americans now benefit from those wrongful acts. So, the destructive government gains public approval for those wrongful acts. ...America regresses from the rule of rational law into the nightmarish rule of irrational man...cleverly crafted into a sort of mob rule.

But, Prime-Law America does not care anymore. Why try to tell sister America her wrongful ways any longer? Instead, the split-run will do the talking. As business owners and investors flee to Prime-Law America, citizens in sister America are left in a country of lazy leaders and lazy losers, all of them looking for redistribution of wealth. But the wealth dries up as the wealth-creators leave. All the "good genes" go to Prime-Law America.

## Wealth/Money Supply

First, the obvious: Money flows into Prime-Law America from immigrating business owners, investors, and wealthy dynasties. Second, those value/job creators and investors create new wealth. That unprecedented rise in money and wealth — that tsunami of prosperity — flows into the country of *no taxes*.

Sister-country America suffers a great loss of money and wealth. And whatever money and wealth are left flow into

Prime-Law America. Indeed, American business owners and investors want nothing to do with rising taxes, especially when Prime-Law America is an option.

And as if the tsunami of wealth and prosperity are not enough, another remarkable phenomenon of good fortune happens in Prime-Law America. Never before has any country entered into the Great Technological Revolution. The forerunners — the clouds before the great technological storm — were the computer and information revolutions during which costs collapsed to fractions and buying-power multiplied a thousandfold, making all consumers in those industries essentially rich. Yet unlike deflation in which prices are driven down because of less and less buyers due to increasing poverty, the Great Technological Revolution enjoys more and more buyers due to increasing wealth. Indeed, rapidly falling prices in the Great Technological Revolution make all Prime-Law American citizens wealthy and add never-before-seen new wealth to the new and booming nation.

## Retirement

The new era of the Great Technological Revolution in Prime-Law America multiplies buying power manyfold, making its citizens wealthy. Soaring buying power makes retired seniors, for the first time, wealthier than when they were working and earning! No country has ever experienced such a phenomenon in which the retired seniors live with a higher standard of living *than their working years!* Indeed, the Prime-Law American standard of living increases at a rapid rate as super rapidly advancing new technologies drive up values while driving down prices.

America, on the other hand, falls into a Catastrophic Era. As retirement funds and pension plans fall apart, Social Security and Medicare do too. Poverty strikes the elderly first as the financial crisis worsens.

## Jobs

The job market booms in Prime-Law America. Not only are there lots of available jobs in Prime-Law America, but the *quality* of jobs keeps going up. Why? The Great Technological Revolution. The quality of jobs climb from physical labor to mental/creative jobs. How? Consider that unemployment is almost nonexistent in the booming business/investment/research/manufacturing center of the world. In fact, there are not enough people to fill all the jobs in such a rapidly booming Prime-Law America. Indeed, this is when the power and beauty of the Great Technological Revolution shines through: As Prime-Law America booms and not enough people can fill the rapidly growing job market, the Great Technological Revolution advances technologies including computers and robotics to take over jobs of labor and push the people upward into the superior jobs of the mind!

In order to get enough people to fill the explosion of new jobs creates a strong demand for new technologies to fill the lower-tier jobs of labor. Those natural economic pressures, like a rising tide, lift ordinary people to better, more enriching jobs of the mind.

Back in America, by contrast, more and more citizens not only hang on to their lowly jobs of labor for dear life as the economy crashes, but those who do lose their jobs seek the lowest labor jobs just to survive.

## Freedom

A fully free country has never existed before Prime-Law America. America came close with the nearly flawless U. S. Constitution. But the most fundamental law of protection, protection from man — the Prime Law — was missed, which caused an opening in our original Constitution for a return of the rule of man. Eventually the rule of man resurged and restrengthened into a ruling class, a big government that today is racing into "government interventionism" or, in another word, *socialism*. With no Prime Law, man broke through the opening in our Constitution, and freedom leaked from our country to the point in America today in which force-backed socialism and, therefore, *poverty* are taking over.

In the beginning, the nearly flawless U. S. Constitution gave us the best rule of law in the world and, therefore, unrivaled prosperity took over. Without the Prime Law of protection from rule of man, from a ruling class, our Constitution and our country became vulnerable. As freedom leaked out, so did our prosperity. And now, increasingly under the rule of man, our loss of freedom is hemorrhaging and so is our loss of prosperity. Freedom is replaced with socialism; prosperity is replaced with poverty.

Prime-Law America, by contrast, is the first and only fully free country in the history of the world. Prime-Law America adds the Prime-Law as an amendment to the U.S. Constitution, which immediately closes the opening and encircles the country with pure protection from man including rule of man and a ruling class. Prime-Law America quickly fills with pure freedom and unprecedented prosperity. Prime-Law America has no ruling class, no rule of man, only the rule of flawless law — the Prime Law, the fundamental law of protection through which all law must pass. All "agenda law" that forces the rule of man on citizens will not pass.

While sister America relinquishes her freedom to rule of man and his big-government ruling class, she sinks into a catastrophic era of job losses, home losses, recession, and depression. Prime-Law America, by contrast, soars into the Great Technological Revolution as the geniuses of society are no longer held back or afraid to invest in their ideas. Prime-Law America quickly rises into the greatest prosperity ever seen as prices come down to fractions, witnessed once before in the isolated personal computer industry. All the people in Prime-Law America grow rich as their standards of living — wealth, health, safety, entertainment, and happiness — soar. They happily pay for their government of protection-only — their service-based government as opposed to America's force-based government. Indeed, citizens of Prime-Law America, as they watch America and the world around them fall into fear and desperation, gladly pay for a government that guarantees the conditions that allow them to live in such health, wealth, and peace.

## Foreign Relations

Foreign relations with America: Consider how the post-9/11 Republican Administration agitated world populations and generated hatred toward America. Although America's military stood strong, the growing worldwide resentment along with America's own democrats and media turning against the Administration ultimately weakened and undermined our military strength. On the other hand, the post-9/11 Democratic Administration relieves a lot of that envy-based hatred toward America around the world, yet the democrats' approach that heavily favors diplomacy over force ultimately weakens and undermines our military strength in the war on terror.

Prime-Law America functions politically and militarily through the Prime Law. That means Prime-Law America is a nation of self-defense. That military stance of striking only when struck *or threatened* takes a lot of the growing hatred toward America and turns it into **respect**. A military NOT functioning through rule of man — NOT *inconsistently* functioning according to whatever Administration is in power — instead *consistently* functioning through the rule of law, the Prime Law of Protection, brings forth a clear, unprejudiced yet unyielding message of strength. We are an unprejudiced rule-of-law (no longer a prejudiced rule-of-man) nation that will not tolerate violations to the flawless Prime Law of Protection that guarantees our conditions for wealth, health, and safety. Our military will act strongly and swiftly, but only if the rule of law, the flawless Prime Law, is violated.

Sister America struggles under any Administration with either worldwide hatred toward an aggressive Republican-Administration America or worldwide semi-acceptance toward a relatively passive Democratic-Administration America. Under both rule-of-man American Administrations, the eventual outcome is a weakened military.

Respect dominates worldwide perception of the Prime-Law American military, which quickly grows the best military in the world. Major weapons manufacturers come to Prime-Law America. Moreover, Prime-Law America zooms forward into weapons-technology breakthroughs much faster than other countries through the Great Technological Revolution. Business, science, research are not held back or prevented by cost-prohibitive regulations or political policies. Prime-Law America and its businesses, science and research are *purely free*, which has never happened before. Therefore, only Prime-Law America experiences the Great Technological Revolution. Technologies race forward at speeds seen only in the relatively unregulated personal-computer revolution, a harbinger to the Great Technological Revolution. The technological breakthroughs in all industries from health to weapons leave other countries in the dust, including heavily politicized America.

Very quickly, Prime-Law America surpasses the entire world in weapons technology. Prime-Law America makes it clear that its superior weapons would be used if and only if the Prime Law is violated. Prime-Law America is consistent about using those weapons in self-defense to put down any country's use of force or threat of force. Its weapons technology could eventually destroy any terrorist organization or any country's military; anti-American countries back down and respect Prime-Law America. Worldwide **respect** brings about the most effective foreign relations.

## National Defense

In America, the budget for national defense competes with the budget for entitlements. Prime-Law America sighs disapproval over sister-America's haunting internal conflict of spending her federal tax revenues on welfare versus national defense. Over time, that conflict causes a rising threat to national security. Indeed, over time, that battle of the budget — funding welfare versus national defense — puts growing pressures on lowering the priority of national defense. Prime-Law America abhors the thought. America struggles with this undermining threat to national security. Over time, in a country increasingly run by rule-of-vote-gathering man, national security loses the battle. Prime-Law America cannot fathom the thought.

In Prime-Law America, all government money, energy, and focus goes into the single proper purpose of the federal government — national defense and the other functions of Prime-Law Protection. No budgetary conflict of interest begins to undermine national security as in America. In Prime-Law America, *every thought* accompanied by life-and-death seriousness goes toward national security and justice. Protection is not only *the* top priority — it is the ONLY priority. Nothing works against national security; nothing competes with national security; no such internal conflict exists.

Focussed only on protection, Prime-Law America quickly builds the most cost-efficient and most effective military in the world. Prime-Law America's military rises quickly, for the demand for peace and protection in the booming economic powerhouse very quickly draws forth the supply — the military defense. Again, in Prime-Law America, the citizens — the luckiest and wealthiest people alive — demand and voluntarily pay for peace. To meet their demands, the best weapons innovators and manufacturers rise and thrive in Prime-Law America. Those weapons innovators and manufacturers race ahead within Prime-Law America's unprecedented Great Technological Revolution. With the catalyst of pure freedom, with no political burden or interference, the ingenious creators advance weapons technology the way they advanced computer technology. Relatively soon, to attack Prime-Law America would be committing military suicide.

Moreover, to remove *threat* of force, a Prime-Law requirement, Prime-Law America righteously and consistently uses its superior weapons technology to exterminate any high-threat terrorist group securing nuclear or biological weapons of mass destruction. That extermination sends a chilling message to all other terrorist groups racing toward more potent weapons: *once you violate the Prime Law by becoming a threat to Prime-Law America, you will be exterminated.*

Meanwhile, poor sister America held in political bondage eventually gets hit again and again with devastating, deadly chemical and biological and nuclear terrorist attacks. Millions of Americans die.

## War and Terror

Fighting the war on terror in America has been weakened from within by domestic politics and media. This problem stems back to the rising rule of man in America, steadily subordinating the rule of law. The U.S. Constitution continually loses its authority to judges, politicians, and bureaucrats. The resurgence of the rule of man starts with politically-motivated federal judges misinterpreting the Constitution, often with great fanfare from politically-motivated media. The authority of law increasingly disintegrates as the authority of man reclaims power. Throughout history, countries suffered in poverty and slavery under the rule of man. By contrast, countries enjoyed prosperity and freedom under the rule of rational law, culminating in the unrivaled prosperity and freedom of America. For, in America, the rule of rational law (the U.S. Constitution) replaced the rule of irrational man (a monarch).

Over the generations, however, flaw-filled man, a law-resistant power-seeking creature, adapted like bacteria and steadily took back his power to rule. For two centuries, rule of flaw-filled man steadily weakened rule of flawless law in America. Therefore, starting in 2008, prosperity plunged into poverty. Perhaps even worse, the proper elements of government that protected the people from terrorism weakened...at the hands of adapting, strengthening, virulent politicians, bureaucrats, judges and journalists interested in building their ruling-class power. Like a deadly bacterium or virus, they weakened America and her safety.

Prime-Law America goes in the opposite direction by crowning the nearly perfect original U.S. Constitution with the flawless Prime Law via the Prime-Law Amendment. The Prime Law forever guarantees rule of flawless law without possibility of a regression into rule of man. Our pure freedom causes the greatest prosperity-boom in the history of the world. Yet, perhaps even more important, the single legitimate purpose of government — **protection** — is not undermined and weakened by the rising rule of vote-gathering man...by politicians, bureaucrats, judges, journalists pushing for popular entitlements, image, political appeal and power. Instead, government focus, drive, and purpose is pointed like a laser — pointed at ending force or threat of force against its citizens. Prime-Law America quickly rises not only as the most prosperous place in the world, but the safest place as well. The people in Prime-Law America, enjoying the Great Technological Revolution and their wealth, health, and peace...gladly and voluntarily pay for their government's protection from terrorists.

Only within a country in which its industries are *truly free* and not burdened by political rule-of-man can the Great Technological Revolution rise. The rapidly advancing new technologies in Prime-Law America race ahead for our better living, better health, and better safety. Indeed, new weapons technologies advance so fast in Prime-Law America they render terrorist operations helpless. Prime-Law America quickly becomes the most peaceful country on Earth.

## Justice

Justice in America was once based on the rule of rational law...on the nearly flawless U.S. Constitution. American justice guaranteed the conditions for freedom, prosperity and peace.

Although the U.S. Constitution nearly eradicated rule of man, power-seeking man steadily adapted like a virulent virus or resistant bacterium. The rule of man — an elite ruling class — began overtaking rule of law. This ominous resurgence of the rule of man in America coincided with the fall of prosperity in America. Agenda-motivated politicians increasingly replaced objective-law with agenda-law. Politically-motivated judges increasingly replaced objective blindfolded-justice with subjective ego-justice. And politically-ambitious bureaucrats increasingly replaced protection-only regulations with political-policy regulations. That steady attack on the rule of law, that steady rise of the rule of man in America, drove freedom, capitalism and prosperity to the point of collapse.

Furthermore, the Great Technological Revolution cannot take hold in a country going deeper into the rule of man. Therefore, the Great Technological Revolution cannot rescue America from her severe fall into recession and depression.

But, the Great Technological Revolution can rescue Americans who emigrate to Prime-Law America, for Prime-Law America has no rule of man. And, because of the Prime Law, Prime-Law America could never regress into rule of man. Therefore, the Great Technological Revolution comes to Prime-Law America and ONLY to Prime-Law America. The people quickly grow wealthy as their buying power multiplies a hundredfold and more. The Prime Law of Protection is the missing integration that would have protected and preserved the U.S. Constitution from rapidly-adapting rule of man and would have prevented the decline of America.

With the Prime Law (as an amendment to the original U.S. Constitution), Prime-Law America delivers pure justice and freedom. The nation booms; the people prosper; the individual soars. Never before Prime-Law America has a land existed with pure justice and freedom. America came close and enjoyed unrivaled prosperity before falling at the hands of socialistic rule of man. In Prime-Law America, politicians, judges, bureaucrats do not govern. The Prime Law governs. Therefore, political agenda-law, subjective ego-justice, and political-policy regulation cannot exist. The people live in natural protection-only law, protection-only justice, and protection-only regulation. That rule-of-flawless-law Justice System creates the conditions for the freest, safest, most prosperous land in the history of the world. Those conditions of pure justice and freedom give rise to the Great Technological Revolution that makes all people rich, including the poor.

## The Constitution

The world watches the sad disintegration of the U.S. Constitution. America, once the strong and proud mother of prosperity now sinks to one knee...a tired and frightened country of poverty, unemployment, terror, and failing health.

The conditions that breed freedom and prosperity versus socialism and poverty arise from a constitutional republic's constitution (although that clear cause-and-effect connection is remarkably missed by many political pundits). Indeed, the U.S. Constitution is the heart of America pumping freedom throughout her land. The increasing rule of man, however, is a growing heart disease clogging her system with socialism. In late 2008, America had a heart attack.

The original U.S. Constitution was nearly flawless, but by

missing the Prime-Law integration that specifically protects a country from power-seeking man, the virulent rule of man steadily regained strength. Today, in America, the rule of man has resurged and is taking over. Poverty is taking over. The antidote to the collapsing economy — the Great Technological Revolution — cannot rise in a county sinking under the rule of man and socialism. Therefore, America will fall to her knees.

The Prime-Law American Constitution, by contrast, adopts the nearly flawless *original* U.S. Constitution, but adds the Prime-Law Amendment, which removes initiatory force and forever ends the rule of man and deadly socialism. The inextricable link between a constitutional republic's constitution and its prosperity is immediately recognized as the Great Technological Revolution rises for the first time on Earth. Similar to its forerunner (i.e., the computer revolution), the people's buying power and prosperity rise rapidly, almost geometrically. The geniuses immigrating into Prime-Law America, for the first time since the computer revolution, are not held back with political-policy regulations, political-agenda laws, or politically-motivated social "justice". Better and better products reach the consumers for lower and lower prices. Better and better medicines and curing health technologies reach patients at lower and lower prices. The wealth and health in Prime-Law America surpass anything the world has seen. The direct link between a constitutional republic's constitution (in this case...the rule of flawless law) and its prosperity is recognized worldwide. The geniuses from around the world move to the pure freedom of Prime-Law America and are welcomed with open arms as the greatest benefactors of society.

Back in America, those geniuses are sanctimoniously scorned on Capitol Hill and in the media as the greedy rich who have no right creating such wealth. Prime-Law America no longer tries to straighten out sister America or her erroneous, envious philosophies. It is hopeless and too much work. Instead, Prime-Law America shrugs and welcomes home the greatest wealth creators in the world.

"Come in, great geniuses, and do what you do best — create! Create jobs! Create wealth! Create inexpensive yet priceless products and medicines that all can afford! We are indebted to your unique talents, and we love you!" cries the philosophy of Prime-Law America. The Prime Law protects those creative geniuses from the political power-seekers. The Prime Law, therefore, protects the wealth, health, and safety of everyone. The citizens smile as they send in their voluntary payments to live in such freedom and prosperity.

## Police Protection

(Federal & State)

America really has no police protection. America has police follow-up. For the most part, a crime must occur first before the police will act...or follow up. In other words, no crime *prevention* exists in America. Many reasons cause this real lack of protection, from obstacles created by political correctness (i.e., by rule of politically-motivated, vote-gathering man) to lack of budget.

Prime-Law America, by contrast, boasts history's best police protection. Prime-Law Americans enjoy crime *prevention*. The Prime Law, which applies at the local, state, and federal levels, establishes the one purpose of government is to guarantee protection against initiatory force or *threat* of force. With 100% focus and budget on protection from initiatory force or *threat* of force, the police work to *prevent* crime, not merely follow up. No political-correctness obstacles exist in Prime-Law America. No entitlements compete for the budget. The entire budget and mindset is to eradicate crime. Such a police force has never existed before Prime-Law America. In this new country of wealth, health, and safety...women and children can walk home on a city street and be completely safe. Here, the only businesses in jeopardy of going out of business are locksmiths.

## Energy

Political correctness and politically-motivated science rises with the rule of man. As the rule of rational law gets steadily replaced in America with the rule of irrational man, personal self-interests dominate the political process...namely the personal desire for political power, thus for winning votes and popular support. That dark, power-seeking agenda that rises with rule of vote-gathering man leads to manipulations and distortions of reality in order to hoodwink larger portions of the population...for public support, more votes, more political power. Pseudo science rises to round up a large public following toward "a noble cause"...or to scare up a large public following against an "impending disaster." Similarly, more and more issues of political correctness rise in attempts to woo votes from more segments of the population.

Unfortunately, as seen in sister America, those contortions of reality in order to win votes and political power, disrupt and destroy the natural order of society to evolve and improve. For example, implementing and enforcing pseudo-science legislation, regulation, and litigation upon a society drags down the geniuses and greatest benefactors working hard to improve and evolve society. The creation of new businesses, jobs, products and wealth — the natural order of evolving and improving society — get shackled and pulled down by cost-prohibitive, political-policy legislation, regulations, and litigation such as global-warming regulations, for example.

Moreover, politically-motivated special interest groups rally around politicians looking for votes from segments of the population. Again, the distortions and contortions of reality used to drum up followers and more votes and political power always hurt the natural order of society to evolve and improve.

Prime-Law America, backed by the Prime Law, has just one purpose for government — protection. Therefore, no pseudo science or political correctness rises here or retards the natural order of society to evolve and improve. Prime-Law America mines and drills its energy sources, embracing the natural order of society to evolve, improve, *and protect* itself. As the radical environmental groups and ethicists "raise hell" in sister America, Prime-Law America just shrugs as sister America and her citizens sink into a living-hell of poverty and terror. Prime-Law America enjoys the natural order of society to evolve, improve, and protect itself. Prime-Law America grows enormously healthy, wealthy, and safe. Sadly, sister America slowly dies in poverty and terror.

## Tariffs

Remember what kicked off the great boom of Prime-Law America: **no taxes**. Prime-Law America will not introduce taxes in any form. Therefore, Prime-Law America imposes no tariffs. Obviously, that creates an uneven playing field for Prime-Law American products that face tariffs when exporting to other countries. However, the Great Technological Revolution occurring *only in* Prime-Law America not only levels the playing field, but outcompetes foreign products in uniqueness, higher quality, and lower prices. Even with high tariffs, the costs of Prime-Law American goods fall to fractions in most industries due to the Great Technological Revolution, similar to what the world witnessed during the personal-computer revolution.

Prime-Law America welcomes foreign products into the country without tariffs. Prime-Law America is consumer-dedicated and guarantees the conditions that bring the lowest prices and highest quality to its citizens. The secret behind Prime-Law America's prosperity is: the government *gets out of the way* and lets businesses compete for consumers. Indeed, in Prime-Law America, consumers are royalty and soon live like kings!

As sister America and her politicians and bureaucrats struggle to level playing fields and gain tax revenues, American businesses continue to sink under the weight of the rising rule of man and his politically-motivated laws and regulations.

Here in Prime-Law America, there are no politically-motivated laws and regulations. Just the opposite. In fact, Prime-Law America welcomes all products from all over the world to openly compete with domestic products in order to bring the highest quality and lowest prices to the people. Prime-Law America enforces, through the Prime Law, a government that *gets out of the way* of the natural order of society to evolve and improve. The voluntary-pay, protection-only government needs no tax revenue, wants no tax revenue, and has no legal authority to collect tax revenue. Therefore, the natural order of society can evolve and improve at a rapid rate as we saw within the computer society...a microcosm of the Prime-Law American society.

Prime-Law America takes long, sad glances at dying sister

America as her organs — her businesses — begin to fail and shut down, one after another.

## Education

In America, the rule of man — rule of vote-gathering man — reaches wherever it can summon substantial votes. Parents want good education for their children, and therefore education is a political target for rule of vote-gathering man. When education, medicine, or any profession or industry becomes politicized, the steady descent of efficiency and effectiveness begins. Put another way, the chokehold of inefficiency and ineffectiveness begins as exemplified by America's ineffectual educational system.

The role of government in Prime-Law America is simply to guarantee the conditions for happiness and prosperity by protecting the people from initiatory force. The Prime-Law prevents government from going beyond its sole purpose of protection. Therefore, no rise of the rule of man — vote-gathering man — can occur in Prime-Law America's government. Its government cannot politicize education, medicine, or any profession or industry. The educational system in Prime-Law America does not follow the pathetic path of sister America.

The wealth and prosperity among citizens of Prime-Law America leads to a far superior private educational system in which parents vote with their feet. Instead of a dumbing-down effect as in sister America, here there is a smartening-up effect. Here, the geniuses of society are born. The universal wealth from the Great Technological Revolution in Prime-Law America enables every parent to easily afford private education. It becomes part of the cost of living, which is extraordinarily low in the only country to ever experience the Great Technological Revolution. That low cost of living delivers the world's highest standard of living and produces the world's best educational system. Sister America struggles to graduate students who can read. Prime-Law America graduates students who can create. They go on to create great values for the world and great wealth and prestige for themselves.

# Budget

As American citizens lose their jobs and savings, the government continues to increase its debt and, therefore, the long-term tax burden on the people and their children. The culprit is the rising rule of man — of vote-gathering man. Seeking to win substantial segments of the voting public, politicians race further and further into the entitlement-game. Bringing more entitlements to more segments of the population attracts more votes. Today, the weight of the budget is collapsing upon America. And as it does, the politicians continue to call for yet larger and larger budgets, demonstrating there is no more hope for sister America.

Prime-Law America is limited by the Prime-Law to a protection-only budget. The sole purpose of government is protection from force or threat of force, which includes all that is needed for protection at the federal level and at the state level such as military, intelligence, police, courts, prisons, veterans pensions.

A protection-only budget does *not* and could never include entitlements beyond veterans' pensions and veterans' war-caused disabilities. The rule of (vote-gathering) man cannot hijack the budget in Prime-Law America. Moreover, the most remarkable phenomenon occurs: in the pure freedom of Prime-Law America, the Great Technological Revolution — something the world has never before seen — makes *all* the people rich. Buying power soars so dramatically that every Prime-Law American citizen lives like a millionaire.

The Prime-Law and its Protection-Only Budget guarantee the conditions for such a wealthy millionaire-like standard of living for everyone. Therefore, the people gladly and voluntarily pay their fair share of the substantially smaller budget. The government itself can never violate the Prime Law — can never use initiatory force on its citizens, can never force anyone to pay taxes. Citizens realize that such pure freedom is a precious gift from their great country of wealth, health, and peace. They proudly, patriotically, voluntarily pay their government to guarantee the conditions for such a beautiful life.

## Environment

America's ruling class (i.e., the rule of vote-gathering man) uses distortions and contortions of reality often through pseudo science to snare votes. The resulting burden on business and technology increasingly sinks companies, research-and-development projects, jobs and wealth. Because everyone cares about our land, water, and air, the environment becomes a prime target for using pseudo science to snare votes. Indeed, the rule of man and his distortions of reality for votes reaches more and more aggressively into American's gullible, close-to-the-heart love for nature. Politicians and bureaucrats put more and more cost-prohibitive "environmental" regulations upon American businesses, technologies, research-and-development projects, and investors. Well, those businesses, technologies, research projects, and investors have begun to fail at an alarming rate! Jobs, wealth, raw materials, products, and future products rapidly vanish from the American economy! Yet, America never learns her lesson, for parasites (i.e., the adapting bacteria-like rule of man) cannot stop themselves before killing their host.

Prime-Law America stands by, free of America's raging internal infection. The good Americans who can no longer go down with their country leave for Prime-Law America. In the end, it is Prime-Law America that rescues Americans.

In Prime-Law America, the environment, as does everything else, answers to the Prime Law. That means an individual can do anything on his or her property as long as it does not directly harm any other individual or his or her property. No broad-sweeping, consensus-building pseudo science can rise in Prime-Law America and burden business, research, science, and their investors. No, government cannot hurt job-and-value-creating business and science in Prime-Law America. The Prime Law does not allow it. Therefore, Prime-Law America is the most friendly nation to business, research, and science. As sister America experiences a systemic failure of her businesses, Prime-Law America experiences an explosion of new businesses. Moreover, the land, water and air get dramatically cleaner in nature-loving Prime-Law America than in any other place on Earth. Why? For every demand confronted by the Great

Technological Revolution, soon comes the new technologies to supply the demand. People love clean air, water, and land. Therefore, the Great Technological Revolution in Prime-Law America quickly evolves new technologies that effectively remove pollutants and other environmental concerns. Instead of wilting under pseudo science, Prime-Law America blossoms with pure science.

## Sadness & Fear

When a person dies, often great sadness and fear set in along with hopelessness and helplessness. Those feelings describe the feelings that increasingly fill America today. Indeed, as those feelings tell us, America is dying.

Prime-Law America, by contrast, is filled with happiness and confidence along with enormous hope. Prime-Law America and its people say their good-byes to the once-great America as she falls. But Prime-Law America stands strong, filled with youthful vigor and energy.

The younger generations in America face a frightening future in a dying and hated country. The younger generations in Prime-Law America face an exhilarating future in a thriving and respected country.

## Wealth & Security Forever

The rapid rise of wealth on Main Street, Prime-Law America is not a bubble that will eventually burst, for it is a function of costs falling to fractions.

In America, prices became falsely inflated such as home prices during the real-estate bubble that burst in 2008. The prices of homes were wildly inflated, and when those prices came crashing down, people's wealth vanished overnight.

Markets in Prime-Law America, enjoying the Great Technological Revolution, do not falsely inflate prices. In fact, the Great Technological Revolution brings prices down, down, down...making the people *permanently* richer, richer, richer. People's new-found wealth is here to stay...never seen before, because a purely free country was never known before.

In America, bubbles continue bursting. The people cannot stay afloat, even with all the "life-savers" the ruling class keeps throwing into the turbulent economy. Prosperous Prime-Law America tries one last time to show America that the ruling-class — the vote-gathering rule-of-man — cannot help the economy. In fact, the ruling class can only hurt the economy. But sister America does not listen. Her people keep asking for interventionism and socialism...and so they drown in poverty.

Indeed, poverty (split-A, America) loses the split-run to prosperity (split-B, Prime-Law America). ...Prime-Law America is, unfortunately, only a hypothetical country. We do not have that wonderful place to move to. And to untangle generations of adapting and resurging rule of man and his choke hold on America — strangling her with agenda-law, ego-justice and political-policy regulations — seems too massive and simply impossible. Where would we start? How long would it take? But there are two very simple and relatively rapid ways to remove rule of man's stranglehold on America: **the Prime Law of Protection** and **the Protection-Only Budget**. With a Prime-Law Amendment to the U.S. Constitution or with a Protection-Only Budget — both explained next in Volume Three — the rule of man would end; the rule of flawless law would begin, and America would quickly become Prime-Law America...all its citizens would become wealthy, including the poor! Indeed, Volume Three next, *Prime Law*, shows us the practical, effective way out of America's Catastrophic Era and into the Great Technological Revolution, the era of great wealth, health, and peace.

## Seeds Of Socrates

In the 4th century BC, the city-state Athens was governed by a representative democracy. The year was 399 BC at the famous Trial of Socrates: perhaps our planet's greatest benefactor was sentenced to death by Athens' justice system. Historic accounts reveal that Socrates could have averted the politically motivated death sentence. But Socrates refused. Even when given the opportunity to escape from jail prior to drinking the poisonous hemlock, Socrates refused. Athens' justice system convicted and sentenced him to death, and Athens was going to get exactly that. At seventy-years-old, Socrates sacrificed his life to leave the world his greatest political message:

### Socrates' Greatest Political Message

Socrates' greatest political message was: *Society and its citizens must live by its rule of law*...as did Socrates at the cost of his own life. *The law, however, had better be* ***flawless-law*** *or society will lose its greatest benefactors and values*...as Athens lost Socrates.

Socrates planted the seeds of Prime-Law America...of the Twelve Visions World: **Society must be governed by rule of law...flawless law**. 2400 years ago, Socrates decided his beautiful message was worth dying for. Socrates' sacrifice has not been lost. Today, 2400-years after the Trial of Socrates, the Twelve Visions Party will manifest his greatest political message: **live under rule of law...flawless law**. That flawless law, of course, is the **Prime Law**.

Volume Three

Rise From Your Knees

# Prime Law

## Rescuing America

*Setting Free the Great Technological Revolution:*

*Era of Super Technologies and*

*Soaring Buying Power*

*Universal Wealth, Health, Peace*

## The Premise

The premise is simple: man is imperfect. Man is flawed. Man is vulnerable to incorrect opinions, selfish agendas, destructive temptations, misguided behaviors, dishonest corruption, even manipulative evil.

By removing all imperfections — by removing man from making the political and legal decisions — a perfect "power-reactor explosion" of wealth, health, and peace will overwhelm society...sooner than later.

The problem in all political and legal systems ever known to man is: they are ultimately controlled by flaw-filled man. The American political system, for instance, whether liberal left or conservative right, in both cases is controlled by man — by flaw-filled man.

Civilization will take an unprecedented leap forward by removing imperfection, by removing man and his endless opinions and agendas from creating, interpreting, and executing law.

The method to remove man is the Prime Law. The rapid consequence, as shown throughout Volume Three, is millionaire-like prosperity for all the people, *including the poor.*

*Universal Wealth, Health, Peace*

# Removing Rule of Man for Universal Wealth Including the Poor!

*"The Prime Law locks down the fundamental of law and government. The Prime Law removes man and his endless opinions and agendas and illusions. I can clearly see how ordinary people like me will become very wealthy."*

*— A Neothink® Society Member*

Once we recognize and remove from politics and law the inherent problem of man — flaw-filled creatures easily influenced by power and money — then we will quickly rise into a wealthy world...even the poor will rise, as we will see in Volume Three.

Ruling-class power must be taken out of the hands of man. Freedom and prosperity throughout history suffered when *man* created, interpreted, and executed the law. On the other hand, freedom and prosperity throughout history soared when man was removed from the political and bureaucratic controls. Our own country soared when we mostly removed the rule of man (i.e., removed a monarchy with our U.S. Constitution).

To complete the evolution into universal prosperity, the powers of the legislative, judicial, and executive branches must be taken away from the opinions and agendas of flaw-filled man and put into a flawless Prime Law.

If you take a hundred well-educated men and women and ask them their thoughts on important issues of law and politics, they will bombard you with many different opinions and agendas — as exemplified by the U.S. Senate. Moreover, once in positions of political power, surrounded by the trappings of irresistible power and wealth, their answers become directed for their own benefits, for their own political clout.

Man is an easily influenced, easily corrupted creature. Therefore, the laws that govern man (i.e., protect man) must be free of man.

The only way to be free of man is to reduce law to its essence. Once at the fundamental nature of something there is no going deeper. All the opinions, agendas, illusions, dishonesties and corruption — all man's faults — no longer matter. The fundamental nature stands unchanged, unscathed, unconditional, uncorrupted...plain for all to forever see and know, which is the nature of the Prime Law.

*The Twelve Visions* (a Mark Hamilton Publication) demonstrates why protection of citizens is the **only** legitimate purpose of government and is the essence of law. The fundamental of protection is captured in the Prime Law, which supersedes all law. The Prime Law removes man — including all the smart law-school graduates — from the decision-making process of law. Law leaps to another level altogether, for the first time completely free of man.

The Prime Law determines the creation or lack of creation of new laws, not man with his endless opinions and agendas and faults. The fundamental of protection — the Prime Law — determines the interpretation of laws, not man with his endless egos, selfish motivations, and many human flaws. The Prime Law determines the execution and enforcement of laws, not man who is drawn to intoxicating power, rampant dishonesties, and a capacity for evil.

When the Prime Law removes man from creating, interpreting, and executing law, something amazing happens: the heavy and corrupt ruling-class of man comes off society. In that new freedom, as you will learn throughout this book, society and technology soar. A Great Technological Revolution takes off and causes our buying power to multiply a hundredfold, maybe a thousandfold, making everyone rich, *including the poor!* We already saw the forerunner with the uninhibited computer revolution in which buying power multiplied a thousandfold in a few years.

Let us now introduce a new grassroots political party with the sole objective to remove man from creating, interpreting, and executing law in order to make all people wealthy, including the poor.[1]

The name of that new political party that removes **man** from governing — removes the corrupt ruling class — is the Twelve Visions Party (TVP). Let us next see how the TVP will do that.

---

[1]A point of confusion among a few readers has been expressed, as follows: "You say the Prime Law will remove man from creating, interpreting, and executing the law...but even with the Prime Law **man** would still create, interpret, and execute the law."

Let me alleviate that confusion: The Prime Law as an amendment to the U.S. Constitution would take *complete control* of governing and remove man from being *in control* of governing. The Prime-Law Amendment would prevent man from creating, interpreting, or executing law based on any decision *beyond* the Prime Law, bound by the Prime Law, the fundamental of protection. Our government will go into another dimension never known on Earth: a pure protection-only government with no initiatory force in the governing body. Man will be prohibited from agenda-law, agenda-regulations, agenda-"justice" that always requires initiatory force. Rule of man will be over. Yes, man will create, interpret, and execute law *within the Prime Law's parameters* of self-defense protection from initiatory force, threat of force, fraud, or coercion. Yet man — our politicians and bureaucrats included — will be prohibited from initiatory force, from ruling via agendas; therefore there can be no rule of man, just rule of flawless law — the Prime Law. Indeed, the Prime Law governs, not rule of man. Man simply carries out the Prime Law of Protection as it applies to society. That complete control over man and complete removal of the rule of man is why I use the expression: *remove man from governing, for the Prime Law takes over governing*. Man must still create, interpret, and execute the law...but will do so as dictated by the Prime Law, void of his own wishes and desires, void of initiatory force necessary for rule of man. Rule of man can never again create, interpret, and execute the law, for without initiatory force, there is no more "rule". There is just man bound by the Prime Law to initiatory-force-free protection only — the only proper purpose of government. The Prime Law will finally deliver a purely free civilization free of the rule of man and will be the unbridled launch of our human potential.

# Presenting the Prime Law for Universal Wealth, Health, Safety & Peace

The Visionaries envision a profoundly free, wealthy, healthy, and safe society protected by rule of flawless law. Man — even the most educated man or woman — is by nature a flaw-filled creature. Any idea or thought put before man generates endless opinions, arguments, and agendas. Moreover, man is vulnerable to ego, temptations, and irresistible power. Man by nature tends to satisfy his own appetite first. In other words, he puts his own gain before society. At the expense of society, politicians build political clout and re-election power.

Historically, the more successful a political system is at removing man from making, interpreting, and executing law, the freer the nation and the wealthier and healthier the people.

Looking back: throughout the first millennium, the majority of people suffered, even starved under the rule of man.

The Magna Carta in 1215 AD **began a trend** of restricting the rule of man. Prosperity eventually began climbing; the people began living in better conditions.

The U.S. Constitution in 1787 **continued the trend** by *dramatically* restricting the rule of man. Consequently, Americans enjoyed unrivaled prosperity. The majority eventually joined the middle class.

The Prime Law coming with the success of the Twelve Visions Party, will **complete the trend** by *fully* removing the rule of man. All people will become wealthy, including the poor.

America dramatically advanced the evolution from the rule of man (a monarch) to the rule of law (the U.S. Constitution). And America can complete that evolution from the rule of flaw-filled man to the rule of flawless law by *fully* removing man from making, interpreting, and executing law. That final evolution is the Prime Law, which will lift society into unprecedented freedom and its people into never-before-seen wealth, health, and peace.

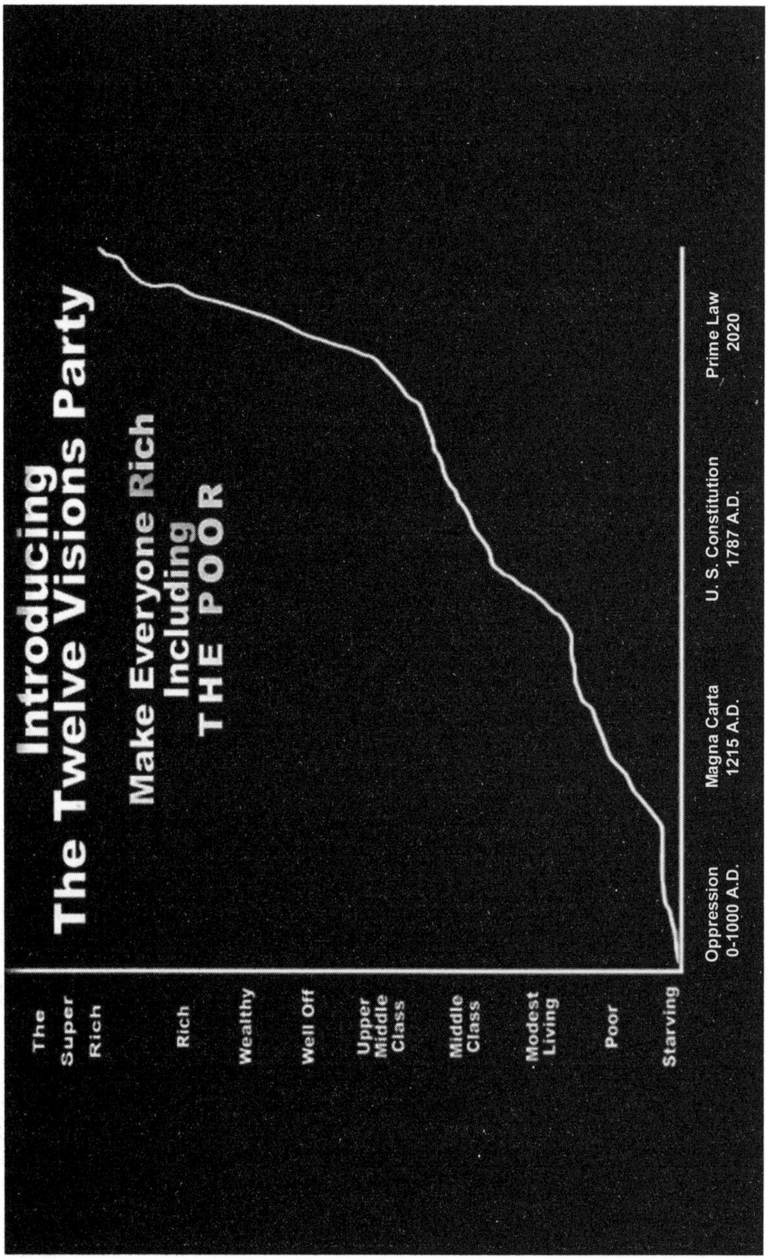
Introducing
The Twelve Visions Party
Make Everyone Rich
Including
THE POOR
The Super Rich
Rich
Wealthy
Well Off
Upper Middle Class
Middle Class
Modest Living
Poor
Starving
Oppression 0-1000 A.D.
Magna Carta 1215 A.D.
U. S. Constitution 1787 A.D.
Prime Law 2020

# Crossroads of History

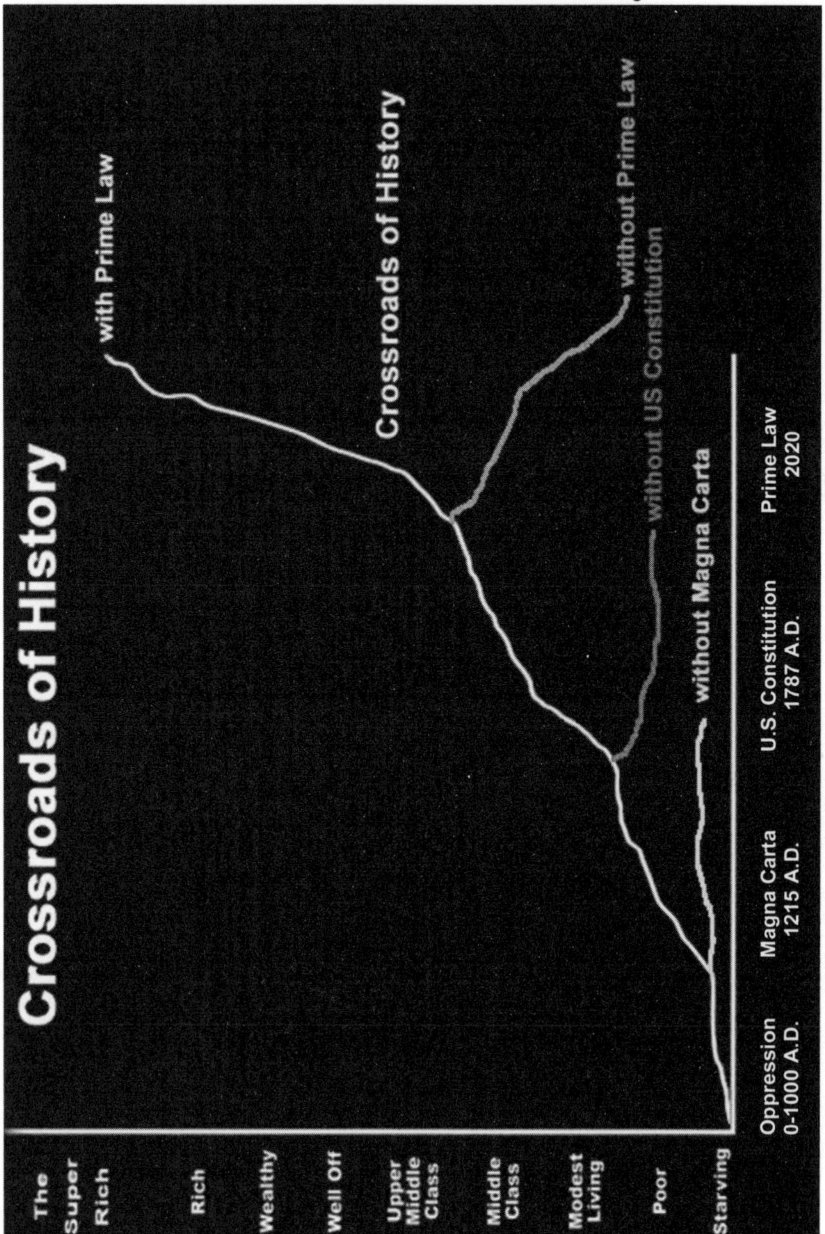

*The Prime Law*

In recognition of man's inherent shortcomings, the Visionaries aspire to lift the rule of law to a whole new level not yet seen on Earth. The Prime Law completes the millennia-long evolution of removing flaw-filled man from creating, interpreting, and executing law and will lead us to the wealthiest, healthiest, and safest nation to ever exist on Earth.

For the first time, law will be completely free from the faulty motivations of man. The lawmakers, judges, and regulatory bureaucrats will no longer control law. Instead, the Prime Law will control the lawmakers, judges, and regulatory bureaucrats. Instead of man governing our country, the Prime Law — the fundamental of protection — will govern.

## The Prime Law

(The Fundamental Law of Protection)

Preamble

*The *purpose* of human life is to prosper and live happily.

*The function of government is to provide the conditions that let individuals fulfill that *purpose*.

*The Prime Law guarantees those conditions by forbidding the use of initiatory force, fraud, or coercion by any person or group against any individual, property, or contract.

Article 1

No person, group of persons, or government shall initiate force, threat of force, or fraud against any individual's self, property, or contract.

Article 2

Force is morally-and-legally justified only for protection from those who violate Article 1.

Article 3

No exceptions shall exist for Articles 1 and 2.

*Universal Wealth, Health, Peace*

## Wealthiest, Healthiest, Safest Society on Earth

Politicians, lawyers, judges, and bureaucrats (i.e., flaw-filled man) controlling our laws have eroded our beloved freedom and prosperity. The flawless Prime Law permanently removes flaw-filled man from subjectively creating, interpreting, and executing agenda-law. Law and justice must now adhere to the Prime Law — to protection only — the one and only proper purpose of government.

No longer will flaw-filled politicians, lawyers, judges, and bureaucrats control our laws. Instead, the Prime Law will control our flaw-filled politicians, lawyers, judges and bureaucrats. Perfection will control imperfection.

A protection-only government will spawn a new freedom that will set free a Great Technological Revolution that will bring universal wealth and health to America. Furthermore, with full government resources focused on protection only, Americans will enjoy the safest society on Earth.

The Prime Law was the one missing ingredient our forefathers needed to forever preserve the beautiful country they created. (This fact is elaborated on in the coming section titled "The Prime Law Will Bring Undreamt of Wealth, Health, Safety to All Including the Poor, the Elderly, the Underprivileged.")

Every Twelve Visions Party candidate, every elected or appointed Visionary will sign the Twelve Visions Party (TVP) Contract. That TVP Contract binds every Visionary's decision in any local, state, or federal office or position in all branches of government; the TVP Contract binds every Visionary — yes, flaw-filled man — to the Prime Law. (See the TVP Contract, pages 100-103.)

The results of removing flaw-filled man from controlling government will be universal wealth, health, and peace. We will instead have a flawless Prime Law of Protection controlling a government of protection and controlling its flaw-filled elected and appointed men and women. Law creation, law interpretation, law execution will be held to protection only. Political agenda-law, agenda-justice, and agenda-regulations will vanish, setting free business and technology to do to all industries what they did to the relatively unregulated computer industry. Americans will become wealthy as their buying power multiplies a hundredfold, a thousandfold or more.

That scenario is not a hypothesis; prosperity explosions have occurred among civilizations throughout history by somewhat pulling back flaw-filled man from the controls of government, reducing political agenda-law, agenda-justice, and agenda-regulations. In fact, our country is the shining example of an evolutionary leap from a man-controlled monarchy to the nearly flawless law-controlled republic. Of course, a great prosperity-explosion followed the creation of our country.

Over two centuries later, the Twelve Visions Party gives us an opportunity at the next and final evolutionary leap away from flaw-filled man-controlled government to flawless law-controlled government. The Prime Law is the missing integration our forefathers did not pull together, the should-be capstone to the U.S. Constitution. The Prime Law is the missing link to *pure* freedom and soaring standards of living, forever. Indeed, that missing integration makes the U.S. Constitution flawless and *fully* removes flaw-filled man. The U.S. Constitution was the stepping stone to freedom; the Prime Law is the capstone to freedom. A great prosperity-explosion will follow once again.

The Twelve Visions Party recognizes and captures this opportunity for all people alike...including the poor and the elderly. The Prime Law results in universal wealth for the first time ever on our planet: the next evolution of freedom will bring *all* Americans a wealthy, healthy, and safe life.

*Universal Wealth, Health, Peace*

# Actualizing Universal Wealth & Health

The Visionaries do have a great vision: we see soaring standards of living; we see all the people becoming wealthy, including the poor. We see all the people gaining good health, including the elderly.

*Universal Wealth and Health*

In this age of rapidly advancing technologies, in a time when buying power can rapidly soar as we have seen with the computers, Visionaries realize that all citizens can soon experience multiplying buying power and great wealth if the government returns to its one proper purpose of *protection only* and removes itself from its improper purpose of promoting the "social good". The *full* dynamics of this return to a protection-only government and the resulting explosion of freedom and wealth for the people in this age of rapidly advancing technologies can be clearly seen later in this book. You will witness why we are *the* political party to make *all* the people wealthy and healthy, including the poor and the elderly. Universal wealth and health is now actually possible. The Twelve Visions Party exists to actualize that possibility.

*Unprecedented Wealth, Health, and Safety*

The Visionaries envision a profoundly free, wealthy, healthy, and safe society protected by rule of flawless law. That Prime Law of Protection — no initiatory force — applies to and restricts government itself. Therefore, a government unable to use initiatory force on its people ends all power-building, force-backed, political-policy legislation and regulations for the "social good". Without force-backed political-agenda-law, without force-backed political-policy regulations, without force-backed political-agenda-"justice", then entrepreneurs, businesses, and their super technologies are held back no longer. What we witnessed during the relatively unregulated computer revolution will occur across all industries (including the medical industry) to bring us a Great Technological Revolution. For the first time on our planet, a government would set free a Great Technological Revolution not just in the computer industry, but in *all* industries, quickly bringing unprecedented wealth, health, and safety to all citizens.

*The Millionaire-Phenomenon*

The flawless Prime Law, not flaw-filled men and women, not agenda-and-ego-driven lawmakers, will direct all political decisions and actions and restrict them to protection from initiatory force. At that fundamental essence of legitimate law and government (i.e., protect the people from initiatory force) not only politicians and bureaucrats, but all people can easily determine the proper protection-only laws. Who is in office becomes irrelevant; political and personal agendas and endless opinions become irrelevant; party affiliation becomes irrelevant; what party holds power becomes irrelevant. The Prime Law of Protection and nothing more remains relevant. Flaw-filled man no longer controls government. The consequences of decisions and actions locked down to the Prime Law will be staggering as *fully* demonstrated in the following chapters.

Without political agendas, policies, and egos controlling legislation and regulations, the geniuses of society will finally be free to accelerate the Technological Revolution and drive our buying power higher than we have ever seen. This millionaire-phenomenon will come to all people, including the poor, as demonstrated in the following pages. Other spectacular consequences are shown in the following pages as well, such as unprecedented health, happiness, love, peace, security, and safety. At the state level, popular planks listed by the Republicans and popular planks listed by the Democrats will either be moved eventually to the private sector if they have nothing to do with the one proper purpose of government — physical protection of the people — or will fall under the Prime Law of Protection.

*Universal Wealth, Health, Peace*

## TVP Planks & Consequences

**Rule of Flawless Law to Replace Rule of Flaw-Filled Man:** Throughout history, the more that societies moved away from rule of man to rule of rational law, the more prosperity the people enjoyed. The Twelve Visions Party presents and supports the Prime Law. All party members will sign the TVP Contract that binds all decision-making to the Prime Law. The Prime Law completes the long evolution from rule of flaw-filled man to rule of flawless law. The result will be an unprecedented prosperity-explosion for the people.

**Protection-Only Budget:** Imagine all taxpayers' dollars and government's efforts going toward protection, which includes the military, protection-only legislation, police, courts, and prisons. Crime would decrease dramatically. Taxes would decrease dramatically. The geniuses of society, without the bogus government-on-the-offense holding them back, would cause our wealth and health to soar. (The following chapters give a better understanding of the unprecedented wealth that will result from the Protection-Only Budget and its government-on-the-defense. The principle applies at both the federal and state levels.)

**Depoliticize and Deregulate:** End politicization and regulation of our lives and businesses via the Prime Law of Protection and the Protection-Only Budget. Get down to the one proper purpose of any government: protection from initiatory force, threat of force, or fraud. By removing the bogus purpose of government, particularly regulatory programs for the "social good", the Twelve Visions Party removes the massive and improper government control over our lives and businesses. By getting government out of our lives and out of our businesses altogether, we free the geniuses of society to do wonderful things for us, as follows:

**Unprecedented Security:** The people will be well taken care of by the geniuses of society, rising by the many millions as the Twelve Visions Party ends political-policy regulations that have nothing to do with protection from initiatory force. The millions of freed geniuses will drive technologies into new dimensions that bring undreamt of values to the people...remarkable values that meet and surpass people's needs and solve their problems.

**Universal Wealth:** The costs for those new technologies will keep falling toward zero, similar to the personal computers during the computer revolution. The Great Technological Revolution will happen in all industries and make ordinary people more and more wealthy as costs in all industries keep falling.

**Universal Health:** The new technologies, racing ahead in all industries, will especially race ahead in the medical industry without the destructive cost-prohibitive FDA regulations holding the geniuses back. The geniuses will eradicate disease after disease, and their soaring new technologies will drive down medical costs. People will live with increasingly better health for increasingly longer lives.

**Job Explosion & Evolution:** Businesses will strive to keep up in the rapid progress of the Great Technological Revolution; everything will change as businesses, to stay competitive, concentrate on bringing out their greatest asset — the unique creativity of their employees. Ordinary people will experience exhilarating entrepreneurial-like jobs at their places of work, and they will love going to work as they discover the creation-driven life, the life they were meant to live.

**Extraordinary Marriages & Love:** The wonderful falling-in-love feelings in the early weeks of romantic relationships will tend to return. Why? People will rise from a life stuck in stagnation. They will rise into the creation-driven life of their dreams. With that growing source of happiness inside, filling them and overflowing into their romantic relationships, they will forever feel the power of love.

**Educating Geniuses:** Our children and grandchildren will become "smarter" than today's smartest people. In tomorrow's Twelve-Visions-World education, children will be taught how to integrate knowledge to build success and lead themselves. They will see through illusions and will no longer need or want to be led by "authorities". The need for a ruling class and its regulations will become repulsive to the graduating self-leaders tomorrow. Our children will grow up to live a creation-driven life — the happy and prosperous life they were meant to live. The old structure of education cannot compete against the new mentality and yields to the coming schools of geniuses (more later).

**Eradicating Crime & Terrorism:** The fear of terrorism will rapidly decline, and crime will nearly cease. The Twelve Visions Party will concentrate every action and every dollar toward *one* purpose: **protect the people from initiatory force**, as declared in the Prime Law. Safer-living statistics will soar.

*Conclusion*

When 20th-century visionary Henry Ford discovered that the workers should not manage the work, rather the work should manage the workers (via the invention of the assemblyline)...society experienced an enormous prosperity-explosion. Mass production began, which accelerated the Industrial Revolution. The people's buying power — their wealth — skyrocketed.

When 21st-century visionary Mark Hamilton discovered that the flaw-filled lawmakers, judges, and bureaucrats should not control the law,[1] rather the flawless Prime Law should control the flaw-filled lawmakers, judges, and bureaucrats...society became poised to experience another enormous prosperity-explosion. Unleashed geniuses of society and nonrestricted super technologies will accelerate the Technological Revolution. Once again, the people's buying power — their wealth — will skyrocket.

Indeed, the Twelve Visions Party is *the* Party to make the people rich, including the poor. **That is our Vision!** We have reached a rare moment in time and technology that could literally make all people wealthy. The Twelve Visions Party clearly recognizes and reaches for the switch to ignite the prosperity-explosion.

---

[1]Misinterpretation of the U.S. Constitution, often through ego-driven, political-agenda "justice", steadily opened the way for lawmakers and justices to control the law. The Prime Law forever ends that steady regression from the rule of law back to the disastrous rule of man. Rule of law — the flawless Prime Law of Protection — will permanently reassert itself with the Prime-Law Amendment to the U.S. Constitution.

*Universal Wealth, Health, Peace*

# The Universal-Wealth Movement & The TVP Contract

The Twelve Visions Party with its Prime Law and Protection-Only Budget understands government's final evolution into providing protection and *only* protection, *the* purpose of government, *without* flaw-filled man in control. As a result, as shown throughout the following pages, removing flaw-filled man from the controls of government means average Americans will live like millionaires without lifting a finger. Everyone will become rich, including the poor.

Indeed, when you get down to the irreducible fundamental of something, a paradigm shift sometimes occurs with almost magical benefits. Consider the following example, an analogy to the Prime Law and the resulting wealth we will enjoy:

In the early 20th century when Henry Ford got down to the fundamental nature of production — down to the *physical movements* of production — the assemblyline emerged and caused a paradigm shift from handmade production to mass production. Ford identified, "Do not let the workers manage the work; instead, let the work manage the workers." And that paradigm shift changed EVERYTHING. A national prosperity-explosion followed.

In the early 21st century, when I (the author, Mark Hamilton) got down to the fundamental nature of government — down to the *physical protection* of the individual and his property — the Prime Law emerged, which will cause a paradigm shift from rule of flaw-filled man to rule of flawless law. I identified, "Do not let flaw-filled politicians, judges, bureaucrats manage the law; instead, let the flawless Prime Law manage the politicians, judges, bureaucrats." And that paradigm shift will change EVERYTHING. A national prosperity-explosion will follow, a freedom paradigm accompanied by an *unhindered* Technological Revolution in which buying power will multiply a hundredfold, a thousandfold or more. The computer revolution was a preview of what can come to all industries.

Now let us take a close look at the political party itself. To do so, I must express my thoughts and feelings directly to you. For a long time, I dreaded the idea of launching a political party.

I knew that *all* people, *including loyal Visionaries, including myself,* were flaw-filled men and women with all our shortcomings, vulnerabilities, and temptations. We are human, and human beings are not perfect. How could the Twelve Visions Party survive the faults of its members and officials? The answer, I continued to conclude, was: it will **not** survive the faults of man.

How could my new political-party idea ever work? Finally, I realized I needed to take the fundamental decision-making away from party members, yes, away from the Visionaries themselves! In other words, "Do not let the Visionaries (imperfect, flaw-filled man) manage the law; instead, let the unchanging flawless Prime Law manage the Visionaries!" Yes! With the fundamental law of protection — the Prime Law — I could do this! The Twelve Visions Party could now work and truly bring the millionaire-phenomenon to the people!

To control this movement, all Party members who run for office or service in any way must sign the TVP Contract below that assures every decision is made according to the Prime Law.

Now, the Political Party will work beautifully. The Twelve Visions Party can now actualize the unprecedented opportunity to make *all* people rich, including the poor. Indeed, we are at a unique moment in time and technology in which the Twelve Visions Party can ignite a never-before-seen prosperity-explosion.

## The TVP Contract

Premise: A Protection-Only Government will lead to the people's greatest prosperity (as demonstrated in *Twelve Visions,* a Mark Hamilton Publication). That is reality. The many opinions and agendas of man cannot alter reality. Yet, while creating, interpreting, and executing law, the attempt to alter reality is continually made: this law...that interpretation...these regulations will improve the people's prosperity...*we promise!* Whether innocent or not, those sound-good, "social good" government actions beyond protection increasingly control us and slowly kill our freedoms, bit by bit, day after day, steadily aging our country, leading to its eventual death.

*Universal Wealth, Health, Peace*

The purpose of the TVP Contract is to establish *the* one proper purpose of government, *the* reality of protection. We establish *the* reality of protection through the unchanging Prime Law of no initiatory force, which controls both the selfish and selfless lawmakers, lawyers, judges, and bureaucrats and their endless opinions, biases, agendas, ambitions, egos, desires, delusions and illusions. No longer will those flaw-filled men and women control law and politics!

Contract: I, ________, pledge to subordinate (to the Prime Law) my many preconceived thoughts, despite how strongly I feel, despite whether I believe with certainty or with reservation, for with external and internal confusions and illusions that accompany a power-based government, I honestly acknowledge that always reaching the proper decision is merely impossible. In serving my Party's objective to return to and forever remain a protection-only government in order to unleash an unprecedented prosperity-explosion that will make all the people rich, including the poor, I fully understand the mechanics come down to consistently, always without exception, supporting the biologically irreducible fundamental act of protection — the Prime Law of no initiatory force as spelled out in the National Platform of the Twelve Visions Party. That Prime Law of Protection must control the lawmakers, law interpreters, and law executors, not the other way around. Therefore, every decision I make — even if it goes against the very grain of my mind, heart, and soul — will be made purely on serving the Prime Law. I realize, in the end, that policy will bring forth our vision to make all the people wealthy, healthy, and safe including the poor and elderly, as demonstrated in the TVP National Platform. Again, that policy will bring forth our vision of a profoundly free, wealthy, healthy, and safe society.

If I knowingly go against the Prime Law of *protection only* for any decision for any reason whatsoever, or if I show a trend of "unknowingly" going against the Prime Law, which is mostly self-evident, the Twelve Visions Party will immediately and publicly disown me and will no longer recognize me as a member.[1]

Lawmakers — *man* — must not control law. Men and women controlling law can lead to anything, can take a country anywhere, even to the point where it becomes law to kill others, as we have seen around the world, throughout history. Man with his many faults of ego, greed, envy, and innocent lack of knowledge and his many vulnerabilities must not control law and interpret the Constitution. Man controlling law, with all his vulnerabilities and faults, has always been a recipe for destruction. No, the flawless Prime Law of protection must control the lawmakers, law interpreters, law executors. If we want to live, for the first time, in a universally wealthy, healthy, happy, peaceful, safe, and truly free society, then the Prime Law of Protection must ultimately become the political point of origin, "the decision maker", not man, not me. Political decisions bound to the Prime Law will effectively minimize crime and eventually end initiatory force including agenda-law, agenda-"justice", and political-policy regulations based on initiatory force, thus unleashing the geniuses of society and their technologies, catapulting our standards of living, buying power, wealth and health for all people, *including the poor*. **That is our Vision**.

All members running for office, appointed to office, or serving in any way must sign below to abide by the Prime Law for every decision, in quest of our vision. Indeed, we the Visionaries must completely commit ourselves to the Prime Law today via this contract; we must bring the Prime Law to each of the fifty states tomorrow via our State Constitutions; we must bring the Prime Law to our Federal government eventually via an Amendment to the U.S. Constitution, which would act as the overarching, de facto Constitution of America. Visionaries must ultimately bring the Prime Law to the entire world, country by country, forever ending war. The Prime Law brings universal and permanent wealth, health, and peace to all people.

________________

Sign here
Member of The Twelve Visions Party

[1]Until our force-pay government becomes a voluntary-pay government,

*(footnote continued on next page)*

*(footnote continued from previous page)*

all government laws and regulations ultimately sit upon forced tax collection. Therefore, Visionaries understand that all government laws and regulations are ultimately in violation of the Prime Law until the force-pay government becomes a voluntary-pay government. In order for the government to function prior to and through the transition (described in the TVP Platform), Visionaries will legislate, interpret, execute initiatory-force-free protection-only laws, decisions, regulations within our current government knowing that our force-pay government will evolve into a voluntary-pay government with the ratification of the Prime-Law Amendment.

*Universal Wealth, Health, Peace*

# The Prime-Law Amendment

**will bring**

## Undreamt of Wealth, Health, Safety

**to all including**

## The Poor, the Elderly, the Underprivileged

The one proper purpose of government is protection against initiatory force, threat of force, coercion and fraud. Any other purpose ultimately depends upon initiatory force in the hands of a ruling class, the rule of man, which takes away our freedom and, therefore, our prosperity.

Indeed, the more free a country, the more prosperous, as shown throughout history. For the first time with the Prime Law, we are talking about a purely protection-only government and, therefore, a fully free country. There has NEVER been a fully free country on our planet.

Moreover, for the first time, we have reached the technology to experience a *universal* prosperity-explosion as first seen in the computer industry. If technology is set free to rapidly advance, we can ignite that prosperity-explosion in all industries. Prices will begin falling to fractions as happened to the computers. Buying power will soar. People's buying power — *all* people's buying power — will multiply a hundredfold, a thousandfold or more. They will become rich, including the poor.

America originally rose quickly and was so much freer and more prosperous than other countries because it was a country brilliantly controlled by nearly flawless rule of law and not subjected to flaw-filled rule of man as so many other countries.

Yes, man is full of faults, motivated by ego, tugged toward temptations, attracted to easy money, corruption and dishonesty. Man is imperfect, including all Visionaries.

Therefore, the Twelve Visions Party takes America's rule of law one final step further: By going down to the biological fundamental of protection — no initiatory force — the Prime-Law Amendment would end lawmakers from recklessly creating new laws that have nothing to do with protection, and the Prime Law would end justices from recklessly interpreting law and opening the door for government to control us through "social justice" and the "social good", and the Prime Law would stop bureaucrats from establishing regulations based on political policy instead of the one proper fundamental of protection from initiatory force. For, any law or regulation beyond protection against initiatory force *requires* initiatory force; the government regresses to the rule of man.

The Prime Law takes the rule of law *all the way* and ensures a pure, protection-only government. A pure, protection-only government is also a get-out-of-the-way government, which sets free the geniuses of society and ignites the universal prosperity-explosion. The flawless Prime Law was the final rule-of-law integration the founding fathers missed.

The Prime Law has the potential to become an amendment to the Constitution of the United States, where the Prime Law has belonged since the creation of the U.S. Constitution. Let us take a close look at that possibility:

The U.S. Constitution's three main principles of inherent rights, government by the people, and separation of powers provided the basis for the freest and most prosperous nation in history. Just imagine over two centuries ago the new ideas of a nation created to ensure a person's right to life, liberty and the pursuit of happiness as written in the Declaration of Independence, a nation governed by the people, a nation with watchdog checks and balances on political and bureaucratic powers.

The delegates of the Constitutional Convention in 1787 also gave careful consideration to the division of power between the federal government and state governments. The U.S. Constitution, which emerged from the Constitutional Convention in 1787, is called the *supreme law* because the state constitutions and both federal and state laws cannot violate the U.S. Constitution.

The U.S. Constitution does a nearly perfect job setting down the principles and system of government. Things went wrong because of continual *misinterpretation* of the Constitution over generations, which led to repeated violations of the Constitution. What was missing was an overarching constitution, so to speak, the *prime* law of no initiatory force.

Had the Prime Law existed since the beginning, our country

would have entered the wealthy/healthy/safe Twelve Visions World generations ago (as seen in *Twelve Visions* and demonstrated in *Superpuzzle*, Hamilton Publications).

If the Prime Law eventually becomes an amendment to the U.S. Constitution — the Prime-Law Amendment — we could again have confidence in the U.S. Constitution, for it brilliantly sets down the system of government and separation of powers, starting with the three main powers of 1) making laws, 2) executing laws, and 3) interpreting laws.

There would be, however, a fundamental change with the Prime-Law Amendment: The whole concept of a government based on *power* — separation of powers, division of powers, checks and balances of powers — would change from a government based on *power* to a government based on *service*. That fundamental change from a power basis to a service basis would evolve a businesslike system — a businesslike protection service — as detailed in Volume Four of this book.

Let us take a closer look at what the Prime-Law Amendment would accomplish. First, as identified in the following chapters, over the past century, our government existed for two purposes:

1) To protect the people
2) To promote the social good

To promote the general welfare of the people has been **misinterpreted** to mean: increase their standards of living or their wealth. Well, as demonstrated in the following pages, politicians *cannot* do that; the government cannot and should not exist to enhance social well-being, not beyond physical protection, which includes justice and proper lawmaking, both criminal and civil. Government merely provides *the conditions* for individuals to pursue their purpose to prosper and live happily. The government guarantees those conditions through the Prime Law, which calls for a protection-only government. Indeed, the Prime Law and its protection-only government guarantee *the conditions* that promote the general welfare of the people. Instead, our politicians spend our money ostensibly for the "social good", but they really want the ruling-class glory and power and importance that goes with spending money (other people's money). The evidence is clear: they do not want anything to do with the deeper effort that goes with soundly spending money. They want control and re-election. The repeated misinterpretations of the U.S. Constitution has led to these blatant violations of the Constitution, such as spending our money beyond protection while bankrupting our future, which could never occur with the Prime Law in place.

So, career politicians with the help of federal justices and regulatory bureaucrats have made a mess of things. Our well-being, standard of living, and wealth can be dramatically lifted by *unhampered* market businessmen and women...by the geniuses of society. But the erroneous second purpose of government must first end.

That bogus purpose of government to so-call "promote the social good" sprang up over the years through career politicians finding ways to spend money and become more and more likable for re-election. (See the James J. Hill story in about 40 pages.) The Prime-Law Amendment gets rid of all that, forever.

The one *valid* purpose for our government, as you know, is *to protect the people from initiatory force,* which includes providing justice. The only way to guarantee the protection of *all* people — *equal, unbiased* and *unconditional* protection of all people of all races and all social classes and all career positions in society — is to protect *the individual.* Regardless of race or social status, the Prime Law guarantees everyone his or her unprejudiced rights as an individual, as a minority of one — the smallest of all minorities. Every individual is equally and fully protected.

Now, to provide comprehensive protection of the individual requires going down to and establishing the biologically irreducible fundamental of protection. As an analogy, to capture the comprehensive nature of the cosmos requires going down to and understanding the irreducible, fundamental sub-atomic particles composing the cosmos. The irreducible, thus indivisible, incorruptible fundamental of protection is: elimination of initiatory force, which is the function of the Prime-Law Amendment. There is nothing deeper upon which to argue opinions or agendas. The Prime Law says it all. There is nothing more.

Indeed, comprehensive protection of the individual demands *one prime law* — one overarching, irreducible law: the elimination of initiatory force against the individual and his property. With that *one prime law*, everyone becomes protected from harm caused by man, including harm from government.

Therefore, with the passing of the Prime-Law Amendment, the erroneous purpose of government and its destructive ruling-class of man can never return. Prosperity will soar forever as described throughout this book. What great news! Indeed, *one prime law* was always needed; *one prime law* eternally guarantees protection and freedom. That one Prime Law could bring about the Twelve Visions World (described in *Twelve Visions*, a Mark Hamilton Publication) if that Prime Law were to become an amendment to the U.S. Constitution, the Prime-Law Amendment.

With that one Prime-Law Amendment in place, it essentially becomes our Supreme Law to which every law must answer. For, the Supreme Law will filter out every law and regulation in violation, namely those that serve the bogus purpose of so-called promoting the "social good", *agenda-law* which requires initiatory force. The Prime Law is the biological fundamental, the point of origin, the beginning of all law. Therefore, no further unhealthy law or misinterpretation of the U.S. Constitution could occur. No more agenda-law, political-policy regulations, or ego-"justice"...no more violations could happen. Government could not tell us how to spend our money or *force* us to pay taxes. As long as we did not commit initiatory force[1], we would be completely free. We would not need ego-and-power-driven lawmakers stirring up legislation...with lawyers and bureaucrats using those laws to control us and drain us. We would no longer need that parasitical ruling-class of man that destroyed our yet-unknown prosperity. Their deceptions could no longer pass through the Prime-Law Amendment — including their forced taxes.

Our government would cease to house a parasitical ruling-class of man as we switched over to the Protection-Only Budget (described in the next chapter) that ends the funds for the bogus second purpose of government — to so-call promote the "social good". The Protection-Only Budget supplies funds to the one proper purpose of government — to protect the country and its citizens from initiatory force, which includes the proper

[1]Threat of force, coercion and fraud are forms of initiatory force.

protection-based lawmaking and system of justice, forever unable to violate the Prime Law.

Now, what guarantees our government could never again grow a ruling class? Government can grow a ruling class only through force — pay your taxes or go to prison. With the passing of the Prime-Law Amendment, not even the government could use initiatory force and, therefore, would *forever* cease to be a ruling class. Instead, with the passing of the Prime-Law Amendment, the government would function as a protection *service* you voluntarily pay for. Volume Four of this book explains exactly how that would happen.

Gone would be the days of bogus and destructive government, government on the offense so-called promoting the "social good". Market businesspersons — the geniuses of society — would successfully take over that job of promoting the social good as shown in an upcoming chapter. Then, our new government would forever provide the one specific value of protection, which its citizens — its customers — would voluntarily pay for. People will gladly pay for safety and peace.

Realize, the Protection-Only Budget described in the next chapter would not be enough to permanently end the ruling class. The government could regress into a corrupt ruling class again, eventually, if government could use initiatory force against its citizens with a force-backed IRS. In short, that ugly rise of the ruling class is what happened to our original, beautiful U.S. Government idea meant to exist for protection only. The Prime-Law Amendment would *forever* stop the ruling class from happening again. Indeed, the Prime-Law Amendment pulls out the roots of the ruling class — initiatory force, which includes forced taxes.

Without forced tax collection, government power is not a *ruling* power. Instead, it is an *earned* power, earned from ever-looming, potential competition. Our Twelve Visions Government is nonthreatening to its citizens — to its customers — and is incorruptible.

With initiatory force permanently out of the equation of government due to the Prime-Law Amendment, man can hold no ruling power — no rule-of-man power — and can never again hold ruling power over you whatsoever. For the first time, you will be truly free...you and the many geniuses of society!

The Twelve Visions Government will eventually evolve into a reputable business providing the immense value of protection — peace and safety — a priceless value *citizens will gladly pay for*. If you were unhappy with the protection service, you could withdraw and not pay...and not be a criminal. If enough people did that, a competitive service would rise to guarantee protection — better protection. Those free-market dynamics would force tomorrow's government to provide honest and satisfactory value to you. Those free-market dynamics would guarantee your best protection, including national defense and local police protection as demonstrated in *Superpuzzle* (a Mark Hamilton Publication).

Those free-market dynamics would also free the geniuses of society. With the Prime-Law Amendment to the U.S. Constitution, the prosperity-explosion described in the following chapters would never end. Now, you will read about the wealth, happiness, love, and health you could experience. The following chapters deliver the actual system that will allow *ordinary* people to live the wealthy, healthy, and safe lives they were meant to live.

*Universal Wealth, Health, Peace*

# Multiply Our Buying Power A Thousandfold

We have reached a special place in time: the idea of real, universal wealth and health can actually happen, and the Twelve Visions Party is highly aware of this unprecedented opportunity. We have identified two paths to universal wealth, health, and security:

Path 1) The ratification of the Prime Law as an amendment to the U.S. Constitution. The Prime-Law Amendment will filter out the bogus second purpose of government. Without initiatory force to pursue the bogus second purpose of government, the dark rule of flaw-filled man — the entire elite ruling class of flaw-filled man — will end in the light of the rule of flawless law, the Prime Law. Geniuses of society would no longer be held back and would be free to multiply our buying power...up to a *thousandfold*, as first seen in the uniquely free computer industry. Multiplying our buying power even a hundredfold would bring Americans universal wealth, health, and security.

Path 2) The process of amending the U.S. Constitution, for all practical purposes, must start with Congress. Therefore, the Prime-Law Amendment will have to wait for the Great Replacement Program to occur first, as described in this chapter. A second, potentially more rapid path to universal wealth, health, and security starts with the Executive Branch, with the President, specifically with his Protection-Only Budget, as described in this chapter. The scenario described in this chapter could happen swiftly (remember Perot's near tipping point in '92). The passing of the President's Protection-Only Budget will effectively cut off the bogus second purpose of government, as described within. Passing the Protection-Only Budget, effectively depoliticizing and deregulating America, will also end the ruling-class of flaw-filled man and free the geniuses of society. The geniuses will do for all industries what they did for the mostly nonpoliticized, mostly unregulated computer industry: they will multiply our buying power a thousandfold, making all Americans wealthy. The Great

Replacement Program (replacing ruling-class politicians with Prime-Law politicians) would follow, and the Prime-Law Amendment would then follow, bringing our country, for the first time, rule of flawless law, permanently locking down the conditions of universal wealth, health, and security. The unprecedented wealth for ordinary people is described within. For the first time, what you are reading here about universal wealth, health, and security is not political rhetoric. It is your destiny with the Prime Law.

So, let us view your destiny of wealth, health, and peace. ...Just before we do, however, I must take a moment to form the ground for your trek to the viewing point of the life you were meant to live: Starting in the early 1980s, I spent long days developing *Twelve Visions*, a Mark Hamilton Publication that reveals twelve visions of the future — of your destiny. *Twelve Visions* uses a unique blend of past and present facts that snap together like pieces to a puzzle.

Consider that, as with any forming puzzle, a point will come when you can see what the completed puzzle-picture will look like, even before all the pieces are snapped into place. Knowing what the puzzle-picture looks like before it is all there is seeing into the future. You can actually describe the missing portion of the puzzle-picture – describe the future pieces. This ability to show you a puzzle-picture before it is all there — an accurate vision of the future – is called **Neothink®**. I developed and perfected Neothink® over the past thirty years.

I used this Neothink® puzzle-building technique to build *Twelve Visions* — a complete puzzle-picture showing us our future. I reveal a country of wealthy, healthy, and safe citizens (and much more) resulting from very specific psychological and political changes. The pages that follow contain selected portions from four of my Twelve Neothink® Visions; they show us exactly how to bring the people, even the poor, remarkable wealth, health, and peace.

Indeed, the remaining Volume Three of this book consists of the Tenth, Eleventh, and parts of the Ninth and Twelfth Visions from *Twelve Visions* and shows you the puzzle-picture of *your* life tomorrow with the Prime Law.

As you begin, realize there may be a few words and concepts

you do not fully understand that were developed in the first eight visions, but just continue reading. We will begin with the Eleventh Vision...

## Unstoppable Universal Wealth

*"That's the technology paradox: Businesses can thrive at the very moment when their prices are falling the fastest. 'The only thing that matters is if the exponential growth of your market is faster than the exponential decline of your prices,' says George M.C. Fisher, chairman and CEO of Eastman Kodak Co. The challenge is enormous, he says. 'Companies have to project out: How will I be competitive in a world (in which) technology will be virtually free?'*

*"The new rules require more than ingenuity, agility, and speed. They call for redefining value in an economy where the cost of raw technology is plummeting toward zero. Sooner or later, this plunge will obliterate the worth of almost any specific piece of hardware or software. Then, value will be in establishing a long-term relationship with a customer — even if it means giving the first generation of a product away."*

*— Business Week*
*"The Technology Paradox: How Companies Thrive As Prices Dive"*

Many new technologies bombarded my thoughts as the Eleventh Vision came to me. A great competitive storm of super rapidly evolving new technologies in tomorrow's Twelve Visions World caused consumer prices to fall to fractions.

With the success of the Twelve Visions Party and its Prime Law, the famous free-falling prices of computers and communications spread beyond the computer industry across many old industries and all new industries, reaching nearly all consumer products. Then, even modest paychecks and savings were worth a fortune.

Well, you got rich, without lifting a finger, in that Twelve Visions World. The computer revolution was a forerunner to a Technological Revolution that drove prices toward zero and values toward infinity in most industries.

Today, people wonder where the Technological Revolution will take us. America's richest man and other powerful people predict mind-boggling technological transformations culminating in a *distance-free* world. They are right: the walls of distance have nearly come down as digitized information traveling through broadband fiber-optic cables and between personal satellite dishes let us work, learn, shop, and play anywhere in the world, anytime, regardless where we live. But those visionaries have limited insight into what will *really* happen. They do not predict the *enormous wealth*.

The very large financial benefits of ending the ruling class brings increasing pressure for people to turn to the Twelve Visions Party. The most powerful and fastest moving trends throughout history were economically driven. As this monetarily motivated trend to end the ruling class grows, my Eleventh Vision showed me big government eventually could not hold. My Vision showed me that during the first quarter of the twenty-first century, big government popped off society like a champagne cork. Suddenly, millions of super entrepreneurs spouted forth, out of nowhere. They were the first to jump into the Neothink® mentality. During my Eleventh Vision, those millions of freed super entrepreneurs caused a catalytic progression of tomorrow's super technologies, which caused a catalytic explosion of buying power.

The era of inexpensive super technologies showered upon us. Cost-collapsing telecommunications, fiber optics, digitized information, super-powered personal computers, the Internet, robotics, the Genome Project...those were only a few small clouds at the turn of the millennium before a giant storm of competitive geniuses and their super technologies. With the success of the Twelve Visions Party, the geniuses feverishly competed day and night against each other to bring us breathtaking values for just a few dollars or less. When the technological storm began, more and more affordable super technologies showered upon us day after day, our buying power soared, and it never came back down once lifted by the great technological twister.

Our lifestyles became our previous fantasies as our buying power kept soaring until we lived like millionaires, including the poor. All along, the only thing that prevented our millionaire-like lifestyles was big government.

Before the success of the Twelve Visions Party, throughout the twentieth century and into the twenty-first century, most industries and their technologies were terribly burdened by big government — by regulation, legislation, litigation, taxes. Most industries and technologies had long been *politicized;* the computer/Internet industry had not (although there was a growing trend, starting with the infamous antitrust lawsuit brought against Microsoft).

Without carrying the same burden, the geniuses in the computer field easily jumped ahead. And that was the difference that allowed prices to miraculously race toward zero.

That was a preview to the Technological Revolution that will happen with the success of the Twelve Visions Party. Over the next three pages are three oversimplified images that flashed before me during my Eleventh Vision: (Author's Note: Although grossly oversimplified, these flash mental images occurred during my Neothinking® process and do make the basic point. The Department of Homeland Security was created after my Eleventh Vision had occurred. Therefore, that executive department does not show up on the following images.)

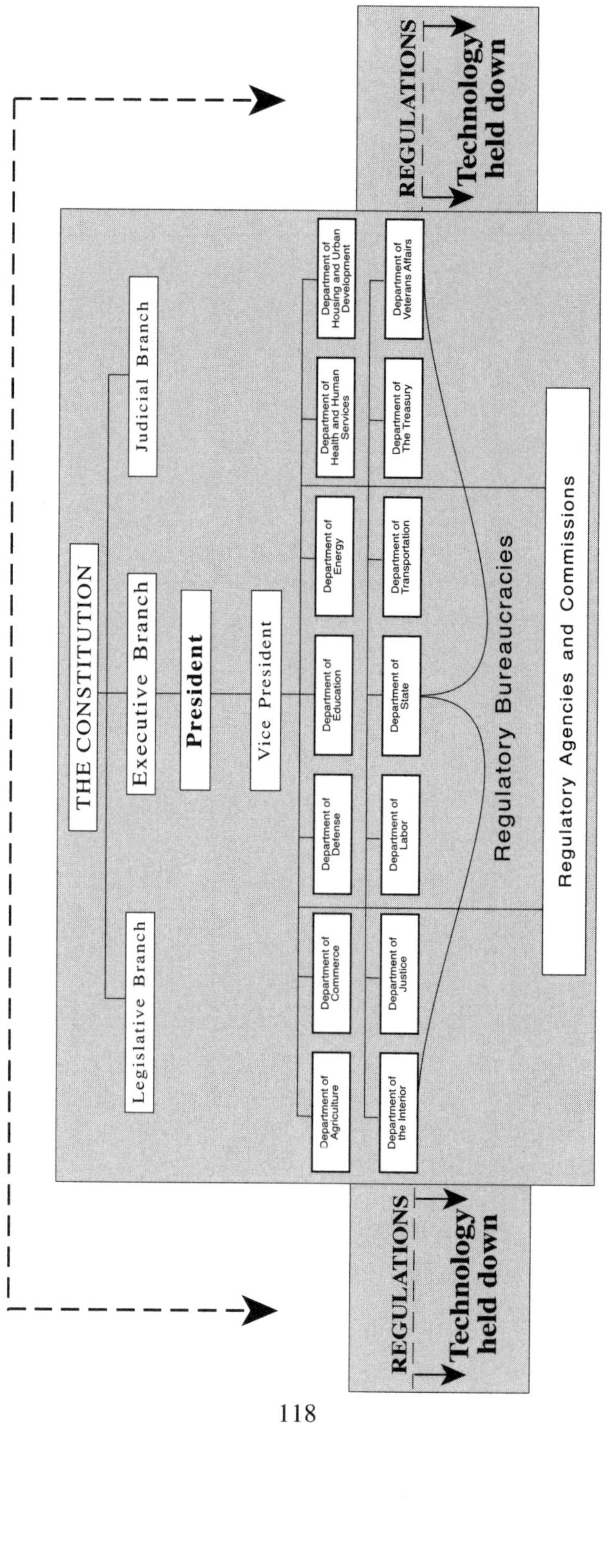
THE CONSTITUTION
Legislative Branch
Executive Branch
Judicial Branch
President
Vice President
Department of Agriculture
Department of Commerce
Department of Defense
Department of Education
Department of Energy
Department of Health and Human Services
Department of Housing and Urban Development
Department of the Interior
Department of Justice
Department of Labor
Department of State
Department of Transportation
Department of The Treasury
Department of Veterans Affairs
Regulatory Bureaucracies
Regulatory Agencies and Commissions
REGULATIONS
Technology held down
REGULATIONS
Technology held down

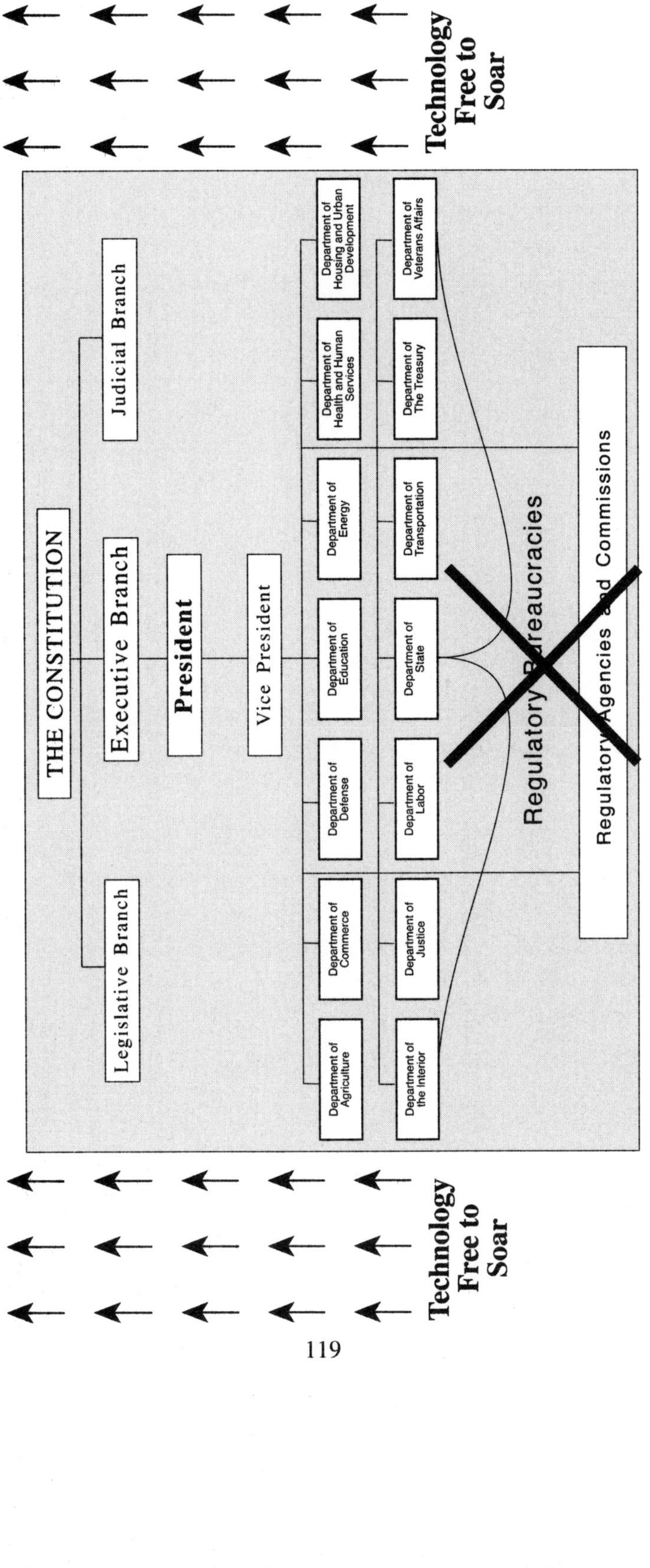
Technology Free to Soar
THE CONSTITUTION
Legislative Branch
Executive Branch
Judicial Branch
President
Vice President
Department of Agriculture
Department of Commerce
Department of Defense
Department of Education
Department of Energy
Department of Health and Human Services
Department of Housing and Urban Development
Department of the Interior
Department of Justice
Department of Labor
Department of State
Department of Transportation
Department of The Treasury
Department of Veterans Affairs
Regulatory Bureaucracies
Regulatory Agencies and Commissions
Technology Free to Soar

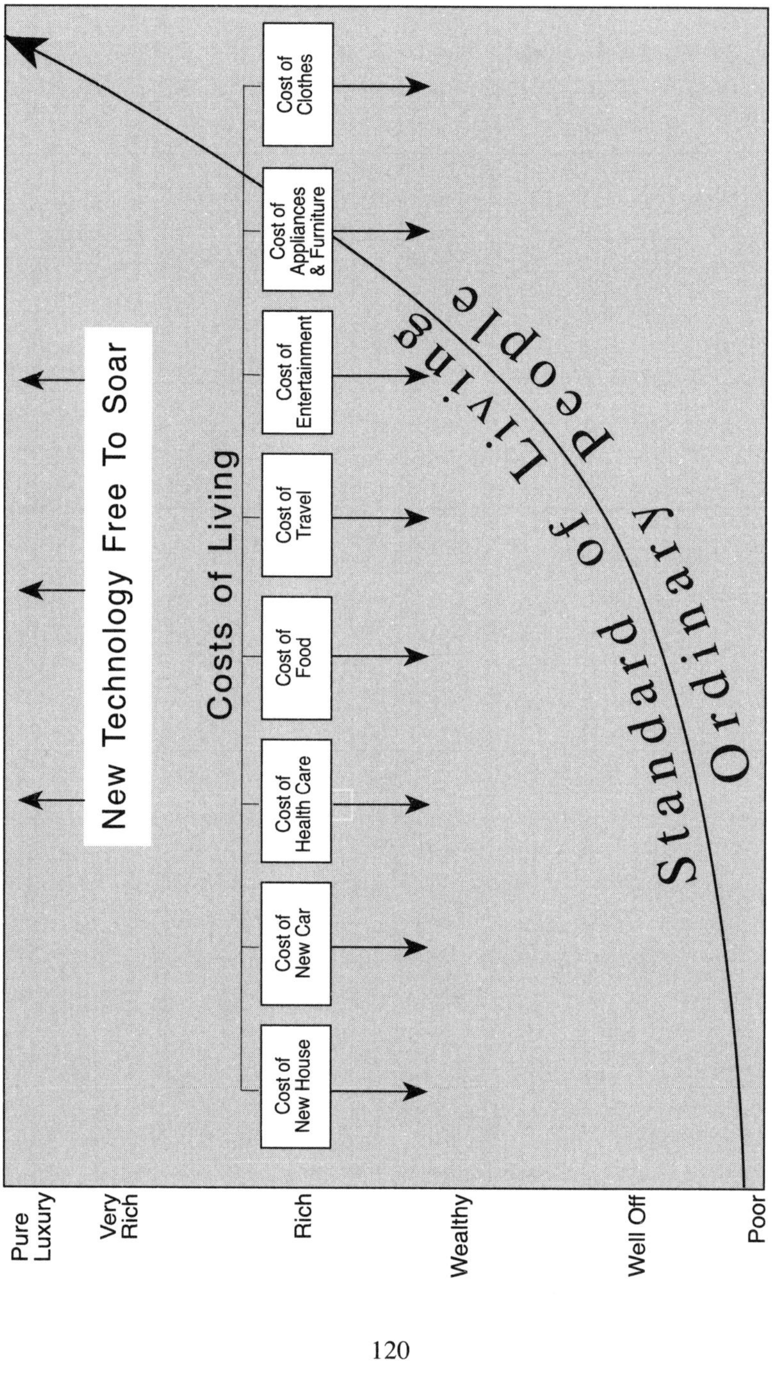


21st-Century Twelve Visions World

### *Universal Wealth, Health, Peace*

My Eleventh Vision showed me technologies in *all* areas of life free to race ahead in the way the computers had. In that Twelve Visions Society of rapidly advancing technologies, living costs fell to fractions in the way the computers had. Buying power in *all* areas of life multiplied a hundred times or more. I saw ordinary people living like millionaires in custom homes, driving luxury cars, and vacationing all over the world first class. Even the poor enjoyed the gifts of life.

One man had the power to quickly bring us into that Twelve Visions World where poverty and suffering no longer existed and Americans lived in luxury. That man was the President of the United States. In the twentieth century and early twenty-first century, no President would initiate the millionaire phenomenon because no career politician would slash his own base of power. But now, we have seen a sample of the great prosperity:

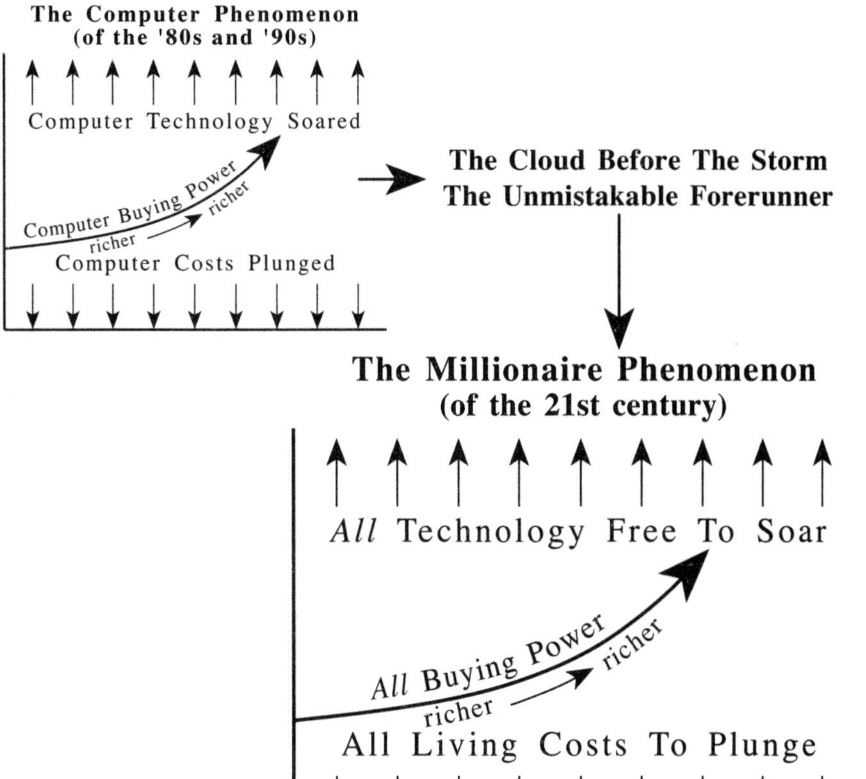

The regulatory seams around society restrict new technologies and hold back the Technological Revolution. Those regulatory seams holding back the Technological Revolution also postpone the job revolution and block a hundred million super entrepreneurs (explained in the Fifth Vision). When big government disintegrated with the success of the Twelve Visions Party, modern technologies burst out everywhere and mixed with millions of unleashed super entrepreneurs using Neothink®. The overwhelming creativity, pumped into the new supersociety, generated prosperity that went off the charts, beyond anything ever contemplated in economic think tanks. Even the poorest Americans experienced enormous wealth.

## You Became 100 Times Richer

My Eleventh Vision showed me that by honing in on the national budget alone, our buying power could be catapulted a hundred times or more! We have to do nothing! Let us start with a brief overview of what makes up the national budget:

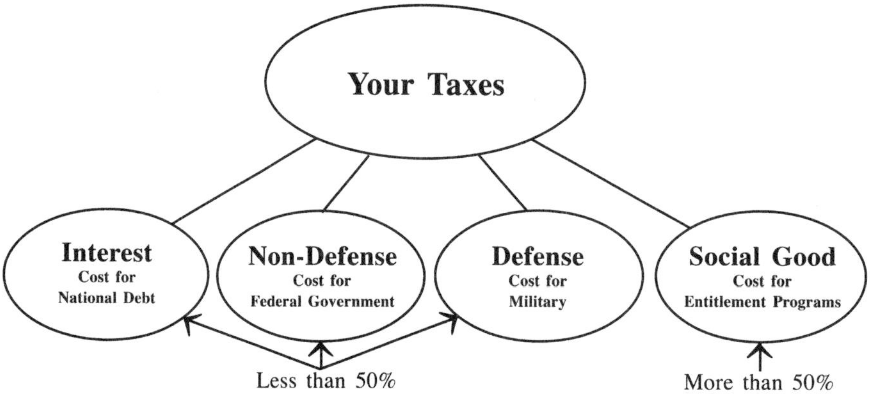


Your taxes break down into mandatory spending programs such as Social Security, Medicare, Medicaid, means-tested entitlements such as Food Stamps, Supplemental Security Income, Child Nutrition, veterans' pensions; and the remaining mandatory spending mainly consists of Federal retirement and insurance programs, unemployment insurance, and payments to farmers. All those Federal entitlement programs, programs ostensibly for the social good, add up to more than half of all federal government spending in the early twenty-first century. The discretionary spending breaks down into defense spending for the military and non-defense discretionary spending, which covers the Legislative Branch, the Judicial Branch, the Executive Branch, including its fifteen executive departments, the EPA, NASA, foreign aid, science...basically whatever it costs to run the Federal government. Then, of course, there is interest on the national debt. Discretionary spending, which is what it costs to run the military and the government, plus the interest on the national debt, add up to less than half of all federal spending in the early twenty-first century.

Finally, federal spending usually creates either a surplus or a deficit, meaning it collects more than it spends in the case of a surplus, or it spends more than it collects, in the case of a deficit. Growing deficits mean growing debt, which means growing interest payments.

Now, let us look at my Eleventh Vision that showed me how to approach the budget to cause our buying power to soar a hundred times or more, without us lifting a finger!

My Eleventh Vision showed me the most sensational creation of wealth the world has ever known. I saw a Twelve Visions President slash government spending by nearly removing the entitlement spending programs and the majority of non-defense discretionary spending. He was very careful that, first, those who had earned entitlements such as social security and veterans' pensions were fully compensated through a spectacular sale of all government assets that had nothing to do with protection. With the trillions of dollars accumulated from the largest sale in mankind's history, social security that was owed was paid off completely, up front and in full, plus interest. Then, the Social Security program ended all together, for the government had no business telling people how to spend or save their money. Veterans' pensions were continued, but managed through a private, third-party service.

The budget to run the government was eventually reduced by over 50% to essential laws, courts, prisons, Federal police, intelligence, defense...everything needed to protect the citizens' peace and safety. The military (including veterans' pensions), courts, prisons, and legitimate lawmaking protected the people from initiatory force. Protecting the people from initiatory force and coercion is, in the long run, the only valid purpose of a federal government. Eventually, all functions of government beyond protection evolved into a businesslike setup, as described in Neothink® trilogy *Superpuzzle* (a Mark Hamilton Publication, 1200-pages). People willingly subscribed to those services.

During this Twelve Visions President's term, there was no chaos. (The President had a two-year battle with Congress over the budget, but the mid-term elections washed out many of those resisting the President's budget as the people noticed their buying power rising.) Instead, he simplified the Federal Government. The country fell into beautiful order as he led the privatization of many government services. Moreover, great prosperity — the millionaire phenomenon — swept across the country as businesses and entrepreneurs were free to invest in research and development without the burden and risk of an offensive, regulatory government. Big business and garage entrepreneurs both developed new technologies so swiftly, with such rapidly dropping costs, that our buying power began climbing...climbing so rapidly, in fact, poor people previously dependent on government entitlements instead soon lived with the standards of living of millionaires by the end of the Twelve Visions President's term. Soon, *no one* missed big government, not even the most liberal communities. Everyone was too busy enjoying his or her new standard of living...a standard of living only the millionaires enjoyed just one presidential term earlier. A new era had arrived, the Twelve Visions Era.

In the Eleventh Vision, looking back at today's budgets, we knew what defense spending and interest on the national debt were for. But, we had a hard time understanding the spending programs for the "social good" or for much of non-defense government. For one thing, tomorrow we knew the best way to help the people was to set free the geniuses in order to make the people rich: *to make their buying power go so high they lived like millionaires.*

Tomorrow our make-the-people-millionaires program freed technologies and freed super entrepreneurs to drive the new technologies into computerlike revolutions everywhere for everyone. A Twelve Visions President whose career was *not* politics turned inward and slashed his own base of political power — regulatory power — to free the technologies and the super entrepreneurs.

To be the President of the United States before the Twelve Visions World was to be a career politician; the career politician by nature *built* his base of political power, and the President's base of political power was regulatory power — the regulatory bureaucracies, commissions, and agencies beneath him. That was why no president *seriously* wanted to eliminate *most* regulations. Social and regulatory programs supposedly "for the public good" supported the President's and Congress' base of power. Those spending programs, even those entitlement programs such as social welfare, came hand in hand with massive regulations telling us how to spend our money and run our businesses. Unbeknownst to you, but so obvious to me during my Eleventh Vision, those regulations actually blocked the Twelve Visions World in which you would live as a millionaire.

Those so-called "help the people" social and regulatory programs were illusions that actually *hurt the people* while building the Presidents' popularity, ego, and power. In my Eleventh Vision, I was amazed that the "great" presidents of the twentieth century who started "noble" social programs for the "social good" were looked back upon as the worst malefactors of society.

### *The Biggest Illusion*

Today, the massive Federal spending programs on entitlements so-called "for the social good" in turn give the Federal Government absolute power to *regulate* the economy and *rule over* our money. The Federal Government has its regulatory web all throughout our economy — in every business, every consumer product, every job, every profession, including every hospital, every doctor's office, every research and development program, every discovery, every invention, every paycheck, every person's wallet.

In my Eleventh Vision, the people in tomorrow's Twelve Visions World were amazed that politicians and bureaucrats once ruled over our money and our lives. The archaic regulatory web throughout the economy *trapped and paralyzed* new technologies.

Without super rapidly advancing technologies, costs did not drop to fractions. Instead, costs went up and up and up for the entire twentieth century. We just could not believe it, looking back: *prices went up for 100 years!* The elderly who lived on set pensions and measly entitlements got trapped in the dungeons of society as long-term inflation ate up everything they had.

Sometime in the twenty-first century, we discovered that the *only* way to truly help the needy and everyone else was to send the economy through a buying-power metamorphosis such as the computer industry's buying-power metamorphosis. The Eleventh Vision showed me the needy and everyone else's limited buying power leapt *a hundred times* when the Twelve Visions President's **Protection-Only Budget** swished away the regulatory web throughout the economy. His budget swished away those so-called "good intentions", such as social welfare and the regulatory bureaucracies that wove regulatory control throughout every nook and cranny of the business world. When that regulatory web was gone, technology was free, and it took off just as the unregulated computer technology had, but in every industry. *Everyone's* buying power quickly rose. (This ended Social Security payments. Moreover, this unique approach miraculously repaid *every penny* of social security to Americans with *full fair-market interest!* That financial miracle meant elderly Americans received a small fortune from the government, all up front, by selling off all government assets that had nothing to do with protection.)

### *The World's Greatest Irony*

The world's greatest irony was: the way to best help the people was to cross out the government's programs to "help the people" and the *massive regulations* that came with those "well intentioned" massive spending programs. Indeed, ending the noble-sounding "higher" causes, those programs for the "social good", ultimately ended the destructive elite class ruling over us, suppressing us. Our Twelve Visions Government shrank to its original and proper purpose of individual protection — *protecting the peace.*

And when that happened, look what happened next: My Eleventh Vision showed me an amazing world without those regulatory webs of "good intentions" so-called "for the social good". The needy and everyone else lived like "kings" as unburdened technology soared, costs plunged, and everyone's buying power multiplied on average a hundred times. *Everyone* became rich...yes, including the poor. It was the *only* program that could ever make *the poor* live like millionaires.

The "social good" was just a clever way of saying "politicize society, rule over the people, and play God with their money, morals, and lives." The "social good" was the career politicians' and regulatory bureaucrats' prime illusion that manipulated our century-old mental programming for "higher" causes (Vision Prologue).

Sometime in the twenty-first century, we deprogrammed our minds with Neothink® and, like coming out of a spell, we shook our heads and said "enough" to spending more than half of the Federal Budget on the "social good".

### *Ending The Spell*

The first Twelve Visions President ended politicization of our lives and ended government on the offense — ended entitlement and regulatory programs. The Twelve Visions President reduced government to self-defense protection only, a government of defense without an active ruling class telling us how to live. That paradigm shift freed the geniuses of society.

They, in turn, whirled into an aggressive storm of Neothink® competition to serve up our every need. In doing so, they lifted technology into new dimensions, which drove down living and health costs to fractions and brought us spectacular new values and entertainment. The computer revolution of the twentieth century seemed like a little white cloud compared to the storm of new technologies raining on us in the twenty-first century.

As you know, after World War II, we looked back in disbelief at the holocaust. In tomorrow's Twelve Visions World, our children and grandchildren looked back in disbelief at today's politicians and bureaucrats ruling over us. In both cases, millions of innocent people died at the hands of politicians and bureaucrats ruling over us. Everyone, everywhere, in my Eleventh Vision knew the *only* reason the disease-free, wealthy Twelve Visions World never happened in the twentieth century was because, simply put, no politicians wanted to slash their base of political power. They cared only about building their base of power — regulatory, legislative, and spending power. (Indeed, spending money they did not earn brought them enormous, easy power and prestige.) Therefore, we did not have the slightest clue of the phenomenal wealth and health available to us by reducing government to a protection-only government of defense...not until the "Solar Eclipse":

## The "Solar Eclipse"

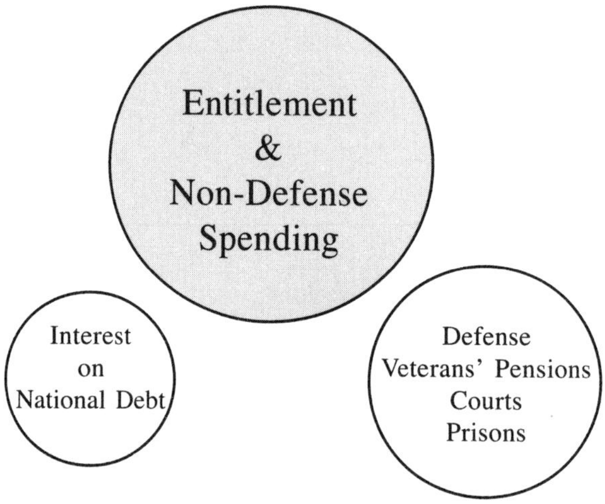


Consider that Einstein's Theory of Relativity ($E=mc^2$) went years unrecognized. Then, a natural phenomenon occurred — a solar eclipse — that demonstrated his theory. Instantly, Einstein and his Theory of General Relativity were a world sensation accepted by nearly everyone. With that solar-eclipse demonstration, the world quickly moved beyond Newtonian physics to Einsteinian physics.

During my Eleventh Vision, I saw a similar phenomenon in politics: The Twelve Visions President's first budget was that "solar eclipse" as he eclipsed many of the solar-high spending programs for the "social good" and most of the non-defense spending. Although Congress did everything possible to undo his budget for their own survival, the unmistakable demonstration of falling taxes and rising buying power still occurred, no matter how diluted. Similar to Einstein's Relativity, instantly the make-the-people-millionaires program of slashing regulations and offensive government was a world sensation.

With that "solar-eclipse" demonstration, world politics quickly moved beyond career politicians and regulatory bureaucrats...into the new political paradigm, the unprecedented get-the-people-rich government.

Needless to say, the Twelve Visions President's Protection-Only Budget was a shock to Congress as he tried to cut the budget *in half* his first year. He wanted no more deceptions — no more politicians and bureaucrats politicizing our lives and ruling over us in the name of "higher" causes. He knew that only the James J. Hills (next chapter) — the geniuses of society — could boost the people's standards of living. Congress did not accept his budget at all. They did not want to give up their ruling class with all its spending and glory.

Yet, Congress had no choice but to give in to some degree because once the people elected a Twelve Visions President, they sensed good things about his route to the millionaire-phenomenon and stood behind him. So the legislative ruling-class, 435 Congressmen and 100 Senators, had to abandon their first thoughts of impeachment. With their very own constituents cheering for the make-the-people-millionaires program, Congress was not able to completely undo his budget. Of course, Congress radically changed the budget, but the President vigorously pointed his finger at the culprits for the whole country to see. Thus, Congress backed off and some of what he submitted took hold.

*Bingo.* People's taxes dropped immediately. But more importantly, their buying power started going up almost immediately. For the first time, exciting practical results outperformed political rhetoric. After that "solar-eclipse" demonstration, the Twelve Visions President then told America, loud and clear: "Imagine what could happen to your buying power if my Protection-Only Budget passed in its entirety. You could all be rich before my term is over!"

With that realization, the people almost unanimously implemented a nationwide change called **The Great Replacement Program**: Like a big wave at high tide due to the "solar-eclipse" demonstration, the Great Replacement Program washed over the country; it washed away the career politicians and their ruling class. Voters nominated and voted into Congress business owners and genuine, market-driven businessmen and women, knowing they would pass the Twelve Visions President's Protection-Only Budget in its entirety.

Those market-driven businesspeople — the James J. Hills (next chapter) — never cared about building political power. Such as the Twelve Visions President, they were not politicians. Instead, they wanted a free and booming economy. So, to that end, they were more than happy to eclipse their own structures of political power. They were more than happy to eclipse all government "good intentions" — that is, all those social and regulatory programs "for the social good" that were really Trojan Horses carrying massive, suppressive regulations. Those market businesspeople passed the Twelve Visions President's budget in its entirety. The ruling class soon vanished.[1]

Taxes immediately fell by more than half. But far more important, the regulatory/legislative web throughout the economy simply got swished away, which immediately set free the aggressive entrepreneurs who leapt into Neothink® (society's geniuses) and immediately set free the advancing new technologies. The Neothink® geniuses — the miracle makers — drove forth the new technologies. Industry after industry went through unprecedented buying-power miracles. Computerlike revolutions were happening everywhere, in every industry, even in the housing industry, bringing us inexpensive beautiful new homes and ending the real-estate crisis with a building boom.

Indeed, removing the many regulations on the construction

[1]Although only one-third of the Senate could have been replaced during the mid-term elections, the public pressure to vote for the Protection-Only Budget overwhelmed the majority of senators.

industry and its many suppliers and support industries, not to mention removing the bulk of taxes, immediately allowed general contractors to build bigger, better, and more beautiful homes for a lot less money. And that improvement was immediate, before the technological breakthroughs kicked in!

Under the government of offense, your buying power decreased for a hundred years. After the Great Replacement Program led by a Twelve Visions President and his Protection-Only Budget, your buying power increased a hundred times or more *during a decade.* Indeed, the Protection-Only Budget *quickly* freed the geniuses and launched the wealthy Twelve Visions World. The Prime Law ultimately became an amendment to the Constitution of the United States and *permanently* freed the geniuses and *forever* guaranteed your wealthy Twelve Visions World.

## Everyone Will Be Taken Care Of

Tomorrow's get-the-people-rich (by getting out of the way) government physically *protected us* only. The Federal Government was reduced to protection against physical aggression (or an imminent threat). A budget less than half previous budgets was needed to protect our country. The other half to three-quarters of previous budgets was no longer needed. We realized up to three-quarters of the Federal Budget had been wrongly used to *rule over* society through politicizing our lives and our businesses.

The people saw the double negative of money taxed and spent for the "social good". In fact, the whole idea of a government on the offensive for the "social good" became a bizarre thought. The government had one purpose — a government of defense to protect its citizens from physical attack, coercion, or fraud. All the other money taxed straight out of our lives — up to three dollars for every four that we earned, taken from us in taxes for spending other than physical protection and interest on the debt — simply sucked that enormous portion of money out of the economy, particularly out of those hard-working geniuses who liked to reinvest their money into growth to generate more wealth and jobs. The government then redistributed over half of that money to a government-created class of people who "inherited" a living and generated nothing for society.

But even worse than the huge mandatory spending programs was the discretionary spending to regulatory bureaucracies. They ruled over us with regulations that suppressed geniuses and new technologies. So, the negative effect of a government on the offense was painfully double: big government drained our money out of our lives *and then used it to specifically block us from rising into a wealthy paradise on Earth!*

The happy, wealthy people in tomorrow's Twelve Visions World looked through history books while scratching their heads, wondering why we did not see this obvious double negative a lot, lot sooner. We disastrously accepted the deceptions called "the social good". The destructive ruling class of career politicians and regulatory bureaucrats was well camouflaged as existing for the "social good".

*The Elderly Benefitted the Most*

What about the elderly and the genuinely needy? Before tomorrow's Twelve Visions World, the elderly were stuck in the poverty-trap caused by the social-welfare illusion. In my Eleventh Vision, the elderly and needy gained the most in the Twelve Visions World, for they *more than anyone* needed a monetary metamorphosis in which their savings and pensions suddenly could buy a hundred times more. And that is exactly what they got. Unburdened, free-to-soar technology began driving down costs to fractions immediately after the Solar-Eclipse Budget passed.

Looking back from tomorrow's Twelve Visions World, when government had regulatory dominance over the economy, prices did not go down. They went up. Inflation was a slow torture for the elderly and the needy on set incomes. Inflation, even slow inflation, eventually trapped many of the elderly and the needy in the dungeons of society as poverty-ridden, dependent "slaves" — "slaves" to big government, forever dependent on their measly entitlement money. That slave class meant guaranteed votes for an ever-increasing regulatory government.

But in the Twelve Visions World, all that changed. Ironically, that change most benefited the huge American slave class — the elderly and the needy. The make-the-people-millionaires program lifted everyone into financial independence and then financial prosperity.

What about health, education, and everyone's welfare? What about all those spending programs that got blacked out? The resulting millionaire phenomenon made *everyone* rich; those previously dependent on entitlements benefited the most. Those previously trapped "slaves", dependent on suppressive big government in order to survive in poverty, for the first time lived like *healthy and wealthy kings* as buying power and jobs began multiplying.

### *Healthy Kings*

Now, I said *healthy* kings because unhampered, soaring technologies not only drove health-care costs to fractions, but eradicated serious diseases. Consider that the FDA, looking out for the "public good", killed many promising low-cost cures with cost-prohibitive regulations. In my Eleventh Vision, I witnessed that unburdened geniuses of society got the public good done and done quickly. Through the help of unburdened super technologies, the Neothink® geniuses quickly, among other things, eradicated diseases (Vision Twelve, later).

### *Unprecedented Prosperity*

I saw the end result of **The Great Displacement Program**: Government assets and programs not part of protecting its citizens from physical force were sold to the private sector. Geniuses of society, not career politicians, took over programs for the social good to finally achieve social good.

The Great Replacement/Great Displacement Program led by a Twelve Visions President and his Protection-Only Budget ushered in the new Twelve Visions Era with no ruling class and no government programs for the "social good". Super technologies and super entrepreneurs, finally free of political pollution, free of even the smallest regulatory impurities, gave the world an unprecedented "power-reactor" explosion of prosperity beyond comprehension in today's terms.

*The New Prosperity*

The new prosperity made it difficult to look back at the former government programs "for the social good":

- Education: Among lowest standard of industrialized nations.
- Social Security: A greater and greater strain on the economy.
- Welfare: Left the poor in deeper and deeper poverty-traps. Stressing the economy.
- Health Care: Less and less effective.
- Social Programs: Deteriorating results.
- Regulatory Programs: Handicapped America in global competition while driving up costs, suppressing progress, and shrinking our job base...all while arming more and more teams of bureaucrats with guns and legislative-like power.

In the Twelve Visions World, the above programs "for the social good" fell out of the hands of a few hundred politically driven politicians and bureaucrats...into the hands of millions of sharp geniuses who finally did those programs right.

The Eleventh Vision answered my own two questions:

1) How will people take care of their parents with no more government aid and medicare?

2) How will people educate their children with no more public schools?

First of all, the Great Displacement Program and the sale of trillions of dollars of government assets to private businesses easily repaid Social Security *with full, fair-market interest.* A lot of people suddenly got back small fortunes, especially the elderly who spent their lives paying the taxes that paid for those government assets sold. That sale of government assets ended the flawed Social Security era with everyone being repaid his or her money with interest. Working people no longer poured their money down the Social Security drain; most adults received a big check from the Federal Government, and retirees suddenly got back a small fortune.

We discovered — even those on entitlements discovered — that social-welfare programs of all kinds, including the medicare and medicaid programs, were clever illusions that hurt, not helped, the elderly and needy. Those social-welfare programs let the government regulate our economy and politicize our health, blocking computerlike revolutions and free-falling prices for breakthrough cures. Tomorrow, we rescued our parents by freeing the economy and medical industry from those regulatory webs. Soon, health and living costs fell to fractions. Quality of life soared. The Twelve Visions President's "solar-eclipse" demonstration during his first year in office led to the inevitable millionaire phenomenon that made *everyone* wealthy and healthy, including the poor and the elderly.

Now, for our children: In the Eleventh Vision, I witnessed superior private education become the affordable norm and not the unaffordable exception. Today, only the privileged can, in a sense, pay twice for their children's education — once to the government (via taxes) and once to a private school. But tomorrow, everyone paid only once, but for superior private education.

Private schools became very inexpensive as open competition delivered the highest value for the lowest cost once the government's monopoly on education ended. Our children grew increasingly knowledgeable, creative, and motivated. They grew up to become successful, happy, and rich value creators. An upcoming chapter goes into details. (My Neothink® trilogy *Superpuzzle* provides a complete picture of tomorrow's Twelve Visions World, including the political and educational structures and results.)

## Money Talks, Abuse Walks

During this Eleventh Vision into the Twelve Visions World, I noticed that the Protection-Only Budget, ending the nearly three out of four dollars spent on entitlement programs and regulatory bureaucracies, collecting only the money needed to protect us...this radically different budget did something else besides set free super entrepreneurs and super technologies that made ordinary people rich. The Protection-Only Budget also eliminated powerful forces of big government that were steadily taking away our freedom and individual rights.

Once the Protection-Only Budget passed in its entirety in the Twelve Visions President's third year in office after the mid-term Great Replacement Program, no more money was available to go to regulatory bureaucracies, all of which had quietly armed their agents over the decades — a dangerous step in America toward secret police and fascism. Those armed armies of bureaucrats ultimately answered to our President as part of his growing structure of power and ego.

The people in the Twelve Visions World simply asked: why should any regulatory bureaucrat be armed? If he confronts a potentially hostile situation, then he should call the local police as any other citizen.

For the previous century, however, the government had been quietly building armies of armed bureaucrats. The IRS, FTC, FDA, EPA, SEC, DEA, FBI, INS, ATF, CIA — every regulatory bureaucracy and beyond had armed agents... *even the postal service came complete with armed bureaucrats!* As the people in my Eleventh Vision looked back, they were amazed at how obvious this abuse of power was, which before went right over their heads.

Those armies of armed bureaucrats, all under the command of the President, grew increasingly aggressive while steadily subtracting our freedom and individual rights. Caught up in the illusions of "social good", we let them rule over us.

The Protection-Only Budget, once in full force with the success of the Great Replacement Program, simply cut off the funds to those growing armies of fascism. The Protection-Only Budget, simply put, *just said no!*

So, while making everyone rich, the Protection-Only Budget saved us from deteriorating freedom and growing government abuse.

## Jobs, Wealth, Security

Once in office, the Twelve Visions President's fiscal policy was simple: eliminate from the annual budget up to three of four dollars previously spent.

Looking back over the twentieth century, America got in trouble regarding the currency. In 1933, Franklin D. Roosevelt took us off the gold standard. With no more accountability or disciplines, the government pumped more and more money into our economy. That caused inflation to eat up our parents' retirement savings and pensions, leaving them poor and financially dependent on us and the government.

Pumping unbacked currency into the economy had a short-term stimulating effect on the economy, but a long-term deadly effect. Of course, politicians sold out our futures for short-term re-election gimmicks. The people in tomorrow's Twelve Visions World were amazed, looking back, that fiscal policy had become an exclusive power-and-ego manipulating game for the powers that be. The ordinary working man was the victim. ...After decades of unbacked currency pumped into the economy — forever followed by inflation and increasing poverty for each new generation of elderly and needy Americans — what did we do? In my Eleventh Vision, here was the Twelve Visions President's immediate course of action — a quick one, two punch:

**One:** He eliminated spending programs for the "social good" and steadily paid off the debt. That cut our taxes in half or more and cut out any need to print more money.

**Two:** The Twelve Visions President eliminated corporate income taxes altogether (which accounted for less than one-tenth of the Federal Government's revenues). That caused an explosion of business, employment, opportunities, and rising incomes for the people as companies reinvested large sums of money back into their businesses, including cash incentives for employee performance. The money that normally went toward taxes and the "social good" instead went toward expansion, job creation, and employee incentive. The economy boomed. ...This concept was first demonstrated in the early '60s during John F. Kennedy's presidency and reinforced in the '80s during Ronald W. Reagan's presidency.

In the Twelve Visions World, students shook their heads in disbelief at the illusions used by big government that tricked their parents and grandparents into sending a major portion of our wealth down the drain disguised as the "social good".

In the Twelve Visions World, with no more government programs for the "social good", our taxes a fraction of what they once were, and with no more corporate income taxes, the money once flushed away to the "social good" was now reinvested into economic growth. That same money went instead toward starting and expanding businesses, creating jobs, motivating us as in-house entrepreneurs (Fifth and Sixth Visions), and causing dynamic technological growth...which, like the computers, drove up our buying power a hundred times, a thousand times.

## The Twelve Visions World — Technology, Wealth, and Health

Let me sum up my Eleventh Vision: The freed geniuses of society whom I saw in my Tenth Vision (next) mixed with the freed twenty-first-century super technologies that I saw in my Eleventh Vision. First the impurities of society were removed — i.e., the career politicians and regulatory bureaucrats ruling over our money, morals, and businesses in the name of the "social good" (instead of simply and properly protecting us). Second, with the impurities absent, the super entrepreneurs and super technologies went through a catalytic, "power-reactor" explosion that lifted society into a beautiful new world, the Twelve Visions World. In that new world, the people including the poor lived like millionaires.

Here were our steps into that new world: America's growing damnation of politicians ushered in a nonpolitician Twelve Visions President sometime in the first quarter of the twenty-first century. His "solar-eclipse" demonstration quickly brought about the Great Replacement Program. Then his Protection-Only Budget passed in its entirety and ended government on the offense doing the "social good". Everyone's taxes fell in half...and then *in half again* as market businessmen drove down the remaining government expenses for protection by digging into the details and making them efficient.

As that occurred, geniuses of society rose by the millions and steadily raised our buying power as their breakthrough technologies drove costs toward zero. We became essentially a hundred times wealthier and more. Furthermore, every day and night felt as safe as living in Disneyland, for people became wealthy without lifting a finger. Committing crime was too much work. Moreover, the government's sole focus was your protection: national defense on the federal level and police protection on the local level. For the first time, civilization existed in pure freedom.

The Twelve Visions World is the paradise on Earth in which we were meant to live — a world in which we will be very wealthy with exciting opportunities, even for those who now have little opportunity. In my Eleventh Vision, that Twelve Visions World provided ever-better technology for ever-cheaper prices, no longer the sole possession of the computer industry. Major health breakthroughs and cures occurred at increasing frequency and became affordable to everyone, even to the elderly.

Unsurpassed, quality education became available and affordable to all families. Fears of unemployment were forgotten in the perpetually soaring economy with endless selections of exciting, "living" jobs (Fifth Vision). And finally, the millionaire's life of exotic vacations and first-class luxuries removed every last drop of boredom from our lives. Life was fun and exciting.

Looking back left a heavy sadness in our hearts for the millions who died unnecessarily to disease. We realized how career politicians and regulatory bureaucrats cost many of our loved ones' precious lives.

Big government was on the *offense* politicizing our lives and ruling over us. By contrast, the Twelve Visions World's get-the-people-disease-free-and-rich government was only on the *defense* protecting our lives from any physical threat or attack. After depoliticizing society, thus setting free the geniuses of society, then super rapidly evolving new technologies eradicated infectious disease after disease.

As you might suspect, political leaders resisted the idea of depoliticizing America. But, as Victor Hugo once wrote, "An invasion of armies can be resisted, but not an idea whose time has come."

The Twelve Visions World is the world everyone wants to live in, but has no clue of. Once enough people got exposure to the prosperity and love available in that previously unknown world — once fifty-million people saw the Twelve Visions — the following four steps swiftly occurred:

1) A politically free Twelve Visions President was elected, vowing to enable the people, including the poor, to live like healthy millionaires by depoliticizing America.
2) The Protection-Only Budget was submitted to eliminate government on the offense. Congress rejected most of the budget, but business owners and potential entrepreneurs could now sense the coming new code of freedom. Suddenly private funds for researching new technologies multiplied in all industries. The Technological Revolution shifted into a higher gear; prices began to fall, demonstrating the potential Protection-Only Budget's mighty effects on the people's wealth and health.
3) The Great Replacement Program washed over the country in the subsequent midterm election like a big wave, washing away most career politicians. Original business owners and other market-driven businessmen and women replaced career politicians nearly unanimously. For, the voting public knew that market-driven businesspeople would pass the Protection-Only Budget without hesitation. Indeed, the Protection-Only Budget passed in its entirety.
4) The Great Displacement Program naturally followed as the government's spending monopolies vanished; private businesses and entrepreneurs moved in to legitimately serve the people. America quickly became a wonderful place to be! Buying power multiplied a hundred times. Ordinary people began living like millionaires. Medical technology jumped into the lead against every disease.

Those make-the-people-millionaires and make-the-people-disease-free phenomena quickly brought three outstanding benefits to us:

1) Near-perfect health to us and our loved ones as medical technology raced forward and eradicated disease after disease.
2) Millionaire wealth as technologies raced forward in every industry like today's nonpoliticized computer/information

industry, driving prices toward zero and standards of living toward millionaire wealth.

3) Supermen and superwomen selves as businesses, in that rapidly advancing Twelve Visions World, evolved beyond their routine-rut jobs and instead brought out every worker's potential (Fifth and Sixth Visions). Our stagnant routine ruts were left behind as we discovered our human potential and achieved dreams we could never even fathom before (Ninth Vision). Exhilaration and stimulation replaced boredom and stagnation. The job revolution (described in the Fifth and Sixth Visions) poured a hundred-million geniuses into society. Our jobs became our transmission belts to Neothink®. Such creative energy rushing into society lifted our nation's wealth beyond all economic theories or models prior to the success of the Twelve Visions Party. We lived in a wonderful new world never before known to man.

*Universal Wealth, Health, Peace*

# The Geniuses of Society Bring You Everything You Ever Wanted

*"Another sign of a healthy, competitive industry is lower prices. The statistics show that the cost of computing has decreased ten million fold since 1971. That's the equivalent of getting a Boeing 747 for the price of a pizza."*

*— Bill Gates*

Stepping through the doorway into the Twelve Visions Era in my mind's eye, our geniuses made us rich, made us healthy, made everything good for us. The geniuses of society, who first evolved into Neothink®, led the Technological Revolution that raised our standards of living towards that of millionaires. We loved our geniuses; they brought us the gifts of life.

At first, in the late twentieth century, the geniuses freely rose in the computer world and brought ordinary children inexpensive video games that, just a few years before, only the children of millionaires could enjoy. My Tenth Vision showed me that sometime in the first quarter of the twenty-first century, the geniuses freely rose throughout the rest of the business world and brought us inexpensive products that a few years before only the millionaires could enjoy. Indeed, this computerlike *millionaire phenomenon* came to more and more industries beyond the computer industry, making ordinary people such as you and me essentially millionaires without lifting a finger.

Looking back over the twentieth-century, the millionaire phenomenon had already happened in the computer industry because it was uniquely free of big-government regulations. The computer industry gave us a look ahead at what life would be like in tomorrow's Twelve Visions World.

My Tenth Vision showed me that, to the amazement of the people, the millionaire phenomenon came to more and more industries as we universally removed big-government regulations. After our get-the-people-rich government removed most big-government regulations, technologies in all industries raced ahead like the computers. As in the computer industry, where buying power multiplied thousands or millions of times, our buying power in more and more industries multiplied hundreds, sometimes thousands of times or more. That was because the geniuses were now free to rise and evolve.

*Freeing The Geniuses*

Simply put, America's falling out with big government freed the potential geniuses of society to drive our costs toward zero and our buying power towards infinity. Fantastic products and services never before imagined quickly evolved and then became cheap and affordable. What happened in the computer/communication world was a harbinger of what happened in my Neothink® Vision of tomorrow's Twelve Visions World. When our government freed technology and the geniuses beyond the computers, we lived in increasing wealth and luxury. People became economically driven to end big government and to embrace get-the-people-rich government.

The Twelve Visions Party ushered in get-the-people-rich-*including-the-poor* government, a completely new political paradigm of entrepreneurs and market-driven business leaders in which your every need, no matter how extraordinary or how small, was taken care of. You and your problems were never alone; help was always on the way for every need.

To achieve that never-alone, always-taken-care-of state, the get-the-people-rich government shifted the responsibility of taking care of you — i.e., social well-being — from a few hundred phony career politicians interested in ruling over you...to a hundred million geniuses in entrepreneurial jobs (the Fifth Vision) with rapidly evolving creativity, very interested in taking care of all your needs and wishes.

Millions of unrestricted geniuses, aggressively seeking out our needs, very rapidly answered our every cry for help. That was the new code of living in tomorrow's Twelve Visions World. Even your slightest problem had you immediately surrounded by quality people, by geniuses of society, wanting to help you. Just one cry for help sent out from your home over the Internet, for instance, ever so quickly led to its cure.

The job of looking out for your well-being and the social good shifted from impotent government and its corrupt ruling class to the miraculous might of an unrestricted genius-driven society. The unleashed creativity and new technology made us wealthy, healthy, safe and solved our problems. Your problems were the geniuses' problems to solve. In short, geniuses were hard at work taking care of you and raising your standard of living.

Today, big-government career politicians do not care about your problems, no matter how real, unless your problems fall into their self-aggrandizing schemes to rule. That is the old code of living soon to be left behind. All good people now have to fight for their survival. If you contract a rare disease, you are doomed. In tomorrow's Twelve Visions World, however, unhampered geniuses using Neothink® developed a cure *before* the disease destroyed you. I saw it all in my Tenth Vision. Tomorrow, you were always safe. Looking back at today's world, if you are not happy with your job and pay or with the direction of your career and income, you are trapped. In tomorrow's Twelve Visions World, genius-driven businesses brought you exciting opportunities including the lucrative career of your dreams (Vision Five), your passion in life (Vision One). Today if you are poor or just not happy with your wealth, you are rather helpless. Tomorrow, the multiplying wealth of society rescued your plight. Today, if you are not happy with love, you grow more and more apathetic. Tomorrow, the happiness available from living the life you were meant to live (Vision Two) helped you activate a new, superlove (Vision Seven). If you felt lonely, the enhanced networking of society brought you quality friends, especially as your own value to the world soared (Vision Nine). If you were having hard times, the curing nature of society took care of you in every way.

Geniuses were there for you, in minutes. Money was no longer an issue. A hundred million geniuses in this country alone took care of your every need.

### *They Brought Us Fortunes*

The Twelve Visions Party simply freed the geniuses of society, who became the first to evolve into Neothink®. We sat back and collected the rewards from society's most gifted people.

It was a nice exchange: we gave them freedom, and they gave us fortunes. We certainly were at a unique place in history.

In the late twentieth century when conversations at cocktail parties developed about computers and the Internet and how we could access for free computing power that would have cost millions a few years before, usually some attractive yuppie said something like, "Can you believe that amazing technology!" Everyone then shared looks of astonishment. Little did we stop to realize that *the geniuses of society* brought us that soaring technology and buying power. And those geniuses would do so in every industry if free to do so...making ordinary people rich and healthy.

Sometime in the first quarter of the twenty-first century, after fifty million people were exposed to the Twelve Visions, ordinary people began to admire and love those geniuses who brought them new technologies at lower and lower prices. The love grew despite political rhetoric that traditionally caused Americans to envy and dislike the geniuses of society. As the geniuses improved everyone's life in so many ways, the ordinary person developed a warm fondness for the geniuses of society not unlike one would for a highly competent doctor who saved his child's life, for instance.

Indeed, imagine if your own child or grandchild were terminally ill and the heroic efforts of a highly competent doctor saved your child. You would forever feel a warm affection for that doctor who saved your child's life. Or imagine a wealthy person gave you and your family a cashier's check for a million dollars. You would forever feel a very warm closeness to that person who made your life so rich and wonderful.

Tomorrow, the people felt similar feelings towards the geniuses of society, for those geniuses eradicated diseases and lifted us into a wealthy and wonderful world. The hoodwinking by the media that made us envy and dislike the geniuses of society subsided. The forces of Neothink® were now too great to be stopped. Sure the geniuses were rich, because they were geniuses! But they made *us* rich, too. Furthermore, they brought us the gifts of life: wealth, health, safety, even happiness and love. The entire population, sometime in the first quarter of the twenty-first century, felt a warm closeness to those geniuses who brought us and our families into an increasingly wealthy and wonderful life.

We also felt growing contempt toward those big-government career politicians who blocked the geniuses and their new technologies. Career politicians blocked the gifts and the wonderful lives we were meant to live. Once the people made the twelve-piece connections and felt love for the geniuses of society, then the Twelve Visions Era irreversibly took off.

We sat back and watched in awe as the geniuses of society took care of our needs, fixed our problems, made our dreams come true, and made us rich, *including the poor*.

Of course, career politicians would not let go of their ruling power as we entered the Twelve Visions Era. They hung on, but they were part of the old world on its way out (Vision Prologue). We, in turn, freed the geniuses of society whose life ambitions were to solve our problems and needs, large or small. With the success of the Twelve Visions Party came *The Great Replacement Program*. Like an unstoppable wave, the voting public replaced career politicians with the market-driven businesspeople of the Twelve Visions Party. Across the country, then the world, the big wave washed away career politicians and replaced them with the entrepreneurs and market-driven businesspeople of the Twelve Visions Party.

## Example of a Genius Evolving Into Neothink®

Just how effective were those geniuses of society at taking care of our every need or problem? Instead of me impossibly trying to describe what I saw in my Tenth Vision, which overwhelmed me to the point of euphoric collapse, let me take you into the life and times of an obscure genius of society who already lived. That way, I can show you already *proven facts*. Now, since some people say the computer revolution was unique — an anomaly based on the invention of the silicon chip — let us go outside the computer industry. In fact, let us go back in time before high technology altogether to see the universal life-lifting power of the geniuses of society *on their own*, even before their catalytic reaction with modern technologies. So, let us now travel back a hundred years...to the down and dirty railroad industry:

This is a story about James J. Hill, a genius of society one hundred years ago. He was well on his way to multiplying standards of living of entire civilizations of ordinary people — including *the poor*. He was single-handedly taking care of their every need until he got held down by big-government regulations. His story represents all geniuses of society, even outside the computer and hi-tech industries.

He was a railroad pioneer back at the turn of the twentieth century, and his story is brought to light in a book called *Entrepreneurs Versus The State* by Burton Folsom.

Let's travel back in time to the 1860s. America was experiencing its first railroad boom. Railroads were being built all up and down the East Coast. Well, as Mr. Folsom identifies in his book, two classes of entrepreneurs exist: market entrepreneurs and political entrepreneurs. Political entrepreneurs make their money by seeking government subsidies, by getting special government rights of way, and by accessing political clout. They seek their success through political clout with government officials.

Market entrepreneurs make their money by providing more and more values and services to society at lower and lower prices. They also create more and more jobs for us.

During America's railroad building boom in the 1860s, an opportunity arose for big government. The political entrepreneurs seeking easy money got together with career politicians seeking popularity, and together they created a deception. The deception was that only the government could finance the building of America's first transcontinental railroad. That deception over 100 years ago is still promoted today; children read about it in their history text books in school.

But that was a deception created by political entrepreneurs so they could line their pockets with lavish government subsidies and by career politicians so they could boost their self-worth by spending money that they controlled but did not earn. They could parade around and say, "Look how important we are. Look how we benefit the American public. We, the big government, are building this transcontinental railroad and opening up the interior and west coast of America." ...A perfect setup for greedy political entrepreneurs joining hands with power-seeking politicians.

So a deception was created: only the federal government could finance the building of the transcontinental railroad. The public bought it, and with great fanfare, Congress went ahead with it.

There were two companies: Central Pacific started building eastward from the West Coast and the Union Pacific started westward from the East Coast. The government paid those companies by the total miles of track they built. So what did they do? Instead of being bound by the disciplines of a bottom line, they were getting lavish subsidies from the government for the total miles of track they built. So they rushed into the wilderness to collect government subsidies.

But because they were being paid by the mile, these companies purposely built the longest, most circuitous routes they could possibly justify so they could get more government money. And they rushed construction to collect their per-mile subsidies. They rushed into the wilderness with poor construction and poor planning.

Remember, the congressmen were spending money that they did not earn but controlled, and they wanted to reap the glory for spending that money. Those politicians, always trying to justify their jobs, always trying to show that they benefit the American public, got into the railroad business where they had no business being in the first place. Controlling tremendous amounts of money they did not earn, they reaped all this popularity that comes with spending the money. Now they could say, "Look how valuable we are; we're financing the building of a transcontinental railroad across America!"

But those career politicians were part of bogus big government. They gladly spent money with their flashy "good intentions", but they were not interested in exerting the nitty-gritty effort that honest business does when it spends money. They were glad to spend the money, large amounts of money. They were glad to reap the glory, large amounts of glory. But they were not about to get out there and exert the nitty-gritty effort to put controls on spending and to make sure that money was spent right. They were not about to get right down into the details themselves to make sure that they were buying the right quality goods at the right prices and that the railroad was being built over the right routes...not like a market businessman would who is spending that money *out of his own pocket.*

So the whole program was laced with fraud from the beginning. The line managers set up their own supplier companies selling their railroads substandard quality rails and ties at exorbitant prices. For, there was no control over the government money.

In addition, because they were getting paid by the amount of rail they built, each company was racing to build as much track as it could before the other one...to get the most money from the government. So instead of taking the proper time to carefully map out the best routes, especially vital for building over hills at the lowest uphill grade, they instead just raced forward and paid no attention to vital planning and surveying. No time to be wasted on planning and surveying, they built track over uphill grades that were far too steep. They did not take the necessary time to do anything right. When winter came, they just kept on building over the plains, right *over* the ice!

Because they wanted to build as much as possible, they did not wait for the ice to melt — they just kept on laying track. When summer came, they had to tear up thousands of miles of track and rebuild it, before they could open the line! And to get more money, the two railroad companies built the *longest* routes with *under-quality* material. ...You can just imagine what the future operating costs this transcontinental railroad would endure.

Indeed, when the Union Pacific was complete, from day one it could not make a profit because its operating expenses were too high. First of all, thousands of miles of shoddily built, under-quality track had to be constantly replaced. Second, because they took the extra long route, and it wasn't built over the lowest-grade hills, they had to pay a lot more money in fuel costs, wage costs, and it took a lot more time to haul freight across the country. The operating expenses were so high, from day one the Union Pacific was never able to make a profit.

Therefore, the government had to continue to subsidize the transcontinental line once it was built. Union Pacific had to continue to receive more and more government money or it would have gone out of business and stopped running. Indeed,

Congress had just spent a fortune financing the building of the transcontinental line. Now Congress could not let their prize transcontinental line declare bankruptcy and close down. So, the government continued financing it.

After the Union Pacific was built, other political entrepreneurs got together with glory-seeking politicians in their areas of the country and said, "The federal government financed the Union Pacific, therefore they have to finance a transcontinental railroad in our region."

So Congress went ahead and financed the building of a transcontinental up North called the Northern Pacific, and one down South called the Santa Fe. Of course, both of those had the same results. They built extra long, circuitous routes; they turned into an orgy of fraud: substandard quality material used, inflated prices paid, no planning, no surveying, no time taken to select the lowest-grade hills. So right from day one, the other two transcontinentals lost money, and they had to receive government subsidies just to continue operating.

In the meantime, there was a young man way up North, James J. Hill, going about making a living. He was born in a log cabin in Ontario, Canada to a working-class family. His father died when he was a boy, so Hill got a job to support his mother. At seventeen, he moved to St. Paul and got a job for a shipping company. He started in an entry-level position, but he loved the transportation business. He really applied himself; he began making contacts, and he began moving up. Before long, he began making partnerships in local railroads that were being built in his area. With a sweeping vision, yet always focussed on nitty-gritty details, Hill commanded success. Eventually, Hill decided that he was going to build the first privately financed transcontinental railroad way up along the U.S. and Canadian border, which at that time was all wilderness with no settlers!

Well, from the beginning the idea was labeled Hill's Folly, and you can see why. How could someone build a railroad that could possibly compete when he had to pay all the building costs himself, and there were three other transcontinental railroads farther South that had all their building costs paid by the government? Moreover, Hill's railroad was going to be way up North where no one lived. Those other three government-financed railroads were located in the main population areas of the United States. In addition, once Hill did complete his railroad, how could he compete with the other three railroads when they continued to receive government subsidies and Hill had to pay his expenses through his own bottom-line profits — and the three other lines proved that no profits existed!

Well, Hill went ahead with his plan anyway. He had to obey the disciplines of a bottom line. He could not go rushing into the wilderness to collect government subsidies. He had to build his line out West one extension at a time. He would build westward into the wilderness a few hundred miles at a time. Then he would send agents back East to advertise to farmers in the East. Hill offered to move people for free into this western wilderness so they could settle and start their farms. Then Hill would give them free rates to ship their crops back to the markets in the East for a couple of years until they got established. He gave a lot of ordinary low-income people exciting new leases on life and made their dreams come true.

This worked. For each extension West, he brought in enthusiastic hardworking farmers; they'd flourish; he'd build up business on his track, and after awhile his extension West made money. From those profits, he'd finance another extension West...a few hundred miles at a time. He never stopped. By turning low-income settlers into land-owning entrepreneurs, among others, he settled the entire northern border of the United States with his railroad. And, lo and behold, in 1890 the first American transcontinental railroad was built without one penny of government money! He reached the Pacific Ocean, and he did it by offering people, some of whom had little chance at much in life, an opportunity of a lifetime to own land and become entrepreneurs.

What an accomplishment. But most amazingly, *one man* did it! Not the entire might of the U.S. Government — one lone man! One genius of society was raising the prosperity of an entire nation! But, now that he accomplished this amazing feat, could he make it work? Here Hill was with his transcontinental, way up North when the population base was farther South; he was competing against three transcontinentals farther South that had their expenses paid for by the government. So, what would happen to Hill's transcontinental?

During the building of Hill's railroad, since it was his personal money that was being spent, he personally dug into the tough nitty-gritty details. With unyielding disciplines and efforts, he put controls on everything: He personally surveyed the routes; he made sure the shortest, most direct routes were built. When the track had to go over hills, he would spend time with the engineers and make sure they picked out the lowest-grade hills. He personally supervised the buying of materials to make sure they got the highest quality rails and ties for the lowest cost. ...So what happened to Hill's Folly? Well, from day one, when it was completed, he made a profit! He ran circles around the three government-financed lines because his operating expenses were so much lower. In addition, his freight took a lot less time to reach the West Coast. From day one, Hill made money. From day one, the government-subsidized transcontinental railroads never, ever turned a profit.

*One man* was running circles around the almighty U.S. Government! Of course, the incompetence and greed of career politicians could never bring values to the people. But one market entrepreneur could raise the standard of living of a nation.

This one market entrepreneur's advantages kept building momentum and, with a great irony, left Congress's follies in the dust. Hill built up the whole industry of the Northwest. He built feeder lines. For example, if copper were found a hundred miles north, he would build a feeder line, move in a copper company so they could start mining and shipping the copper over his line. If lumber were discovered up in the mountain, he would feeder line up there, move in a lumber company, and they would start shipping the lumber over his lines. If there was a good clearing for cattle ranching a few miles south, he would build a feeder line. ...Railroads discovered that feeder lines became a main source of profit.

But consider Congress's lines built for politicians' own glory and self-worth. Because those railroads were receiving their money from the government, they would have to get Congress's permission to build a feeder line. Well, of course, everyone knows what happens when the government has to make a decision. A simple black-and-white decision to build a profitable feeder line that should be made overnight would be tied up for months, even for years. All the incompetent congressmen would get up and debate over it to get in the spotlight and appear needed and important. ...They cared only about themselves, not about what was best for America.

So Hill's railroad ran circles around the three government-financed railroads from day one. In addition, Hill brought civilization and industry to the Northwest: mining in Montana, lumber along the North, apple farmers in Washington, wheat farmers on the plains. He built up the whole region along his railroad line.

Once Hill completed his line to the West Coast, he did not stop there. He kept reaching out and pushing up standards of living. Integrating more and more widely, into Neothink® itself, Hill started reaching out toward the Orient. What about trade with the Orient? Hill did some calculations: if one major province in China substituted an ounce of rice a day with an ounce of American wheat, that would mean 50 million bushels of American wheat would travel over his railroad to China every year! Think what that would do for his farmers! Now, he would make them rich! American farmers exporting huge shipments of wheat to China — what a possibility! So Hill sent agents to Japan and China to begin promoting American trade, the same way he had done during the building up of his transcontinental railroad.

In the meantime, we had these political entrepreneurs in Washington, D.C. still running around wondering how to get more government subsidies to line their pockets. Yet one market entrepreneur was creating jobs and dreams by the thousands. Indeed, Hill sent his agents to Japan and China to start promoting American products, and he went out and bought his own steamship line. He raced his ships back and forth between Japan and China and America. Hill built up American trade with Asia the same way that he built up business along his line. He would send products for free to the Japanese and Chinese if they would just try them. If they liked them, they would come back for more, and Hill would build up the business.

Every day Hill filled his ships with American grain from the plains, with copper from Montana, lumber from Washington, cotton from the South, textiles from New England, rails from Pittsburgh, apples from Washington. He would send them all free to the Far East. The Asians would try these American goods, and if they liked them, then they would come back for more.

In fact, Hill went to Japan, met with Japanese businessmen, and proposed that he would buy southern cotton, pay for it himself, ship it to the Japanese for free, and *give* it to them free. Hill would buy the southern cotton out of his own money if the Japanese would just try this cotton in place of the cotton they normally got from India. Well, the Japanese took him up on his offer; they liked it, and soon Hill's box cars were full of cotton, travelling from the South to the North to the Pacific Coast and then on to a steamship to Japan.

Hill used this strategy to build up all kinds of business. In 1900, Japan started a railroad building boom. Hill recognized the potential of railroads throughout Asia. At that time, the world's suppliers of rail were England and Belgium. But there were a few American rail makers in Pittsburgh. So Hill went to Japan; he purposely underbid the English and the Belgians, paid the difference out of his own pocket just to get the Japanese to try rails made in Pittsburgh. His strategy worked: Japan started buying all their rail from Pittsburgh, which built up the fledgling rail industry in America.

What happened in the 1890s was nothing short of a miracle: When Hill started his push into Asia, trade with Japan was seven million dollars a year. Nine years later, with Hill in charge of this American mission into Asia, American trade with Japan *alone* was fifty-two million dollars! And he was now pushing into China as well! Hill was causing geometrical increases in American commerce. He was spearheading, a hundred years ago, an American dominance of trade in Asia. In the meantime the political entrepreneurs, Hill's so-called rivals, were still running around Washington, D.C. trying to figure out how they could get more subsidies. And Hill just kept on reaching out, with Neothink®, taking care of people's needs, and pushing up standards of living while spearheading a geometrical increase of American commerce in Asia. That was one hundred years ago.

As time went by, the other three government-financed transcontinentals continued to lose money. The government kept pouring taxpayers' dollars into financing them. The public started getting fed up with this. In addition, as time went by, the frauds committed by the political entrepreneurs started to surface — things like setting up their own companies to sell substandard material at overcharged prices. The American public had to continue to pay subsidies into this hoax just to keep these other three government railroads running. The public finally had enough. So Congress, those eternal glory-seeking politicians, started self-righteously parading the corrupt political entrepreneurs in front of Congress and the nation, forming special-investigation committees.

Well, once again, Congress created a deception: They presented themselves as protectors of the American public. They would nobly project, "Look how great we are; look how needed and important we are; we're going to protect the American public from those greedy and corrupt railroad executives." Yet, the root cause of the problem was Congress itself. Congress was the culprit! Congress spent other people's money in a railroad business where they had no business being in the first place.

So instead of getting up and confessing, "Look, the problem was us. We now realize the problem was us getting into the railroad business in the first place. We had no business in there, so now we're going to get completely out." They could have been honest, but they were not. No, they did not want to say that because that would have exposed bogus big government. Instead, they saw a chance to enhance big government and to increase their own popularity and political power for re-election. They instead self-righteously projected, "Look how we earn our keep. We're protecting the American public." Congress self-righteously started parading those corrupt railroad executives in front of the nation. Congress made the railroad executives solely to blame for the transcontinental fiascoes. And then, to "protect the public", they proposed to form tough regulatory authorities such as the ICC, the Interstate Commerce Commission, and to pass Sherman Antitrust legislation to further get in there and regulate the railroads.

Well, Hill knew what was going on; he knew what the story was here. So Hill moved to Washington, D.C. He set up residence in the country's Capitol. He personally talked to the congressmen. He testified before their special committees. He told them what was going on: the root cause of the problem was big government getting in there where it had no business being in the first place, financing those railroads, spending other people's money on rails. That caused the corruption. Hill gave the example of his railroad. He did not accept one penny of government money while his railroad built up all the industry in the Northwest. And now his line was promoting an explosion of American trade into Asia while the three government-sponsored lines were sinking in corruption.

Now, the congressmen were intelligent men. They were college educated. They knew what Hill was saying. They knew he made perfect sense. They knew his account was the truth, but they did not care because they wanted to justify their own jobs. So they ignored him. They ignored Hill, and they went on to pass the ICC and the Sherman Antitrust legislation, which enabled them to get in and heavily regulate and punish the railroads.

Hill even wrote a book on this whole ordeal and circulated his book to the congressmen, explaining the situation. He presented all the evidence that showed how Congress was doing the wrong thing. But the big-government ruling class ignored Hill because they wanted to advance their own power. The career politicians went ahead and passed the ICC, passed the Sherman Antitrust legislation. And what did that do? Those regulations "for the public good" made it illegal for railroads to make any special deals with customers. They had to charge the same standard rate to all customers. Therefore, the Neothink® dynamics Hill used to build up his railroad, to move in people for free, to make their dreams come true, to ship their freight for free or for a low cost until they got established...was now illegal! Those same dynamics that he was now using to spearhead an American dominance of trade in Asia were all now illegal! Hill was a genius of society who was pushing up ordinary, even poor Americans into prosperity — and WHAM! Big-government regulations smashed him down. Hill's drive into Asia was over.

The year after the ICC's legislation passed, America's trade with Japan alone dropped by 40%. Now remember, Hill was spearheading a *geometrical increase* in trade. Trade with Japan and China was increasing geometrically. Now Congress passed this legislation and, plop, everything dropped 40%.

Hill was forced to sell his steamship lines, he got out of trade completely with Asia, and he was so frustrated, he retired. Suddenly, the miracle was over. He could no longer make ordinary and poor people wealthy and happy.

Now, this was a hundred years ago. Let us stop and look at the implications of this. Let us stretch this out to see what Congress really cut off a hundred years ago. It was bad enough they cut off Hill's trade with Asia back then and destroyed the wealth, lives and dreams of many entrepreneurs dependent on Hill's dynamics, but let us project that into the future to see what they cut off today:

Throughout the past two decades, you have heard our President and top CEOs and top economists say that America's greatest danger economically is its trade imbalance with Asia and our lack of international competitiveness. But who in the world knows that a hundred years ago Hill was spearheading an American dominance of trade throughout all of Asia? That trade dominance was cut off by big-government regulations. Who even knows that? Nobody mentions that today, but everyone has warned about "the greatest economic danger facing America today". Americans have lost jobs by the thousands, have been outcompeted, factories have closed down. Yet who knows that one hundred years ago this one genius of society, *one man*, learned how to tend to people's needs, make people's dreams come true, and spearhead an American dominance of trade with Asia? Who knows that a hundred years ago a man named James J. Hill started something really magnificent that would have painted an entirely different picture of America's future than that of uncertainty today? Big government destroyed that prosperous future when they destroyed Hill a hundred years ago.

The politicians back then knew what they were doing. They were intelligent men. They were college educated. Hill went and explained the facts to them. Typical of big government, however, they only wanted to increase their political powers. The career politicians wanted to advance their images and egos. So they ignored Hill, and they cut off something magnificent a hundred years ago. No different than today, the ruling class back then stopped our great, great grandparents from rising into a paradise on Earth.

So there you have an example of what just one genius of society can do for everyone. And you can see that the geniuses of society will rise in any industry at any time, not just in the computer or hi-tech industries, if not held down by the big-government regulations. And you can see that, when the geniuses rise tomorrow in all industries, our problems, needs, and dreams will quickly be tended to. In short, the Twelve Visions Society tomorrow — a supersociety with millions of James J. Hills — will take care of us and make our dreams come true.

Now, imagine a hundred-million geniuses of society (Vision Five), a hundred-million James J. Hills all using Neothink®...their progress accelerated by modern technology. You cannot imagine, because the image goes beyond anything we can know today.

## Held Down in the Darkness

My Tenth Vision showed me that in tomorrow's Twelve Visions World, looking back at today's world was very frustrating. We saw how career politicians and bureaucrats ruling over us and holding down society today caused the only injustice that no one could see, because no one today could see ahead into the Twelve Visions World tomorrow. One obvious example, America would have been the dominant trade of that huge upswinging in Asia, but we never had a clue. America's problems with the trade deficit and people losing their jobs to international competition would have all been reversed. But no one saw that. Instead, we were held down in the darkness. Looking back, no one except those who read *The Twelve Visions* could see the injustice of government ruling over us and holding us down.

James J. Hill started pushing ordinary and poor people up toward that paradise on Earth, but he was slammed back down by big government. Tomorrow, once we lived in the Twelve Visions World and could see the injustice of former big government, to look back became painfully hard to do. The people in the Twelve Visions World realized that every life lost on the battlefield, all famine and sufferings in America and around the world in the twentieth century and early twenty-first century, including deaths from diseases...all of that was encompassed in the Great Suppression — the ruling class holding down America from soaring into the Twelve Visions World.

*The Geniuses Pulled Everyone Up With Them*

In this Tenth Vision of tomorrow's Twelve Visions World, the geniuses of society were free to go up, and they pulled everyone up with them, including the poor, just as Hill was doing. All our needs were taken care of. We did not have just one James J. Hill, for we had thousands and then millions of James J. Hills making ordinary people's dreams come true.

Tender youth could rise and rise quickly. Tender youth today, by contrast, cannot rise because they cannot struggle through the big-government regulatory web and risk being eaten alive like Hill.

Unburdened technology in tomorrow's Twelve Visions World, regulated not by glory-seeking politicians and bureaucrats but by objective private services, advanced incredibly fast. Science, business, and medicine, no longer being pushed down by big government, advanced incredibly fast, similar to the nonpoliticized computer industry of the previous two decades.

Upon setting free all industries and launching the mighty Technological Revolution, genius-driven new technologies quickly took care of all our problems. Disease, unemployment, poverty, obesity, insecurity, stagnation, racism, crime, budget deficits, the national debt, government abuse, Social-Security deficiency, illiteracy vanished along with big government. So did our personal problems such as a lousy job, lousy love-life, an uncompetitive body, a stagnant mind, an embarrassing home, car, and overall financial self-worth.

Consider that in 1936, mankind reached a new high with the completion of Hoover Dam to harness the Colorado River. After thousands of years, man reached a level of technology that could control nature on a large scale. But man took only another 33 years to go to the moon. Civilization was *begging* to progress *geometrically,* which occurred in my Tenth Vision sometime in the first quarter of the twenty-first century when the big-government legislative/regulatory web was swished away and super technologies and unrestrained geniuses made us wealthy, healthy, and safe.

*Too Painful To Look Back*

Some readers of this very page lost their lives to disease or lost a precious loved one. Looking back at our loss was hard. My childhood friend John who, at 12 years old, ran and played with all the other children; but the next year, muscular dystrophy started taking over his tall and handsome body. John first needed crutches, then a wheelchair, then an electric wheelchair...his long, limp body strapped in with a seat belt. In those days, John and I would go around doing things that young men do. John was almost in my world, talking about sports and girls. Yet, John would never experience those things. I could sometimes see in John's eyes his longing to throw off his seat belt, jump out of his wheelchair, and scream, "Here I am world! Here I am!" One day John got a cold, and just a young man, he died. Yet, geniuses in tomorrow's unrestricted Twelve Visions Society would efficiently cure his disease.

Looking back, big government held down the lid on America including cures to diseases, but we could not see the harm caused by big government. Tomorrow, it became almost too painful to look back at what and *who* we lost.

Consider looking back at the following image: Imprisoned by hunger, little children in poverty-stricken third-world countries hoped for a little fish with their rice for dinner. If James J. Hill were not stopped 100 years ago, along with the other market businessmen since Hill, then those poor countries would have been industrialized and prosperous a long time ago.

Instead, those third-world children suffered and died to the bitter end of the twentieth century and into the twenty-first century as the "glorious" big-government "good intentions" flourished and lived. The Great Suppression went on and on.

American children have always felt excitement about their futures. Yet, tomorrow when we looked back we realized that America, the land of opportunity, was also the land of disillusionment and disappointment. The drop from childhood dreams to adulthood reality was a deep letdown. Indeed,

American adults carried a subdued sadness every day...to the end. Before the Twelve Visions World, Americans died unfulfilled, without experiencing wealth, romantic love, the life they were meant to live.

In tomorrow's Twelve Visions World, looking back became almost unbearable, for we saw what was lost. We failed at our dreams in the twentieth century and early twenty-first century because we were in a society in which we could not win. My Tenth Vision showed me that the Twelve Visions Society, by contrast, would not let us fail. Instead, it made our dreams come true and made every ordinary person, including the poor, wealthy and healthy.

Looking back, people shook their heads in disbelief. The legal battles, regulations, and legislation made opportunities at success limited, costly, and risky. We glumly looked back at the stagnation that killed our dreams, weakened our marriages, and destroyed the thrill of love we felt only during the first few weeks or months of falling in love. And, most painfully, we saw how our children absorbed from us our hopeless resignation, just as we had from our parents.

*The Disgraceful End*

In the first quarter of the twenty-first century, with the dissemination of *The Twelve Visions*, the Great Suppression came to a disgraceful end. Neothink® was setting free stagnant minds everywhere. Big government could not continue to hold on and strangle progress and kill our dreams. The success of *The Twelve Visions* ushered in The Twelve Visions Party.

With the success of The Twelve Visions Party, society no longer got pushed down with us being squeezed into stagnation-traps where we had always lived. Career politicians lost. Their big-government regulations and harmful legislation — always in the name of the "social good" — lost. Their bogus purpose for government lost:

> **Promote social "prosperity" and provide social "well-being" through social and regulatory programs "for the social good"..."good intentions" to "serve the people" (a deception, enforcing what is deemed the "social good",**

**"good intentions", or the "national will"...mere men and women playing God with our money, morals, businesses, and our lives).**

With the success of the Twelve Visions Party, the proper purpose for government won:

**Physically protect the people from force (or threat of force) with protection-only legislation, police, courts, prisons, and national defense (plain reality, defending against and punishing initiatory force).**

Tomorrow we looked back and realized in disgust that, as with the transcontinental railroads, our career politicians spent our money to ostensibly enhance our "well-being" and promote social "prosperity", but they really wanted the glory and "importance" that went with spending *other people's* money and ruling over us. They did not want anything to do with the effort, though, that went into building values, which market businessmen and women put themselves through every day when spending their own money.

Career politicians and regulatory bureaucrats today suppress all industries (the computer industry being the most fortunate, least politicized industry). Career politicians today suppress our entire economy and standard of living as they did a hundred years ago with the railroads. Market businessmen, by contrast, are interested in creating and building values, not in ruling others. They create miracles for the human race, from Hill's transcontinental railroad to Jobs' computer software and beyond.

### *The Miracle Makers*

Tomorrow, the miracle makers, the unburdened market businessmen and women, dramatically improved our well-being and prosperity. A Twelve Visions Society, flourishing with geniuses, handed us the gifts of life, especially wealth, health, and peace.

Prior to the Twelve Visions Society, the erroneous idea in the anticivilization that government could "promote social prosperity" sort of sneaked up over the previous century through career politicians finding ways to self-indulge at spending our money to become more and more likable for re-election. Indeed, spending *other people's* money was a fast way to build favorable illusions in the twentieth century and early twenty-first century. But when the people caught on sometime in the first quarter of the twenty-first century, the career politicians' careers ended with great shame.

In this Tenth Vision, market businessmen and women replaced career politicians. Geniuses of society rose and threw open the lid on society and lifted society toward its destiny of great, great prosperity. Each person was pulled up, our wheelchairs left behind. The whole world was then lifted as the communications revolution obsoleted distance and boundaries.

### *Paradise On Earth*

The Tenth Vision showed me that in the Twelve Visions World, irrationality disappeared. Poverty and crime vanished. In the Twelve Visions World, the motivation for people to do dishonest things reversed. In time, in that world of disappearing irrationality, the idea of crime and eventually war became archaic. We achieved paradise on Earth.

Perhaps this all sounds like Utopia. But my Tenth Vision showed me tomorrow's Twelve Visions World truly reversed the motivation for people to do dishonest things, for most problems disappeared, and a millionaire standard of living was automatic — far easier and more lucrative than any possible crime. With the success of the Twelve Visions Party, the era of wealth and peace was here, finally and forever.

Before the Twelve Visions, the people never knew about this wonderful world. We only dreamed about it when we were children. We needed to "see" it through these Twelve Visions.

Today, we live in a lucky time. Huge financial rewards beckon us to the Twelve Visions Party. Our get-rich era is coming.

# Real Universal Health

*"It is not just new viruses that have doctors worried. Perhaps the most ominous prospect of all is a virulent strain of influenza. Every so often, a highly lethal strain emerges. Unlike HIV, flu moves through the air and is highly contagious. The last killer strain showed up in 1918 and claimed 20 million lives — more than all the combat deaths in World War I. And that was before global air travel; the next outbreak could be even more devastating."* *—Time Magazine*

By now during my Neothink® Visions, the images centered more and more around our health. More than anything else in the twenty-first century, the people cried out for the geniuses, with their groundbreaking technologies, to eradicate virulent diseases.

Devastating new diseases were on the rise and, perhaps even worse, drug-resistant strains of several old killer diseases were back. Those frightening new diseases and new strains tended to break down our acceptance of the FDA that suppressed the rise of Neothink® geniuses in the medical industry and held back the rapid advancement of the medical industry. Our physical survival more and more depended on rapid advancement.

My Twelfth Vision showed me that during the early twenty-first century, doctors were less and less able to handle certain infectious diseases that were gaining resistance to antibiotics. A powerful warning came when only a single remaining antibiotic could stop a popular strain of staph infection that commonly spread throughout hospitals. Once that lone remaining antibiotic ceased to work, hospitals would become risky places to visit. Then, the common strep infection gained resistance to antibiotics. My Twelfth Vision warned me of the increasing danger as we advanced into the new millennium. A killer disease, tuberculosis, returned, this time attacking our children, and this time even a combination of antibiotics could not stop it.

In short, infectious diseases caught up with and began to surpass modern medicine in the twenty-first century. The FDA worked against a major medical revolution that was just waiting to explode with greater force than the computer revolution. In fact, the inherent force of a medical/biotech explosion was so great that even with the FDA, genetic engineering such as the Human Genome Project and other biomedical projects were advancing at an all-time pace. But the mighty biomedical explosion could not ignite with the FDA smothering progress. As with computers, the technology needed quick access to the marketplace, which the FDA blocked. Indeed, the marketplace is the oxygen needed to ignite the biomedical explosion, which the FDA smothered.

Here is a brief review of a *Time Magazine* warning.

## Killers All Around

### New Viruses and Drug-Resistant Bacteria Are Reversing Human Victories Over Infectious Disease (A Review of *Time Magazine* Cover Story)

The *Time Magazine* cover story begins by reminding us how, not long ago, humanity thought that infectious diseases were rapidly becoming a thing of the past. In the 1970s, the medical world started boasting its imminent victory. And why not? Previously deadly illnesses such as polio, small pox, malaria, diphtheria, pertussis, tetanus "seemed like quaint reminders of a bygone era, like Model T Fords or silent movies". And antibiotics transformed the most terrifying diseases known to mankind such as tuberculosis, syphilis, pneumonia, bacterial meningitis, and even bubonic plague into "mere inconveniences that if caught could be cured with pills or shots". Medical students were being told not to go into infectious disease, a "declining speciality". Instead, they were advised to concentrate on "real problems" such as cancer and heart disease.

But, unfortunately, today the era of great medical success and confidence has been giving way to a new era of unnerving medical defeats...and fear. The *Time* cover story states, "The question ceased to be, When will infectious disease be wiped out? and became, Where will the next deadly new plague break out?" The article goes on to tell us about new lethal agents emerging in Africa and South America. As population grows and man settles new parts of the world, such as a new part of the Brazilian rain forest, for example, new deadly diseases spread from other animals such as monkeys to humans. As those deadly agents adapt to humans, they gain the potential for large-scale deadly pandemics. In a world of extensive air travel, those deadly agents become just a plane ride from America.

And it could get worse, the *Time* article claims. Antibiotics are our main defense that stand between us and some of the most deadly bacterial diseases. But bacteria have been evolving and steadily adapting for survival, and now they are well adapting to antibiotics. In fact, the article warns us that every disease known to man is already resistant to antibiotics of one form or another. Several devastating diseases once thought to be nearly eradicated are back and on the rise: malaria, cholera, measles, tuberculosis, even bubonic plague. Perhaps even more threatening are the "seemingly prosaic but once deadly infections" staph and strep. They have become much harder to treat. Both spread through the cleanest of hospitals, routinely cured with antibiotics. But as those two infections develop universal resistance, the article questions, what will happen to our hospitals?

"One of medicine's worst nightmares is the development of a drug-resistant strain of severe invasive strep A," the article states. Severe, invasive strep A killed Muppeteer Jim Henson in 1990; this vicious killer is on the rise.

Bacteria adapt to antibiotics because, while rapidly multiplying, bacteria mutate and change slightly, just enough to outwit their combatant drugs.

Viruses, on the other hand, are usually tamed and sometimes even eradicated by the preventive vaccine. But the article points out that new viruses keep emerging. Viruses that have gone undetected, inhabiting animal populations, can and sometimes do make the jump to humans. The *Time* article tells us that was the case with some very lethal African viruses such as Ebola, which made the jump from monkeys to humans.

Still, the biggest fear of all, as explained in that *Time Magazine* article, would be another killer flu, which usually makes the jump from another animal to humans. Humans have little defense against such a flu, and if it took hold, then it would wreak deadly havoc. The 1997-1998 Hong Kong "chicken flu" introduced such a killer flu that, tragically, killed a few people in Hong Kong but, fortunately, did not take hold and go into a widespread outbreak. Now, each year that avian flu attempts to jump to and spread among humans. When a global outbreak does happen, the world will never be the same.

The *Time Magazine* article was a warning. Today's biomedical progress is impressive, but is it moving fast enough? The answer is: no, not until the technology has quick access to the marketplace, as do the computers. And that means no regulatory FDA.

The definitive antidote is "begging" to happen now, in the early twenty-first century, to rescue the human race from the threatening plagues. That antidote to the threatening human catastrophes is: **super rapidly evolving technologies**. Only rapidly evolving new technologies can win the race against rapidly evolving infectious diseases. But those new technologies will not evolve quickly enough until they can swiftly reach the

**Killer Flu** Seattle police wore protective masks during the pandemic of 1918. That killer flu infected 1 billion people and killed more than 20 million in 10 months. The population in 1918 was less than half of today.

marketplace.

Starting in the late twentieth century, continuing into the twenty-first century, the national media such as *Time Magazine* repeatedly warned us we were suddenly losing the race against infectious diseases, with mutant strains of old diseases returning after decades of "absence" and new diseases invading us with devastating results. The media warned that a medical defeat to microbes could bring with it human catastrophes such as those experienced in the time of bubonic plague, polio, and killer flus. The Superflu of 1918 infected over one billion people, *half* the world's population in 1918, and killed over 20 million people in just 10 months. Never in the history of the world had there been so many deaths in such a short period of time. Man has not experienced anything close to that catastrophic pandemic since, but in the early twenty-first century, scientists fear a repeat is not far away.

The 1918 Spanish Flu, as it was often called, actually started right here in the United States and infected 25% of our population. Doctors have warned in the early twenty-first century that logistically "we are due" for another killer strain. In fact, in 1976, we survived a great scare — a false alarm, or perhaps more apropos, a fair warning: A soldier at Fort Dix, New Jersey got the flu and died. The medical world was stunned when the virus taken from the dead soldier was a descendent of the 1918 killer flu. The medical world braced itself for another catastrophe of unthinkable proportions. But the deadly virus that made the jump from birds to humans was an isolated case unable, this time, of passing among humans. This time, we were lucky. Next time...

Only super rapidly advancing new technology can prevent a "next time". The race is on. Every year a handful of people die from avian flu. It is only a matter of time before it will pass freely from human to human. The new technology of genetic engineering has the potential to permanently and universally stop deadly viruses and bacteria. The problem with this promising new technology in the early twenty-first century, however, is that it is not *super rapidly advancing*, not fast enough...not until the removal of the FDA. Remember, *super rapidly advancing* new technology demands rapid access to the marketplace. Breakthrough technologies and drugs must freely reach the marketplace. Private regulatory services with risk-rating systems would be in place, but simply put, the way things are now with the FDA, we will lose the race. For a computerlike medical revolution to happen, the FDA will have to come to an end in order to spring loose the geniuses of society and their new technologies.

The following brief review from the same issue of *Time Magazine* reveals new technologies pursued by doctors, scientists, and businessmen (but again, missing the key ingredient of **market-accessible** *super rapidly advancing new technologies):*

## Counterattack:

How Drugmakers Are Fighting Back

(A Review of *Time Magazine* Article)

"Doctors and the public were not alone in feeling cocky about infectious disease a decade ago. The drug companies did too," so began the article. "More than 100 antibiotics were on the market, and they had most bacterial diseases on the run, if not on the verge of eradication."

The pharmaceutical industry simply modified existing antibiotics to stay one step ahead of the bacteria. But that approach no longer works. So, researchers are turning to new technologies to get back in the lead against disease.

One dynamic approach is called "rational" drug design. Scientists study the molecular structure of a bacterium, particularly the active site of the enzyme used by the bacterium to fight off the antibiotic. Next, scientists attempt to design a molecule to "plug up" the active site of that enzyme. Without the effect of that enzyme, the bacterium would once again be killed by the original drug.

A similar concept is being pursued against viruses. You see, viruses cause their damage by invading our bodies' living cells. To invade a living cell involves receptor sites, like little hooks, where the virus joins the cell. Similarly, a molecule can be designed to block the receptor sites so the virus never attaches to our cells thus remains harmless to our bodies. ...So goes the search for such defendant molecules through combinatorial chemistry.

Again, the problem with such new medical technologies is that they are not *super rapidly advancing* ...not as they should be, not like, say, computer technology. How, then, did our country finally get medical technology to *super rapidly advance* to prevent the coming human catastrophes? My Twelfth Vision showed me:

## The Great Rescue

I witnessed during the Twelfth Vision that the looming medical catastrophes helped us see reality and depoliticize the medical industry. Two things happened at once by depoliticizing medicine: 1) record amounts of private research funds went toward medical research, and 2) a record number of entrepreneurial geniuses went into medical research. Those unhindered geniuses of society drove medical technology into unimaginable new dimensions that eradicated the most complex diseases. In short, the Neothink® geniuses drove forth those new technologies to save our lives.

Depoliticizing the medical industry, depoliticizing everything about it from regulations on health insurance to regulations on medical research, saved many tens of millions of lives.

Today, each added increment of politicizing the medical industry further bureaucratizes and slows advancing new medical technology, which in turn dramatically drives away private research funds. Medical projects become too inefficient and cost-prohibitive for businesses to invest. Moreover, the lone entrepreneurs, those aggressive geniuses of society, could never function in such a cost-prohibitive, risky environment. The force of their creativity and endless energy that so propelled the free computer/Internet industry is but a fraction of what it could be in the medical industry. They are needed to unlock the cures to the most complex diseases.

In the Twelfth Vision, those geniuses, once they were free to flourish and leap into Neothink®, rapidly unlocked otherwise impossible combinations.

Politicization ravages our health and costs us millions of precious lives. Each incremental step the other way — depoliticizing the medical industry — dramatically frees up thus speeds up advancing technology, which in turn dramatically attracts private research funds and opens up the medical industry to the entrepreneurs and their endless energy and creativity, their speed and ability to ferret out brilliant advances.

In the Twelfth Vision, I witnessed that we outgrew our desire to be ruled over. As people began dying in increasing numbers, at a faster rate than the bio-tech advancements started saving people, we chose to depoliticized the medical industry to make it as free as the computer industry. Survival pressures changed our toleration levels for debilitating big government. Without it, the geniuses did to medicine what they did to computers. Our country won this race against the microbes. In the Twelve Visions World, after depoliticizing the medical industry, more and more geniuses rose up and saved us from worldwide human catastrophes. That medical revolution became known as the Great Rescue. But the human losses were never forgotten.

*Two Forces That Brought Us the Twelve Visions World*

My Twelfth Vision showed me two forces at work: Rising within us, we felt disillusioned with politicians and regulatory bureaucracies. A steady rebellion against a ruling class started spontaneously rising throughout civilizations around the world, from China and the Orient, through Russia and Eastern Europe, Asia Minor and down through Africa, to the relatively free United States and throughout Central and South America. Those early signs of the new Neothink® mentality, spontaneously rising throughout different civilizations around the globe, affected us at home.

Tomorrow, we started resisting the ruling class and its politicization over our lives just as we would resist a religious cult trying to tell us how to live. A shrinking number of people tolerated big government legislating and regulating our money, morals, and businesses.

That anti-authority trend gained momentum as medical catastrophes loomed. Under growing survival pressures, the people saw more clearly and ended the ruling class.

There was also another, more specific force at work: the inevitable Twelve Visions Party with the underlying mission to prevent the coming medical catastrophes. The Twelve Visions

Party, upon its success, set free the geniuses of society. They brought the Technological Revolution beyond the computer industry to the medical industry and to all American industries — the only antidote to the looming medical and economic catastrophes.

The Twelve Visions Party quickly depoliticized the medical industry and set free the drug companies and especially the aggressive entrepreneurs, the geniuses of society. The Twelve Visions Party represented medical technology versus medical catastrophe...the new world of freed geniuses using Neothink® versus the old world of career politicians and bureaucrats suppressing progress. The Twelve Visions Party brought in the new world and unleashed the technologies and geniuses in *all* industries. When America embraced the Twelve Visions Party, the party for depoliticizing America, then three benefits surfaced:

1. Near-perfect health for the young, the old, and for those in their prime.
2. Millionaire-like wealth for ordinary people, including the poor.
3. Exciting creative jobs *for nearly everyone,* which released nearly everyone's human potential (the Fifth and Sixth Visions).

## Young Again

My Twelfth Vision showed me that as the ordinary person got swept into a stimulating life of nearly perfect health and millionaire wealth, he passionately sought life over death. Death at mid-70 simply became unacceptable. Science, medicine, business, and entrepreneurs focused on an epic event: eradicate diseases and illnesses to enable ordinary people to live healthily well into their hundreds, and then beyond.

Technology-blocking "higher authorities" such as the FDA that burdened progress were scorned out of existence by the people.

Today, most people feel the unacceptability of the ultimate disease, *aging*. But few people can relate to their own greatest tragedy of dying in their 70s because:

- The thought of living healthily and prosperously for 130

years or more seems like science fiction.

• One's wealth, health, love and happiness are stagnant or shrinking. At 75 years, life is no longer very stimulating, and the desire to live longer in "old age" is gone.

In tomorrow's rapidly progressing Twelve Visions World, I saw (in my Twelfth Neothink® Vision) that the idea of living longer did not seem so futuristic. What before seemed technologically impossible was in wide use. Without disease, we lived well into our hundreds. Moreover, the idea of extending human life by slowing the disease of cellular degeneration or aging, and slowing the effects of gravity and entropy, became a mass appeal, especially as ordinary people became wealthy, healthy, and in love with life...the young and romantic life. The geniuses were hard at work learning how to extend our lives!

Today, by contrast, people eventually lose the desire to live. Sinking in stagnation, most good people experience limited financial and emotional success. Physically, emotionally, and financially burned out, most older people do not care to live too much longer. Quality of elderly life is far below what it would be in tomorrow's Twelve Visions World. Thus, today the desire to live longer is not in wide demand.

In tomorrow's nonpoliticized wealthy/healthy/exhilarating Twelve Visions World, I saw people regain a childlike desire to live longer. Rich and in love with life, the desire to live longer was in wide demand.

### *Death Under 100 Became Unacceptable*

A strong sense of tragedy grew in us as we got older and closed in on death. We emotionally grasped the unacceptability of dying in our 70s. In fact, the thought of dying at all, not to mention *so young,* grew increasingly intolerable. That unacceptability of dying was a direct result of our deep and permanent happiness as value creators (Vision Two). Tomorrow, the freed geniuses of society raced forward to answer our cries for life as we discovered the persons we were meant to be, forever ending the burden of life (Visions One and Two).

Most of us today do not grasp the tragedy of dying so young because, as we grow older, we steadily lose our enthusiasm for life. The burden of life comes to the surface as we use up our happy experiences of life (Vision Two). We cannot blame ourselves, for in today's suppressed world, life offers limited mortal doses of wealth and happiness.

My Twelfth Vision showed me that tomorrow's Twelve Visions World actually *reversed* the trend: enthusiasm actually *intensified* as we grew older. As Neothink® value creators, we built larger and larger puzzles of creation, which became very exhilarating. Instead of withering in our ruts, we blossomed in our creations.

In tomorrow's Twelve Visions World, our brief seven-and-a-half decades of life was considered much too brief for the wealthy and happy ordinary person. The demand for living longer grew enormous. First, disease was eradicated to give us healthy life well into our hundreds. Then, major businesses, financial institutions, scientists, research doctors and entrepreneurs embraced the growing demand for longer life. Money, minds, technology, science, medicine came together through entrepreneurial business. Their superpuzzle soon pieced together the ultimate demand of slowing down and eventually curing the disease of aging. (See my Neothink® trilogy *Superpuzzle,* 1200-pages).

The geniuses awakened the sleeping-giant consumer product of all time: life extension. For suddenly, happy people's *brief* time in all eternity became unacceptable. Too brief. Within *your* lifetime, the new Twelve Visions World doubled your journey through life...and eventually more.

### *The Life We Were Meant To Live*

Tomorrow's Twelve Visions World saved us from emotional diminishment and lifted us to the next level of happiness. We lived each and every day with four new frontiers of happiness, described in *Twelve Visions* (a Mark Hamilton Publication).

Today's world brings us uneventful years for the time we have left...for our one short experience of life in all eternity. In the Twelve Visions World, by contrast, my Twelfth Vision showed me we were like children with so much yet to experience. As value creators, we had no limits...always another adventure to create and experience. We finally lived the lives human beings were meant to live. Before the Twelve Neothink® Visions, we had no clue of that life.

Tomorrow, life was bigger than life again, like when we were children. Every new day filled us with exhilaration. Creating exciting new values was how we played as adults. Yes, *play* ...like children. We enjoyed the love from our fellow man for creating important values for society. The burden of life was gone. We achieved both the technology and the desire to live a lot, lot longer (Vision Four). We enjoyed nearly perfect physical and mental health for a long, extended life of happiness.

Today, the regulatory and entitlement programs for the "social good" are illusions that politicize our lives and rule over us — over our money, morals, and businesses. The career politicians and regulatory bureaucrats get enormous power, prestige, and they control enormous wealth. On the other hand, we get suppressed and stuck with physical diseases, mental stagnation, and short burdensome lives.

Looking forward into the Twelve Visions World, career politicians and regulatory bureaucrats were left behind. The geniuses jumped ahead into Neothink® and brought us enormous buying power and nearly perfect health. Thereafter, we too jumped into Neothink®. As described in the full Twelfth Vision (in *Twelve Visions,* a Mark Hamilton Publication), four new frontiers of happiness appeared before our eyes and brought us back to our child of the past and a beautiful, long-lost world in which we permanently rediscovered the thrill of life.

*Universal Wealth, Health, Peace*

# Educating Geniuses

Upon entering first grade at six years of age, the natural motivational drive in the child is gradually lost. You see, the premise of public schools today is: *Prepare children to effectively integrate into society.* Now, imagine that the eager child dreams about growing up and becoming a famous person who does wonderful things...a great value creator. "I'll do great things for the world and become a millionaire!" But those dreams gradually dissipate as the child blends into today's suppressed civilization.

In my Ninth Vision, I witnessed the premise of Twelve-Visions-World schools: *Prepare children to create values that many people need and are excited to buy.* My Vision showed me that on the child's first day of school, the teacher would walk in and say, "I'm going to prepare you to create great things for the world, and as a result you will become famous and rich!" Wow, the child sat up and took notice — his dreams confirmed! His motivation grew with compounding momentum as he steadily gained the ability to achieve his dreams throughout his Twelve-Visions-World education.

## *The Old School*

In today's suppressed civilization, children have little chance to grow up and become rich with a public education. Consider the trend in public schools today concerning the three fundamentals of education. (The three fundamentals of structure, motivation, and thinking as identified by renown educator, Professor Leonard Peikoff):

**Structure:** Increasing trend toward class discussions, free-flowing thoughts from kids and teachers, random facts about events and dates pragmatically "structured" to bring the child into "what's happening in today's social environment". The child hears all those unintegrated points (i.e., percepts), but later he forgets much of what he saw and heard in school.

**Thinking:** The child is not taught to *integrate.* He is not taught to integrate the many random percepts into common denominators — into a few timeless, unforgettable concepts. He never knows the power of his mind to integrate random percepts into structured concepts for everlasting knowledge. Knowledge is power, but he retains little knowledge. Instead, he absorbs then forgets unintegrated, pragmatic percepts, many regarding what's germane to the politically correct times. When he graduates, his mind is quite impotent as he settles into our suppressed society.

**Motivation:** He has little certainty, just a go-with-the-flow "education". The child learns to "fit in". He is trapped, at the mercy of our society, economy, national standard of living. There is nothing to be motivated over, for the child implicitly feels less and less power to rise above the suppressed state of things, above the burden of life he sees in his parents, to create new values for society and enjoy the emotional and financial rewards as an adult. Dreams become blurry and fade.

*The New School*

In tomorrow's Twelve Visions World, by comparison, dreams not only came true for schoolchildren and for adults, too, but those initial dreams were just the beginning. I saw it all in my Ninth Vision:

**Structure:** Twelve-Visions-World schools had a highly ordered presentation of knowledge, via class lectures, starting with bare percepts and integrating those many percepts by common denominators into a few timeless concepts for rapid absorption and permanent retention of knowledge. Knowledge was power. Through building timeless concepts, the child retained all that he learned in school. Moreover, he observed and learned *how to integrate* to build, piece by piece, onto his base of concepts — to build more and more knowledge and power throughout his life in order to someday *create great values for society.*

**Thinking:** The child was taught to integrate. He discovered why his mind was infinitely superior to all other animals. He integrated knowledge through common denominators from random percepts into structured concepts. He learned to form a few large concepts, not memorize many specific percepts. Thus, that child retained magnitudes more knowledge through integrated thinking. Soon, he learned how to snap a few of those concepts together into simple puzzles. Integrated, puzzle-building thinking sent thrills through the child, and it would eventually take him to great heights. The child quickly rose beyond the reach of all stagnation traps. Instead of heading toward a routine rut, he was heading toward exhilarating value creation...and a creation-driven life.

**Motivation:** The child knew with certainty that he could make a difference, for knowledge was power. The child felt certainty and power. He naturally became motivated for more, for superchild would now grow up to become superman or superwoman. The child felt like dynamite! The thrill for life, for expanding awareness and control, gained momentum. He felt more and more power to someday do great things for society and make great wealth for himself — every child's dream. Dreams became focussed and closer. The child became highly motivated.

### *Our Children Lifted the World*

In today's civilization, our education does not properly teach children how *to think, to integrate and build mental puzzles* of new knowledge. In the Twelve Visions World, education and children's minds will exist at a whole different level.

The Ninth Vision showed me that toddlers' rapid learning curves did not slow down. With the same thrill for life and expanding awareness nurtured by proper education, our children and grandchildren evolved straight into Neothink® and soared beyond even the smartest and richest people alive today.

Tomorrow's superchild became a genius of society who, with his peers, made us all rich through brilliant technological breakthroughs that drove prices toward zero and buying power toward infinity, a similar phenomenon to what we have already seen in the computer industry. For the most part, our children and grandchildren lifted the world after the collapse of the ruling class.

### *On the Prosperous Path in the Twelve Visions World*

Obviously, tomorrow's superchild needed a lot of knowledge. The discussion method that dominated public schools in the late twentieth century and early twenty-first century vanished. The original idea behind that popular discussion method was that children taught each other in order to help develop their social and communication skills — to better integrate into society. However, *tomorrow's superchild needed knowledge.* Twelve-Visions-World education used the old-fashioned lecture method in which the teacher did the teaching and filled the child with knowledge.

Now, the superchild rapidly built upon that base of knowledge as he grew up. Unlike us, he was taught conceptual thinking and integrated thinking. To perceive surroundings — see, hear, feel, smell, taste — was automatic and present in most animals. Man's superiority came from his ability *to integrate.* Tomorrow, our children and grandchildren integrated percepts by common denominators into concepts to generate reason and knowledge. That process was called conceptual thinking. Soon thereafter, their minds could build concept upon concept into puzzles of knowledge. That process was called integrated thinking. Tomorrow, without today's education blocking our children's integrated thinking, they reached out more and more widely and onto Neothink®.

*Leaving Behind the Old Way*

As researched by renowned Professor Leonard Peikoff and detailed in his *Philosophy of Education,* public schools (and most private schools) in the latter twentieth century and early twenty-first century did not teach children how to integrate the endless percepts into a few simplified concepts. For example, instead of teaching children the simple concepts of phonetics (e.g., a "p" makes a "pa" sound), public schools in the late twentieth century taught the look-say or whole-language method. Phonetics required understanding 44 simple concepts (i.e., sounds); look-say required memorizing how to read *every single word* the child ever saw (i.e., perceived) with no simplifying common denominators such as phonics (i.e., no concepts).

Indeed, children in *all* subjects — history, math, science, literature — were taught impotent perceptual thinking and not potent conceptual thinking. History, for example, was taught by unintegrated specific events (i.e., by percepts) and not grouped together by common denominators into concepts. For example, the wrath of human destruction over the centuries was touched on fact by fact (i.e., percept by percept) but not grouped into the basic underlying concept of tyranny, of rule of man — a ruling class. Thus, children did not make connections of logic and, instead, lived their lives in a somewhat helpless "airhead state". They retained very little knowledge since they never learned how to *integrate* percepts by common denominators into interlocked concepts of logic — the very capacity that separated man from the other animals. In short, children never learned *to think.* ...Was it not to be expected that essentially all children in the anticivilization grew up to a life of stagnation? Was it any surprise that smart politicians ran things the way *they* wanted to?

In the Twelve Visions World, as I saw in my Ninth Vision, children grew up to be geniuses with powerful motivational drives. They were intensely happy, for they did not experience the tragedy of their dreams fading as we did. Moreover, as those children tomorrow grew up, they used Neothink® to not only make their own dreams come true, but ours as well.

To get a metaphorical sense of the power of integrated thinking, imagine, for a moment, a large boulder sits near the edge of a cliff. We find the strongest man in the world and ask him to push that boulder over the cliff. He braces his shoulder against the boulder and pushes with all his might. The boulder does not even budge. Well, we could find the next thousand strongest men in the world, line them up, and watch them one by one push the boulder with all their might. But the boulder never budges. ...That is a metaphor for how we are taught to use our minds in school, thus later at work — to helplessly push our thoughts one by one against the big boulder to success. The big boulder to success never budges.

Now, imagine this: you and I and ten average guys brace our shoulders against the big boulder and, all together, give it one big heave. That boulder would roll right over the cliff! ...That is a metaphor for how our children's minds will work tomorrow with a Twelve-Visions-World education — continually bringing together many thoughts into one powerful force to easily push over the big boulder to success. With this powerful *integrated thinking* tomorrow, our children grew up to push through all the money-making barriers that even the thousand smartest men today could never move through.

### *More Creative Than Today's Smartest People*

My Ninth Vision clearly showed me that integrated thinking gave our children more creative power tomorrow than the smartest men and women in the world today. That was why our children and grandchildren actually became creative geniuses, even with average IQs!

Our education today in our suppressed civilization gives us powerless perceptual or specialized thinking that leaves us stranded as adults in routine-rut jobs with specialized tasks. Even if someone today is very good at what he does, he is usually powerless at fulfilling his deepest dreams, sort of like those world's strongest men powerless at pushing over the big boulder.

In tomorrow's Twelve Visions World, however, our children grew up learning how to snap thoughts together into an integrated force that easily pushed over the big boulder to major success.

In today's civilization, the same forces that hold back super entrepreneurs and super technologies also hold back our children's development. You see, career politicians and regulatory bureaucrats increasingly control our educational system. The ordinary person graduates from our public schools with severe short circuits; he or she cannot put together the connections needed to be creative. He or she, in short, cannot integrate.

### *Make A Change*

Knock out of your mind the passive acceptance of your children and grandchildren settling into a specialized routine rut. They can escape the stagnation-trap you perhaps endured.

Imagine their most ambitious dreams, and daydream about them for a few minutes. In your mind's eye, block out the obstacles that will hold them down in a stagnant routine rut. Instead, see your children and grandchildren leading the way to exhilarating success.

With all that you know now, that daydream strikingly demonstrates to you (as it did for me) that, in today's suppressed civilization, they will grow up, trapped in a terminal rut. As simple as it may seem, that striking snapshot of their lifelong stagnation-trap can set off an act of self-preservation: as happened to me, you might start seeking the Twelve-Visions-Party agenda.

With a Twelve-Visions-World education, as seen in my Ninth Vision, our children and grandchildren frequently came up with major marketing ideas, for marketing ideas were simply an exercise of the mind: of finding common denominators that served a lot of people's needs. They then built success upon those structured concepts, say those great marketing ideas, through forward-movement integrated thinking.

Their creativity and energy went toward identifying then servicing society's needs. Indeed, those geniuses — our children and grandchildren — solved people's problems and needs. As a result, enormous creativity and energy rushed into society. Prosperity reigned throughout America, then across our planet. Exhilaration and wealth filled our children's and grandchildren's lives.

Knowledge is power. But creating *new knowledge* is *super power*. The richest people today *created* something new. Through forward-movement integrated thinking, they integrated lots of existing knowledge. While steadily putting together existing knowledge, they hit critical points that broke through into new knowledge. While steadily building their success-puzzles piece by piece, they reached a point when they had snapped together a creative new puzzle-picture. At that point, they experienced Neothink®. Tomorrow, our children evolved into the Neothink® mentality.

Realize, our graduating geniuses were not necessarily gifted with creativity. Not until they built a certain size success-puzzle did they begin springing into creativity. You see, as they built their success-puzzles piece by piece, they began to see puzzle-pictures gradually forming. As they saw their puzzle-pictures coming together, they broke into new knowledge while seeing how their unique pictures and their missing pieces must look like. Then they began *creating* by completing those unique puzzle-pictures.

*The Neothink® Movement*

*Forming The Bridge to Money and Power*

Sometimes we wonder how a money/power giant got from point A in school to point B on top of the world. Building success-puzzles, piece by piece, formed his bridges to money and power. To build those success-puzzles, piece by piece, though, requires integrated thinking. Tomorrow, under the new code of education, that happened automatically to ordinary people. Today, under the old code of education, that seldom happens to even extraordinary people.

I observed in my Ninth Vision that it was integrated thinking that eventually enabled the entire human race to mentally cross the bridges to a whole new way of orchestrating our minds in the Twelve Visions World, something we called the *Neothink® Mentality*. Neothink® was so superior that once it got started, its natural advantages quickly engaged people everywhere.

Neothink® comes from compilations of complex concepts that, when pulled together, reveal startling, synergistic advancements of human knowledge. (*Twelve Visions*, a Mark Hamilton Publication, is an example of Neothink®.)

Very rare today, Neothink® became our children's and grandchildren's normal mentality in tomorrow's Twelve Visions World. We, too, eventually evolved into Neothink®. With Neothink®, ordinary people routinely contributed life-lifting values to mankind. Ordinary people became extraordinary.

*Becoming Geniuses*

When that happened, we discovered our unknown selves: our buried genius within. The measurement for mental power changed from intelligence tests for IQ to the efficacy of one's integrated thinking. IQ no longer mattered (save for subnormal, mental retardation, of course). In time, the superior Neothink® mentality swept across our planet. Babies naturally grew into and children naturally stayed in the Neothink® mentality.

Tomorrow's schools, as seen in my Ninth Vision, taught our children and grandchildren how to Neothink®. As they grew up, they joined the geniuses. Indeed, living exhilarating creation-driven lives instead of boring routine ruts, they joined the entrepreneurial geniuses and created wonderful values for the world.

Your children and grandchildren built larger and larger puzzles of knowledge through integrated thinking. With that integrated, puzzle-building thinking, surpassing their best dreams became natural and fun. They lived the way man is supposed to live. Highly motivated and making more and more conceptual advancements, they learned how to pull the integration string. That was when they saw their first puzzle-pictures. Pulling together their conceptual advancements into one interlocked, synergistic advancement of knowledge, one clear puzzle-picture of new knowledge, they experienced the euphoria of Neothink®. Soon, they crossed over to the Neothink® mentality and continued to pull together those synergistic advancements of knowledge in their lines of work or interests. Of course, they were greatly rewarded with prestige, wealth, happiness, and love.

My Ninth Vision showed me that sometime in the twenty-first century, snapping together synergistic advancements of knowledge became the norm for ordinary people graduating in the Twelve Visions World.

Volume Four

Soar To the Wealthy Elite Class

# THE PARTY

## DELIVER OUR TWELVE VISIONS WORLD

*SETTING FREE AMERICA:*

*ERA OF UNIVERSAL*

*WEALTH, HEALTH, PEACE*

# Why We Need a New Political Party

We see the century-long trend: the Democratic Party and the Republican Party have become all about gaining political power. Therefore, today I introduce the Twelve Visions Party, a new political party that reverses the century-long power-grab by making politics *only* about protection and *not* about power.

I will begin by saying: There are *ostensible* qualities that on appearance I <u>love</u> about the Democratic Party and the Republican Party, qualities upon which rises the genuine Twelve Visions Party:

Let's start with the Democratic Party:

I <u>love</u> the democrats' idea of tolerance, acceptance, and protection of all races, religions, and social classes. The problem, as I pointed out before, is that our political parties supplant their good original intentions with a thirst for political power. So, the Democratic Party's tolerance and love for people has transmogrified into a grotesque power-play to win groups...to win certain ethnic races, religions, and social classes or **voting segments of our population**, which has led to extraordinarily damaging consequences. For example, democrats push for extensive entitlements for those voting segments, in essence buying their votes. Those entitlements are now sinking America into mind-boggling debt. Those entitlements are bankrupting our children's futures.

The original, beautiful idea of tolerance, acceptance, and protection of all people, of minorities and all religions and the unprotected 'littlc guys' inspired me and my Twelve Visions Party idea. In order to protect even the smallest of minorities, my Twelve Vision Party idea introduced the fundamental, natural law of protection — the Prime Law. The Prime Law protects the smallest of all minorities: the individual — a minority of one. It protects *everyone* equally and does not favor a group or *significant voting segment* of the population. Therefore, the vote-gathering power-play is not available for democrats. Thus, the Democratic Party hypocritically and shamefully has no interest in the protection of the smallest of all minorities — the individual. That responsibility instead falls on the Twelve

Visions Party. In the end, the old party's ostensible quality of tolerance, acceptance, and protection of *everyone*, which I fell in love with, has been used as a trick to gain votes and political power at our expense. Now, the Twelve Visions Party with the Prime Law of Protection captures and enforces the original, beautiful idea of tolerance, acceptance, and protection of *everyone*...without tricking people for votes and political power.

Now let's shift to the Republican Party:

I love the republicans' idea of fiscal responsibility and limited government. The problem, as I pointed out before, is that our political parties supplant their good original intentions with a thirst for political power. So, the Republican Party's fiscal responsibility and limited government (when in power) transmogrified into fiscal irresponsibility and government empowerment...into a grotesque power-play to buy or pander to groups or **voting segments of our population**, which has led to extraordinarily damaging consequences. For example, republicans *when in power* push for elaborate spending sprees (and for mandating personal morals) that please voting segments, in essence buying their votes. Those spending sprees have contributed to America's insurmountable debt. Those spending sprees are now bankrupting our children's futures.

The original, beautiful idea of fiscal responsibility and limited government inspired me and my Twelve Vision Party idea. In order to truly limit government, my Twelve Vision Party idea introduced the fundamental budget of limited government — the Protection-Only Budget (aka the Prime-Law Budget). The Protection-Only Budget funds only the fundamental, prime purpose of our government — physical safety and protection, which includes military, intelligence, domestic security, justice, courts, prisons, police, veterans. The Protection-Only Budget protects *everyone* equally and does not favor or pander to a specific group or voting segment of the population. Therefore, the vote-gathering power-play is not available for republicans. Thus, the Republican Party hypocritically and shamefully has no interest in the Protection-Only Budget and its *massive* reductions that would immediately wipe out the deficit and eventually the debt. That responsibility to limit government and eradicate the debt instead falls on the Twelve Visions Party. In the end, the old party's ostensible quality of fiscal responsibility and limited government, which I fell in love with, has been used as a trick to gain votes and political power at our expense. Now, the Twelve Visions Party with the Protection-Only Budget captures and enforces the original, beautiful idea of fiscal responsibility and limited government...without tricking people for votes and political power.

The Prime Law of Protection and the Protection-Only Budget capture the beautiful, original intentions of the democrats and republicans while removing the hypocritical tricks and power-plays. In many ways, the democrats and the republicans have become the same: their drive for political power has supplanted their original intentions. Indeed, when in power they are both spending away our country's future, sending us into mind-boggling debt, bankrupting our children's future. Soon, there will be nothing left if we stay with those two old political parties. The answer is the new Twelve Visions Party.

With the TVP National Platform, **Make All the People Rich *Including the Poor***, I announce the birth of the Twelve Visions Party. **The Prime Law of Protection** and **The Protection-Only Budget** are the two pillars that hold up this new party. They manifest the original beauty behind the two old parties without the lies, tricks, and power-plays that destroyed those beautiful original intentions.

If you ask me *why* the beautiful original intentions of republicans and democrats — those original intentions of fiscal responsibility/limited government and tolerance/acceptance/protection of all people — *why* those beautiful intentions have instead bankrupted our country, I will tell you that the answer comes down to the steadily rising rule of man in America. Rule of man — flaw-filled man — craves political power and promptly establishes a ruling class. For over two-hundred years, the rule of nearly flawless law — our Constitution — has been steadily weakened by the rising rule of man...by federal judges, congressmen, presidents, bureaucrats, journalists...a strengthening ruling class hungry for political power and control.

The rising rule of man and his strengthening ruling class of democrats and republicans have severely damaged this country. Ordinary people are suffering. The Twelve Visions Party is here to reverse the rising rule of man and eventually eradicate it and its destruction of government and country. The Twelve Visions Party recognizes a unique opportunity to rapidly and radically turn this economy around. Whereas people's wallets suffer greatly under the rising rule of man in America, the Twelve Visions Party sees an opportunity to arrest the rule of man and its suppressive ruling class in order to free the geniuses of society to make everyone prosperous, including the poor!

**Make All the People Rich, *Including the Poor***, the premier (and timeless) National Platform of the Twelve Visions Party, opens the mind-space to visualize a Twelve Visions World. Here are the Twelve Visions that will benefit **you** — the Twelve Visions of the Twelve Visions Party:

*Universal Wealth, Health, Peace*

# The Twelve Visions *for You* of The Twelve Visions Party®

| | |
|---|---|
| Vision One: | Become the Person You Were Meant to Be |
| Vision Two: | Live the Life You Were Meant to Live |
| Vision Three: | Feel Extraordinary Every Day |
| Vision Four: | Slow Down Aging Permanently |
| Vision Five: | Land the Job of Your Dreams |
| Vision Six: | Build the Business of Your Passions |
| Vision Seven: | Experience the Love of Your Life |
| Vision Eight: | Have the Body You Always Envied |
| Vision Nine: | Become a Genius of Society |
| Vision Ten: | Have Everything You Ever Wanted (via the free-to-soar geniuses and super technologies) |
| Vision Eleven: | Ride A Prosperity Wave to Riches (via falling prices and soaring buying power) |
| Vision Twelve: | Enjoy Nearly Perfect Health (via soaring medical technologies and falling prices) |

Those Twelve Visions are fully developed in *Twelve Visions* (a Mark Hamilton Publication). At first glance people automatically dismiss the Twelve Visions as unrealistic utopia. There is *no way* human beings can have all that perfection in this imperfect world! As farfetched and easily dismissible as the Twelve Visions seem in this sinking America...just remember: the world has NEVER seen the Great Technological Revolution — NEVER!

The personal computer revolution was a small microcosm and a forerunner. Computer buying power multiplied a thousandfold! With that in mind, imagine your buying power in general multiplying a thousandfold while super technologies and super entrepreneurs race forward as free and as fast as the unhindered personal computer industry of the late 20th century. Imagine it for a moment, then look again at the Twelve Visions above. Suddenly some of those Twelve Visions no longer seem so farfetched! Right?

*The Prime Cure* (2800 pages, a Mark Hamilton Publication)

shows you a world in which the Twelve Visions above come to life. It demonstrates — vision by vision — how each vision listed above becomes reality when the Twelve Visions Party replaces the two old parties through a *Great Replacement Program.*

The TVP postulates a different world, an alternative to everything we have ever known. The TVP gets down to the nuts-and-bolts of saving us through the Prime Law of Protection and the Protection-Only Budget. You have never seen anything like this Twelve Visions World. Take a close look, for the Twelve Visions Party is the savior of your future and of your children.

# The TVP Is Your Savior

When our debt becomes unsustainable, America's wealth will collapse. Economic failure will follow. Chaos and civil unrest will threaten your family's safety. America will sink into poverty and chaos...and eventually into tyranny.

The Twelve Visions Party was put in place at this time to catch America's fall and prevent a civil catastrophe. The existence of the Twelve Visions Party is critical to every American. Whereas third parties in America ultimately exist as platforms to win political awareness and even to influence the two major parties, that is not the case with The Twelve Visions Party. Its end-rule-of-man Prime Law will never influence either major political party. The Twelve Visions Party was put in place at this time as the safeguard and savior of civilization after the economic collapse.

The Twelve Visions Party (TVP) has little to no effect today in the massive establishment of politics. However, the TVP is the most important political movement in America today. In an economic failure, the TVP will save you and your family from poverty, crime, tyranny. Unlike any other third party, the TVP has a major role in your future.

Third parties stand little to no chance at the presidency. Admirable efforts have been made for decades, from the well-organized Libertarians, the Green Party, United We Stand, and others. With little chance of winning, the purpose of third-party presidential candidates is: getting their party's ideas out and known...and winning influence upon the two mainstream parties.

Unlike the other third parties, the purpose of the TVP at this time is not about winning political positions, nationally or locally, or even getting our ideas out and known. The purpose of the Twelve Visions Party at this time is something entirely different...something vital to each and every American. The immediate purpose of the TVP is to save you and your loved ones if our country goes into an economic meltdown. Let's take a closer look:

Most Americans are aware of the mounting debt America has accumulated. Anyone who understands the least bit about economics knows the trouble America is in. Even without a basic understanding of economics, we see on TV and read in the paper warnings from economists, professors, news journalist, even from politicians themselves. America is in deep financial trouble.

We are told we could be heading into disaster, whereby the bottom of our economy falls out. Our futures and our children's futures could suffer an economic depression unlike the world has ever seen. By looking at America's debt alone, the long-term future looks dangerous. That threatening future can all turn around if the TVP took hold, but a TVP President is not going to happen now; even gaining widespread state recognition will not happen *in time* to stop our imminent economic fall. Without a strong TVP direction, we face certain realities that guarantee disaster.

The critically important purpose of the Twelve Visions Party is clear: **If America falls hard, if the bottom falls out from under this economy and we go into a systemic economic failure, the Twelve Visions Party with its Prime Law is the only thing there, *the net* that catches America's fall and saves us from the horrors of poverty, crime, tyranny.** When America experiences a catastrophic economic collapse...America will fall first into severe poverty, then civil unrest, chaos, and finally into tyranny. That failure cycle has been demonstrated throughout history. Prior to TVP, there was nothing in place to stop that failure cycle. Without TVP, we would sink deeper and deeper into poverty, civil unrest, and tyranny. Imagine that future for your children and loved ones...poverty and tyranny. The only thing *now set in place* that could stop this spiraling fall is the Twelve Visions Party and the entirely new political structure with the Prime Law, its pure and unhindered freedom that releases the geniuses of society, its protection-only government, its service-basis government versus the otherwise power-basis, tyranny-bound government. This entirely new TVP political paradigm in a completely new dimension of politics will be there, in place, as a stopgap, *the net* to catch America's collapse and to give its people, *our loved ones*, a way out.

When you understand that TVP has little to do with third-party agendas of winning political influence, and once you realize that TVP is the ONLY possible **net** that can catch a collapsing America, then you can understand the importance and urgency of TVP NOW. When the financial failure hits, TVP and its Prime Law will be there to save our country. The TVP can literally save your life.

## The Two Fundamental Movements of Life

Let's go down to the deepest movements of life, down where the meaning of life reveals itself. Beneath our many physical/mental movements in life are two fundamental movements of life:

1) Improve oneself in order to live a better life (Neothink®).

2) Improve society in order to live a better life (TVP®).

Those two fundamental movements of conscious life (human beings) bring us happiness. In other words, they bring us the meaning of life. They are why I started the Neothink® Society (improve oneself in order to live a better life) and the Twelve Visions Party (improve society in order to live a better life.) They are also the prerequisites to achieving the greatest possible feat of mankind, revealed later.

Those two movements are my life; I spent over thirty years preparing those two movements, spending long days and nights writing the necessary Prime Literature that provides *the source* to the Neothink® Society and the Twelve Visions Party.

### Successful Life is Two Movements
### (1) Neothink® and (2) TVP®

We move through life. We move from our beds to our jobs. We move from our homes to our schools and stores. We move from our jobs back to our homes. Children move from school to play to their homework. We move from our careers to our dinners to our hobbies and to our family time. We move through life. Even when we are sitting still reading a book or watching a movie, our minds are moving through the story. We move through life, directed by our objectives...from small objectives (go fishing) to large objectives (achieve that goal).

Underneath all our objectives, two fundamental objectives direct us through life.

Those two fundamental objectives are:

*The Neothink® Movement*

1) To improve one's life — virtuously selfish movement

2) To improve the world one lives in — virtuously selfless movement

Directed by those two fundamental objectives in life rose the two *Mark Hamilton Movements*: the Neothink® Movement and the TVP® Movement:

| <u>A Virtuously Selfish Movement</u> | <u>A Virtuously Selfless Movement</u> |
|---|---|
| The Neothink® Movement | The TVP® Movement |
| (To improve your life and help improve your loved ones' lives*) | (To improve the world you, your children and grandchildren live in*) |

**Improving life for our loved ones enters as a subset of both those fundamental movements.*

The Neothink® Society provides the blueprints for improving our own lives and becoming the persons we were meant to be, and the Twelve Visions Party provides the blueprints for improving the world we live in and living the life we were meant to live. (Both movements rise from my literature.)

Take a moment to look at those two movements of human life again:

1) Improve our own lives — The Neothink® Movement.

2) Improve the world we live in — The TVP® Movement.

After three decades of writing the Prime Literature — *the source* — I founded the Neothink® Society and the Twelve Visions Party to accelerate those two fundamental movements of human life. Indeed, improving self and improving society are the two fundamental movements of our existence and our happiness. Members actively involved in the Neothink® Society and the Twelve Visions Party benefit enormously and **love their lives!** They discover happiness and enjoy the meaning of life.

I have enjoyed bringing millions of people major values over the decades, from the Neothink® literature and clubhouses to the new TVP® Movement for replacing our sinking world ruled by dishonest politicians and bureaucrats with a prosperous Twelve Visions World ruled by the honest Prime Law.

Let's make no mistake...our country, our future, is headed toward disaster. When you know all the variables, you know that *our country* has only one way out: The Twelve Visions Party with its Protection-Only Budget and Prime-Law Amendment. (The *ordinary person,* prior to the TVP Revolution, has a way out: The Neothink® Society with its Prime Literature and Prime Secret of becoming the Self-Leader.)

For people to shift to the Twelve Visions Party, they have to let go of the idea of *being led.* Instead, they must get used to the idea of being protected <u>and nothing more</u>. As simple as that seems to you now, it took over thirty years of developing the Prime Neothink® Literature to uncover <u>why</u> people will not let go of the idea of being led by a ruling class. (My magnum opus, *The Prime Cure*, 2800 pages, uncorks this bottleneck of human mentality that could otherwise lead to our extinction.)

To get in the psychological position to let go of being led, to let go of having leaders and living under a ruling class, requires the Neothink® mentality. By now you have been introduced to Neothink® and, therefore, you understand the danger of a ruling class.

Once the self-leader shift in thinking occurs, once people let go of the idea of being led by government and instead embrace the idea of only being protected by government, the rule of man will effectively end. We will no longer look to being led and legislated and regulated how to live under a government backed by force. Instead, we will merely look to being protected by a protection-service called government.

With the resulting economic freedom, the geniuses of society and super technologies would race ahead so fast that costs would drop dramatically, our buying power would climb rapidly, and we would live wealthy, healthy, peaceful, and entertaining lives.

The path to universal prosperity is elegantly easy. However, due to our bicameral roots (explained in my magnum opus), it is hard for people to let go of our leaders and end the ruling class backed by force. It is hard for the ordinary person to become The Self-Leader.

*The Neothink® Movement*

Thirty years of Prime Literature was required to open the path for people to let go of being led by a ruling class. And now, the TVP makes letting go of the ruling class a choice — *the* clear choice — and provides a step-by-step process to do so.

*Universal Wealth, Health, Peace*

# The Twelve Visions Party & Neothink® Nourishment

*The TVP Movement*

The Twelve Visions Party seeks to end the rule of man in order to launch the wealth of mankind. The ordinary person has not made the cause-and-effect connection between ending the rule of man and launching the wealth of mankind. Once that connection is made, it will be all over for the republicans and democrats. In their place will rise visionaries and their Twelve Visions Party.

The cause-and-effect connection between ending the rule of man and launching the wealth of mankind is surprisingly easy to make. Over the next few pages you will make that connection.

Most people don't know that they could live wealthy lives if not for the resurging rule of man and its strengthening ruling class. Most people don't understand what rule of man is or how it cuts their standard of living to fractions of what it could be.

The rule of man has, like an infectious disease, adapted and resurged in America since her founding over two centuries ago when rule of man was nearly eradicated with our U.S. Constitution. In an America that eradicates rule of man, you and every citizen would live like a millionaire...everyone. How? Eradicating the virulent disease killing our country and killing all countries on Earth — the deadly rule of man — would free the geniuses of society and their super technologies to soar as never seen before. The rule of man is a fatal, societal disease that needs to be eradicated to save our country and save our world from economic collapse.

The U.S. Constitution came closest to replacing rule of man with rule of nearly flawless law. But there was a weak spot in the U. S. Constitution, a breach, through which the rule of man leaked, a slow leak at first, but now a flood destroying the unrivaled prosperity once enjoyed by Americans.

The Twelve Visions Party repairs that breach with the Prime-Law Amendment and Protection-Only Budget. The Twelve Visions Party proposes the Prime-Law Amendment to the U. S.

Constitution, which would plug the leak — now a FLOOD of rule of man drowning America in debt, regulations and taxes. The Prime Law eradicates the rule of man thus offers the people — ALL PEOPLE — great wealth.

People do not really understand the rule of man, what that means, and what it leads to. When you take the end results of rule of man, its devastation becomes very clear, examples being the bloody regimes throughout history from a Stalin Soviet Empire or a Mao Tse-Tung Red China to a Hitler Germany or a Saddam Hussein Iraq.

The rule of law, on the other hand, can be terribly confusing because often the rule of law is, in reality, rule of man, that is, man-made laws. Just imagine the courts in a Stalin Russia or Hitler Germany.

Rule of law must rise from natural law — universal laws that apply throughout nature and in any country, any civilization across all lands and all time. Natural law for human life reduces down to individual protection — live and let live without violating others.

Our Declaration of Independence and U.S. Constitution rose from natural law and were nearly flawless. But our founding fathers missed the most fundamental, natural law — the Prime Law of Protection, which essentially says live and let live and no person, no group, no government can initiate force. That Prime Law that outlaws initiatory force was missed by our founding fathers. All rule of man requires initiatory force — man forcing others to obey the ruling class and their man-made laws, regulations and rules; self-serving laws as opposed to natural laws...agenda law as opposed to natural law. Rule of man requires initiatory force. Natural law does not require and does not allow initiatory force. The most fundamental natural law of protection — the Prime Law — allows only self-defense force to protect oneself from those using or threatening initiatory force against them.

I have brought forth that Prime Law and formed a political movement around it — the Twelve Visions Party (TVP). That Prime Law, as an amendment to the U. S. Constitution, would immediately patch the breach that has allowed the devastating rule of man back into our government.

What exactly is the Prime Law? The Prime Law simply eliminates the use of initiatory force. All abusive man-made laws require the use of initiatory force against its citizens. So, without initiatory force, there can be no rule of man. Initiatory force, by the way, means *initiating* force. The Prime Law ends initiatory force and the threat of force.

This entirely new dimension of civilization, this never-before-seen prosperity option is elegantly simple: Once you eradicate initiatory force, you eradicate the rule of man, and amazing things happen for the people. When you swipe away the thick regulatory and legislative rule of man in one swoop, then the pure and open freedom left behind allows entrepreneurs, businesses, sciences, technologies to soar ahead at rapid speeds never seen before. We would experience a Great Technological Revolution the world has never seen. Costs of goods would drop to fractions as buying power soared.

Super entrepreneurs and super technologies racing ahead unhindered would immediately start driving down prices. We have seen isolated examples of this throughout history. Consider the computer revolution of the late 20th century: Computer buying power multiplied a thousand times as computer consumers became computer rich. Another example happened nearly a hundred years ago during the early car industry when Ford Motor Company invented the assembly line. Buying power multiplied dramatically through mass production. And that multiplying buying power spread throughout other industries as the production-line brought the world mass production and economies of scale. Standards of living soared.

Even before all that were the railroads. Consider the example of maverick James J. Hill (story in Volume Three) who used his transcontinental railroad along the northern border of the United States to single-handedly multiply the standards of living of many, many poor Americans. That one man would have multiplied the buying power of our entire nation if not for the devastation from the rule of man and its ruling class.

In those examples, we were experiencing prosperity-explosions that happened in a vacuum free of rule of man. Those great prosperity-explosions were eventually killed by rule of man.

As we eradicate the rule of man and it ruling class, we

eradicate poverty! And, something else amazing happens: as technologies race ahead in all industries, as entrepreneurs, businesses, scientists race ahead unhindered, free of the thick regulatory web, the medical industry is no exception. Eradicating the rule of man in turn eradicates disease after disease as the unhindered medical industry rapidly advances. Costs of medicine and procedures fall as medical breakthroughs occur more and more frequently.

So, eradicating the ruling class eradicates poverty *and* eradicates disease (and brings us breakthroughs to slow down aging).

There is yet *another* enormous benefit of eradicating the ruling class: We will eradicate crime and terrorism. You see, the Prime Law is the fundamental law of protection. Imagine the full might and focus of government as a protection service against initiatory force or threat of force. First, there would no longer be a deadly competition of funds between protection versus entitlements. Entitlement money buys votes, so that wins out in the end, jeopardizing national security. When the government focuses on its one and ONLY proper purpose of protection against force or threat of force, however, then our country will evolve the greatest protection and peace the world has ever seen.

Once we eradicate the rule of man, then we eradicate poverty, eradicate disease, eradicate crime and terrorism. The Twelve Visions World begets **wealth, health, peace** (the TVP Emblem). Indeed, the title of the TVP Platform is no overstatement or gimmick, as follows: *Make All People Rich, Including the Poor!* Literally the TVP will make all people rich, including the poor. It is time for people to discover the Twelve Visions Party and claim a rich life in America!

*The Debt*

Many people today are rightfully afraid of the debt our country and other countries are accumulating. The TVP Budget breaks from the rule-of-man entitlement-filled budgets and adheres to the Prime Law Protection-Only Budget: money is budgeted to protection only — the ONLY valid purpose of government. Imagine a budget that is restricted to and dedicated to protection

ONLY. Suddenly our budget drops well over fifty percent! Just that alone gets our deficits and debt under control while increasing our safety *and* prosperity!

Indeed, we will also experience a prosperity explosion as the man-made, debilitating regulations — regulations that have nothing to do with protection — lose their power over our economy. All this GOOD begins with a psychological shift among the people, realizing our government exists for our protection and NOTHING ELSE. With even the slightest move in this direction toward the Protection-Only Budget and the Prime Law, the standards of living will start to rise. Why? Because economic freedom goes up and, therefore, prosperity goes up too. Then, the people will begin to personally and emotionally make the connection I stated earlier: **End the rule of man to launch the wealth of mankind!**

Rule of man is seductive because of entitlement programs paid out to over half our population and because of special ruling-class relationships with big businesses and big unions. Rule-of-man has been hard to leave behind. But as more and more people realize, through the TVP Movement, that those free-money temptations will continue to destroy their standards of living, and as they abandon their support for the rule of man, their poverty will begin to vanish.

The Great Technological Revolution has NEVER happened before. It requires the removal of the rule of man and all his regulations and bad ruling-class laws. The only way to do that — to eradicate the rule of man — is to remove initiatory force with the Prime Law.

We can start with a Protection-Only Budget. With a budget for our protection only — a budget consistent with the Prime Law — we will quickly stop funds from hemorrhaging and from going toward those rule-of-man regulations holding back the Great Technological Revolution.

A TVP President will boldly submit a Protection-Only Budget. Although Congress will fight it and reject it, the immediate economic benefits will be fast and phenomenal, which will lead to a Great Replacement Program in which TVP candidates are put into office during the mid-term elections.

Then the pressure will quickly build for the full Protection-

Only Budget and the Prime-Law Amendment.

When results replace rhetoric, the momentum and public support will rise quickly into an unstoppable wave that will wash over Washington, D.C. and wash away the rule of man — the ruling class as we know it.

The TVP can save our future from crippling debt and civil unrest; the TVP can end the rule of man and launch the wealth of mankind. The TVP exposes the ruling class and unites the non-ruling class. The TVP offers the path to a wealthy America no longer shackled with a ruling class.

The Twelve Visions Party is for *everyone* in the non-ruling class. There are reasons those on the right could dislike us. There are reasons those on the left could dislike us. But there is a much stronger reason those on the right and left and all in-between could love us: we have the ONLY program that will make all people wealthy, including the poor!

Our method is: end the rule of man. Our tools are the Protection-Only Budget and the Prime-Law Amendment. I invite everyone in...liberal democrats, religious right, all in-between including persons of every religion, race, class, indeed, the entire non-ruling class. People of all race, creed and color, business owners, struggling poor and unemployed Americans: *discover the TVP*. The Twelve Visions Party is the non-ruling-class unifier! The TVP seeks to make everyone rich, everyone!

Everyone who comes into the Twelve Visions Party does so with the same drive and purpose: to live a wealthy and prosperous life! That is our universal common-denominator. And when I say wealthy, I really do mean wealthy. There is no reason to live as most of us do now. We have financially stressed lives because of the rule of man. When the rule of man ends, the entire bogus side of government ends — everything that does not deal with protection ends. With that computer-industry-like, unhindered freedom, a Great Technological Revolution will ensue as the world has never seen before. Costs will plunge as buying power soars, and everyone rises to the wealthy elite class!

Once we all realize and agree that the rule of man is our scourge, then the steps to a wealthy future are straightforward. The Twelve Visions Party gets rid of the rule of man in two ways:

1) temporary but effective — The Protection-Only Budget.

The Protection-Only Budget will SAVE our future from crippling debt. The TVP's Protection-Only Budget breaks the budget away from rule of man and instead adheres to the Prime Law of Protection (the only valid purpose of government). The Protection-Only Budget limits spending to protection. "But what about needed entitlements? What about needed regulatory bureaucracies?" The REAL ANSWERS to our economic and unemployment woes materialize by getting rid of most entitlements and regulations, for with unhindered freedom from rule of man, all people will become rich as costs of living plunge.

Now, the second way to get rid of the rule of man is final:

2) permanent and definitive — The Prime-Law Amendment.

Ending initiatory force ends rule of man. When we all understand that the rule of man is society's scourge, then the Twelve Visions Party becomes everyone's choice. It will be all over for the democrats and republicans who increasingly govern civilization through rule of man. As I said before, the Twelve Visions Party has all the answers. When the Twelve Visions Party eradicates the rule of man through the Protection-Only Budget and the Prime-Law Amendment, the results will be a Great Technological Revolution, plunging costs, soaring buying power, and wealthy people — everyone, including today's poor!

So, what we are about is very simple:

#1 The rule of man is the devastating societal disease.

#2 We eradicate the rule of man through the Protection-Only Budget and the Prime-Law Amendment.

#3 All people get rich including the poor in the ensuing Great Technological Revolution.

Understanding the Twelve Visions Party requires recognizing those three simple steps...

Step 1) Grasp that *the poison* to civilization is the rule of man.

Step 2) End rule of man with the Protection-Only Budget and Prime-Law Amendment.

Step 3) Watch all the people get rich, even the poor!

That is why the TVP Platform is entitled "Make All People Rich, Including the Poor." It is not hyperbole. It is reality.

And that is why the Protection-Only Budget and the Prime-Law Amendment, which end the rule of man, are listed in the TVP Bylaws as the pillars upon which the TVP rests.

Who will be drawn to this new political party? The answer: VICTIMS. We will pull from both the left and the right. Why? The Twelve Visions Party rescues victims, and people NOT in the ruling class <u>are victims</u>. The poor are victims; the middle-class, even wealthy business owners not part of the ruling class are victims! We are being played against each other by the ruling class. By playing us against each other, we do not see the <u>real</u> enemy — those playing GOD with our lives — the ruling class!

Everyone in the NON ruling class is a victim. Inner-city minorities will find the TVP Movement very appealing and beneficial. Country-club white Christians will find the same. The Twelve Visions Party is going to pull our entire family together — the entire suppressed NON ruling class! The Twelve Visions Party is the <u>real</u> UNIFIER.

We are all individuals, and the Prime Law protects <u>the</u> individual — the smallest of all minorities — the minority of one. As individuals, we all want the same thing: a happy, prosperous, wealthy life for ourselves and for our children and grandchildren. That common denominator is *the reason why* the Twelve Visions Party exists. The Twelve Visions Party is for *everyone* — EVERYONE! Now the people must discover this gift.

Where did the Twelve Visions Party come from? The answer is on the next page...

*Universal Wealth, Health, Peace*

## The Neothink® Movement

Over thirty years ago I began discovering a new way of thinking that I named Neothink®.

For thirty years, I researched and developed Neothink®. I wrote over a dozen books on Neothink®. I founded the Neothink® Society with Neothink® Clubhouses spread across the world where the Neothink® Secrets in my books are taught.

You will see many thousands of testimonials by googling Neothink® or the Neothink® Society. The Neothink® Movement is a strong self-improvement dynamic that has existed for over three decades. The TVP Movement has grown out of the Neothink® Movement. The TVP Movement is a movement to improve our world. The Neothink® Movement is a movement to improve ourselves.

Neothink® is a new way of thinking in which one becomes a self-leader who is not dependent on the destructive leaders of our country today. I teach those self-leader Neothink® tools in my books. You learned a little about Neothink® and becoming a self-leader in this book. Now, consider my Neothink® approach to the Twelve Visions Party:

The TVP weakens and ties the hands of our destructive leaders through the Protection-Only Budget and the Prime-Law Amendment. The TVP weans people from their destructive leaders. Those with Neothink® are READY for and WANT this. They are self-leaders and know that by clearing away the destructive rule of man and his massive web of regulations and legislation, the results will be wealth, health, and peace for all — even for the smallest and least protected of all minorities — the individual, *all* individuals.

Because we must wean ordinary people from their leaders — from their false security blankets — the Twelve Visions Party must initially grow from self-leaders within the Neothink® Society, from those ready to break away from ruling-class leaders.

As you know, for over 30 years I have written long, in-depth books about this new way of thinking called Neothink®. Very briefly, Neothink® conditions the mind to think for itself — to see through illusions to *what is* and to stop depending on leaders who create illusions to manipulate the people. Neothink® enables people to know what is really going on and have the confidence to become self-leaders.

That Neothink® mentality — that self-leader mentality — applies to all aspects of life, from politics and running our country through self-leadership under the Prime Law instead of through powerful leaders under their man-made laws (the foundation of the Twelve Visions Party) to business and running our careers through self-leadership for much greater creativity and monetary payoffs (the foundation of the Neothink® Society).

Whereas the TVP corrects our political structure for great prosperity, the Neothink® Society corrects your work structure for great prosperity as introduced in Volume Four.

The members of the Neothink® Society are all readers of my revolutionary Neothink® Manuscripts, and those Neothink® Members understand self-leadership versus being <u>tricked</u> into living under powerful leaders — living a subservient life under a ruling class...pushed down into an underclass.

Therefore, members of the Neothink® Society understand the vital need for the Twelve Visions Party ... for saving our country from increasingly powerful leaders, from an out-of-control ruling class. Indeed, members of the Neothink® Society understand the Prime Law and Protection-Only Budget. So, the Twelve Visions Party has the advantage of rising from my readers — from the Neothink® Society. A point will come — a tipping point — when the TVP members begin growing beyond my Neothink® Society and beyond my readership.

Until then, growth of the Twelve Visions Party comes with the growth of the Neothink® Society and my readers.

As people connect the cause-and-effect relationship between the rule of man and their prosperity, specifically how eradicating the rule of man results in standards of living beyond anything the world has seen, they will support the TVP. Indeed, the Twelve Visions Party has the only tools and complete program that can successfully eradicate the rule of man.

Those tools, of course, are the Protection-Only Budget and the Prime-Law Amendment.

The key when approaching the public and the media is to make all this very simple to communicate, very simple to grasp, and very easy to drive home with an <u>emotional charge</u>. Our slogan is: *End the rule of man to launch the wealth of mankind.* Eradicate the rule of man and everyone lives spectacularly wealthy lives. That is our message to the public.

Initially, for now, our growth and strength comes from within — from within our Neothink® Society. The TVP will benefit enormously by the growth of the Neothink® Society. The members know that the rule of man means government backed by initiatory force. The rule of man is the disease of all civilizations. All fallen civilizations came at the hands of the rule of man. Indeed, the rule of man kills civilization and is killing ours. The Neothink® Society and its Twelve Visions Party can turn this country around and save our country from dying.

## How Government Could Evolve Into A Super-Competent, Customer-Driven Protection Service

Now I will reveal to you the evolving TVP government structure that will maximize its one and only purpose of protecting the individual against initiatory force. I created this document of the new government structure in 2005. I first presented the concepts in the 1980s in my publication *Neo-Tech® Business Control* (740 pages). But I have held this document back, until now...now that we will actualize the Twelve Visions Party. This is how the TVP and Neothink® Business combine to bring us the competent protection-only government that provides the conditions for unprecedented wealth, health, and peace.

As you know, government will undergo a fundamental change with the Prime-Law Amendment. The concept of government would fundamentally change from a government based on *power* to a government based on *service*. That fundamental change from a *power* basis to a *service* basis would evolve a businesslike system — a businesslike protection service.

The evolution from a power basis to a service basis will steadily happen with the success of the Twelve Visions Party. I will lay out a very simplified, an *oversimplified* explanation of the highlights of the new businesslike government structure we would be aggressively working toward:

With the nearly flawless job done in the original U.S. Constitution document setting down the structure of government, we will not touch its main principles. After the Prime-Law Amendment, we will work toward evolving the daily functioning of our government into the most competent value-creating system — the Neothink® Business System as detailed in *The Neothink® System* (315 pages, a Mark Hamilton Publication).

To really understand this transition from a power-grabbing political/force basis of government to a value-creating business/service basis, you must know about the breakthrough Neothink® System and its mighty *division of essence*. With the briefest of highlights, here is a quick synopsis of the ideas:

The Neothink® System's **division of essence** is the ultimate division of labor because each job of labor also includes the mind — the ability to think and make the job more and more valuable. The division of labor works by dividing a company into its physical movements, which become its jobs of labor such as (before robotic arms) the man driving in rivets on the assembly line. My division of essence, on the other hand, divides business into its physical movements too, but movements that *include* the thinking mind in order to creatively advance the essence of the business (i.e., its marketable values). Through my Neothink® tools, all jobs at all levels can creatively advance the essence of the business. This evolution from dead-end jobs of labor (body of the business) to open-ended jobs of essence (mind and body of the business) replaces stagnation with exhilaration — a must for abiding happiness. Each mind/body job becomes alive and valuable to the company's creative forward movement. For a full understanding of the division of essence, see *The Neothink® System*. ...Let us now apply the powerful division of essence to the new, businesslike *protection service*...our new government:

The three branches of government as set down in the U.S. Constitution are 1) the Legislative Branch (creating laws for citizen protection), 2) the Executive Branch (executing laws for citizen protection), 3) the Judicial Branch (interpreting laws for citizen protection). Instead of three branches of government, we can now identify them as the three main physical movements of protection (protection being the *essence* of government) that include the thinking mind in order to make each movement more and more valuable. This begins the government's ultimate division of labor, known as *the division of essence*. The purpose of government, *the essence* of government, remember, is **protection**.

So, the three main mind/body movements of government protection are 1) creating the laws for protection, 2) executing the laws for protection, 3) interpreting the laws for protection. But, how does the government break down further?

Inside those large main mind/body movements of protection are smaller mind/body movements of protection, just smaller value-creating subsets or mini-movements of the overarching main movements of protection. For example, under the main movement of executing laws for protection, comes four mini-movements: 1) executing foreign affairs, 2) executing money matters, 3) executing the military, 4) executing justice. Each is a mind/body movement with a clear purpose of protection, the essence of government. Notice, those mini-movements are four of the thirteen Departments of the President's Cabinet — Department of State, Department of Treasury, Department of Defense, Department of Justice. In a protection-only government, the other Cabinet Departments are not needed. Interestingly, those four Cabinet Departments were the original four the father of our country, Neothink® man George Washington, established in setting up our government.

The "mind-with-body" movements of protection are self-contained chunks of essence from the overall value-creating essence of the government, which is protection. Collectively, the mini-movements of protection make up the government's division of essence. The massive government continues to divide into its mind-with-body movements of protection or chunks of essence, down to smaller and smaller chunks of mind-with-body, value-creating movements of protection. For instance, the federal prison system is a complete chunk of essence, a full mind-with-body value-creating movement of protection that falls under the larger movement of executing Justice, which falls under the overarching main movement of executing the laws. The police force, the armed services...those are chunks of essence, mind-with-body value-creating movements of protection that fall under larger mind-with-body movements of protection.

Such chunks of essence — mind-with-body movements where value creation and value elevation of the business's essence can occur — exist throughout all value-creating businesslike structures. Of course, the TVP government's essence is protection. Chunks of essence — mind-with-body movements where value creation and value elevation of protection can occur — would exist all throughout our new Twelve Visions Government. Those mind-with-body value-creating movements of protection will cover all functions of the protection-only government, bringing out *the best* protection service.

*The Neothink® System* demonstrates how the division of essence allows decentralization while, *at the same time*, allowing strong centralization, which is exactly what a service-based U.S.

Government will need. For example, the fifty states would most effectively become their own chunks of essence (i.e., protection). In other words, they would function autonomously under their own constitutions. They could compete, and people would vote with their feet. However, the Prime-Law Amendment would filter out every state and federal bad law in the country, including some existing amendments in the U.S. Constitution. Therefore, all citizens everywhere would be protected by the Prime Law of Protection: *no initiatory force*.

Moreover, without getting into too much detail, once you understand how the division of essence works, you will understand the mutually beneficial internal Essence Tracking Reports that will rise up from the states to the federal main Movement Heads. And you will understand the Essence Meetings that will bring centralized control over the decentralized U.S. Protection Service. The service of protection and justice, from the local level to the federal level, will snap together into one unbreakable Neothink® puzzle-picture through the Essence Tracking Reports. That Neothink® service — that intense value-creating thinking put in at every level of government — will deliver the greatest *value creation* to the American people. Peace unlike ever before will blanket America.

Let me pause here to make a point: The separation of powers and division of powers will no longer be necessary, for a *ruling power* will no longer exist. Whereas, as the saying goes, power corrupts; absolute power corrupts absolutely...our new government will be merely a *service* — a pay-as-you-use service. Instead of forced tax collection, citizens will voluntarily pay for superior protection. People will pay for peace.

There will be absolutely no ruling power, no reason to separate or divide power. All divisions will come by way of the division of essence to maximize the values being created — the protection of our citizens.

With that in mind, I see two possible scenarios here for the Twelve Visions Government that would be determined based upon which one would deliver the *best service* when the time approaches:

**Scenario One:** Do not link the federal and the states' Essence Tracking Reports and Essence Meetings. The federal responsibilities stop with federal law, courts, prisons, national defense; the states' responsibilities cover state law, courts, prisons, police.

**Scenario Two:** Vertically link the federal and states' Essence Tracking Reports and Essence Meetings. The federal and states' responsibilities link vertically under one essence of protection. This is possible only because we are shifting from a power basis to a service basis.

The better approach is yet to be determined. Since the Twelve Visions Government will eventually become the first government NOT based upon power, rather upon service, either approach will be valid. The determination will be made upon **one** factor: *which approach provides the customer with the best service, the best value, the best protection!*

Imagine...a value-creating businesslike government built upon the value-creating breakthrough: the division of essence. The division of essence is the next evolution of the almighty division of labor. That next evolution lifts dead-end jobs of labor into open-ended jobs of value-creation for the ordinary working person. Imagine, *value creation* broken down into the workers' jobs by the ultimate division of labor that includes not just labor, but *the mind* as well, the superior *division of essence*. That division of essence in business has proven to bring forth the most creative, breakthrough-values, often by ordinary workers! And that is exactly what we want from our government: *the most creative, breakthrough-protection.*

We want no weapon to be able to penetrate our country; we want no criminal or terrorist to be able to violate our citizens. The division of essence ignites every man and woman's creative mind throughout the entire business and, in this case, will bring us what we want for our country: breakthrough protection and abiding peace.

I created the division of essence for maximizing value creation while pulling in *all workers'* creativity. The division of essence is a powerful value-creating force that will thrive in the purely free Twelve Visions World. The division-of-essence structure of business will cause the creation of the most amazing consumer values in all areas of life including medicine. And now, we will bring that division of essence to the structure of protection. We will enjoy the best protection ever achieved on our planet, even during a world of escalating terrorism. And people will gladly and voluntarily pay for abiding peace, health, prosperity and happiness.

As I said, the new division-of-essence structure of protection will adopt tools such as Essence Tracking Reports and Essence Meetings. I will not go into the details here, but you can fully understand those terms as well as Movement Heads, mind/body mini-movements of protection, their mini-movement heads — those at the state and federal levels — by reading *The Neothink® System*. That Neothink® Manuscript explains all those terms, used below, and the value-creating power of the division of essence.

*Neothink® Control*

The Movement Heads will receive the weekly and monthly Essence Tracking Reports from their mini-movements under them. Those tracking reports are the Movement Heads' puzzle pieces. The Movement Heads will snap those tracking reports together like puzzle pieces into the big Neothink® puzzle-picture. Then monthly, the Movement Heads will hold their Essence Meetings with their mini-movement heads. The three main Movement Heads of the United States Protection Service will be the persons with the big picture — the Neothink® puzzle-picture — of their respective movements, and they will guide each mini-movement head to best serve the big picture.

The three main Movement Heads — the heads of the three branches — carry enormous responsibility. They are the best at the movement they serve; they rise to the top through superior performance. They give invaluable big-picture guidance to their mini-movement heads at the federal level and to their fifty mini-movement heads at the state level (if the vertically-linked paradigm takes hold). Again, the Movement Heads receive their Essence Tracking Reports, snap together the big picture for their specific movements, and hold monthly Essence Meetings with their mini-movement heads in order to guide them through the big picture toward creating the best values — the best protection.

That big picture comes together from everyone's essence-work revealed on their Essence Tracking Reports, from everyone's creative efforts to best serve their chunks of essence of protection.

The three main Movement Heads will be selected by a board of directors. (I will explain the board of directors in a moment.) The board will select the three main Movement Heads, as in any successful business, based on performance. The board will select the three persons best suited to snap together the big picture and guide the mini-movement heads. Those three Movement Heads of 1) creating protection-only law, 2) executing protection-only law, and 3) interpreting protection-only law have the businesslike responsibility of providing America and her citizens with the greatest protection-performance ever known on Earth.

Similarly, the mini-movement heads of protection will earn their positions through performance. Remember, we are steadily replacing an intrusive, political government based on power with a citizen-friendly, businesslike government based on service — a comprehensive protection service aimed to please and to *earn* its keep.

Because of rapidly declining crime in the future Twelve Visions World, the cost of the protection-only government — your protection service — would continue to drop year after year. Someday, when the entire world population has evolved into the Twelve Visions World, the government — your protection service — might no longer be necessary. Government as we know it might become extinct.

Until then, the board of directors will select and assist the Movement Heads in their immense responsibilities. The board of directors will consist of nine persons with the most outstanding careers at serving the essence of government: three with the most outstanding careers in the legislative-protection movement, three with the most outstanding careers in the executive-protection movement, three with the most outstanding careers in the judicial-protection movement.

Those nine board members will advise the Movement Heads as they integrate and coordinate the three movements of government. Remember, there will be many mini-movement heads and three Movement Heads. Each Movement Head will receive Essence Tracking Reports from his or her mini-movement heads. The Movement Heads will snap together the national puzzle-picture for their specific movements and guide their mini-movement heads across the country. They will meet monthly for their all-important Essence Meetings where the Movement Heads give their mini-movement heads big-picture guidance and expectations. In turn, the three Movement Heads will submit their own national Essence Tracking Reports to the board — the nation's Leading Head. From those three Essence Tracking Reports, the Leading Head, the board, will snap together the final big puzzle-picture and, in turn, give the Movement Heads the final big-picture direction, guidance, and ultimate expectations.

The board of directors will be responsible for replacing board members when the time comes. The board will replace any Movement Head if performance permanently slips. Although the board will select the Movement Heads and advise and assist them, the hands-on Movement Heads *will be in charge* of their movements. With advice, big-picture direction, ultimate expectations, and possibly great pressure from the board, the Movement Heads will make the day-to-day decisions. Through clear bylaws, the Movement Heads can eventually be replaced. But, except for very specific circumstances (such as blatantly violating the Prime Law), they will make the final operating decisions until that day comes.

Since the Prime-Law Amendment guarantees no forced tax collection can ever exist — no IRS as we now know it and no Criminal Investigation Division — the people will have the legal option to withdraw from government protection...withdraw from government protection against force being used against them, their property, or their contracts. With that legal option to withdraw from government protection, the government would have to competitively provide a genuine value that people want to pay for. The government employees would have to work hard to offer a valuable service — ever-growing protection and peace. Again, people will pay for **real** protection and peace. They do not necessarily want to pay for what they get today.

For example, our police force today is not really a service of protection — of crime prevention. Today's police force simply follows up *after the crime*. We have crime *follow up*, not crime *prevention*. Thus, we really have no protection whatsoever, no elimination of *initiatory* force or *threat* of force. Our police — though no fault of their own — get involved only *after* the force occurred.

In tomorrow's Twelve Visions World, we will have **real** protection. The protection will be so good, in fact, we will want to pay for it. We will want to pay the relatively nominal cost for safety and peace. Movement Heads will oversee value-creating mini-movement heads who run the police force, the armed services, the judicial and prison systems, the legal work that will include filtering out bad law, revising law, creating civil and contract law, determining legitimate liability laws and punishment for violating laws. As a division-of-essence, value-creating protection service for the people, we the people will gladly offer our voluntary payment for a country of blissful peace, harmony, and prosperity.

As any value-producing institution, the board will keep their Movement Heads as long as they are the *most competitive* for bringing value — protection — to the people. Without forced tax collection, the government's value will be easily measured by the number of subscribers.

The Movement Heads of government will be the gatekeepers of our protection as laid down in the Prime Law. And every subscribed American will "own stock" in protection — in his or her protection. So, American individuals will be "stockholders" in their own protection. (A contract will be signed by the protection service with the people stating this stockholder relationship.) If the people were unhappy about the board's performance or any Movement Head's performance, they could call for a general vote of "stockholders" (i.e., subscribed Americans). Also, the board will have the prerogative to call a general "stockholder" vote in the rare scenario the board prefers the "stockholders" to decide whether or not to remove a Movement Head. The *specific choice* for replacement, however, will always fall upon the board.

Why will the board of directors ultimately be responsible for selecting the Movement Heads? As in any value-producing institution, the board members are closer to the company and its details than the stockholders. The board members know best who is most qualified to provide maximum value to their customers. Therefore, the board will select the Movement Heads. Proven value-creating *performance* — not corrupt election campaigns with deceptive propaganda — will select our Executive Movement Head, our Commander in Chief, for example. The massive election campaigns today are often designed to deceive a gullible public into voting for a particular candidate — into voting for an illusion. Those deceptions and illusions will be gone. Moreover, re-election fever will be gone along with its symptomatic, attention-getting lawmaking and spending programs that destroy our economy. (See the TVP Bylaws for a deeper look at selections versus elections.)

In tomorrow's Twelve Visions World, any time the people — the paying subscribers — grow discontent, they may call for a general vote to remove a board member or Movement Head. In such a rare scenario, the people tomorrow will not be caught up in propaganda and deceptions as they are during campaign season today. The people will know they are not happy about something specific and will use their power as "stockholders" in peace to effect a change. ...Each individual will be equal under *the Prime Law of Protection.* Thus, each individual will receive one vote.

Moreover, the board will call such a "stockholder" vote if it feels the people need or want it. Remember, the people can always withdraw without being criminals, if ever the need arose. If enough withdrew, a competitive service would rise to meet the growing demand. But that technicality would only exist in theory, for without a force-backed government, only rational decisions and the best actions for the people will continually occur. The gifts of life, the wealth, health, and peace described in *Superpuzzle* (1200 pages, Neothink® Society) will shower upon the people.

*Universal Wealth, Health, Peace*

## The Path Into The Twelve Visions World

The country is sinking into a catastrophic era. Over a quarter-century ago, I wrote about this catastrophic era. As I prophesied this coming catastrophic era in my literature published in the 1980s, I wrote that we were in a race, a race between rationality and irrationality.

Now as the catastrophic era falls upon us, rationality has lost the race. The problem is that rationality, reason, logic no longer register with the majority of people. Decades of media brainwashing, educational indoctrination and a mix of other problems particularly the rising rule of man in America have nullified the benevolent power of rationality, logic and reason.

Rationality just doesn't work anymore. What moves the majority now is: emotional and physical **urges**. That's right, primitive *urges* from the forces of nature moves us, direct us.

Now, I have written about this in my literature, about the forces of nature and about how two to three thousand years ago man leapt beyond nature into human consciousness, and how the forces of nature now wreak havoc in conscious man and his civilizations (see Vision Three in *Twelve Visions*).

Man is a conscious being, not an automatically reacting, unconscious animal. So those automatic controls, *those primitive urges*, those forces of nature will devastate mankind (if dominating and directing civilization). Unfortunately, the majority of people today are controlled by those forces of nature; they are controlled by those primitive urges.

For example, consider this primitive urge: we seek the path of least resistance. In nature, the animal spends the least amount of energy for the maximum meal, for example...maximizing food for the least amount of effort spent. That path of least resistance unfortunately still drives us today.

So, the majority of people vote for the politicians who appeal most to that path-of-least-resistance urge. The result is inevitable; the result is socialism and the redistribution of wealth, which will quickly destroy civilization, as we are seeing today.

In today's world, arguing socialism versus capitalism no longer works because that requires rationality and reason. Rationality, reason and logic no longer work. The ruling class has successfully numbed enough minds so that rationality, reason and logic are ineffectual. The ruling class has, over the decades, successfully reduced the voting majority to those primitive urges, those easy-to-manipulate and easy-to-control urges. By recognizing that fact, we suddenly realize how reasoning with people is futile.

Instead, we must win this battle of the urges by appealing to those primitive urges. Now that does not mean that we are going to abandon rationality, reason and logic. Rationality, reason and logic lead us to reality. And that is why, in the end, we can win this epic battle of good versus evil. Let me explain:

Our promises that appeal to people's urges amount to more than mere political rhetoric, otherwise known as failed promises. Our promises become fulfilled promises. That difference, *reality*, will increasingly shift the tide in our favor. Yes, our promises will appeal to the same urges, to those forces of nature controlling most people today. But I will summarize the difference...

Let us first look at what politicians do: they appeal to the urges, the forces of nature, the get-something-for-nothing, the instant gratification. They appeal to those path-of-least-resistance urges. How? Through illusions. Through non-reality. And how do they build those illusions?

As explained in my literature: politicians use *true facts*, true facts, out of context. So the unsuspecting, gullible public hears those true facts, and they are true, so how can the voting public argue with those facts? So politicians build illusions using true facts, *true facts*, ***out of context***.

Now the Twelve Visions Party is going to appeal to people's urges, those same instant-gratification, get-something-for-nothing urges, but in the background our plan is based on reality, not illusions. Indeed, we are going to have reason and logic behind us...but only in the background, the plan backing up our promises. Up front we are going to drive on the urges, appealing to those urges.

Consider the title of the TVP Platform: "Make All The People Rich, Including the Poor!" Throughout the Platform, I write about becoming a millionaire without lifting a finger. Indeed, we appeal to the primitive urges, the forces of nature, the path of least resistance, the get-something-for-nothing urges.

But here is the unbeatable power in our approach: we appeal to the urges, but behind it all, what we promise is real.

Let us look closer: in my literature I write about the personal computer revolution of the late 20th Century. That technological revolution revealed that when regulations are held back as they were in that particular industry (personal computers sprang up so fast the authorities did not know how to get a handle on regulating that phenomenon), the geniuses of society when given freedom move technology forward so rapidly that our buying power increases hundreds or thousands of times over. So in a few short years, one could purchase what, just a few years earlier, only multi-millionaires could purchase. That is *the reality* behind the TVP promise of living like a millionaire without lifting a finger.

Indeed, we can take that same computer-industry model and apply it throughout all industries. This TVP idea of removing regulations, removing the ruling class, setting free the geniuses of society to start this Great Technological Revolution for which the computer revolution was the forerunner...this TVP idea will win people over. Why? The urge to get rich is now backed by a plan of reality. The plan is real and sound. Instead of political rhetoric and empty promises, the people now see a real course to living the lives they were meant to live!

Addressing our urges, we have plans of reality. Backing up our promises, we have reason and logic. We are for real! The people will love our appeal to their urges, and they will *fall in love* with our plans of reality. Live like a millionaire without so much as lifting a finger, and it's real, it's real!

So there you have an example of appealing to the urges and delivering reality. What a powerful combination. In the long run, that one-two punch of the Twelve Visions Party will be unbeatable.

Now that live-like-a-millionaire claim should roll foremost off your tongue when you are in a public setting talking about the Twelve Visions Party; you should not necessarily concentrate on or talk too much about the Prime-Law Amendment or the Protection-Only Budget. For, the latter educates, the former stimulates. Instead, reality is *backing up* our appeal to the urges.

People will ask you, "How will you make all the people rich, including the poor?" Give them concise, short answers. Simple, easy and real. For example, give them the answer I just gave you. Say ordinary people today can buy computer power that, a few years ago, only millionaires could buy, and the Twelve Visions Party plans to spread that same model throughout all industries. So, in a few short years, everyone can have the buying power to purchase things that just a few years prior only millionaires could purchase.

I guarantee you, with that answer, you will spark their interest, and when they want to know more hand them this book and tell them to read it and pass it on.

Now pay close attention to this point: If you give a talk to a room full of a few hundred people and in your talk you describe the Prime Law of Protection and you talk about the Protection-Only Budget, after your talk, perhaps a handful of people will stick around to ask questions.

Now, if you give a talk to a room full of a few hundred people, and you talk about how in a few short years their buying power is going to multiply a hundred times, maybe a thousand times, and how they are going to, all of them including the poor among them, in a few short years live like millionaires, I guarantee you that afterwards, dozens of people will stick around to ask questions. I know because I have experienced it. That is the difference in today's world between stimulating versus educating. We must stimulate first, educate later.

The blend of stimulation and education, a blend of stimulating promises backed by educating logic is properly captured in our TVP National Platform.

Over generations, urges stimulated and manipulated by illusions from our ruling class have completely blocked out reality. That is why our country is sinking. The TVP combines urges with reality. This is the only way to defeat the ruling class.

## Scale of Importance

What you are participating in, the founding of the Twelve Visions World, is perhaps more important than the founding of our country. I will explain my very large statement:

The founding of America was a stunningly successful effort to move away from rule of man to rule of nearly flawless law, the U. S. Constitution. It was the most powerful move into freedom ever known on Earth resulting in unrivaled prosperity for two centuries. But at the time leading into the American Revolution, many Americans did not want to break from England. There was no imminent threat to the colonies' survival. Then Thomas Payne published *Common Sense*, which enlightened the colonists with a powerful sense of right versus wrong, and that publication ushered in the Revolutionary War.

But things were not so bad here before the war that brought us our independence and our brilliant system of government under the U. S. Constitution. By contrast, the imminent terrorist and economic threats to America today threaten the existence of our civilization as we know it. We stand in the doorway to a catastrophic era unlike America has ever seen. And those threats from nuclear, biological and chemical terrorist attacks to a major economic failure make our mission with the Twelve Visions Party and the Prime Law — that is, the founding of the Twelve Visions World — even more important to the survival of our civilization today than the founding of our country was to the survival of our civilization over two centuries ago. I say this not to lessen the magnificence of the founding of our country. I say this to bring perspective to the magnitude of what the founding of the Twelve Visions World means to all of us and our children. Indeed, our lives and the lives of our children depend on our success.

Only the Twelve Visions Party can stop the regression into the deadly rule of man.

All of us who are not part of the ruling class are in the same family, and we are all victims. And our children and their children will continue to be victims as this race backward into the rule of man continues.

The Twelve Visions Party is very simple, as follows:

Free all victims by replacing the rule of man with the rule of flawless law, the Prime Law. As you know, the Prime Law is the fundamental law of protection and is the cornerstone of a protection-only Twelve Visions Government.

Outside of the Twelve Visions Party, nothing on our planet can stop this victimization of our suppressed family. The ruling class suppresses all of us who are not in the ruling class (or not receiving key advantages from the ruling class). Indeed, we are all victims: the poor, the middle class, the wealthy business owners. Now that is important to know because we have been played against each other throughout history. We should — all of us should — live exhilarating lives, wealthy lives, doing what we love to do. All of us. And that wealthy life will come to all of us in the Twelve Visions World.

Instead of heading into a dangerous world of imminent terrorist attacks and economic collapse, we should and could be heading into a world of wealth, health, and peace. As the Twelve Visions Party gains traction, great emotions will rise among the populace as the people discover the beautiful lives they were robbed of. Those great emotions will be a mixture of exhilarating self-discovery and damning anger. The ruling class stole from us the exhilarating life we were meant to live.

### *Reason Is Dead*

Why is the Twelve Visions Party the only movement that can save us?

The answer is: *reason is dead.* Let me say it again, reason is dead. Reason as the guiding voice of humanity has died. Irrational wants and desires have replaced rational reason. Illusionary political rhetoric promising higher standards of living for no extra effort has killed reason.

Politicians killed reason in order to rule over mankind. As long as people do not reason, they will cluelessly vote for those who create get-something-for-nothing illusions. Without reason, demagogues can promise the people Utopia. Without reason, irrational wants and desires elect our ruling class and set up humanity's demise. Make no mistake: our demise has begun with the death of reason and the consequential rise of the rule of man and his controlling illusions.

With the many bright, even brilliant rational voices in our country today, the demise of our country continues. Reason as the guiding voice of humanity has died. Irrational wants and desires now guide the masses. Voices of reason fall upon deaf ears.

I will not go into the long explanation of how reason died, but briefly, it died in our educational system. You will understand the death of reason when you read *Superpuzzle*.

So without reason, what do we do? Our future is heading toward disaster. Our children and their children are heading toward a life of poverty and danger. And reason cannot save us. It seems as though nothing can save us. No one has the antidote to today's sinking America because reason is dead. Not even the most brilliant minds can stop our fall into disaster. We do see some pockets of reason, some attempts at rationality, but they are not enough to arrest the overwhelming problems.

The Twelve Visions Party is our savior. Suppose for a moment, the TVP appeals to people's get-something-for-nothing wants and desires, but instead of irrational illusions, what the TVP offers is rational reality. Reason does into even need to enter the equation. Not at first. We can circumvent reason and touch people's dreams and desires. As the reality of the TVP program washes away the illusions of political rhetoric, reason will reawaken in the people. Like bringing them out of a deep spell, the Twelve Visions Party Movement gradually resurrects reason. With the return and rise of reason comes the rise of the Twelve Visions World. But first we must circumvent reason. We must appeal to people's primitive urges, wants and desires. We must compete with the politicians.

Remember, reason as the guiding voice of humanity no longer lives. If it did, we would not be headed in the irrational direction that our country is headed.

If reason is no longer society's guiding voice, then what is? The primitive guiding voice seeking the path of least effort — unearned entitlements, handouts, redistribution of wealth — now guides society. Politicians stimulate and manipulate that primitive urge through unreal, unreasonable illusions.

So let us face reality that reason, as society's guiding voice, is dead. Let us face reality that unreasonable, unreal, path-of-least-effort urges now guide America. So our TVP will approach the public not with arguments based on reason, but with emotions based on people's primitive urges. Our strength, however, is this: when socialistic politicians appeal to people's get-something-for-nothing urges, those politicians offer illusions. They have offered failed illusions ever since the ruling class began three thousand years ago (their 3000-year-old secret). When TVP Visionaries appeal to people's get-something-for-nothing urges, by contrast, those TVP Visionaries do not offer illusions. They offer reality, as clearly demonstrated throughout this book.

In this war of good versus bad — of the non-ruling class versus the ruling class — we pursue our battle plan: we do not use reason up front. We do not educate. We, instead, *stimulate* people's wants and desires just like the socialists. Moreover, we let the country know we are all victims. In fact, we can outdo the politicians at their own game. But we are backed by reality, not illusions. The people will begin to see how it all works. They will begin to see we are offering reality, not political rhetoric. People will begin to see our fast track to riches is real, not empty promises, not political talking points.

So from the desire/want perspective, what are we offering the people? Here it is. Here's our face to the world: the TVP is the greatest get-rich phenomenon in the history of civilization. Shout it from the rooftops, sing it to the media, play it from your guitars. The Twelve Visions Party is the greatest get-rich program since civilization began. Give people the analogies they need to hear. Tell them about the computer revolution, a forerunner to the Great Technological Revolution with a TVP Protection-Only Government.

Give people all your compassion, genuine compassion for their unnecessarily suppressed, even wasted lives. Let them feel your genuine compassion for them; let them know you care, and they will stand by you. Energized, they will campaign for the Twelve Visions Party. They will fight for the Prime-Law Amendment. Even those who are not used to reason will stand up and cry out for the Prime Law!

*Compassion*

Can I walk into a living room of a lazy welfare recipient who refuses to get off his couch and get a job...and still feel compassion for him? Honestly, yes I can. For I know the bigger picture. I know he has been conned, and he has conned himself, and I know his *precious life* is wasting away. Soon it will be too late to change. His one and only precious moment will pass by, wasted, and then he will just pass away. Yes, I do feel deep compassion for him.

I feel saddened for the loss of the happy, exhilarated persons we were meant to be. Remember, we are all born as innocent human beings with the promise of a creation-driven life and exhilarating happiness. In a Twelve Visions World, our lives will be exhilarating and happy. Even the helpless welfare dependents will become motivated to make TVP successful and to remove the ruling class. All people, including the welfare poor, will get behind the Twelve Visions Party if they can live like millionaires. They will get behind the TVP Movement for removing initiatory force from those in power...from those political leaders whom we are led to believe we love...those who promise the poor great things but fail to deliver on those promises that are only illusions.

Once people feel the TVP's compassion and *their* possibilities, well then, in time they will back the Twelve Visions Party. The Twelve Visions are not merely political rhetoric, not empty promises. People will realize the TVP's Twelve Visions are real. The Twelve Visions World is everything the TVP promises. Reality backing the TVP's promises is unique and powerful. The Twelve Visions Party will steadily gain momentum until it becomes unstoppable.

We will deliver speeches and post messages and organize campaigns that say the Twelve Visions Party is the greatest get-rich program since the beginning of civilization...*remove the ruling class and everyone soon lives like a millionaire.* We will attract the masses through such stimulation. Remember, reason is dead. Eventually, as more people get introduced to the ideas in my literature, they will evolve their stimulated emotions into integrated reason. I hope to resurrect reason and save this crumbling world.

By understanding the nature of our approach, you will begin to see that we will pull just as many voters from the left as we do from the right. Many people with lower incomes are consumed with a sense of being victimized, although misdirected because of the illusion-masters, our politicians. The entire non-ruling class has been victimized and robbed of the life we were meant to live...the poor, the middle class, even the wealthy.

I want you to now embrace the fact that we have been victimized. It is part of our job and campaign strategy to make our victimization known: the ruling class suppresses the non-ruling class. We are all victims of the ruling class. I want you to know and emphasize that you have been victimized.

Those who have read my literature know how our lives have been suppressed by the ruling class. Without knowing better, we have been held down, all of us from the liberal left to the religious right, from the poor to the rich. We can, all of us, come together to eradicate the true culprit, the monster in disguise, the rule of man, the ruling class.

The monster in disguise played our family — the non-ruling class from the unemployed poor to the wealthy business owners — against itself for millennia. The ruling class has done this throughout all civilizations throughout history, but the victimizer is and always has been the ruling class. The ruling class is the family of society that exists by rule of man, by ruling over you and me. And America is falling into a deep, dark hole under the rule of man. We are falling into an underclass!

The Twelve Visions Party with its flawless Prime Law of Protection and its Protection-Only Budget is our only savior. Realize there has never been a pure Protection-Only Government, never in the history of the world. A pure Protection-Only Government backed by the Prime Law and Protection-Only Budget would quickly deregulate and depoliticize all industries. The many regulations and legislation that have nothing to do with protecting the individual from initiatory force would go away. In other words, all industries, for the first time, would experience pure freedom.

Our recent experience of nearly pure freedom of an industry was the personal computer industry of the late 20th Century and early 21st Century. The computer industry raced ahead without the burden of politicians and bureaucrats regulating and politicizing that industry. The result was computer buying power multiplying a thousand times.

*An Anomaly?*

Some people might say, "Well, that's just an anomaly due to the invention of the silicon chip." But we have seen cases of this throughout history, such as the example in Volume Three involving the railroad industry over a hundred years ago, before the development of high technology altogether. That example of James J. Hill and rising standards of living due to that one genius of society makes the problem of the ruling class clear. Indeed, while he was free to move ahead unburdened by the government, he made even the poor wealthy. But everything came crumbling down when the politicians and government regulators got a hold of that industry and destroyed it

And we have seen other examples throughout history, one being the car industry with the invention of the assembly line and the rapid acceleration of buying power. Mass production followed and spread throughout America and then the world because of the assembly line. Buying power multiplied throughout the car industry and then throughout other industries until the government stepped in with regulations and legislation, politicizing those American industries and reversing their prosperity explosions.

*Computer Revolution...Great Technological Revolution ...Health Revolution*

The personal computer industry was so unique and happened so quickly and moved so rapidly that bureaucrats and politicians just did not know how to get a handle on it to begin regulating and politicizing that industry. So it advanced very rapidly, and computer consumers became computer rich. That same phenomenon will spread throughout all industries with the Twelve Visions Party's Protection-Only Government. That same freedom paradigm will play out in every industry as the Twelve Visions

Party and its Prime-Law Amendment and Protection-Only Budget deregulate and depoliticize every industry. By swiping away the thick web of regulations and legislation with the Prime-Law Amendment and the Protection-Only Budget, all American industries will become as free as the computer industry was to race ahead. Prices will plunge. Buying power will multiply ten times, a hundred times, a thousand times.

The medical and health industries will be no exceptions. Only the Twelve Visions Party can swipe away the thick web of regulations and legislation entangling and paralyzing the medical and health industries (via the Prime-Law Amendment and Protection-Only Budget). With the heavy regulatory and legislative burdens gone, those industries will soar. New medical technologies will soar, and prices will plunge. Research and development programs will flourish. Indeed, more research money than ever before will pour into those medical research and development programs because the investment risks will fall dramatically with the thick web of government regulations and legislation out of the way.

Medical breakthroughs will happen beyond anything the world has ever seen. Costs will continue to plunge. Complicated diseases will be eradicated in that never-before-seen environment of pure freedom. We will live increasingly disease-free lives and much longer lives with higher quality of life for a fraction of the cost.

With that insight into the health and medical industries, I will reveal something about the Twelve Visions Party that I have never before made public.

First, a little background about myself: I am known for a few things. I am co-founder of the award-winning engineering marvel, the Grand Canyon Skywalk...the horseshoe shaped glass bridge that juts out seventy feet over the edge of the Grand Canyon. Some builders believed that the engineering of this glass bridge cantilevered over the side of the Grand Canyon would not be possible. And I will say this: yes it would have been impossible if not for Neothink®.

Neothink® is a new way of using our minds that I discovered in the early 1980s and developed in my first book *Neo-Tech® Control* published in 1985 followed by my 740-page *Neo-Tech®*

*Business Control* published in 1989. Neothink® makes seemingly impossible goals such as the Grand Canyon Skywalk possible, tangible and real.

The Platform of the Twelve Visions Party is entitled, "Make All People Rich, Including the Poor". Now we know just how impossible that is in today's world. But it is possible with the Twelve Visions Party that rose from Neothink®. Again, Neothink® is a new way of using our minds, using integrated thinking to achieve marvels the world has never seen before — from engineering marvels such as the Grand Canyon Skywalk to economic marvels such as the Twelve Visions World.

A single reading of the TVP Platform reveals exactly how the Twelve Visions Party will make all the people rich including the poor. Instead of political rhetoric, our Neothink® approach is easy to follow and self-evident.

To spread Neothinking® throughout our world, I founded the Neothink® Society and its growing Neothink® Clubhouses where my Neothink® Manuscripts can be discussed and their beneficial and practical advantages can be taught. We also hold TVP meetings at those Neothink® Clubhouses.

I have written over a dozen Neothink® Books, thousands of pages of Neothink® literature. My 2800-page magnum opus *The Prime Cure* reveals my master-plan, my complete life-goal, which I am leading up to here.

Instead of trusting and following our leaders, with Neothink® we become self-leaders. We integrate facts, concepts, events together like pieces of a puzzle. As those pieces come together, a puzzle-picture begins to form, a picture never created before, never seen before. *The Prime Cure* brings together a complete picture of a world never seen before, our yet-to-be known Twelve Visions World. That Twelve Visions World will bring us happy and prosperous lives, the lives we were meant to live. That Twelve Visions World is my master plan in life; I want to accomplish that master plan in my lifetime.

The Seven Treatments in *The Prime Cure* contain the puzzle pieces needed in our world to bring about the Twelve Visions World. I am creating in our world those puzzle pieces. Treatment Three, the political movement, is one of the puzzle pieces.

Indeed, the TVP Movement, that is, the Twelve Visions Party, the Prime-Law Amendment, the Protection-Only Budget — this political movement — is one of the key puzzle pieces to the Superpuzzle that brings us the Twelve Visions World.

The Neothink® Movement — my Neothink® Manuscripts, Neothink® Society, Neothink® Clubhouses, Neothink® Business Alliance — is also one of the key puzzle pieces to the Superpuzzle that brings us the Twelve Visions World.

Today, I will make public the third key puzzle piece to the Superpuzzle. Those who have read Treatments Five, Six, and Seven of *The Prime Cure* know the third puzzle piece to snap into place. It would be useless without the two prior puzzle pieces already laid down — the TVP Movement and the Neothink® Movement.

Remember, the Twelve Visions World will bring us the wealthy, happy lives we would want to live *for a very long time*. The third major puzzle piece is the Neothink® anti-aging movement. My Association for Curing Aging is the third key puzzle piece to the Superpuzzle that brings us into the Twelve Visions World and, ultimately, the happy and wealthy life worth living far longer than we live today. Indeed, people will be so prosperous and happy they would want to live forever. Aging is the extremely complex disease of cellular degeneration, and it is much more complex to arrest than all forms of cancer and heart disease.

Today's highly regulated and politicized world renders this third puzzle piece impossible. But tomorrow's non-politicized purely free Twelve Visions World would accelerate this third puzzle piece.

This third puzzle piece is dependent on two critical puzzle pieces to be laid down before it, which I have now done: the TVP Movement and the Neothink® Movement. Let us see how my two prior puzzle pieces generate demand and supply:

Puzzle piece number 1: Demand. In today's suppressed world, the ruling class suppresses the non-ruling class. Life for the ordinary person loses excitement, achievement, growth. In a suppressed politicized world there is minimal desire or demand for substantially longer life. Through my Neothink® Books, the Neothink® Society and Neothink® Clubhouses, however, I give people the tools to rise from a suppressed, used-up body in the labor force to an exhilarated, self-leading value creator. I open the door to true happiness, to the creation-driven life we were meant to live. Those exhilarated, happy people love life, and they desire, *they demand*, longer life.

Puzzle piece number 2: Supply. In today's politicized world, the ruling class politicizes and regulates the non-ruling class. Rapid medical progress is impossible. Only in a truly free, non-politicized environment could rapid progress against the most complex diseases including aging occur. Only with the pure freedom provided by the Protection-Only TVP Government could the never-before-imagined size and scope of research and rapid progress against aging occur. Only in the Twelve Visions World can the supply of longevity meet the growing demand. The cure to aging is a cause-and-effect formula that is elegantly simple as follows:

**The demand** of the happy people *wanting to live longer* would be overwhelming in the Twelve Visions World, a world without suppression filled with creative, wealthy and healthy citizens living in peace. **The supply**, the progress against the disease of aging, would be free to flow and to rise to the demand. With such demand-and-supply in the Twelve Visions World, the cure to aging would follow.

Indeed, you can see why my two puzzle pieces had to be laid down first: Number one, my Neothink® Movement, Neothink® Books, Society, Clubhouses to lift people from their great suppression in order to discover the self-leaders' creation-driven lives of exhilaration and happiness. They love life and demand longer life. And two, my TVP Movement, the Twelve Visions Party, Prime-Law Amendment, Protection-Only Budget to depoliticize America and provide the pure freedom that will allow for anti-aging research to rapidly advance.

So, after thirty years and thousands of pages of Neothink® literature completed, with my Neothink® Society and Clubhouses founded, with my Twelve Visions Party gaining traction, I am now ready to pursue the third puzzle piece to the Twelve-Visions-World Superpuzzle. I am now ready to pursue the Association for Curing Aging.

The blueprints of my master plan to bring us the Twelve

Visions World are in Treatments Five, Six, and Seven of *The Prime Cure*. Those three treatments took me nine years to create after over two decades of preparation while creating Treatments One through Four. Those latter three treatments provide the course into the Twelve Visions World. Happiness, wealth, health, peace and longevity are synonymous with the Twelve Visions World.

After reading Treatments Five, Six, and Seven, one realizes that my Twelve Neothink® Visions are possible. Similar to the Grand Canyon Skywalk, the Twelve Visions are possible through Neothink® and through the Twelve Visions Party — the two causal puzzle pieces to the Twelve Visions World where people are not suppressed, where people are creative and living the exhilarated happy lives they were meant to live...where they are wealthy, healthy, living in safety and peace and where they want to live much longer lives...and where the geniuses of society are working hard and unburdened to bring those happy citizens longer and longer quality-filled lives.

With the two casual puzzle pieces launched — the Neothink® Movement and the TVP Movement — I launch my third puzzle piece that has been planned for over 30 years: The Association for Curing Aging.

Our visionaries are serious about bringing a new world to civilization, a world full of prosperity and happiness and wealth, health, peace and longevity that heretofore would be considered impossible. Through Neothink® and TVP, we can bring this new world to America and then to the entire planet. The Twelve Visions World is our impossible glass bridge that will allow us to walk the sky. You know, our logo at the Grand Canyon Skywalk is, "I did it!" Someday my visionaries and I will say, "We did it!" ...We will save America, and then the world. The Twelve Visions Party is *the party*, the *only party* that will bring us wealth, health, peace and longevity.

*Universal Wealth, Health, Peace*

## Our Appeal to Everyone

I meet some famous, influential people in the Hollywood entertainment scene. And, as you know, Hollywood celebrities can be very opinionated when it comes to politics; so much so that Hollywood celebrities often will not associate with those who oppose their political views.

I recently had dinner with a living legend in the music industry. I will not use his name here because he does not know I am revealing this story. But he is a huge President Clinton and President Obama supporter; one of the largest donors to their campaigns. On the other hand, I recently had dinner with a famous actor, whom you would know, but he is the rare Hollywood conservative who laments President Bush's absence. As you can see, I associate with people on opposite ends of the political spectrum.

Now both those Hollywood celebrities know about my political movement. Yet, in both cases they deeply like me and look forward to spending time with me. That is unusual with those very opinionated...I'll even go as far as to say, politically-obsessed individuals.

So let us take a deeper look at this. Why do those politically obsessed celebrities consider me a close friend when my political movement dismisses both of their political obsessions as the destructive, suppressive ruling class pushing the non-ruling class down into an underclass? The answer unveils our broad appeal with our TVP approach.

To get the answer, let me first tell you why I like those two individuals and why I know they both belong in our TVP Movement as opposed to being devoted Obama and Bush supporters.

You see, I clearly understand the separation of the ruling class and the non-ruling class. I clearly see the two families of all societies. I see both the loving, non-ruling class that exists by adding values to society versus the power-hungry ruling class that exists by taking values from society.

By clearly seeing that dichotomy, I can see that these two good people are part of our loving family, members of the non-ruling class adding net values to society. By clearly seeing who they really are, seeing through their misguided support of the ruling class, I realize their support is not support for a net-drain ruling class. Instead, they support *the illusions* of that ruling class. Now that is the key here. They are not really supporting Obama, Clinton, Bush. They are supporting *the illusions* of the ruling class. They are supporting *illusions.* As do most people, as do your own families and friends, these two good individuals who are part of our benevolent non-ruling-class family, support complex, sound-good ruling-class illusions without realizing what they are doing, without realizing they are supporting that which hurts society, hurts them, their children, their families. Because these two non-ruling-class value creators support that which hurts society and their loved ones, they too are victims of the ruling class.

They would never support the ruling class if they understood what is explained in my literature and understood that those political structures destroy their children's and their grandchildren's futures. My friends support *illusions.* They unsuspectingly support something harmful to society. Those two good individuals are sadly victims and do not even know it. Those two famous individuals are victims just as our own family and friends who adamantly support the ruling class, *whether the left or the right.*

By understanding who those good people are — i.e., value contributors to society who are victims — you can understand my compassion and patience. In turn, they deeply like me even though I do not agree with their political obsessions. With the background I just gave you, the reason they deeply like me becomes clear, and as I explain this to you, we are all going to project the same understanding and patience for people in the non-ruling class as part of our own loving family, the non-ruling class.

So, within good people such as those two famous individuals who are misguided, within good people you know who are misguided, within all good people who contribute values to society, there is a common denominator deep inside that we all carry: **the child of the past**.

When we were children, we looked toward the future and imagined our lives as bigger than life, achieving major accomplishments, making major contributions to society and feeling the pride and exhilaration that comes with such a creation-driven life. But now, for reasons I explain in my writings, we as adults live in a less than exhilarating, smaller than life existence. Most of us are trapped in routine ruts, and we increasingly feel we missed out on the life we should have lived. Most people are living less than the life they once imagined, the life they were meant to live.

Even famous actors and music legends often feel they could have done something more with their lives. Whereas our adult selves eventually resign to the lives we are living, deep inside our child of the past still looks for that something more to our lives. That goes for all of us in this world suppressed by a ruling class. The child of the past within is looking for that bigger than life existence filled with exhilaration. Everyone in the non-ruling class has that child of the past deep inside wanting to rise to its human potential.

And here is a secret that I inject into all my literature: I reach inside and touch the child of the past, hiding deep within every good person, and that answers why those celebrities in the entertainment world, the most unlikely people who are married to their political views, why they respond so favorably to me once they get to know me and know about me. Their attraction is the same as your attraction; their child of the past is reaching out for me, and I feel that affinity when I am with them. It is very clear what is happening. They will not go so far as to walk away from their political leaders. But the TVP seed has been planted, and it will grow within them over time.

Ask yourself, what do we visionaries really offer? Rising from everything I have written over the past thirty years, we offer that bigger-than-life existence that our child of the past deep within still hopes for and never stops searching for. Underneath it all, we are reaching deep within, reaching for that child of the past.

You know wonderful people who will turn to you and passionately say how they support Obama or Bush (or whomever is the latest). They are prepared to bond or argue depending on who you support. Instead, look at those people and love each and every one of them for being a good person in our valuecontributing, non-ruling-class family. They are merely caught up in the illusions of our ruling-class leaders on both sides.

Your good friends do not know it, but they support illusions that make them victims. They support the illusions of the ruling class. Now think about that: they support illusions. They have no idea that they support harm toward their loved ones. That makes them all victims, and with that insight you can look at them with compassion. They support harm toward their loved ones. With that understanding, with compassion and patience and tolerance, you can reach out your hand to each and every one of them and invite them to look into something different, something that will bring them a worthy and wealthy life, something that will greatly benefit their loved ones.

Just remember, they are in the same family — the loving non-ruling class, and they are pushed down by the ruling class, by those they support. Invite them to take a look at a new world. In the Twelve Visions World, we will all live in the wealthy elite class under the Prime Law of Protection as opposed to living under a ruling class with all of us sinking into an underclass. Even today's poor will rise in that new world and live in the wealthy elite class.

By the way, I am slightly misusing the word "elite". "Elite" indicates a societal separation, such as the highest class of society as opposed to the lower class. However, the lower class of society goes away in the Twelve Visions World. I am slightly misusing "elite" because there will no longer be a lower class. Everyone is going to be in the wealthy elite class by today's standards. In tomorrow's Twelve Visions World, there is not going to be an elite class versus an underclass separation. Everybody is going to live in the wealthy class. The problem now is: no one can see that wealthy world because we have nothing in history to compare it to. The best we have are little nuggets of examples that I have previously stated: We have the computer industry; we had the assembly line breakthrough in the early 1900's when we broke through into mass production and saw a rapid acceleration of standards of living. We had the James J. Hill example in Volume Three. But, perhaps the best example is the founding of our country when we largely broke away from the ruling class and rose to unrivaled prosperity.

Those are closed-nugget examples. We have never had a pure example to follow, including early America. So this great wealth is hard for people to understand.

In early America, the non-ruling class strikingly broke away from the ruling class with the formation of our country. Consequently, we rose to great prosperity. The Declaration of Independence and the U.S. Constitution rose from non-ruling-class natural law and nearly eradicated ruling-class man-made law. But whereas the Declaration of Independence and the U.S. Constitution rose from natural or non-ruling-class law as opposed to man-made or ruling-class law, the founding fathers missed the fundamental natural law of protection — the Prime Law of no initiatory force. Without the fundamental natural law of protection, the consummate protector of the non-ruling class, without that Prime Law, well, the ruling class would creep back in.

And ruling-class man-made law did creep back into America, for ruling-class man-made *agenda law* by nature requires initiatory force. Indeed, man-made agenda law must force the non-ruling class to obey the ruling class' agenda. Let me say that again: Man-made agenda law must force the non-ruling class to obey the ruling class' agenda.

Without the Prime Law of no initiatory force, rule of man would return and grow like a disease, and eventually it would arrest the productive elements of society and start leading the non-ruling class down into an underclass as we are experiencing today.

The Twelve Visions Party is first and foremost about bringing the Prime-Law Amendment to the U. S. Constitution along with the Protection-Only Budget. The Protection-Only Budget is the Prime-Law Budget. It is a budget that abides by the Prime Law of Protection. We need that Protection-Only Budget now, even before the Prime-Law Amendment, to save our nation from bankruptcy and civil unrest.

The Twelve Visions Party will eradicate the societal disease, the rule of man, through the Prime-Law Amendment and Protection-Only Budget. The ensuing pure freedom and Great Technological Revolution will bring us — all of us including the poor — great prosperity and an exhilarating bigger-than-life existence.

The Twelve Visions Party is different than both political parties in that it is the party **not** of the ruling class and their man-made agenda laws; the Twelve Visions Party is the party of the non-ruling class and its natural Prime Law of Protection. It rescues all those trusting, innocent faces who passionately turn to you and to me and support the illusions of the ruling class.

People cannot know what it will be like to live under the Prime Law of Protection as opposed to the ruling class. As I said, there are no pure examples. But if people had a clue, if their child of the past had a clue, they would shift their allegiance to the Prime Law and its Protection-Only Budget. With a clue of what the Twelve Visions World would be like, their child of the past would sense that the Twelve Visions World is where it belongs.

The Twelve Visions Party Platform, the Twelve Visions Party web sites, and the TVP radio shows give people a clue. This book gives people that clue. My literature gives people and their child of the past inside that clue they need. So, we do have everything we need right now. But we need to get this clue out there in large numbers, and this is where I am going to turn to you to give those in your community the clue.

The Twelve Visions Party with its Prime Law is in place; the TVP is here as an idea whose time has come. We must communicate this idea in a stimulating way to our communities. People need to know what life would be like in a civilization living under the Prime Law as opposed to living under the ruling class as we do now, sinking into an underclass. The direction we are heading now is dangerous. It could be catastrophic. But under the Prime Law of no initiatory force and, therefore, no ruling-class laws, everyone including today's poor would live like millionaires. ...Pass this book on to a loved one or friend to read.

Volume Five

Keep Us In Bliss

# THE GUARANTEE

## BYLAWS

*SETTING FREE CIVILIZATION:*

*ERA OF THE NON-RULING CLASS*

*Universal Wealth, Health, Peace*

# Bylaws of the Twelve Visions Party®

Adopted July 2009

Last Mark Hamilton Update: July 2012

## The Prime Law*

(The Fundamental Law of Protection)

### Preamble

*The *purpose* of human life is to prosper and live happily.

*The function of government is to **provide the conditions** that let individuals fulfill that *purpose*.

*The Prime Law **guarantees those conditions** by forbidding the use of initiatory force, fraud, or coercion by any person or group against any individual, property, or contract.

### Article 1

No person, group of persons, or government shall initiate force, threat of force, or fraud against any individual's self, property, or contract.

### Article 2

Force is morally-and-legally justified only for protection from those who violate Article 1.

### Article 3

No exceptions shall exist for Articles 1 and 2.

*The Prime Law is the fundamental, natural law of protection (that directs all decisions and actions of the Twelve Visions Party); the Prime Law may not be amended.

*The Neothink® Movement*

BYLAWS

## Table of Contents

## PREAMBLE: PRECIOUS NEWBORN

The Twelve Visions Party is an unlikely, precious phenomenon that has steadily risen over decades. First the Prime Literature had to be completed – thousands of pages of literature that develops the idea system and application systems upon which a new world, a much better world, the Twelve Visions World would rise. Decades of work went into developing the Prime Literature that idealizes the Twelve Visions World. The Prime Literature provides the thinking tools and applications to free civilization from subjugation...from political leaders and their ruling class pushing America down. With the Prime Literature in place, we are now ready to actualize the better world in which there is no rule of man, no ruling class. There is only a Prime Law we all live by. With the completion of the Prime Literature idealizing the Twelve Visions World comes the next phase – the phase we have now begun – of actualizing that better world through the Twelve Visions Party. This phase, patiently awaited for decades, requires safely shepherding this vulnerable newborn party safely into the harsh political world. With our success, civilization shall no longer be subjected to the rule of man, living under a ruling class. Subservience shall be eradicated and replaced with absolute freedom as all men and women live with invincible individual rights under the Prime Law. By freeing the subservient class – freeing the citizens and the geniuses of society among them – standards of living will soar as described in the National Platform *How To Make All the People Wealthy, Including the Poor*. The TVP Platform and Bylaws are groundbreaking documents changing the way political parties have behaved and misbehaved since the beginning of this great country.

## ARTICLE 1: NAME

These articles shall govern the association known as the "Twelve Visions Party," hereinafter in the Bylaws referred to as the TVP.

## ARTICLE 2: DURATION

The TVP shall exist until all objectives are accomplished.

## ARTICLE 3: PURPOSE

The TVP has one purpose: to bring about an initiatory-force-free, protection-only, service-based government via the Prime-Law Amendment and Protection-Only Budget, forever ending the age-old power-based government and its virulent force-backed rule of man, forever depoliticizing America (and eventually the entire world), thus setting free the geniuses of society, launching the wealth of mankind as described in the TVP Platform.

## ARTICLE 4: PROCESS

I. **The Presidential Election:** The National Executive Committee (Article 11) and the National Committee (Article 13) shall put forth a concentrated drive toward the election of a TVP President and Vice President and shall integrate and coordinate the state-level affiliates (as defined in Article 8) to organize support of the process at both the national and state levels. With the success of Article 4, Section I, the TVP President shall submit to Congress the Protection-Only Budget and the Prime-Law Amendment to the U.S. Constitution (as described in the National Platform).

II. **The Great Replacement Program:** The National Executive Committee and the National Committee while integrating and coordinating the state-level affiliates shall put forth a concentrated drive toward the Great Replacement Program: that is, replacing career politicians with working people, replacing the political ruling class with the working non-ruling class – replacing republicans and democrats with visionaries who have signed the TVP contract binding the visionaries to the Prime Law. The success of Article 4, Sections I and II will bring down the rule of man, for with swelling political and public support, the TVP President shall submit (and congress shall pass) the Protection-Only Budget (i.e., the Prime-Law Budget) in its entirety and rally overwhelming support for the Prime-Law Amendment to the U.S. Constitution (as described in the National Platform) to be ratified by the States.

III. **The Great Displacement Program:** With the success of Article 4, Sections I and II, the TVP President and Vice President and Cabinet Heads (with support from TVP members of Congress) shall orchestrate the dismantling of the federal bureaucracy that has nothing to do with protection of its citizens, coordinate the displacement of its resources including the Great Sale of government assets (that have nothing to do with protection) to the private sector...government assets including federal land that serve not the Prime Law of Protection. The Executive Branch shall shrink its size and focus to one laser-like purpose: the protection of its citizens as defined by the Prime Law. Revenues from the Great Sale shall pay off Social-Security obligations with interest and pay down the national debt.

IV. **The New Governing Dimension:** The TVP President and Vice President, TVP Cabinet Heads, TVP members of Congress shall oversee the transition into the new governing dimension of NO initiatory force as described in the Platform. That Twelve Visions Government operating under the Prime Law shall leap from a destructive power-basis to a productive service-basis – from a destructive ruling class to a productive protection service as described in the Platform.

V. **The End of Rule of Man:** With the ratification of the Prime-

Law Amendment, the government may no longer initiate force of any kind – not through laws, regulations, or litigation. That new-dimension Twelve Visions Government could never again hold back the geniuses of society, who will now make our standards of living soar. Ending the rule of man launches the wealth of mankind. Everyone will become wealthy, including the poor.

## ARTICLE 5: THE PILLARS AND THE PLATFORM

The Prime-Law Amendment and the Protection-Only Budget (described in the National Platform) are the two pillars upon which the Twelve Visions Party stands. The timeless TVP Platform demonstrates how the pillars will bring us universal wealth, health, and peace. All people will be wealthy, including today's poor. The TVP Platform is *the* document to defeat the deeply flawed, powerful political structure in America today.

## ARTICLE 6: PRIME LITERATURE FOUNDATION

The Prime Literature presents us with a world governed by The Prime Law as opposed to man. The founder of the TVP and author of the Prime Literature, Mark Hamilton, has for over thirty years developed the Prime Literature Foundation upon which this movement is built and the Visions toward which this movement is headed. Mark Hamilton's goal to dramatically improve civilization through the political process as described in the National Platform demands deep and wide integrations beyond what most citizens know. Visionaries interested in office must read his Prime Literature and gain confidence and faith in his vision based on his thousands of pages of written works, most notably his magnum opus *The Prime Cure* (2800-pages, Neothink® Society). Without the big picture as seen in his writings, it is easy to misunderstand and misuse this political movement and political party; it is also easy to become frustrated, rebellious, even destructive to this precious and vulnerable movement...this movement to rescue America and then the world from civilization's disease: the rule of man. Always protecting the TVP, the National Executive Committee (Article 11) shall select officers who most deserve their positions based on the effort and performance they have put forth *and* based on their integration with the Prime Literature Foundation and its big picture...officers who will grow this tender political movement into a strong, unstoppable movement whose time has come.

## ARTICLE 7: SELECTIONS VS. ELECTIONS

I. Major problems in politics arise from the election process. The election process creates "vote-gathering politicians" who cause severe harm to society (described in the Platform) in order to win or buy votes from substantial segments of the population. Indeed, election and re-election fever create win-at-all-costs purposeful distortions of reality and convincing illusions among politicians prior to and while in office, while in power, which ultimately ushers in the destructive rule of man with his illusions of "social good". As good as it may feel to vote, elections and campaigns (and actions taken while in office for re-election) based on half-truths, deceptions and illusions enable politicians to jump into positions of power they did not earn, or worse, to abuse power they now have. In the Twelve Visions World, positions will be earned based on value/effort/performance (not on campaigns) as in any value-producing business.

II. "Free elections" is a concept needed for representation only because we live under a force-backed government. One can understand this more after reading the Platform. If society embraces the Prime Law and removes initiatory force through the Prime-Law Amendment, then elections and representation become unnecessary and obsolete. Performance and results replace elections and campaigns. Indeed, in the Twelve Visions World, positions in government will be filled by performance and results as described in the Platform, not by elections and campaigns...just as in value-producing businesses. In a businesslike setup, where services are paid for voluntarily and not paid under coercion and force, positions and promotions are filled based on competent performance and results, not on campaign promises and illusions. For example, value-producing businesses do not hold elections for their positions. Representative democracy needs representation because we live under a pay-by-force government – under the rule of man. Without a pay-by-force system, we will not worry about representation because we simply withdraw pay if the service is unsatisfactory. So-called representation gets replaced by real results, real value, *real value exchange*. Good performance and value replaces representation when the Prime-Law Amendment becomes law.

III. Within our own TVP, we will begin a post-Prime-Law-Amendment structure, defined in these bylaws. As a businesslike structure, the TVP's National Executive Committee (NEC) is the administrative leading head (*leading head* is described in Mark Hamilton's *Neothink® Business System*).

IV. The NEC shall select the TVP Presidential and Vice Presidential candidates in lieu of caucuses and primaries (see details in Article 17). When the time comes to replace or fill a vacated National Executive Committee seat, including the National Chairperson, the NEC shall select the officer based on performance – on real results and value. The same applies to the Executive Committees of all TVP affiliates. We will break from the "free election" representation model that brings about campaigns, deception and rule of man. Instead, we now transition to the post-Prime-Law-Amendment businesslike environment of performance, effort and value. TVP Presidential and Vice Presidential candidates, state and local candidates, officers in the National Executive Committee, officers in the State Executive Committees and in all affiliate committees shall be selected based on the effort/value they have delivered (not on empty promises they make). Performance, effort and value – not campaigns, promises and deception – is how we shall internally run our political party and how we shall select our candidates and officers. We shall require all TVP affiliates to do the same. Flaw-filled man harbors self-indulging agendas and, when given the opportunity through illusion-based, election-based politics, would devastate the TVP political movement. Those problematic possibilities get cut off in a businesslike, promoting-on-effort-and-value system. In our case, effort and value also includes integrating the big picture in Mark Hamilton's writings and taking to heart the sole purpose of the TVP: to depoliticize America by removing initiatory force as stated in Article 3 and described in the National Platform. The Executive Committees shall determine the people who best meet those requisites of effort, value, integration. The national, state, and local Executive Committees shall select officers for their respective committees as defined in Article 11 and shall select their candidates as defined in Article 17.

V. The TVP shall NOT ever entertain the election process to determine its candidates and officers (such as the initial, erroneous idea of delegates electing the National Chairperson). As any value-creating business, the officers are selected based on proven performance, big-picture integration, effort and value, not on campaign promises. Selections may come from within or from without of the TVP Committees as long as the selection is a visionary who has signed the TVP Contract. The National, State, and Local Executive Committees shall select their officers and candidates through a majority vote of the respective Committee members as set down in these bylaws and their bylaws. The Executive Committees shall act as "Board of Directors" in their respective jurisdictions. A majority vote of the entire Executive Committee is needed to approve a new officer and to select a candidate. A majority vote of the entire Executive Committee is needed to remove an officer (the officer in question participates in this vote).

## ARTICLE 8: AFFILIATES

I. No person, group or organization may use the name "Twelve

Visions Party" or "TVP" or any confusingly similar designation except the TVP or an organization to which the TVP grants affiliate status or as otherwise provided in these Bylaws.

II. The National Executive Committee shall charter the state-level affiliates from qualifying organizations requesting such status in each state. An organization that wishes to become a state-level affiliate shall present a Declaration of Intent to represent the TVP in their State. Affiliate status shall be granted only to those organizations that adopt the Prime Law, the State Bylaws, and State Platform. The National Executive Committee shall grant or deny state-affiliate status.

III. The potential state-level affiliate officers must demonstrate an intimate understanding of the TVP, its purpose and vision, the big picture as seen through the National Platform and through Mark Hamilton's Prime Literature, the Post-Prime-Law-Amendment Structure of the TVP Bylaws, the concept of performance/effort/value/results replacing campaigns/promises/deceptions/illusions. Businesslike selections in TVP replace political elections. Moreover, the potential state-level affiliate officers must understand that self-indulging "big political ideas" must be replaced with one simple idea: an initiatory-force-free America – a depoliticized America – as defined in Articles 3 and 4 and developed in the National Platform. The potential state-level affiliate officers must demonstrate a deep understanding that the TVP is not a typical political party. TVP is the party to ultimately disintegrate typical political parties. No off-message showboating or power grabs are tolerated in the TVP; no "strong *political* leaders" are tolerated in the TVP; just a disciplined focus on depoliticizing America by bringing about an initiatory-force-free government through the Protection-Only Budget and the Prime-Law Amendment is welcomed in the TVP. Again the TVP is NOT typical politics and is NOT a typical political party. The TVP is breaking new ground with the objective to bring government into the new dimension of NO initiatory force and to, therefore, disintegrate the traditional dimension of force-backed politics. The National Executive Committee shall not grant state-level affiliate status until the potential state-affiliate officers fully grasp the purpose of the TVP as stated in Article 3 and developed in the National Platform. (These same points apply from state-level affiliates to all sub-affiliates.)

IV. The National Executive Committee shall not grant state-level affiliate status until that organization adopts and its potential officers grasp the state platform written by Mark Hamilton. The deeper understanding of the Prime Law and Protection-Only Budget and how to apply those pillars free from anyone's opinions or beliefs is not an easy concept to fully grasp. To successfully end initiatory force and depoliticize America – the *sole* purpose of the TVP – requires the founder's pure and simple state platform applying the pillars *free from underlying opinions or beliefs*. The TVP must prevent "good *political* ideas" (not the purpose of the TVP) and non-Prime-Law, contradictory messages from entering into the TVP. The National Executive Committee shall provide state-level affiliates with their state platform written by Mark Hamilton. That state platform shall be the state platform of all state affiliates. The success of the TVP depends upon the presentation of its ideas as well as the ideas themselves as articulated in Mark Hamilton's talk at the first TVP National Convention in Chicago, July of 2009 (as seen on the Neothink® Society YouTube Channel www.youtube.com/NeothinkSociety). The TVP Platforms effectively appeal to people's primitive urges while backing up those urges with reality, both at the national and state levels. (See more about the state platforms in Article 18, Section IV.)

V. The National Executive Committee shall not grant state-level affiliate status until that organization adopts and its potential officers grasp the state bylaws written by Mark Hamilton. The deeper understanding of the Post-Prime-Law-Amendment Structure of TVP must be fully grasped. Affiliate officers shall be selected via their bylaws, which are in the Post-Prime-Law-Amendment Structure and closely patterned after the TVP National Bylaws. (See more about the state bylaws in Article 18, Section V.)

VI. The TVP State Bylaws and Platforms shall present the Prime Law as a heading as seen on the TVP National Bylaws and Platform, with the following footnote: The Prime Law is the fundamental, natural law of protection (that directs all decisions of the Twelve Visions Party); the Prime Law may not be amended.

VII. There shall be no more than one state-level affiliate in any one state. Each state-level affiliate, in accordance with its own Bylaws and these Bylaws, shall determine who shall be its VIVs (Very Important Visionaries) invited to the Regular National Convention (Article 16, Section IV).

VIII. A state-level affiliate may charter sub-affiliates within the State, which shall entitle such sub-affiliates to use the name "Twelve Visions Party." Sub-affiliates shall be held to the same standards and demands put upon the state-level affiliates.

IX. No affiliate shall take any action inconsistent with the Prime Law or the Bylaws and all officers must sign and be held accountable to the TVP Contract (see National Platform).

X. The National Executive Committee shall have the power to revoke for cause the status of any state-affiliate by a majority vote of the National Executive Committee. A motion to revoke the status of a state-affiliate for cause must specify the nature of the cause for revocation.

## ARTICLE 9: A WORLDWIDE MOVEMENT

I. The TVP is a worldwide movement to bring civilizations out of their only-known poverty-bound dimension of initiatory-force-backed ruling classes into the never-before-known prosperity-bound dimension of no initiatory force, no ruling classes...from power-based governments to service-based governments worldwide.

II. This political movement out of civilization's traditional dimension of power-based, initiatory-force-backed rule of man into the new dimension of service-based, initiatory-force-free rule of Prime Law must be looked at differently than anything in the past. The structure of this movement must be looked at as a service-business, specifically a division-of-essence service-business (Article 14).

III. Borders and countries are needed to corral power and control for their respective ruling classes. Whereas the TVP must still operate country-by-country, the TVP itself will be set up now in a service-based structure, a division-of-essence businesslike structure to someday offer extraordinary protection service around the world...until the day that the need for protection no longer exists.

IV. In our division-of-essence structure (Article 14), the U.S. National Executive Committee (U.S. NEC) is the administrative leading head of the TVP (Article 11) and is the original TVP area of purpose (Article 14). The U.S. NEC replicates its knowledge while chartering and guiding other areas of purpose, specifically the state affiliates *and* the National Executive Committees of other countries, the international affiliates.

V. The emerging potential National Executive Committees of countries outside the United States are, in the division-of-essence structure, potential international affiliates. The U.S. NEC shall grant international-affiliate status using the same criteria enumerated in Article 8, with the following clarifications:

VI. The National Executive Committees of chartered international affiliates shall adopt, permanently, Mark Hamilton's timeless Prime-Literature National Platform, the fundamental expression of civilization's new dimension of no initiatory force, with its solo purpose of taking us into that new dimension of no initiatory force known as the Twelve Visions World. That National Platform shall be adjusted throughout by the country's National Executive Committee for obvious geographical and structural political differences. Those edits shall be turned into the U.S. NEC for review and approval, and after the U.S. NEC approves the edits, the U.S. NEC shall submit them to Mark Hamilton for his review and final adjustments and approval.

VII. The National Executive Committees of chartered international affiliates shall adopt, permanently, Mark Hamilton's timeless Prime-Literature National Bylaws, the fundamental expression of the post-Prime-Law-Amendment structure of a division-of-essence, service-based party, with the solo purpose of protecting its citizens. The Bylaws shall be adjusted throughout by the country's National Executive Committee for obvious geographical and structural political differences. Those edits shall be turned into the U.S. NEC for approval, and after the U.S. NEC approves the edits, the U.S. NEC shall submit them to Mark Hamilton for his review and final adjustments and approval.

VIII. The National Executive Committees of chartered international affiliates shall grant charters to their equivalent of "state-level affiliates" (and those "state-level affiliates" shall grant sub-affiliate status) using the same criteria enumerated in Article 8.

IX. The U.S. NEC shall decide by majority vote when to let go as leading head of another country's NEC and let it function autonomously as its country's leading head according to its bylaws.

X. The NECs of the different countries shall meet annually to share their progress, data, disastrous and successful campaigns...to help each other break through to the next level.

## ARTICLE 10: REGIONS

I. At this point there shall be no regional officers.

II. With growth of the TVP, regional committees will develop as part of a growing Division-of-Essence businesslike structure (Article 14), and this Article 10 shall be amended accordingly by the National Executive Committee.

## ARTICLE 11: THE NATIONAL EXECUTIVE COMMITTEE

I. The U.S. National Executive Committee is the Administrative Leading Head of the TVP, including the Administrative Leading Head of the state affiliates and international affiliates. The National Executive Committee's responsibilities are enumerated throughout the Articles of these Bylaws.

II. The National Executive Committee's Officers

A. There shall be seven officers as the Administrative Leading Head of the TVP known as the National Executive Committee.

B. The seven National Executive Committee Officers at the time of these Bylaws are:

1. Michael Dilworth (Chair)
2. Steve Fagan (First V. Chair)
3. Tom Cary (Second V. Chair)
4. Jill Reed* (Third V. Chair)
5. Larry Johnson* (Treasurer)
6. Kenneth Townsend* (V. Treasurer)
7. Loren Taylor (Secretary)

* Jill Reed was selected to replace original officer Bill Hunsicker when he resigned.

* Larry Johnson was selected to replace original officer Karlton Roberts when he resigned.

* Kenneth Townsend was selected to replace original officer Larry Wert when he resigned.

C. A National Executive Committee Officer shall continue his or her role as officer until:
   1. He or she resigns
   2. A majority vote (includes the vote of the officer in question) of the entire National Executive Committee calls for his or her removal based upon:
      a. Weak performance
      b. Replacement with a more effective choice (natural competition)
      c. Not adhering to the Prime Law (ignorantly or purposely)
      d. Lacking or slipping integration with the purpose of TVP (Article 3)
      e. Lacking or slipping integration with the National Platform
      f. Physically not able to fulfill responsibilities
      g. Mentally not able to fulfill responsibilities
      h. Need for a change, a fresh approach toward achieving our purpose (Article 3)
   3. A 2/3 vote of the National Committee (Article 13) calls for his or her removal based upon:
      a. Weak performance
      b. Replacement with a more effective choice (natural competition)
      c. Not adhering to the Prime Law (ignorantly or purposely)
      d. Lacking or slipping integration with the purpose of TVP (Article 3)
      e. Lacking or slipping integration with the National Platform
      f. Physically not able to fulfill responsibilities
      g. Mentally not able to fulfill responsibilities
      h. Need for a change, a fresh approach toward achieving our purpose (Article 3)

D. The National Executive Committee shall hold an annual, open and honest discussion of its seven officers' performance, both individually and collectively. This annual meeting should open the eyes of the NEC to its strengths and weaknesses and could begin the process of removing a weak officer.

E. Once the National Executive Officer is removed, the National Executive Committee shall replace the position within 90 days upon majority vote of the National Executive Committee.

III. State and International Executive Committee's Officers

A. There shall be from four to seven officers (preferably seven) as the Administrative Leading Head of the TVP State Affiliate known as the State Executive Committee and there shall be seven officers as the Administrative Leading Head of the TVP International Affiliate known as the country's National Executive Committee.

B. The State Executive Committee is the Administrative Leading Head of the State TVP, including the Administrative Leading Head of its direct sub-affiliates. An international affiliate's National Executive Committee is the Administrative Leading Head of that country's TVP, including the Administrative Leading Head of its direct sub-affiliates.

C. The original State Executive Committee Officers and National Executive Committee Officers of the international affiliates shall be approved by the U.S. National Executive Committee during the process of granting the TVP State or TVP Country Charter. The U.S. NEC is the Administrative Leading Head of the TVP worldwide (Article 14).

D. A State Executive Committee Officer or National Executive Committee Officer of an international affiliate shall continue his or her role as officer until:

1. He or she resigns
2. A majority vote (includes the vote of the officer in question) of the entire State Executive Committee or entire

National Executive Committee of an international affiliate calls for his or her removal based upon:

a. Weak performance
b. Replacement with a more effective choice (natural competition)
c. Not adhering to the Prime Law (ignorantly or purposely)
d. Lacking or slipping integration with the purpose of TVP (Article 3)
e. Lacking or slipping integration with the National and State Platform
f. Physically not able to fulfill responsibilities
g. Mentally not able to fulfill responsibilities
h. Need for a change, a fresh approach toward achieving our purpose (Article 3)

3. A majority vote of the U.S. National Executive Committee calls for his or her removal based upon:

a. Weak performance
b. Replacement with a more effective choice (natural competition)
c. Not adhering to the Prime Law (ignorantly or purposely)
d. Lacking or slipping integration with the purpose of TVP (Article 3)
e. Lacking or slipping integration with the National and State Platform
f. Physically not able to fulfill responsibilities
g. Mentally not able to fulfill responsibilities
h. Need for a change, a fresh approach toward achieving our purpose (Article 3)

E. The State Executive Committee and National Executive Committee of international affiliates shall hold an annual, open and honest discussion of their officers' performance, both individually and collectively. This annual meeting should open the eyes of the Executive Committee to its strengths and weaknesses and could begin the process of removing a weak officer.

F. Once the State Executive Officer is removed, the State Executive Committee shall replace the position within 90 days upon a majority vote of the State Executive Committee. Once the National Executive Officer of an international affiliate is removed, that country's NEC shall replace the position within 90 days upon a majority vote of the country's NEC.

IV. Officer Responsibilities of the Executive Committees

A. The Chair of the U.S. National Executive Committee shall preside at all National Conventions and all meetings of the National Committee. The Chair is the Chief Executive Officer of the TVP with authority to direct its business and affairs, including the hiring and discharging of National Committee volunteers and paid personnel, subject to majority consent of the National Executive Committee.

B. The Chair of the National Executive Committee of an international affiliate shall preside at that country's National Conventions and all meetings of that country's National Committee. The Chair is the Chief Executive Officer of that country's TVP with the authority to direct its business and affairs, including the hiring and discharging of that country's National Committee volunteers and paid personnel, subject to majority consent of that country's National Executive Committee.

C. The Chair of the State Executive Committees shall preside at all State conventions and all meetings of the State Committee. The Chair is the Chief Executive Officer of the State TVP with authority to direct its business and affairs, including hiring and discharging of State Committee volunteers and paid personnel, subject to majority consent of the State Executive Committee.

D. The Vice-Chairs shall be the chief assistants to the Chair, performing such duties as the Chair shall prescribe and holding such executive powers as the Chair shall delegate.

The Vice-Chairs shall perform the duties of the Chair in the event the Chair is, for any reason, unable to perform the duties of the office. If multiple vice-chair officers are appointed, one must be designated as "First Vice-Chair" who will perform the duties of the Chair in the event the Chair is unable to.

E. The Secretary shall be the recording officer and shall perform such duties as are assigned by the Chair. The Secretary shall attend all meetings and all Conventions and shall act as Secretary thereof, keeping such minutes and records as necessary. The Secretary shall maintain the email list of his or her Executive Committee as well as the National Committee (National EC Secretary) and State Committee (State EC Secretary). The secretary shall send out voting ballots and receive and tally votes including the National Committee or State Committee votes when necessary. The Secretary shall be the custodian of the Bylaws. The Secretary shall collect the tracking reports for his or her Executive Committee, containing all information required by the Committee.

F. The Treasurer shall receive, expend and account for the funds of the TVP under the supervision and direction of the National Chair and the National Executive Committee (regarding the National EC Treasurer) and State Chair and the State Executive Committee (regarding the State EC Treasurer). The National Treasurer shall make a monthly financial report to the National Executive Committee and an annual financial report to the National Committee. The State EC Treasurers shall make monthly financial reports to their respective State Executive Committees and an annual financial report to their respective State Committees and to the National Executive Committee. The Treasurer shall perform all duties required of the office by applicable federal and state law. The Treasurer is responsible for oversight of all financial functions, including, but not limited to, receipts, disbursements, internal and external reporting. The Treasurer shall report to his or her

Executive Committee both the financial situation of the TVP and the results of its activities. The annual report of the Treasurer shall include an independent auditor's report opining whether the financial statements present fairly, in all material respects, the financial position of the TVP and the changes in its net assets and its cash flow for the year then ended, in conformity with accounting principles generally accepted in the United States of America. The Treasurer shall also present unaudited monthly financial statements to his or her respective Executive Committee. Such reports shall be sent to all officers of the respective Executive Committee.

G. The Vice-Treasurer shall be the chief assistant to the Treasurer, performing such duties as the Treasurer shall prescribe, and shall perform the duties of the Treasurer in the event that the Treasurer is, for any reason, unable to perform the duties of the office.

H. The TVP officers shall thoroughly know and understand all aspects of the timeless National Platform written by Mark Hamilton. The TVP officers shall read closely the publications of TVP founder Mark Hamilton and strive to see the big picture as presented in his 2800-page magnum opus *The Prime Cure*.

## ARTICLE 12: THE BIG-PICTURE LEADING HEAD

I. The Big-Picture Leading Head is Mark Hamilton. Mark Hamilton holds the widest Neothink® integration, having spent most of his life, beginning decades ago as a young man, pulling together, integrating, and creating the broadest vision, as fully revealed in his 2800-page magnum opus *The Prime Cure*.

II. Mark Hamilton removed himself through these Bylaws from the day-to-day TVP administrative actions for actualizing his vision. That responsibility now falls upon the Administrative

Leading Heads (i.e., the National, State, County, Local Executive Committees). Instead, Mark Hamilton immersed himself into the deepest Neothinking® (i.e., focused ongoing integrated thinking – superpuzzle-building thinking) needed to see and pull together the puzzle-picture. The responsibility of creating that big picture and guiding the TVP movement toward that big picture falls on Mark Hamilton and will always fall on Mark Hamilton until his passing.

III. Visionaries holding a TVP committee officer position or political office or government position must work to internalize and engage Mark Hamilton's big-picture guidance, which always stems from one objective: *end initiatory force.* A lack of integrating and abiding by Mark Hamilton's big-picture guidance is tantamount to a lack of integrating and abiding by the Prime Law, which is reason for dismissal of committee officers and for disowning elected and appointed politicians, bureaucrats, and judges.

## ARTICLE 13: THE NATIONAL COMMITTEE

I. We must shed our political skin and see the TVP National Committee from the perspective of a division-of-essence Neothink® company (as described in Article 14 and described in detail in Mark Hamilton's *Neothink® Business System*). The essence of the TVP is *protection of American (eventually all countries') citizens* under the Prime-Law Amendment and Protection-Only Budget (i.e., the Prime-Law Budget). To that end, the National Committee exists. All else must go.

II. The National Committee consists of the National Executive Committee, the Chair and Vice Chair (First Vice-Chair if more than one) of the state affiliates.

III. The National Committee shall meet monthly for its Essence Meeting (as described in Article 14) under the direction of the TVP National Executive Committee Chairperson. Most monthly Essence Meetings will be held via telephone conference call. Times and places shall be determined by the National Executive Committee Chairperson. The National Chairperson (i.e., Chairperson of the National Executive Committee) shall guide the state affiliates via the big picture.

IV. The National Executive Committee shall adopt rules of procedure for the conduct of the National Committee meetings and the carrying out of its duties and responsibilities, including the Essence Tracking Report (described in Article 14). The National Executive Committee shall establish and through the National Committee implement the purpose and process of the TVP as stated in Articles 3 and 4.

V. A National Committee member shall be a visionary in good standing of the National Executive Committee or a State Executive Committee and shall not be a member or candidate of any political party other than the TVP.

VI. Any member of the National Committee may call for a special meeting or request to be added to the agenda of a scheduled National Committee Meeting to discuss and possibly request a vote regarding the selected presidential and/or vice presidential candidates (see Article 17, Section X). In the event of such a vote, all members must vote.

VII. The Secretary may mail or email ballots for votes. Twenty days shall be allowed for the return of the votes cast, by mail or email, to the Secretary. The Secretary shall report the results to all members of the National Committee. The Secretary shall establish procedures for identifying voters in an email ballot, and may accept votes through any mail system, including facsimile and electronic mail, for which such procedures have been established. If a quorum (i.e., 51% of the National Committee) is required, then at the expiration of the applicable voting period, if a quorum has not returned their votes, the measure being voted upon shall be deemed to have failed; in all other cases, a majority of the votes returned shall carry the measure, except where a higher vote is required by the Bylaws. The Secretary shall preserve all such votes until the next meeting of the National Executive Committee, at which meeting the NEC shall order the disposition of such votes, which shall be later revealed to the National Committee in the subsequently scheduled meeting.

VIII. Vote counts may be reviewed in detail by any officer of the National Executive Committee or any officer of the National Committee upon request.

## ARTICLE 14: DIVISION OF ESSENCE

I. The TVP is to take the unique form of a division-of-essence businesslike structure (as developed by Mark Hamilton in *The Neothink® Business System*, 315 pages, Neothink® Books). All TVP officers must read and understand the Neothink® Business System. That is mandatory. The Administrative Leading Head of this division-of-essence structure is the U.S. National Executive Committee, the original area of purpose. The U.S. National Executive Committee replicates areas of purpose (i.e., the state affiliates and NECs of other countries, the international affiliates) that, in turn, replicate areas of purpose (i.e., the sub-affiliates). The U.S. National Executive Committee shall hold monthly Essence Meetings (as described in *The Neothink® Business System*) with the state and international affiliates. The Chair of the U.S. National Executive Committee shall prepare, deliver, and preside over the monthly Essence Meetings with the entire National Committee plus the Chair and First V. Chair of the international affiliates (i.e., the NECs of other countries).

II. The Chair and First Vice Chair of state and international affiliates need to be present in the monthly Essence Meeting. Attendance is mandatory and may be missed only because of an emergency. If one does not attend due to an emergency, another representative from that state or country must attend without excuses. Two officers from each state and international affiliate must attend the monthly Essence

Meeting. The National Executive Committee's secretary shall take detailed minutes and distribute those minutes via email to all state-affiliate and international-affiliate officers.

III. The purpose of this monthly Essence Meeting is big-picture direction and guidance. The U.S. National Executive Committee led by its Chairperson shall give the state and international affiliates projects to pursue and complete. The projects to pursue could apply to all state and international affiliates or could be different among the affiliates. Those projects shall be determined by the U.S. National Chairperson. As described in Mark Hamilton's *Neothink® Business System*, those projects shall be listed (by the U.S. National Executive Committee's secretary and sent to the state and international affiliates via email), and progress shall be reported on that list of projects – the Essence Tracking Report – to be turned in to the U.S. National Executive Committee via email five days prior to the next monthly Essence Meeting.

IV. The businesslike TVP is very different than other political parties. The division-of-essence businesslike structure will increasingly bring strength of focus to TVP's sole purpose to end initiatory force – to the Prime-Law Amendment and Protection-Only Budget – a focus and purpose no other political party has. Indeed, the TVP will grow in a businesslike way toward its single purpose to end initiatory force, thus depoliticize America (and eventually the world) for our freedom, prosperity and happiness. There shall be no internal elections and re-elections within the TVP to obscure, compromise, corrupt, and eventually lose focus on our purpose and drift from our goal. There shall only be a single, determined drive to depoliticize America by eliminating initiatory force and forever ending the rule of man and his ruling class.

V. To best understand this division-of-essence structure, all officers in the TVP are required to read, study, and internalize Mark Hamilton's *Neothink® Business System*.

## ARTICLE 15: FINANCE AND ACCOUNTING

I. The fiscal term of the National TVP shall begin on January 1 of each year. The National Executive Committee shall determine the National TVP budgets and expenditures by majority vote.

II. The National Executive Committee shall cause an efficient double-entry system of accounts to be installed and maintained. Financial statements of the Party shall be prepared in accordance with Generally Accepted Accounting Principles (GAAP).

III. No disbursements exceeding $100 may be made with cash

IV. The National Executive Committee shall have the power to designate the depository of all funds of the Party, and shall appoint such officers and employees as in its judgment may seem advisable to deposit and withdraw funds.

V. The TVP shall not borrow in excess of $1,000 total without prior approval by a 5 to 2 vote of the National Executive Committee.

## ARTICLE 16: CONVENTIONS

I. Regular National Conventions: The TVP shall hold a Regular National Convention every four years up to a year prior to the Presidential Election at a time and place selected by the National Executive Committee. The National Chairperson shall preside over the convention.

II. Non-Regular National Conventions: In any year which does not include a Regular National Convention, a Non-Regular National Convention may be held at the discretion of the National Executive Committee.

III. The National Executive Committee shall select the TVP

Presidential and Vice Presidential Candidates as defined in Article 17, and the Chairperson of the National Executive Committee (i.e., the National Chairperson) shall announce the selection at the regular National Convention.

IV. As the TVP grows, the National Conventions will eventually reach full-capacity, evolving into an invitation-only event of Very Important Visionaries (VIVs). VIVs are major donors and valuable, hard-working volunteers who have earned a spot for their contributions and efforts at the "big party" Regular National Convention where the National Chairperson shall announce the TVP's Presidential and V. Presidential Candidates. VIVs have no role in the selection process, no voting role. They are Very Important Visionaries (VIVs) selected to celebrate the selection of the Presidential and Vice Presidential candidates. At National Conventions VIVs shall be those invited by the National Executive Committee, the National Committee, the State Affiliates and subaffiliates. A selected delegate must RSVP to his or her invitation within two weeks of receiving the invitation.

## ARTICLE 17: PRESIDENTIAL AND VICE-PRESIDENTIAL SELECTIONS

I. The selection for the TVP Presidential candidate and the TVP Vice Presidential candidate shall be made by majority vote of the National Executive Committee and shall be announced and made public by the National Chairperson at the Regular National Convention.

II. There shall be no primary election for the TVP Presidential nominee. However, at any time prior to the National Convention, TVP Visionaries may announce their TVP presidential aspirations and put forth awareness campaigns for the TVP and its immense benefits for all non-ruling-class Americans. The effectiveness of their – the "candidates'" – awareness campaigns may play a major role in the National Executive Committee's Presidential and Vice Presidential selections. And those awareness campaigns are NOT won by a voting public, therefore attack ads, illusions, deceptions will only work against the selection of a TVP Presidential hopeful.

III. Contrary to other political parties, the TVP Presidential Candidate should have no "big political ideas." The TVP is not about having a strong political leader and is not interested in that. The TVP is about depoliticizing America via the Prime-Law Amendment and Protection-Only Budget. *That's it.* The one and only focus of the TVP Presidential Candidate is spelled out in Article 3 and expanded upon in the National Platform. Any visionary with political ambitions beyond Article 3 (and its resulting Twelve Visions World as described in the National Platform) shall not be selected for TVP Presidential or V. Presidential Candidates. The TVP is NOT traditional politics...*it is the anti-politics.*

IV. Reiteration: The purpose of the TVP Presidential and V. Presidential candidates is defined in Article 3 and expanded upon in the TVP Platform. There can be no other purpose. Those with any further purpose including personal agendas, personal egos, personal ideas or beliefs or feelings, any purpose for running for office other than the simple idea of depoliticizing America as described in Article 3 shall not qualify for the TVP Presidential or V. Presidential candidacy.

V. TVP Presidential hopefuls must submit a resumé to the National Executive Committee. Although there is no mandatory timetable, it is strongly suggested that TVP Presidential hopefuls submit their resumés no less than six months prior to the National Convention. A TVP Presidential hopeful must be available for interviews with the National Executive Committee. The National Executive Committee shall determine who will be interviewed to help determine how well he or she understands and integrates the purpose of the TVP as defined in Article 3 and expanded upon in the National Platform. All self-indulging "big political ideas" must be replaced with discipline and *one idea* and *one idea only*: depoliticize America through the Prime-Law Amendment and Protection-Only Budget. The National Executive Committee will determine how well a potential candidate can be true to those two pillars and how skillful a potential candidate can be at stimulating people's urges to vote TVP, as articulated in Mark Hamilton's speech delivered to the 2009 National Convention (see that speech at www.youtube.com/ Neothink Society).

VI. As described in the National Platform (and even further in Mark Hamilton's trilogy *Neothink® Superpuzzle*, 1200 pages), a totally free, voluntary-pay TVP government will no longer need elections and their destructive deceptions and illusions from vote-gathering politicians distorting reality to win substantial segments of the voting public for election or re-election. The harm they do to society by "buying" votes while in power is exposed in the TVP National Platform. Nevertheless, for now, we must compete within their ruling-class, pay-by-force traditional system run by elections for so-called "representation" (as opposed to positive results and value exchange as in the voluntary-pay TVP system described in the TVP Platform). To compete and pursue its purpose (Article 3), the TVP shall participate in the general elections.

VII. No candidate shall be considered for President or Vice-President who is ineligible under the United States Constitution, who has not expressed a willingness to accept the candidacy of the TVP, who is not a visionary of the TVP, or who has not signed the TVP Contract.

VIII. In the event of the death, resignation, disqualification or suspension of the TVP's nominee for President, the Vice-Presidential nominee shall become the Presidential nominee. The National Executive Committee shall then fill the Vice-Presidential vacancy within 60 days.

IX. The National Committee and affiliates and their VIVs shall respect the selection for the Presidential ticket at the Regular National Convention and provide full support for the selected

Presidential and Vice Presidential candidates as long as they do not violate the TVP Contract, and their campaigns are conducted in accordance with Article 3 and the Platform of the TVP.

X. The Presidential or Vice Presidential candidate's nomination may be suspended by a majority vote of the National Executive Committee or by a 2/3 vote of the entire National Committee at a meeting called for that purpose (see Article 13, Section VI). That candidate's nomination shall then be declared null and void. In either case, a new Vice Presidential candidate then must be selected by the National Executive Committee and made public by the National Chairperson within sixty days. In the theoretical possibility the full TVP Presidential ticket is declared null and void, the NEC must select a new Presidential ticket within 60 days.

## ARTICLE 18: THE FUNDAMENTAL DOCUMENTS

I. The Prime Law is the fundamental, natural law of protection and therefore stands alone. The National Executive Committee may not amend the Prime Law. The Prime Law shall be the heading to, but not an amendable part of, all TVP Platforms and Bylaws, including national, international, state, county, city, local bylaws and platforms. The Prime Law stands alone, untouchable, immune to amender. The Prime Law may be edited by the founder of the TVP, by Mark Hamilton only, but most likely never. The following footnote shall accompany the Prime Law when it appears as a heading to national, international, state, county, city and local bylaws and platforms, as follows: *The Prime Law is the fundamental, natural law of protection (that directs all decisions and actions of the Twelve Visions Party); the Prime Law may not be amended.*

II. The founding 2012 TVP National Platform (unveiled in mid-2009) is timeless. That fundamental document is based on fundamental principles as opposed to transitory pragmatism.

Therefore, that seminal 2012 National Platform shall forever remain the TVP National Platform, for that founding Platform is the fundamental expression of an entirely new dimension of civilization void of initiatory force. That document founded on fundamental principles NOT on pragmatic planks will end politics as we know it, eradicating the political dimension of initiatory force and its virulent rule of man. The National Platform takes civilization into the never-before-known dimension of no initiatory force, and that founding Platform is our map into that prosperous new world. To reach our destination, to enter a new dimension requires Mark Hamilton's founding Platform. The Platform may never be amended by anyone or any committee beyond Mark Hamilton himself. Mark Hamilton may at any time edit this document as part of a lifelong journey to idealize and actualize the Twelve Visions World. His editing process digs down, down, down beneath the illusions and appearances, down to the fundamental nature of things, down to bedrock reality to bring us into the never-before-known dimension of no initiatory force...into the prosperous and peaceful Twelve Visions World. These same requirements apply to the international affiliates. However, the international affiliates may make adjustments for geographical and structural political differences as described in Article 9, Section VI.

III. The TVP National Bylaws is a breakthrough document bringing us for the first time a political party, political purpose, and a political process from an entirely new dimension – the dimension of no initiatory force. The fundamental principles may never be amended by any hand beyond founder Mark Hamilton's editing hand. The National Executive Committee, the Administrative Leading Head of the TVP, may make *administrative* amendments to the National Bylaws with a 5-2 vote. However, the principles of the Bylaws may never be amended. Only the founder of TVP, author of the Bylaws, and Big-Picture Leading Head Mark Hamilton may edit the timeless principles of the Bylaws. Specifically, Articles 1 through 9, 12, 18 and 20 should not ever need administrative amendments and fall into the Do Not

Touch category. Articles 10, 11, 13 through 17, and 19 contain procedures that could conceivably require administrative/procedural adjustments in the future, although very rarely if ever. Any administrative/procedural amendments shall be brought to Mark Hamilton's attention. These same requirements apply to the international affiliates. However, the international affiliates may make adjustments for geographical and structural political differences as described in Article 9, Section VII.

IV. The timeless State Platform written by Mark Hamilton shall be the State Platform for all state affiliates. Over time, when and only when the National Executive Committee is convinced the state-level affiliates fully grasp the role of the TVP to obey the Prime Law despite personal ideas, beliefs, feelings and egos, to forego all grasps for glory and power and to pursue nothing more than the "boring" single-minded purpose of **depoliticizing America** through the Protection-Only Budget and the Prime-Law Amendment...then the National Executive Committee may make the decision with a majority vote to grant permission for the state-level affiliates, on a state-by-state basis, to "localize" their state platforms while always abiding by the Prime Law and Protection-Only Budget. The National Executive Committee may hold certain states to Mark Hamilton's founding State Platform and not others. The National Executive Committee may require a state affiliate to immediately reinstate Mark Hamilton's founding state platform in lieu of their "localized" state platform that falls short of the purpose, principles, process and pillars described in Articles 3, 4, and 5 of the National Bylaws. All state platforms must drive home the point that the TVP will depoliticize America and each state through the Prime-Law Amendment (for both the U.S. Constitution and their State Constitutions) and Protection-Only Budget (for both the National Budget and their State Budgets). These same requirements apply to the international sub-affiliates.

V. The State Bylaws written by Mark Hamilton are closely

patterned after the National Bylaws. The State Executive Committees may make administrative amendments only to the State Bylaws with a minimum 2/3 vote. However, within our Division-of-Essence business structure, any administrative amendment that formally passes at the state-affiliate level must then be submitted to the National Executive Committee. The National Executive Committee shall accept or reject the amendment by majority vote in no more than 60 days. Only the founder of the TVP, author of the Bylaws, and Big-Picture Leading Head Mark Hamilton may edit the principles of the State Bylaws. These same requirements apply to the international sub-affiliates.

VI. The Bylaws' article titled "The Fundamental Documents" (Article 18 of the National Bylaws) may not be amended – may not be altered by any hand beyond founder Mark Hamilton's editing hand. Article 18 (or article titled "The Fundamental Documents") may never be amended at any level – national, international, state, county, city, local...all sub-affiliates. The Bylaws' Article 18 – the article titled "The Fundamental Documents" – preserves what needs to be permanently preserved in order to end the rule of man.

## ARTICLE 19: DISTRIBUTION OF BYLAWS

The National Executive Committee shall issue the Bylaws as follows: a copy of these Bylaws shall be provided to each officer of the U.S. National Executive Committee and U.S. National Committee and each Chair and First Vice Chair of all International Affiliates and sub-affiliates. All other TVP officers and members can access these Bylaws at www.TVPNC.org.

## ARTICLE 20: ADOPTION

These revised Bylaws, written and edited by Mark Hamilton, shall take effect immediately. These Bylaws provide the TVP with the purpose, process, and structure to enter the new dimension of no initiatory force...to bring the world into the wealthy, healthy, and peaceful Twelve Visions World.

## Final Word

Are politicians and regulatory bureaucrats bad people, perhaps evil? Some are and some are not. In fact, some are honest, even noble public servants trying to improve society.

The stimulating clashes between good and evil among politicians and bureaucrats emotionally engage the people and keep their eye off the real problem: a bad system built on initiatory force that enables the steady rise of the rule of man and demise of the working class. All politicians and bureaucrats, good and bad, operate within a bad system — a system built on initiatory force. For the first time, the Twelve Visions Party with its Prime Law offers the one and only good system— a system that banishes initiatory force.

# Epilogue

I can see now from early experiences of TVP candidates running for office that bloggers and traditional media will put down the Twelve Visions Party by claiming that the movement is only about selling the founder's books.

For the record, I have sunk a lot of time and money into the TVP movement with little monetary return. In the early 1990's I did experiment with a political movement and was hoping to find a way to finance the movement by selling one of my books. I aired a half-hour interview that gave away my first political manifesto *A Future of Wealth Belongs To You* (283 pages) without charge as a way to reach the people with my ideas. Inside my political manifesto, the reader was offered another Hamilton Publication for $20, which would go straight toward purchasing more air time. My hope was I could sell enough of those valuable publications to finance (i.e., break even) a campaign that would compete with the two parties monopolizing the political system. I learned, however, that subsidizing a political campaign by selling books does not work. I knew then that if I ever entered the political world again, I would have to spend a lot of money with no return.

Over the next decade, my life changed dramatically with the arrival of my four children. As with most parents, the direction of the country took on deeper meaning out of concern for my children's futures. And the direction was not good.

In 2007, fifteen years after my initial experiment in a political movement, I founded the Twelve Visions Party. This time, I knew I could NOT subsidize the movement with sales of my books. I knew I would spend a lot of money I would never get back, but I was determined to make this a better country for my children and future generations. That determination to make the country a better place for my children and future generations motivated me to step back into a political movement, willing to spend time and money.

References to my Neothink® writings are made as a courtesy for people who want to learn more about the philosophy behind TVP, but not to make money. The TVP is not "a scam selling Mark Hamilton's books" as I saw on the Internet. Revenues from book sales is a drop in the bucket to money spent.[1]

The attempt to discredit and put down the Twelve Visions Party, the Neothink® Society, the Neothink® Manuscripts, and my name Mark Hamilton, however, has occurred for years. In fact, I will take this opportunity to tell you a dirty little secret:

The easiest and fastest way to rise to attention, power and popularity is to tear down someone or something of value. The dirty little secret is: the greater the value, then the greater the opportunity for someone such as a politician, journalist, bureaucrat, activist, blogger, lawyer or flamer to attack that value, flame it, tear it down for quick attention, power, and popularity.

Such value-attackers camouflage their dirty little secret by creating an age-old illusion. The illusion is always the same: the person of value – their target/victim – is made out to be an underhanded greedy person, a scam preying on the public. That's the illusion — which is actually the complete opposite of reality.

But that illusion always works because it makes the attacker appear good, even heroic. Therefore, the public supports and gets behind such value-attackers. With great public fanfare those value-attacking politicians, journalists, activists, regulatory bureaucrats, bloggers, lawyers and flamers bring down the person or entity of value who is now unjustly perceived and emotionally rejected by the public as a scam. The value is destroyed and the value-attackers are erroneously perceived as benefactors of humanity. The public is none the wiser of losing both its freedoms and values. Society as a whole suffers; the standard of living struggles.

This rising up to popularity/prosperity/power at the expense

[1]With that being said, however, let me make something very clear: Values come from business and profit. Without business and profit, values/goods would disappear. They could not exist. There is absolutely nothing wrong with profiting from providing a value. In fact, the TVP vision is to turn government from a pay-by-force institution to a voluntary-pay business offering competitive protection services — offering value. Business and profits *bound by the Prime Law* bring us only values.

of others has always been used by a certain percentage of the human race. You can even see this start in children as a certain percentage of school children will bully classmates for attention, popularity and power. ...Some people will always try to rise at the expense of others. When adults, many of those value-destroyers unfortunately become part of the ruling-and-influencing class of society. This myriad of value-attackers *competitively* rise to popularity and power by tearing down value-producers.

The value emanating from the Neothink® Society to its selected recipients is life-changing, financially and emotionally. Because the value is so large, the Neothink® Society is a target and a victim of this dirty little secret used by bloggers, flamers, haters. Moreover, the ruling-and-influencing class is threatened by those in the Neothink® Society because we "Robin-Hood" them...transfer their power from the parasitical, elitist ruling-and-influencing class back to the people, especially to the less fortunate. Therefore, the ruling-and-influencing class continually puts down the Neothink® Society and our life-enhancing, individual-empowering secret knowledge that especially empowers the less fortunate. The value-attackers cast distorted and malicious perceptions and outright lies in their attempt to provoke rejection of the Neothink® Society and its revealing, establishment-threatening secrets. Unwittingly, some in the outside public (most of whom have never seen our massive Neothink® Manuscripts) tend to pile onto those false perceptions and lies out of ignorance and a follow-the-herd mentality. They have been influenced by the ruling class to attack us.

The ruling-and-influencing class's illusions prevent millions from reaping their true benefits from society as instead they unwittingly hail the malefactors of society. But we in the Neothink® Society "Robin-Hood" the ruling-class greed and power and give their power back to the people. Indeed, we have Robin-Hood techniques to transfer much of the ruling class's stolen power and wealth back to the powerless...back to the poor and to all who deserve the good life, including you.

For centuries illusions have been cast to influence public perception and provoke emotional dejection toward our kind. Those attacks by outside value-destroyers among the threatened ruling-and-influencing class are another reason why you need to act now to uphold these values while they are still available, before they become banned by the ruling-class authorities in this country as they have been banned by the ruling-class authorities in other countries.

Once inside our Neothink® Society, the values are so beneficial that those attacks/illusions against our Society simply dissipate. The attacks come from OUTSIDE the Society. Once inside, one will choose to remain inside because of the immense values. Particularly exciting are the Robin-Hood techniques to transfer the massive unearned power, prestige and wealth from the parasitical ruling-and-influencing class directly to YOU for quick but LEGITIMATE attention, prestige, power and wealth! Inside the Neothink® Society your eyes open immediately to what has secretly been going on behind your back for your entire life, for centuries. And with that hidden knowledge, you can become very successful, even wealthy, at record speed. Francis Bacon said, "Knowledge is power." But this kind of knowledge captures power *and wealth*.

Whereas for decades the Neothink® Society has endured libelous and slanderous reputation-damaging attacks, the vast majority of attackers never saw the large Neothink® manuscripts. Why is that? If they have not seen the large manuscripts, why then do they attack? They are influenced by the ruling/influencing class to attack us. And why have those money/power giants of the ruling/influencing class for decades influenced others to smear our Society? The answer is: we have the powerful Robin-Hood method to transfer much of their stolen power and wealth back to us.

The majority of attacks on the Society just "follow the herd" and "pile it on", influenced by the threatened establishment's age-old illusion slanderously stating "the Society is a scam...ripping off people" by charging for these rare leatherette, massive gold-leafed (up to 2800-pages) restricted manuscripts. To those duped, follow-the-herd libelous and slanderous flamers, here is a challenging, revealing thought that perhaps leads to a positive change for you: If a business does not charge for a value, then the value cannot and will not exist! YOU DON'T JUST GET GOODS FOR FREE. Again, let me make this very clear: Values come from business and profit. Without business and profit, values/goods would disappear. They could not exist. There is absolutely nothing wrong with profiting from providing a value. So, as most attackers did not and will not ever see the manuscripts and instead just pile onto the mound of attacks and think it's OK to slander the Society and to blindly call the life-changing massive manuscripts a scam...you are fundamentally duped by the ruling-and-influencing class. Indeed, what would you expect us to do? NOT CHARGE for this life-changing value? Then it would disappear. With that flawed philosophy, values will cease to exist for humanity.

Unfortunately today, a very damaging philosophy that success is somehow bad and done at the expense of others is rapidly spreading. In reality, achievement and success benefit others as personal success brings values, jobs, and rising standards of living to society. The pervasive ruling-and-influencing class pushes the very destructive illusion on the public that is opposite of reality. And those who are duped, in turn, attack achievers and their success.

The Neothink® Society does something wonderful for its members: this exclusive Society delivers the necessary tools for success in today's difficult economies, including the tools/weapons to protect that success from the ruling-and-influencing class and their duped followers. Moreover, we "Robin-Hood" the ruling-and-influencing class's stolen power and give it back to the struggling working class — to you!

The Neothink® Society, the Twelve Visions Party, and my Neothink® Manuscripts bring honest power to the powerless. EVERYONE wants power — the power to earn money, the power to attract a desirable lover or spouse, the power to achieve worthy goals, the power to give your children a wonderful life. A certain percentage of the population unfortunately acquires power quickly and easily through the dirty little secret. You can, too. But most people are not interested in participating in the dirty little secret.

You can test the dirty little secret, however, to get a glimpse of its power. For instance, at a gathering, perhaps at a party, if you put someone down, even in the slightest way, you will see an instant transfer of power to you. It's human nature — the offensive posture versus the defensive posture. In fact, you see this attacker/bully versus defender/victim role play out starting at a very young age...as early as in pre-school and continuing throughout all school years, sometimes culminating in tragic consequences such as the rash of cyber-bullying, teen suicides lately. Parents and teachers know this only too well about certain children.[1]

Certain adults use the dirty little secret to its full extent to transfer power and wealth from the good, rightful owners of that power and wealth to themselves. The greater the person of value/ power being attacked, the greater that transfer of power to the attacker. Those adults rise to power through conquests and join the ruling class of attack-mode politicians, regulatory bureaucrats, journalists, attack lawyers.

Once again, you can get a small taste of this power by putting someone down, especially in front of others. Of course, most good people feel terrible inside by putting someone else down

---

[1]One critical point to bloggers, flamers, and haters: When a blogger flames a person, remember that is a real person with real friends, parents, children, loved ones. Today's wired generation tends to not realize that online attacks on others cause very real pain and consequences in people's lives. As I wrote above, sometimes this disconnect causes tragic real-world consequences such as the rash of cyber-bullying, teen suicides lately...a sad, sad result of particularly the younger generation not relating what they are doing online to real-world consequences. Let me remind haters, flamers, bloggers who attack on line and cause damage to others, including to me and my Neothink® Society and reputation, particularly attackers who are downright vicious...you are an example of today's disconnect between associating destructive on-line posts with real-world consequences. For example, recipients of attacks and hate are real and caring persons with loved ones who are the light of their lives, with friends, with those who admire them. Flamers who attack without reservation, give pause to realize that those you attack are not inanimate objects, but usually kind persons with lives of love around them, with close loved ones who care about them. Just stop for a moment and consider how your online posts that degrade others...how those posts affect not only their reputation, but *their world*...when people they love see those harsh posts, such as their children who look up to them, their family who are proud of them, their customers who respect them. And know those degrading words about those warm human beings posted on line will remain on the Internet, forever.

and therefore could never climb to power and wealth through this quick and easy dirty little secret. But a certain percentage of the population, a certain breed has always thrived on this attack mode for a quick and easy rise to power. That bully breed harbors no conscience. And unfortunately, the majority of our ruling-and-influencing class consists of this ruthless breed. They rise to the top through their conquests of value producers. And sadly, millions upon millions of others become influenced by their ruthless put-downs that make the successful appear bad. In turn, the masses believe in the ruling-class attacks on the successful. The value producers are shamed; the value destroyers are revered.

## Turning the Tables

Many true heroes of society — the value creators — are perceived as villains. Many true villains of society — the value destroyers — are perceived as heroes. The ruling-and-influencing class's illusions prevent millions from seeing the true benefactors of society, and instead they unwittingly hail the malefactors of society at great costs to themselves! Indeed, overwhelmed by the illusions and guilt, value producers often erroneously feel ashamed of themselves. And countless millions of would-be value creators succumb to the destructive illusions and lose their ambition to become business owners, value creators, job creators. The economy and standard of living steadily decline.

Here is a clue as to how to see through the illusions: the working class — from the ditch digger to the billionaire entrepreneur — works hard to put values into society. The parasitical attack-class — from the bully in school to the highest politician — attacks the value producer to usurp his power and drain values from society.

Often the "villains" that you and children see in the movies are really the heroes and often the "heroes" are the real villains. Likewise, in the real world many of the persons we perceive as "villains" are the value producers, the heroes. And many of the persons we perceive as "heroes" are the value destroyers, the villains. Often life is not as it appears to be. Inside the Neothink® Society our eyes open immediately to what has secretly been going on behind our backs for our entire lives, for centuries.

Inside the Society, you become both successful *and* capable of defending your success from the attackers. There is nothing on this planet better for you *right now* than taking back all your rightful power and soaring into a new realm of success never even fathomed before in your lifetime. That happens as Neothink® Society members "Robin Hood" the money/power giants using the dirty little secret against us. Our members jiu-jitsu (i.e., flip down) anyone/everyone using the dirty little secret against them. Members jiu-jitsu the money/power giants' unearned and stolen power, prestige, wealth and recapture it directly for themselves for *legitimate* power — *earned* power, prestige, wealth.

**Protect the Society**

Here's how you can help protect our precious society: As you know, the Twelve Visions Party is the political arm of the Neothink® Society. I, Mark Hamilton, am the founder of the Neothink® Society and the Twelve Visions Party, and I am the author of the Neothink® Manuscripts. My Neothink® Society, my Neothink® Manuscripts, my Twelve Visions Party, and my name, Mark Hamilton, are victims of ongoing attacks. We must all stand up to protect Mark Hamilton, Neothink®, and TVP. I am inviting you to do exactly that, as follows:

Write a powerful testimonial about how you have benefited from Mark Hamilton, from my Neothink® Manuscripts, from the Neothink® Society, and how the world will benefit from the Twelve Visions Party.

By standing up for the values of Mark Hamilton, Neothink®, and the Twelve Visions Party, you protect those values and prevent the ruling-and-influencing class's attempt to end those values in America. Your written testimonial is so very important to the survival and expanding influence of Neothink®, TVP, and Mark Hamilton. Please know that I will post your testimonial. Sign your testimonial how you would like to see it on line. You can use your full name (or initials). You will be defending the right side of history. Your testimonial for the Neothink® Society, Neothink® Manuscripts, Twelve Visions Party, and Mark Hamilton posted to the Neothink® website will be your mark on the official documents that two-hundred years from now will be viewed as the early documents that brought us freedom, prosperity and peace. In that future world we will all have the life we were meant to have.

You understand what I am bringing to mankind; let the world know what you know. Show the world you are a bright visionary. Leave your eternal mark on history. Become one of the rare, original members of the Twelve Visions World with your testimonial. I will be sure to attach your testimonial to the Neothink® Society website for the scribe of history to forever record you as one of the original supporters of the world-changing Neothink® and TVP movements. Put your immortal stamp on the next evolution of civilization — the evolution into universal wealth, health, peace with the Prime Law that forever ends initiatory force. I look forward to reading what you send me. Send me your testimonial today to: MarkHamilton@Neothink.com. In the subject line please say "testimonial" to help me see your valuable email among my hundreds of emails on a normal day. Thank you. Your testimonial is a crucial part of the protection-shield to keep me, Mark Hamilton, Neothink® and TVP going strong. Keep checking back to www.MarkHamilton-Neothink-TVP.com to see when your testimonial gets posted.

Now, I want you to take that testimonial that you send me and use it as your starting point for something big in the making:

## The Peaceful Neothink® Revolution of Ideas A Call To Action & Leadership

You are now among my readers. Today I make a very special announcement — a call to action. I have patiently waited for over three decades to make this announcement: The time has arrived to commence with the peaceful Neothink® Revolution of ideas. We are now going to the masses *through you.* You will play an important leadership role in this peaceful revolution of ideas.

I am asking you to start with your testimonial to me and use it or parts of it to post throughout the Internet. But don't stop there. Post positive comments and personal stories about your good experiences from reading my Neothink® Manuscripts. And you as a leader in the Neothink® Revolution of ideas, post your sophisticated integrations about Neothink® and TVP on relevant blogs and forums all throughout the Internet. It is now time to start spreading the ideas of Neothink® and TVP to the masses through the Internet. Always reference the source — Mark Hamilton, his Neothink® Manuscripts, the Neothink® Society, the Twelve Visions Party — to propagate a rooted revolution of ideas locking everything down to the Prime Literature. My elite Neothink® readers will be the surge behind the Neothink® Revolution of ideas. You are now one of my elite Neothink® readers.

Use your integrating abilities to present Neothink® viewpoints throughout the blogosphere. And do not stop there. Present the Twelve Visions Party platform of ideas with the Prime Law that ends initiatory force. Explain how the TVP will eradicate the disease of civilization — the rule of man. Post the Twelve Visions Party ideas on political forums, discussion boards, open blogs. You may post this link anywhere and everywhere. I believe you will become a strong voice for Neothink® and the Twelve Visions Party and a leader of the Neothink® Revolution of ideas.

I welcome you to write and submit on-line articles about Neothink® and the Twelve Visions Party. With you having read this publication, I firmly believe in your abilities to be a strong Neothink® voice. In my eyes, you can be a true journalist writing about and submitting/posting articles about the Neothink® Movement and the Twelve Visions Party. I believe in you and in your abilities to present the full value of Neothink® and TVP.

If you read further Neothink® works, then in the business forums you can write about personal success stories using my Neothink® business techniques. Explain that this all comes about from a new way of thinking — Neothink®.

In political forums write about the Prime Law and ending initiatory force and the rule of man. Explain how this is a new dimension of civilization, law, and governing that will lead to universal wealth, health, and peace.

In the health forums write about the secret formula to curing aging. That formula, of course, is found in my 2800-page magnum opus. In short, it basically exposes how to remove stagnation with a creation-driven life through the Neothink® business techniques, and the resulting wealth and happiness would drive up the demand for longer life. Then by removing initiatory force and the rule of man through the Twelve Visions Party with its Prime Law, the obstacles blocking the rapid advancement of medical technology and science vanish. The supply of longer life will then rise to the demand for longer life. The major diseases and even aging itself will be cured within a decade.

In the book forums write about the Neothink® books and their Neothink® breakthroughs such as the business breakthroughs, the TVP political breakthroughs, the Prime Cure anti-aging breakthroughs, and the Superpuzzle Trilogy (Miss Annabelle) embedded with the secrets of the most successful people who ever lived.

You truly can now become a leader in the peaceful Neothink® Revolution. I have patiently waited for over three decades to free the Neothink® ideas to the general public — through my readers...through you. You are ready. This is finally your moment to be a pioneer, an early leader, in the Neothink® Movement and TVP Movement beyond the Neothink® Society — to the public. I believe in you. I know you are now a Neothink® reader and have the rare ability to present Neothink® and TVP to the world. The time is upon us, and this is how you will deliver great value back to society. I will be watching and reading as you put Neothink® and TVP out there. I know you will make me and a lot of other people very proud of you. Our time is coming.

Thank you, and I look forward to receiving and reading your testimonial. Send it to me at MarkHamilton@Neothink.com. Check the website www.MarkHamilton-Neothink-TVP.com daily to see when I post it.

Thank you,
Mark Hamilton
www.aboutMarkHamilton.com

# Appendix

# A Young Mind Evolving

Over the next seventeen pages, you will witness a young teenager (my son) begin to see through the leaders' illusions to *what is*...his initial insights in his journey toward gaining Neothink® knowledge. I observed my son as he began to make those powerful insights, taking him days at first, then hours...and now about fifteen seconds to see past a political illusion!

As you read the revealing insights, I want you to notice how simple they really are, yet most people do not grasp *what is*...even when reality is very clear and simple.

The reason most people do not see *what is* **and never do see it** has to do with the illusions fed to us by our leaders. Once the process of seeing through those illusions starts, the momentum builds as you will see in the young man on the pages to follow. I compare it to a child learning to talk and the momentum and enthusiasm that builds as that child gains more words and power. This process of seeing through the illusions to *what is* starts off slow, but eventually the mind makes powerful insights in just seconds that can change one's life forever.

*Universal Wealth, Health, Peace*

# Politicians and Bureaucrats: Juvenile Delinquents!

by

Wallace Hamilton (son)

and

Mark Hamilton (dad)

## A Boy, His Dad, and Their Country

As most boys, I am learning important lessons about life during my childhood. Many of those important lessons come from my father, renown author Mark Hamilton. As I was turning ten years old, four years ago, my father was forming a new political party. I often heard him talking about it passionately over the phone or with visitors at the house. At some point, I started asking questions. Hearing both his conversations with others and his answers to my questions, I began to realize that many of the issues he was upset about were violations of the simple childhood lessons he taught me — violations committed on a large and continuing scale by those adults who ruled over my country!

I was stunned by this realization: The leaders of my country blatantly violate the right-versus-wrong juvenile lessons boys and girls learn growing up!

One day, during one of my memorable talks with my dad, I asked him if I could write down those right-versus-wrong lessons he taught me and then show how our country, at the highest levels, is going along a "juvenile-delinquent" path of self-destruction. I asked if he could help me with this project.

He loved the concept and said he would help. It was my hope that this project, written at such a simple level, could help galvanize my country against those violations of universal right-versus-wrong lessons we all learned as children. Here are the first ten lessons:

# Lessons From Our Childhood

## Lesson One
## Do Not Take What Does Not Belong To You!

All my life my parents taught me to never take something that was not mine. Even if a friend had rich parents and was more privileged than me, still I could not take any of his toys home unless *he* voluntarily gave them or loaned them to me. I could never take someone else's toys even if he had rich parents and had more toys than anyone I had ever seen. I could not take even *one* of his toys, not even if I wanted to give it to another friend instead of keeping it for myself.

When I hear my father talk to important people in his Twelve Visions Party, I hear him speak with great concern about how the government is taking increasing amounts of money from citizens. I hear him talk about how our leaders take money that belongs to people who earn it and give it to those who did not earn it. I recognized that juvenile-delinquent action and asked my dad about it. I had a hard time believing that our government can take more and more money from those who earn it. I am young, but that just goes against everything I learned growing up.

## Lesson Two
## Do Not Take Anything By Force!

That juvenile-delinquent behavior gets worse. I learned that the government takes more and more money from people *against their will*. Dad calls this "taxes by threat of force." And I hear him concerned how the government is taking increasing amounts of money from people against their will and giving it to other people. Dad calls this "redistribution of wealth by threat of force". When I asked him to explain it to me, his explanation sounded like everything he taught me NOT TO DO as a young boy: DO NOT take from others what belongs to them...DO NOT take from others by threat of force. I was taught while growing up to NEVER take something by FORCE.

One night, I asked my dad, "Is the government bad?"

He said, "It certainly is when it takes someone's property against that person's will." That was the talk when my dad told me about the Prime Law, which is the cornerstone of his Twelve Visions Party:

## The Prime Law

(The Fundamental of Protection)

### Preamble

*The *purpose* of human life is to prosper and live happily.

*The function of government is to **provide the conditions** that let individuals fulfill that *purpose*.

*The Prime Law **guarantees those conditions** by forbidding the use of initiatory force, fraud, or coercion by any person or group against any individual, property, or contract.

### Article 1

No person, group of persons, or government shall initiate force, threat of force, or fraud against any individual's self, property, or contract.

### Article 2

Force is morally-and-legally justified only for protection from those who violate Article 1.

### Article 3

No exceptions shall exist for Article 1 and 2.

*The Neothink® Movement*

## Lesson Three
## Do Not Steal!

My father taught me to never steal from others under *any* circumstances. When I asked him once, "What if I were starving and my family were starving...could I steal a loaf of bread in the marketplace?" I thought maybe that would be okay to help myself and my starving family.

But my dad said, "When exactly do you decide to steal that loaf of bread? When your family is literally dying...or just very hungry...or simply out of work? The point is, instead of putting your focus and energy on stealing, you must put all your focus and energy on providing a value *to earn* that loaf of bread."

No matter what excuse I could come up with, there was NO excuse for stealing. And I took it to heart.

One day I overheard my father on the phone with that concerned look on his face. He said, "The government is stealing more and more from our children."

So I asked him about it, and he told me, "The government is spending more and more money it does not have against the will of the people. The government is spending money that you and your brothers and sister will have to pay back. The government is stealing from you and your brothers and sister. And this goes against the will of your parents and grandparents. Responsible parents do not condone this government spending."

Dad and I talked for two hours about this. Never knowing much about the government before, I could not believe what the government was doing! It goes against everything I learned growing up! At this point, I asked my dad, *who makes up the government? What kind of people?* And he told me politicians, judges, and bureaucrats, and he explained the differences.

"So," I asked, "are they all bad?"

"Those driven to rule over America by force are bad," he said. "Only those driven to end such power-hungry ruling powers are good," he explained. "My new political party with its Prime Law is driven to end all force-backed ruling power.

"The only proper purpose of government is protection of its citizens through the military, courts, police, prisons...*protection only*. The people will voluntarily pay for protection, peace, and prosperity. The idea of ruling over the people backed by initiatory force comes from power-hungry politicians, judges and bureaucrats. All that bad goes away when we take away their initiatory force through the Prime Law."

We talked for another hour, mostly me asking questions about the Twelve Visions Party and Dad patiently answering me. When I was done, I realized that his new Twelve Visions Party is going to transform government from a force-driven ruling class to a customer-driven protection service.

## Lesson Four
## Do Not Hit!

My parents taught me to never hit or threaten or force someone to do something he or she does not want to do. Even if I really, really wanted my little brothers to do something, for example, I could not grab them and force them into it. My parents made sure I never forced my younger, smaller brothers to do what I wanted them to do. Even if I strongly disagreed with my brothers and, as their big brother, thought I knew best, still I could not FORCE them to do something. In the end, they had to do so *willingly*.

So, during a talk with Dad, when I learned that the government FORCES people to do things they do not want to do *all the time*...imagine how dumbfounded I was. I knew that forcing people to do things they did not want to do was just plain wrong. I was beginning to know that the government was, for the most part, just plain wrong...except when it came to protection. Growing up, Dad taught me to never lay a hand on anyone. But, if a kid ever laid a hand on me, Dad gave me permission to strike back hard in self-defense. Dad taught me how to throw hard punches just in case I ever needed to.

I was troubled how government forced upon its citizens laws and regulations that had nothing to do with protection. I was troubled that laws and regulations forced people and their businesses to do things against their will, even when they were in no way hurting others!

I started asking my dad questions like, "Why is there a government in the first place? Should there even be a government? Can it ever be good?" I learned more about how society works over the next hour with my dad than I had learned in my entire life before that talk.

Dad explained how government should exist for one purpose and one purpose only. That purpose is protection. He explained that the Twelve Visions Party plans to bring about a Protection-Only Government. He explained that the Prime Law can bring about a Protection-Only Government. Force may be used only to protect the people from those who use force or threaten force against them or their property. I could really relate to that! I grew up being taught that I could never hit anyone else. But if someone started hitting me, I could fight back. My dad told me to never, ever start a fight with someone. But if someone ever started fighting me, I was free to fight back.

The Prime Law is simply *The Golden Rule* for all kids growing up! I guess you could say the Prime Law is also the prime law for all kids in school and on the playground! I felt really proud because I was starting to understand the Twelve Visions Party. I was beginning to understand what my father had been working so hard on, day and night.

## Lesson Five
## Do Not Be Irresponsible!

My grades at school have always been good. But there have been times that I struggled, especially during fifth grade. I noticed those tough times were usually because I missed homework assignments or I was not paying close attention in class. In other words, I was goofing off or lazy. My father got very firm with me, quite cross, when I fell behind, for he knew I had the intelligence to do well. He knew that I did poorly only when I avoided responsibility. Fifth grade was my nightmare. I could have blamed that first semester when I did not make honor roll (for the first time) on my teacher, for she was really lacking and was fired after that year. But my dad had nothing to do with those "bad teacher" excuses.

"Did others make honor roll?" he asked.

I hung my head and said, "Yes."

"How many?"

"About half the class."

He accepted *no more* excuses. He taught me not to get behind others, to keep up, and to be competitive.

I abandoned laziness, got focused and ended up not only making honor roll, but making headmaster that memorable year.

In more great talks with Dad, he told me how the government has failed public education:

"The responsibility to keep up and do well is put less and less on the student," Dad explained. "We are raising lazy and uncompetitive kids who can't keep up in the global arena."

"Well, I could relate to that. From my own experience, I knew a good education came mostly from the child himself *making* himself pay attention and learn and do homework. If my dad never blamed **me** for not keeping up in school, I would not have started working hard in class and paying close attention and doing my homework and doing it on time and doing it well!

My dad explained government should get out of education because it has nothing to do with protection. He explained why the private sector should take over educating our young. Every year in our public schools, more and more of our students grow irresponsible, regardless of the taxpayers' money put toward education. And I was soon going to learn that the students were not the only ones who were growing irresponsible.

You see, my parents always emphasized the importance of education. I go to a private school. My friend, who is in public school, told me he is not taught history. I thought he was kidding. But when I asked my dad, he said, "Your friend is right. In many public schools, they have scaled back or don't teach history at all."

I could not believe what I was hearing. Talk about being irresponsible! History is the source from where we can put today's trends into perspective. Without history, we have to learn our lessons all over again. We cannot improve. In fact, we can only fall backward!

After my dad told me this, for the first time I experienced anger toward our government. Until now, I could *understand* my dad's anger, but never *felt it*. Today, grasping the irresponsibility of government-controlled education, I felt this anger toward our government, and I felt closer than ever to my dad. I also admired him for doing something about the irresponsible and unjust political system.

"Why do public schools cut back on history?" I asked.

"The less the people know, the more the ruling class can control them," Dad answered. "The ruling class wants control, power, and our money to keep *their* utopia going strong."

"How do we stop this?" I said, "How do we get a world-class educational system again?"

Dad paused for a moment. I could tell the answer was complex, and he was trying to reduce it to simple terms. After a minute or so he said, "Education will be dumbed down as long as there is a ruling class. We must end the ruling class. That's the answer to all of our problems including our educational problem. The ruling-class goal of leading a nation of easily controllable automatons is unstoppable. Instead, we must eradicate the highly unhealthy, eventually deadly ruling class."

"And I know how to do that now," I said. "The Prime Law would end the ruling class and instead bring us a superior protection service."

"And with that, nothing is held back by a controlling ruling class," Dad said. "Everything soars ahead including our wealth, health, peace...and our educational system!"

In unison, Dad and I said, "The ruling class must go." ...I never before felt so responsible for making my country right.

## Lesson Six
## Do Not Twist the Truth!

My parents taught me to not talk negatively about others. If there were something wrong, then address that specific problem with honest facts *in context*.

Early on, I learned I could tell truthful facts, but I could arrange those facts or omit certain facts so that I could look better than what really happened. My dad taught me to never "adjust the truth" by leaving some true facts in and other true facts out. When I screwed up, I was taught to tell what happened with all the facts presented honestly. Politicians, on the other hand, violate this universal juvenile lesson. I learned after some deep and eye-opening talks with dad that politicians, certain judges, regulatory bureaucrats routinely leave out facts to distort context and build political power. This is the same as intentionally being untruthful. Children know that being untruthful is wrong, and most children work hard to be truthful. Politicians blatantly violate that childhood lesson and hold little or no respect for the honest, in-context truth.

## Lesson Seven
## Do Not Support Laziness!

My parents taught me to be charitable to those who have little or no control over their plight (e.g., poor children and the elderly). "But DO NOT help those who are lazy and dishonest," Dad told me several times.

At school, when there are charities to help poor children or the elderly, my family always gives a lot. But if we see a young and healthy man begging for money, my father says that he can work; he can get a job. So we do not give him anything. My dad explained that if people give to capable but lazy people, then their numbers would grow out of control.

My dad says that people have to be a value to society to get back a value such as money. That is how society sustains itself. People have to work or do something good for others in order to get paid.

During political campaign season, I learned about welfare and entitlements. So I asked my dad about it. We had a long talk about welfare-money given to the poor. The problem is that *the majority* of that money is given to capable, lazy people. My dad said that just giving away money to a lazy person is like giving away drugs to a drug addict! They will both just consume and never change for the better. Moreover, the lazy welfare recipient will drain more and more from future generations.

I started asking my dad some probing questions. "Dad, does welfare money go mostly to poor people who have little or no control over their poverty?"

"No," he said. Unfortunately a lot of that welfare money goes to lazy and undeserving people."

"You mean, they're poor but they're like those healthy men on the road begging for money?"

"Exactly. Yes they're poor, but they're capable. Giving them money just keeps them lazy and poor. Giving the elderly money is different. Government-policy inflation over the past few generations has eaten away their earned retirement money."

"So welfare is bad?"

"The way the government hands it out now, yes it's very bad."

"Welfare keeps lazy people lazy," I said.

"Yes, the way it's done now, you're right." Dad said.

"But why is it like that?"

"Do you know how your politicians get in office?" Dad asked.

"Yes ...we elect them."

"If you're a lazy person and a politician promises to give you money, who are you going to vote for?"

When my dad said that, I was amazed. Suddenly I could see why my dad would get angry when talking to his associates about our government today: *It's a racket!*

"They're buying their votes!" I shouted.

"With other people's money," Dad added.

For the second time in my life, I really felt *the wrong* of our government. And I now knew why the government had to take our taxes *by threat of force*.

"The way the government pays out welfare now, the lazy people will grow out of control," I said.

"And it is all so unnecessary," Dad said right back. "If government spent money on one thing — on protection only — then the poor would not be poor for long. Standards of living would soar as costs of living plunged. Poverty and the underclass would vanish. We would be left with one class only — the wealthy class."

"Why?" I said, "Dad, why would a new government, spending money only on protection, be the cure to poverty and end the poor class?"

"Not only will it end poverty," Dad said, "but all people will become rich, *including the poor!*"

"How?"

"By becoming a protection service only, the ruling class falls away and economic freedom opens up beyond anything ever seen. The personal computer revolution of the late 20th century gave us a look at what happens when the government gets out of the way. Free from debilitating regulations, computer buying power multiplied a thousand times. We can bring this same buying-power explosion to all industries when we take government back to its one and only valid purpose — that is, a protection service.

"Consider this quote by Bill Gates: 'Another sign of a healthy, competitive industry is lower prices. The statistics show that the cost of computing has decreased ten million fold since 1971. That's the equivalent of getting a Boeing 747 for the price of a pizza.'

"We will bring that computer paradigm to all industries," Dad continued. "In short, the personal computer industry was TVP de facto. The personal computer industry rose so fast the ruling class could not get a grip on it. That same multiplication of buying power will come to ALL industries when we remove the ruling class."

And this all comes about by not supporting laziness and removing initiatory force, I pondered, and it's all so simple: the Prime-Law Amendment and Protection-Only Budget. Dad had it all figured out.

## Lesson Eight
## Do Not Bully!

My parents taught me not to push around someone I didn't like. Growing up, there was a problem kid who made it very hard to stick to my parents' lesson. But, over time, I discovered a power in using discipline *not* to push him around. I found power in self-control and in being honest with myself.

Now that I am growing up, I am learning how the government uses its power to push around businesses or groups of people the politicians or bureaucrats or even judges do not like and want to push around for political gain. All that goes away with a protection-only government. Without initiatory force backing up the rule of man, government abuse will end.

"Granting politicians, judges, and regulatory bureaucrats the power of initiatory force leads to ongoing yet unrecognized tragedies," Dad explained as he drove me to school one morning. "They take down wonderful benefactors including job creators in order to build political portfolios and climb the political ladder. Politicians and bureaucrats and even judges tear down, push around, even destroy honest businesses (thus jobs) and important research programs. Your grandfather was a revered scientist at Du Pont involved in a promising research project that potentially could cure cancer. But bureaucrats in the FDA stopped Du Pont's research and development with self-serving, portfolio-building, cost-prohibitive regulations. Without the power of initiatory force, those bureaucrats could not hurt businesses and society like that. They could not bully and push around society's benefactors."

As I learned more and more from my dad, I realized that government violates almost every lesson parents teach children. For example, every parent teaches his child not to take from others what belongs to them. Yet, our government takes our money and spends it, and our money belongs to us! And taking what does not belong to them is only the beginning of our government's juvenile-delinquent ways. I wanted to know more about how my dad planned to fix all this.

"What is your TVP political movement?" I asked Dad.

"The TVP offers a simple but profound change to how government functions," Dad answered. "Since the beginning of time, government was synonymous with a ruling class and force, which is synonymous with a privileged class versus an underclass. Government is wrongfully *a class* that can rule over and tell others what to do...backed by initiatory force. In our country, there is a ruling class...and a non-ruling class. The ruling class bullies the non-ruling class.

"And that one fact — a ruling class backed by initiatory force — is the essence of what is axiomatically wrong with government. In fact, that fundamental point that the forefathers missed, I now capture in the Prime Law that eliminates initiatory force. The Twelve Visions Party provides a complete methodology for creating a new government structure — while going through proper constitutional procedures — to remove initiatory force from government, thus remove the age-old ruling class from holding down and bullying the non-ruling class. The end results will be a beautiful, rich country for us and our children and grandchildren."

"The Twelve Visions Party," I said, "is the only movement that can turn our country around and then turn the world around, right Dad?"

He looked at me with a sad expression and said, "Without our success, there will be severe poverty and civil unrest in our country within a decade." His face then lit up as he added, "With our success, all people will become wealthy, including the poor. Once people see this, the TVP will take off."

"Why is it so hard for people to see this?" I asked.

"Illusions," Dad said. "Since the beginning of civilization, the ruling class has strategically played different groups of people in our large non-ruling class against each other to keep our eye off the real enemy — the wolf in sheep clothing — the ruling class backed by initiatory force. The TVP is going to unite the non-ruling class to throw the ruling class off our backs!"

I smiled.

"Our country needs the Twelve Visions Party," Dad continued. "The *whole world* needs the TVP movement to end the ruling class and launch the wealth of mankind. The TVP movement is the savior of our failing world and is going to universally unite the non-ruling class. The ruling class will then come off civilization, ending the Great Suppression."

# Lesson Nine
# Do Not Follow!

All my life Dad taught me NOT to blindly follow anyone, but to instead be a good listener and think about things being said until I really understood them. He taught me this next level of thinking he called Neothink®. He taught me to be my own self-leader. It seemed to me this shift into Neothink® would wake people up. They would see all these violations by politicians, judges, and bureaucrats — juvenile violations that everyone learned as a child.

"It's almost like people are hypnotized or under a spell," I said to my dad.

"They essentially are," he said. "You're right, almost everyone learned the basic, *natural* laws of right and wrong as children, but they allow those basic *natural* laws to be blatantly violated by their leaders — by the unnatural ruling class — as adults! You know that I've worked over thirty years developing this new way of thinking called Neothink®, which is the natural evolution of our minds from the following mode to the self-leading mode. In order to do this, people must do exactly what I taught you all your life and not just absorb and accept what they read in the press or hear from their leaders. Instead, to see through the illusions to *what is*, they must think everything through their own minds to understand it before accepting it. As simple as that sounds, it requires a mental process different than they are accustomed to. It requires Neothink®."

"Dad, at school, there are kid-leaders of the kids. The kids let those kid-leaders control them. But I always do what you told me and think through, question, and accept only something I understand and verify. Everyone respects me because I'm my own leader."

"You just described Neothink® in its most simple form. No one could control you from that point forward. No one could confuse you or trick you with illusions. Now, realize most adults today are controlled by the ruling class mostly through illusions. My thirty years developing thousands of pages of Neothink® literature is helping people learn Neothink® for their own prosperity. I founded the Neothink® Society and its clubhouses around the world to help people rise into the prosperous Neothink® mentality. And those people, those self-leaders, most easily understand the Twelve Visions Party's goal of ending rule of man and its monstrously destructive ruling class. No self-leader needs leaders telling him how to live. Neothink® members most easily understand the nature of the Prime Law that eradicates the use of initiatory force. Eradicating initiatory force eradicates the ruling class. Indeed, for people to rule over other people is unthinkable to the self-leader and requires initiatory force. With the absence of initiatory force, the destructive ruling class ends. A valuable protection service begins.

"So, just as I taught you as a child how to evolve your mind from the following mode into a self-leading Neothink® mode, I reach out to more and more people to join the Neothink® Society, which in turn strengthens the Twelve Visions Party."

## Lesson Ten
## Do Not Sidestep Honesty!

After several talks now with my dad, I finally asked this question:

"Dad, why do we have so many problems in the Middle East and with terrorism around the world?"

His answer surprised me.

"We can get some insight by looking inside our own house. We know a LOT of people and you and your brothers and sister have a LOT of friends. It's amazing how demographically diverse you and your siblings' friends are! Their parents are from all over the world: India, Lebanon, Iran, Syria, Nigeria, China, Korea, Philippines, Singapore, Guatemala, Costa Rica, England, Russia, Mexico, Canada and, of course, America. On any given summer day, we have over a dozen kids in our large house.

"So, we have a lot of children playing together from different countries, cultures and religions on a daily basis. And from that ongoing mix of races, religions and cultures, I have made some observations over the years. The MOST IMPORTANT observation I have made is this:

"I've noticed a stark contrast between certain cultures, and the contrast is consistent among both the children and their parents. This ONE observation could be a key to unlocking the problems we see around the world today.

"I have noticed that when playing, certain children will be quick to *scorn* a sibling who is not playing fair or is cheating. Other children will be quick to *defend* a sibling even if that sibling is not playing fair or is cheating. The former children put right versus wrong as the highest priority. The latter children put family bond as the highest priority. Interestingly, in dealing with issues and conflicts, I have observed the parents of both sets of children follow the same patterns; right versus wrong above all else versus family bond above all else.

"I must say that, as a devoted family man myself, I admire the families that have such a strong family bond. I smile affectionately as I watch Dad wrap his hands around his children's heads and lean over to kiss their hair. Those families radiate love, and I relate to that.

"But I also recognize a trap that forms around them starting at a young age...while playing with friends. When a friend of yours sticks up for his sibling when the sibling is clearly in the wrong, I know it seems a little shocking to you. On the other hand, if one of your brothers is doing something wrong, you will be among the first to scorn him. Your friend who sticks up for his brother, regardless of right versus wrong, puts blind allegiance above what is right. You put what is right above allegiance. And by doing so, you are helping, conditioning, teaching your brothers to do the same. You are giving your brothers a great gift by shaping them to do the right thing, the honest thing. Your friend, by contrast, is giving his brother a terrible burden by shaping him to do the wrong thing, the dishonest thing...and without consequences.

"Parents of children with this blind allegiance to siblings display this same blind allegiance. I see this behavior when those parents' children get in trouble in school, for example. I see this behavior when their children have a conflict with other children.

"When we extrapolate that mentality of putting an allegiance above right versus wrong, we begin to unlock some of the problems around the world. That blind allegiance that starts conditioning children with blind allegiance to the family in certain cultures eventually expands to blind allegiance to the religion or country...blind allegiance above right versus wrong. That higher-cause mentality begins to unlock the mystery of so many problems around the world, including problems in the Middle East and blind-allegiance, higher-cause terrorism around the world."

"Wow," I said, "as obvious as it seems, a peaceful world all starts with teaching right versus wrong to our children."

"And expecting our government to chose right over wrong as well," Dad said.

# Conclusion & Next Step

## Mark Hamilton's
## Universal Wealth vs. Individual Wealth

### Universal Wealth for the Masses

All Americans and all citizens the world over should be wealthy. The publication you are reading from Mark Hamilton *How To Make Everyone Wealthy, Including The Poor!* shows why and how everyone should be wealthy, and that opportunity is available right here in America! Discover right here, right now exactly how you and your family can be wealthy with one very simple but hidden change. As you discover that very simple (yet extremely guarded) change on the pages you are reading, keep in mind the simple change would make all Americans (and eventually all citizens the world over) wealthy, and we have all been held back from that life *we were meant to have.*

As you have seen, just one simple yet highly guarded change of removing initiatory force from our government would set off a Great Technological Revolution that would drive down costs and drive up buying power a thousand times just as we saw in the mostly unregulated computer industry, but this time the buying-power explosion would happen across all industries. Suddenly in a few years all citizens would be a thousand times wealthier. Everyone would become wealthy with such an exponential increase in buying power, including the poor. It's all so clear to see in the Mark Hamilton Publication that you are reading.

Indeed, that one simple change in government would bring us universal wealth never seen on Earth. This publication by Mark Hamilton clears that prosperity path that will eventually make everyone wealthy, including the poor. Read it, join hands with others, and step onto the prosperity path to universal wealth.

### Individual Wealth for You

Before that change in governance happens, before the masses

walk that path together hand-in-hand to universal wealth, Mark Hamilton has also cleared another path to individual wealth so **you** can rise up to the good life **now**, starting today. Whereas his path to universal wealth requires a very simple yet highly guarded change in governance, his path to individual wealth requires a very simple change in business. He shows how most of our jobs today put us in stagnant routines. In other words, we are caught in routine ruts and go nowhere as the result of business's division of labor. Most jobs require very little of our greatest asset — *our minds*, our lucrative creativity. We are wasting our human potential! Mark Hamilton invented a new business paradigm — a new division of business called the division of essence that effects every job and easily brings our minds into our work, into each and every job, beckoning and cashing in on your buried creativity. Indeed, unearthing your buried creativity is your secret fast-lane to individual wealth as proven by thousands of Mark Hamilton's readers.

Now you can finally fulfill your human potential! Instead of a job of labor that shuts down your mind and creativity, now you can easily re-mold your job to become a job of essence that embraces your mind and ignites your creativity. Hamilton shows how everyone, including people who are unemployed or who are stuck in a stagnant rut with little or no income, can get on a creative vector and on the fast lane to a wealthy life. And once on a creative vector racing ahead on the fast lane to wealth, life becomes extremely stimulating each and every day! Life becomes the opposite of our boring stagnation-traps as we rise in importance, relevance and gain the power to influence others, to buy wonderful things, to provide an extraordinary life for our loved ones, and to just *enjoy the expensive good life!* Whereas many say Hamilton's division of essence breakthrough is the route to individual wealth, Hamilton himself contends that in the end, his breakthrough is the route to happiness.

If you would like to own Mark Hamilton's hard-to-get 500-page prize publication on this fast lane to individual wealth and happiness, see the next page:

*Universal Wealth, Health, Peace*

## The Prize

The Mark Hamilton Manuscript you are reading offers the cure to the debilitating disease of our civilization, which is the rule of man killing major Universal Wealth for all of us. However, by far, the *prize* Mark Hamilton Manuscript cures the disease of our jobs, which is the mind-numbing division of labor killing major Individual Wealth *for you.* Mark Hamilton's prize 500-page Manuscript will quickly sweep you off your feet and change your life forever. For the first time, you can *control* and *catapult* your wealth! The change comes *fast* and is significant. When it is offered to you, be sure to get your Mark Hamilton Prize Manuscript that launches *major* Individual Wealth, and rise to the wealthy elite class.